Kate Pavelle

ZIPPER FALL

KATE PAVELLE

Dreamspinner Press

Published by
Dreamspinner Press
5032 Capital Circle SW
Ste 2, PMB# 279
Tallahassee, FL 32305-7886
USA
http://www.dreamspinnerpress.com/

This is a work of fiction. Names, characters, places, and incidents either are the product of the author's imagination or are used fictitiously, and any resemblance to actual persons, living or dead, business establishments, events, or locales is entirely coincidental.

Zipper Fall
Copyright © 2013 by Kate Pavelle

Cover Art by Aaron Anderson
aaronbydesign55@gmail.com

Cover content is being used for illustrative purposes only
and any person depicted on the cover is a model.

All rights reserved. No part of this book may be reproduced or transmitted in any form or by any means, electronic or mechanical, including photocopying, recording, or by any information storage and retrieval system without the written permission of the Publisher, except where permitted by law. To request permission and all other inquiries, contact Dreamspinner Press, 5032 Capital Circle SW, Ste 2, PMB# 279, Tallahassee, FL 32305-7886, USA.
http://www.dreamspinnerpress.com/

ISBN: 978-1-62798-063-0
Digital ISBN: 978-1-62798-064-7

Printed in the United States of America
First Edition
September 2013

To my family, especially to those members who will never read this book because it's naughty but who love me enough to encourage my writing adventures anyway!

This book would not be in your hands without the enthusiastic words of support from my fans. My Beta Hit Squad offered their selfless help in making the manuscript ready to face the light of day, and P.D. Singer was very kind to correct my rock-climbing technical specifics. That being said, all errors are still mine.

CHAPTER ONE

My best friend, Reyna, and I sat at the Barking Shark, celebrating Friday. Every week, like clockwork, we sat perched on tall barstools by one of the round tables in the corner, eating bar food for dinner and drinking beer. I had tucked my silk tie into my jacket pocket as I tried to keep stray bits of food off my starched dress shirt. I kept toying with the ends of my hair as I listened to her latest tale of woe.

"Azurri's an asshole." Reyna lifted her beer bottle and sipped, marking the top of the bottle with her red lipstick. "He's a *fucking* asshole," she elaborated somewhat, shook her head in disbelief, then patted her lips with a napkin. Her chestnut-brown eyes flashed in the dim light of the bar. "Of all the bosses I've ever had, he's the rudest, nastiest, loudest sonovabitch I've ever worked for. He has absolutely no ability to delegate, he gives me the most boring grunt work imaginable, and then he complains over having to stay late." I watched my best friend belch, covering her mouth delicately in discreet affectation. Her fingers, graceful and strong, hovered over a bowl full of complimentary nuts and pretzels. She stirred the contents with a long, red nail until she found a cashew, picked it out with precision, and ate it. She was crushing the nut between her teeth in an act of determined, stubborn catharsis. Her face was flushed, her scowl accentuated by severely plucked and angular eyebrows. I've always admired her waist-long, crimson hair that threatened to escape her ponytail and barely disguised a realistic tattoo of a life-size banana spider on the nape of her neck. It exemplified her "no guts, no glory" attitude I knew and loved back in college. If I weren't into guys, I'd have asked her out on an official date a long time ago, but we've established that being best friends is our ideal relationship.

"Sorry, girlfriend." I hummed, waving for another round of Belgian Lambic. "At least you have an interesting job description. You work with major accounts. What you do matters a bit more than just putting advertisements together."

I pressed my lips into a tight line, suppressing a sigh. Two years out of college, I still cultivated the youthful air of innocent fun, every inch of me a bachelor, my sense of purpose still being somewhat fuzzy around the edges. My outward manner and appearance, which my critics described as "a mere air of civilized decency," didn't always correspond with my private endeavors—endeavors that were much aided by my five-foot-eight-inch athletic body. I am a creature of the night; when she was still alive, my mother used to say I should be wearing sunscreen because I tend to break out into wicked freckles. I am good at all kinds of things, but none of them seem to matter: I know climbing, lock-picking, and good beer. Aside from these important personal facts, I'd also like to share that my job is meaningless. After all, nobody gives a damn about advertising unless a video goes viral on YouTube. The product of my hard work becomes trash as soon as it's removed from the mailbox, billboards get tuned out, flashy magazine ads are cut up for children's school projects, and TV commercials get muted. My job is worse than watching moss grow.

Maybe that's why I enjoy breaking into people's houses so much.

Life can be incredibly boring at times, and in order to make it worth living, I need a bit of zing to spice up my dull routine. I've always been like that, and besides, I have always been able to talk my way out of anything. My mother used to say I'd make her go prematurely gray with my wild skateboarding antics. After a while, skateboarding wasn't enough, and I started rock climbing. Small risks turned to bigger risks, except I didn't want to endanger my climbing buddies by doing something really crazy on the rock face. Instead, I discovered the thrill of occasional and strictly recreational break-ins. Two years ago, I took my first souvenir. I knew it would be missed, which made the experience even more thrilling. Heightening the risk heightened the excitement. Last year, I wore a distinctive ring for a few days. I got away with it, which was almost disappointing, because it was a Superbowl ring. I ended up wiping my prints off and sending it to the local TV station, and its return made the news because anything having to do with the Steelers makes the news. I rode that high for almost a whole month.

I always prepare for my B&E with meticulous care. It has become a soothing ritual by now, and I don't deviate from it, because without careful planning and execution, I wouldn't be able to get away with my occasional adrenaline fix. I also have a strict code of conduct, and I adhere to it on every job:

Never take sentimental items (and keep them).

Steal only from the rich.

Don't get caught.

I guess the last rule would be the most important one, and I'm pretty darn good at what I do, since I've been burgling for almost ten years and haven't been caught yet. It all started in high school with my dog-walking job: I had been given the keys and unsupervised access to many a house in our Pittsburgh neighborhood. Taking the dogs out to do their business and burn off excess energy using a tennis ball and racket had given me unmitigated pleasure, along with much-needed extra cash. I'd been so good, so painfully responsible—until one time when I had forgotten to bring my client's key. I had heard the dog whining by the door, his bladder full to bursting, but going back home would have taken at least half an hour. As luck would have it, I had been in the midst of reading Lawrence Block's mysteries at the time. Since his protagonist is a burglar who moonlights as a soft-spoken bookseller during the day, I was no stranger to the *idea* of picking a lock. I had in fact been practicing at home using my sister's hairpins, and my dog-walking predicament had seemed like a natural opportunity to try out my new, hard-won skills. If Bernie Rhoddenbar could do it, well....

I had chosen an awl from my Swiss army knife and my sister's hairpins, which I carried around "just in case." It had taken me ten long, focused minutes to make the simple lock click open. My muscles had trembled from exhaustion, but the thrill of victory had sent chemical happiness coursing through my veins. It had occurred to me at that moment I didn't need a dog with a full bladder on the other side as an excuse to experience that heady, exhilarating feeling of victory again.

This formative experience allowed me to discover that there was no better way to get that awesome adrenaline rush than casing a place of residence, learning when it would be empty, and finding an illicit way of entry. Sometimes I just need to pick the lock to the front door. In other cases, more inventive means of breaching the fortress are necessary.

Another firm rule: No cat-burglar stuff. Cat burglars are people who break into homes while people are still there, preferably asleep. That's not only creepy, it's also dangerous. It's a good way to get your chest ventilated with a pistol the resident inherited from his grandfather and still keeps around for sentimental reasons.

"…so he'll be out of the office next week. Yay!" Reyna squinted at me. "Hey, Wyatt. Are you even listenin'? Azz-hole's going on a vacation for a week, so he'll be off my back."

Vacation. A successful stockbroker's going on a vacation.

Hmmm….

I knew I shouldn't have even formulated the thought, but there it was: suddenly I was possessed with an overwhelming urge to break into Mr. Azz-hole's chateau. Of course, that would break another rule: don't steal from people you might know, even if only through other people.

"Maybe he's just grumpy from his commute," my mouth said, seemingly detached from my body.

"Nah," Reyna said, tossing her head to get her long hair out of her eyes. "He walks to work. He lives right on the corner of Bellefonte and Espada Way—you know, right where that coffee shop is? I had to deliver some papers one day when he made me stay late, that jerk."

Now, I knew better than to pursue this train of thought, but I have always had a curious fascination with knowing how other people work. Nothing gives me more insight into a person's psyche than having a chance to walk through their private domain, to breathe the air they have breathed, and to rifle through their personal possessions. Just by looking through his drawers, I would be able to tell why Mr. Azz-hole is the way he is. His taste in books and clothing would most certainly be very different in private than in public. Much like my beloved literary protagonist, I also felt that extra frisson of excitement run through my body when I found the difference between my victim's private self and the public persona they put on for our benefit.

I even know why I am so curious: my family and I aren't terribly close anymore. I'm on my own, an adult child of a dysfunctional family, and peeking into the lives of strangers fills me with a sense of temporary satisfaction; it's as though I *belong* again. My father won't talk to me because I dated his arch-enemy's son; my mother died on the operating table—under his arch-enemy's scalpel—and my brother and sister are off in college.

No, I should stop.

Stop now. Go back. Take a trip out of town.

"What's his place like?" my mouth asked Reyna while I sat aghast in my body, along for the ride.

MY TWISTED sense of curiosity led me to spy on my new target at his Shadyside address within a day after I found out about his impending absence. Then, after keeping an eye on his third-floor apartment over the weekend, I was gratified to see him—the bane of my best friend's existence—exit the front door with an overnight bag in his hand. I shifted from foot to foot, thinking about having to use the bathroom exactly as my stomach began to squeak for lunch. Just about then he got into his taxi and left.

When somebody gets into a taxi with a piece of luggage, it generally means they'll be gone for a while, but relying on this truism is unwise. It is always prudent to call before breaking in. And once you approach the residence, it's imperative to ring the doorbell. This prevents the burglar's unexpected contact with dogs, house sitters, irate spouses—and the local police department. I took a deep breath and went home to eat lunch. As I walked away, I began to formulate a plan.

I knew what I would wear and what I would bring along, as well as how long it would be safe to stay. And, of course, I had to call his home number first to make sure he was really gone.

Jack Azurri's apartment was in a turn-of-last-century apartment building lush with neo-classical embellishments chiseled into its stone façade by long-dead Slovak immigrants who made Pittsburgh their home. Typical for this part of town, it was five stories high, with wide parapets connecting the adjacent windows along each floor. Its façade was covered with a vining Art Nouveau floral motif, and its chased-brass-and-glass door pointed to the importance of its residents. In my professional career as a burglar, I have learned to assess the inner characteristics of buildings by examining their external architectural elements. Just looking from across the street, for instance, I could already see the ceilings would be tall. That could be both good and bad—it meant a longer rappel off the roof and a possible lack of an elevator. It could also indicate a resident population flush with cash and collections of small, easy-to-fence *objets d'art* they would never realize were missing. I'd take just enough to feel Reyna was properly avenged, and my profit would contribute extra funds to our best-friends tropical vacation.

THAT afternoon, nervous yet excited, I called the number for Mr. Azzhole's residence. Nobody picked up. If you want to break into a place, your best bet is to do it during the day while wearing a service uniform. People will remember the uniform, not your face. As for me, looking like a computer-repair tech with a messenger bag full of tools lent an air of verisimilitude to my disguise. The plan was to just walk up to the door and knock. If anybody opened, I would just pretend I'd gotten out on the wrong floor.

My dark blond locks and tendrils were temporarily tamed under a dark, microfiber skullcap. The repairman hat I wore over it had a sewn-in half wig with short, dark hair attached around the perimeter. My blue-striped shirt sported a tag embroidered with the name *Lloyd* and a logo for my supposed employer, WTF Service. Clad in navy chinos and black, crepe-soled shoes for a quiet approach and a fast getaway, I sauntered in, striving to look tired. Three in the afternoon on a Saturday, and to all uninitiated observers, I was stuck working.

The building's doorman sat behind a chest-high marble counter, trying to follow a ball game on a portable television.

"Hey. What's the score?" I asked, pitching my voice a bit deeper than usual.

He uncoiled his long body, carded his stringy black hair with his fingers, and spared me a glance. "Three-two, bottom of the sixth, bases loaded."

"Oh man." I let out an exasperated moan. "I coulda been at that game. Had to give the tickets away—just when the Pirates might actually win!"

"No shit?" The doorman, a Mr. Haus according to his name tag, turned toward me.

"Yeah. Then a client called. Wants to have a virus removed off his system and new RAM installed. Can't get a thing done now. Poor jackass." I blew out some hot air. "Sucks working Saturdays, but a man's gotta do what a man's gotta do."

"Yeah." Haus's eyes flicked back toward the game. "Strikeout! Shit!"

"Wow, damn. That coulda been sweet. Three more innings, though."

Haus glanced my way. "They shouldn't have benched Gonzalez. Here, you sign in here. Where're you goin'?"

I signed my fake name and time of entry. "Mr. Azurri. Third floor."

"He's gone."

"Yeah. He told me in no uncertain terms he wants the system running like a Swiss watch by the time he's back, too. Loud bastard. He gave me a key."

"He sure is a loud bastard." Haus nodded with a sneer, his eyes on the game again. I peeled away from the counter and headed toward the elevator. Nobody attempted to stop me.

Azurri's door had a regular lock and two dead bolts, which told me he knew a bit about not putting all his eggs in one basket. I knocked on the door and rang the doorbell with the knuckle of my finger, mostly for the benefit of his neighbors. Nobody opened the door to see who was in the hallway. I snapped on latex gloves and reached for the picks in the bottom of my tool bag. The regular lock was butter soft and turned almost on command. The deadbolts took a bit more convincing. After a bit of patience, I felt rather than heard a sharp metallic sound, and a tendril of thrill ran up my spine as the tumblers turned and aligned, and the mechanism yielded to my desires.

As soon as I was in, I locked the door again so nobody would disturb me. Then I did a quick walk-through. The apartment had two bedrooms, two bathrooms, a huge dining room, and a living room separated into what at first glance seemed to be a junkyard jammed with yard-sale goods with only a small, modern oasis of order with a flat-screen TV.

I've said before that I can judge the character of a person by the way they keep their dwelling and belongings. Looking around, I'd have guessed Mr. Azz-hole suffered from a split personality disorder. His kitchen was immaculate. His freezer contained not only five gourmet frozen dinners but also the fairly common stash of cash. Lots of people hid their emergency funds in the back of their freezer, thinking it was so clever and original.

Frozen assets: about five grand.

Not much for a successful stockbroker. I palmed the icy Ziploc bag and slipped it into my cargo pocket. The act of theft sent familiar, spine-tingling warmth across my shoulder blades, wrapping me like a warm hug. I was focused and my hearing sharpened to a point where I filtered out even my own heartbeat and the hum of the refrigerator. I froze for a second, halted by the sound of the elevator opening and closing again. A few moments of stillness passed before I dared to exhale and examine my surroundings with a keener eye.

One of the bedrooms was right over Bellefonte Avenue. The room's dark, elegant furniture was complemented by several

Tokugawa-era Japanese prints. The nightstands, the bureau—all clean. Azurri's personal effects must have been minimal. How surprising, then, that the second bedroom—the one with a window onto the alley and the fire escape—was cluttered with boxes piled on top of one another, with full bags of material ensnaring my feet. I didn't even bother wading in because I didn't care for bruising my shins on odd pieces of furniture. I felt a brief sense of relief that I chose not to enter via the fire escape. Had I tried to climb in through the window on the other end of all that junk and make my way across in the dark, I'd have sounded like two raccoons fighting in a garbage can.

The bathrooms were both clean. The first was empty of towels and toiletries altogether; the other held personal items and first-aid supplies. A plush, black cotton terry robe hung on the door, waiting to wrap its owner in warm comfort. Its pockets were free of diamonds, cash, or contraband. So were all other potential hiding places in both bathrooms: the toilet tanks held only water, there was nothing terribly valuable in the cabinets, and the plumbing access contained only pipes and a dead spider.

The dining room, on the other hand, had every single surface covered with collectible objects of various sizes. There were four half-opened cardboard boxes on the floor.

How did this seemingly neat and tidy individual amass such a wealth of knick-knacks? I walked through, not spending much time. Only a few items caught my attention. There were four English silver candy dishes, circa 1820s, and since their design and quality varied, I picked one of medium value; the nicest one would have been the first to be missed. I found a fabulous carving of a tiger, probably an antique ivory piece with ruby eyes, but the way it was displayed told me its absence would be noted, so I left it.

Thirty minutes had passed and I knew I had to get out soon. Computer maintenance wasn't all that complicated these days, and the guy downstairs might start to get suspicious. I looked around, frantic to find the magical third secret treasure to satisfy me. One more thing... just one more little thing.

My eyes fell on a midsize painting centered over the dining-room sideboard. The subject matter was neo-classical, but the quality...

awful. I peered a little closer. A decent frame was being wasted on a cheap print with a paint-like acrylic layer on top. Mr. Azurri might have been an asshole, but judging from his other decorations, he was a man of taste when it came to art, so why would he display such fake trash in such a prominent location?

The frame seemed a tad thick. I jostled it with a gentle hand and almost jumped when it swung to the side on a column of piano hinges and revealed a small wall safe.

Bingo!

Safecracking was something of a hobby of mine, and my fingers itched with the desire to turn the dial and make the mechanism sing for me. Time, however, was not on my side. I closed the painting. There would have to be another visit.

TWO days passed since my illicit adventure. Tuesday at work paled in comparison with the thrill of the untouched safe in the wall, and I was aching to get out of the office. My venture had earned $5,380, mostly in hundreds—enough for a Caribbean getaway for both Reyna and me. The antique candy dish of wrought silver sat on my dining table, where I could admire its fine workmanship.

As I sipped my tea that night and ate chocolate-dipped orange peel out of my newly acquired and soon-to-be-fenced silver candy dish, I thought back to the apartment. I could never get in the same way again. And next time, it would have to be a night job. The summer was pleasantly warm, and it wasn't unusual for people to leave their windows open. I had eased the locks of the old-world type casement window frames in the bedroom just so I could push my way in later tonight.

ELEVEN o'clock could never come soon enough as the far-away wall safe kept crooning its siren song. I barely resisted biting my nails. My microwave clock showed I still had ten minutes to go before departure when, impatient, I pulled on my lightweight, dark green jacket and a baseball cap, hoisted my black backpack, and headed out the door. I walked, using the next twenty minutes to calm down and control my adrenaline levels. I still could back out. I didn't have to go through with it. The idea died young: it was like paying the entry fee to a public swimming pool and then talking myself out of getting into the water. There was no way I wasn't getting inside that apartment tonight.

Two blocks away from Azurri's apartment, I ducked inside an entryway and stuffed my jacket and baseball cap inside the bag. I caught my hair up in my black skullcap, hiding every single strand by feel alone. The black hood of my sweatshirt covered my head as I continued to my target area.

The windows in the corner of the third floor were dark. I dialed the number on my cell phone anyway, but nobody picked up. I sucked in a deep breath.

Shit. I was really going in. I did my phone-check routine, making sure it was on vibrate and the camera flash was off. I also set it on redial, just in case someone was home and I had to distract them—even though that never happened. As a last step, I covered the phone's screen with three strips of electrical tape. That way, if I had to use it in the dark, I wouldn't make a target out of myself.

The service entrance in the alley wasn't equipped with an alarm, and the lock wasn't hard. Somebody must have miscalculated, thinking there was no point protecting a self-closing door next to a Dumpster. I slipped in like a shadow and took the service elevator all the way up. There was a narrow staircase from the fifth floor to the roof. I took it to an unlocked door. It creaked only a little as I pushed it open, but even that little sound almost made my heart stop. I scanned the flat, asphalt roof and the vents and chimneys to my left. The edge of the roof was to my right. Working fast, I reached inside my backpack and slipped a climbing harness over my black cargo fatigues. I slid my silenced phone into a secure side pocket. The other pocket held my flashlight. I pulled a coil of climbing rope out of the backpack and fastened it to a sturdy chimney. Before I knew it, my feet were anchored on the rim of the ledge and, with the rope wound behind my butt and through my self-belay device, I leaned back over the abyss.

I grinned as the thrill of being suspended over a street threatened to overcome my senses— alone in the dark, unseen. Slowly, I slipped my soft black shoes down the side of the building in careful steps as I fed extra rope through my harness. The soles of my feet felt every contour of the vines and flowers carved into the acid-rain roughened stone, giving me extra purchase. I descended past the glowing fifth-floor window and the dark fourth-floor window, and I had just started to breathe a bit harder when, finally, the third-floor window appeared. I stood on the generous parapet and unclipped myself and let the rope hang by my side. Slowly, I pushed in the glass panes.

Lights from the streets illuminated the Spartan bedroom interior as I slipped in, landing in a crouch. The white carpet gleamed pale amber, reflecting the sodium lamps outside. I look around and froze.

The bed was occupied.

At this point, I should have climbed out the window and back up the building and gotten out of there. Yet I stood here, conflicted between running away and getting a little closer. The bed's owner was sprawled naked on his back, his head and shoulders shrouded by the shadows. The stark city glow, barely impeded by sheer curtains, accentuated the shady contours of his trim abdomen and his well-muscled legs. I stopped in my tracks, feeling as though a Grecian marble statue from a nearby museum had been placed on this stranger's bed, displayed for my eyes to feast upon. He was incredible, beautiful in the unearthly glow, and I felt like a lost man, captivated by the sight of his physical beauty. Even if I weren't into guys, I think I would have gotten hard.

He stirred. I broke from my stunned reverie and looked around fast. The dark corner of the room to my left was my only hope, and then I realized a closet was there, with its door cracked open. I ducked into the shadows, moving fast. I blessed my luck and slipped inside, not making a sound. My breathing came in short, shallow breaths, and my heartbeat felt like a drum against the wall of my chest. I fought to maintain absolute silence. I heard Jack Azurri stir. His bed creaked. Then there was the soft patter of his feet, almost muffled by his lush carpet.

I hope he won't kill me on sight.

I swear I'll never do this again.

I heard him piss in the bathroom next to me, and I breathed a deep, silent sigh of relief. Maybe, just maybe, I didn't have to voice any rash oaths just yet.

He flushed and washed his hands.

More footsteps, this time in my direction. Once again I began to negotiate with the powers that be.

"Fuck, it's hot." The low, sexy growl shot an arrow of heat down my spine.

I heard him draw the curtains aside and open the window even wider. The heavy evening air stirred, and even more light poured in from the street.

My heart sang in relief.

The mattress creaked as he got back in bed. So far so good. I'd have to wait until he was asleep before I could make my exit out the window, which he, being such a considerate gentleman, had opened even wider for my convenience. I didn't dare attempt cracking the safe with him there. In fact, I barely dared to breathe. I waited, wondering why the hell he wasn't on a vacation like he should have been.

Light snoring reached my ears, and I pushed the closet door to the side a little more, just enough to get out comfortably. With painful slowness I peeked around the wooden panel.

There he was, now fully lit by the dramatic glow from outside, legs spread apart, sporting a significant boner. You would think I would be no stranger to that part of male anatomy, but being single, it had been a while since I had seen a full-grown specimen. Also, I had never seen one from someone's closet while hiding in there, trying to avoid detection. This situation had all levels of awkward written all over it, and as my mouth went dry, I felt a hot blush rise up to my cheeks. All the same, I wasn't quite willing to look away.

Light pollution was the burglar's enemy under ordinary circumstances, but right now I felt grateful for its ubiquitous, eerie glow. This guy, no matter what Reyna had to say about his personality, had the goods. Neon lights, flashing from outside, reflected off the smooth planes of his muscles as he twitched, giving a slight moan.

Sleep, dammit.

Sleep didn't come to him easily that night. Soon, I saw his powerful thighs tense up as his hand crept to his groin. He reached his fingers to skim his stiff shaft. I heard him gasp and knew that even though he might have looked as though he was in the dream world, he wasn't even close to being asleep. I sucked in my lower lip, working hard to control my breathing. Before me was a Greek god come alive, parts of him veiled in shadow, mysterious and beautiful. He was a gorgeous specimen of a man and— Well, I'd been raised better than to intrude, except I'd never seen a man as perfect as him laid out on display like this.

Blood rushed to my dick and I bit my lip as I struggled not to whimper with desire. Damn but was he ever so beautiful. He was a gorgeous specimen of a man, and I'd have done a lot to go out there and join the party—except I wasn't keen on him introducing me to the local police department.

Slowly, my hand crept down, past my raging hard-on and inside the cargo pocket of my pants. I flipped my phone open and turned the camera on. There was just enough light for the device to record what was going on before me. Fighting not to touch myself, I kept my phone trained on the bed.

Somewhere in the back of my mind, a little voice nagged, reminding me of my solid upbringing. Surely taking a video of someone in such a delicate moment was beyond the pale. I had no words for it, no justification. I was a thief, though, and I'd never have this man—no chance of that. I could keep this little personal memento, though. An insignificant souvenir to be played a few times and then erased. I just could not avert my eyes as my breath turned into short, shallow pants.

Azurri slid a neck roll under his hips. He reached for something on the bedside table, and I heard a familiar click of a lube bottle. When he touched his delectable specimen of a dick again, I heard his hiss of pleasure. I wanted to be the one doing the touching. He undulated his hips in thrusts both small and intense as his slick fingers did the grab-and-twist around his shaft. Then he spread his feet apart and reached his other hand down to his ass. I saw him stroke around his hole as he let out soft, delicate gasps of pleasure. When I saw his finger plunge through the tight ring and heard him moan in reaction, I wanted to be the one that made him make sounds like that. Another digit... he gasped, panting and cursing, his two fingers embedded and pulling at his opening, his slick hand pumping his engorged cock. I hoped he'd come soon. I had only so much self-control, and my phone had only so much memory left...*yesssss*.

His voice was a growl and a moan and it resonated as thick ropes of jizz briefly luminesced in the neon lights outside. He pulled again and his hips rose off the bed in a spasm of pleasure so hard, it yanked the fingers out of his ass. More pearlescent liquid came out in an arc, then more again, and just when I thought he would either levitate entirely or throw his back out, his body crashed down onto the sheets and all I heard was the sound of his loud, raspy pants. A few minutes later, he sat up on the bed, still playing with himself. His eyes were closed and his mouth pulled back in a languorous smile, and all of a sudden, I wanted to know whom he had been thinking of as he came. I wanted it to be me, but there was just no way we would ever even meet. He was beautiful and relaxed, and I really wanted to toss the phone and go to him and lick the come off his chest and kiss him until he forgot his own mother's name.

Oh God, how I wanted that man.

I watched him walk to the bathroom again. When the water ran, I used the cover of its noise to shut my phone and slip it back in my pocket. I didn't get to use the screen to aim, but even if the video didn't show much, I wouldn't forget the details for a long, long time. In not too long, he climbed back on top of the sheets, hugged a pillow, and this time he fall asleep for good. The scent of his cologne, barely discernible before, increased with his increased body heat and mingled with the musky smell of sex. As I stood in his closet, his suits kept caressing my back, emanating that very same heady scent, and it was all I could do not to roll my eyes back in my head, lean back into all that luxurious fabric, and pass out. It was at least an hour before I could trust myself to move out the window and scale the wall to reach the safety of the roof. Once there, I coiled my rope around my hand and elbow and pulled it up with tired slowness. With klutzy fingers, I untied the other end from the chimney and stowed it in my backpack. My harness came off next, and I dropped it into the bag. With my gear secure, I flopped behind the chimney in exhaustion. Going up is a lot harder, even if you weren't distracted by the way your body and mind reacted to the spectacle below. After I wiped the sweat off my face with the sleeve of my shirt, I hid my climbing gear in a cooling vent for the next time.

Then I realized I'd just considered doing it again.

My thoughts drifted to the stranger sleeping three floors below. I felt my cock spring to attention again and groaned in frustration. Maybe I could still go to Frankie's Bar and Lounge. That would be the surest way to meet a hookup and get my needs met—except my needs were no longer simple: I wanted Jack Azurri, not some random stranger whose name and visage I could tune out in the heat of the moment. In the absence of Jack, maybe Kai would do. He was big and strong and almost as gorgeous as Azzuri, even though a bit on the shy side, I thought. He never said much, like he was scared of being found out, and my efforts at getting to really know him had fallen flat to date, but he was still an awesome lay. Except I hadn't seen Kai in a while, which meant he was probably unavailable, maybe even living the high life somewhere other than Pittsburgh. Azz-hole was already sated and fast asleep; I was the one haunting the rooftops, needy and alone.

I shrugged, sprawled on the asphalt roof, and unzipped my pants. I felt like I couldn't function in my current state; best get it over with. It would take but a few minutes before I could find relief, gather myself, and go home.

CHAPTER TWO

IT BECAME apparent to me almost immediately—after I was done panting over my illicit video of Jack Azurri for the third or fourth time, anyway—that Cupid had played a rather vicious prank on me. I was infatuated, smitten, and hormonally insane. As far as I could recall, I'd never fallen so fast for anyone, or so hard. This time I didn't even know of any of the guy's redeeming qualities. I knew his name, home address, housekeeping habits, and occupation, and had it on a good authority that he was an utter asshole at work.

Still....

Here it was, the short footage so hot, it threatened to turn my cell phone into a puddle of molten plastic and twisted wires. The video I took of Azzuri in the middle of the night threatened to singe circuits, both electronic and neural. I leaned back in my office chair and closed my eyes. The feel of the sensuous brushes of his expensive suits against my back was indelibly embedded in my neurophysiological pathways. The scent of his aftershave mingling with the intoxicating, musky scent of sex lingered in the back of my mind. That body endowed with the strength and poise of Discobolos—a Grecian ideal, lean-limbed and muscled, his eyes sultry in repose. And, oh God, that voice. I no longer needed to play the recording; my utterly twisted mind rewound it to the very beginning and recreated every hiss, gasp, and pant from memory. That particular roar at the end was so expressive and intimate and primal, I wanted to hear it over and over—hell, I even considered making it my ringtone.

The physical manifestations of my sorry state left me irritable and distracted. I stopped by Frankie's Bar and Lounge to see if Kai was there, hoping the redhead could alleviate my pain.

"Nah, he ran into some issues, stayed here for a couple of weeks, and disappeared," Larry said while pouring me a beer. I thanked him and looked around. Nobody in the upper bar looked anything like Azzuri, Kai had mysteriously disappeared, and I didn't feel like braving the anonymous sex atmosphere downstairs. I finished half my drink and, thinking sleep sounded good just about now, walked the two miles back to my apartment building.

REYNA might be happy that "Azz-hole" was gone on personal leave, headed for points unknown, but I couldn't think of Jack Azurri by that nickname anymore. As unattainable as he was, I still found him to be enticing, tempting, and devastating. And let's face the fact that despite her being my best friend, Reyna was hardly a stellar employee.

Tuesday found me in my office with my eyes half shut and cheeks flushed. I visualized Jack getting out of his bed and padding around, just the way I had seen him from my hiding place in his closet: stark naked and gorgeous, illuminated by the slow flashes of neon signs and the steady glow of sodium street lamps. I imagined him walking off to the kitchen, reaching for a glass, slipping it under the ice dispenser, and getting some ice water in the middle of the night.

Ice.

Frozen assets.

I imagined him opening the freezer and reaching into the back left corner. Empty. Over five grand disappeared overnight.

I wondered how he would look when he was angry. Suddenly I didn't want him to feel angry, violated, sad….

Shit. I've never felt guilty before—that's why I always selected my donors with such careful precision. Except this one wasn't selected so carefully. With this one I'd broken a slew of my own rules: the guy was personally known by a friend, the house wasn't cased well enough, I returned a second time, I entered while he was home, and I allowed it to become personal. This series of events robbed me of that cool detachment which had, up until now, allowed me to dehumanize the victims of my extracurricular activities. Jack Azurri was now a real person, and my sudden pangs of guilt were as new as they were unwelcome.

"Mr. Gaudens." Auguste Bernard Pillory III ghosted to my office door with his usual, otherworldly elegance.

My eyes popped open and I sat up ramrod straight. "Yes, boss."

"Are you feeling well?" Pillory frowned the slightest bit. He allowed his handsome and finely sculpted face to show a hint of concern. Considering his usual, stoic expression, he may as well have shouted a red alert. He had the sort of silky, raven hair women envy and consider a waste on a man's head, bound in a professional ponytail with his usual flair, a sure sign a client meeting was somewhere on his schedule.

"Wh-why do you think I'm not well, boss?"

He drifted in like silent fog, his thin lips pressed in a face as pale as porcelain. "Your face is red. Your expression—are you in pain? I have that new client for you for tomorrow, but I can reassign him to Yamada, if you're coming down with something. It wouldn't do to infect the whole office."

Unable to withstand his scrutiny, I stood. "Thank you for the offer, but I'm alright… just something I ate. I'll be right back." I headed for the bathroom. The hallway carpet would soon show a well-worn path between my office door and the facilities unless something drastic changed in my personal life. A quick peek under the doors of the other stalls confirmed I was alone. I locked myself in the handicapped stall, unzipped my trousers, and let them drop along with my briefs. I sat; the cold porcelain of the water tank was soothing against my back. I pulled my cell phone out of my pocket, and there he was. I kept the sound turned so low, only I could hear.

My right hand almost mirrored his.

I won't go into further details. Suffice it to say I was back in my office within ten minutes, my face cooling off and my hair slicked back to disguise the moisture clinging to it.

I felt somewhat more functional as I reached for the thick manila folder left by Auguste Bernard Pillory the Third. A new account. Hmm. And I was to meet their vice president tomorrow. From the look of it, Black, White, and Blue, LLC was a fairly small, but successful, personal investment outfit. Further growth and expansion was part of their strategic plan—thus their need for an advertising campaign. The names of the partners were a bit unusual, but hey—whatever. As long as they liked my presentation. I was to meet Mr. Schiffer tomorrow.

A thorough analysis of Black, White, and Blue's current customer base revealed new, logical places for strategic expansion. It didn't take much to alter a boilerplate proposal to fit my new client's needs and e-mail it to Pillory for approval. After lunch, Pillory granted his go-ahead, and I quickly morphed the document into a PowerPoint presentation.

Then I kicked back, stretched my legs out under my desk, and situated my laptop in front of me. To all outside observers, I was busy at work. If only they knew. As it happened, I had more than one project to plan.

WORK would have been going well, had it not been for the awful, gnawing feeling of guilt that wouldn't let go of me no matter how hard I tried to will it away. I worked hard. I focused. I put my cell phone away, having copied the video onto a separate flash drive. I used the image of the angelic, debauched face as my wallpaper.

Not safe. Definitely not safe.

Then I just sat there, berating myself for being paranoid that somebody would recognize the face on my laptop's wallpaper as one of post-coital bliss. Only I knew what it was. What could possibly happen? He was just another handsome, sleepy, smiling man. Jack's room was poorly illuminated and light and shadow played with the ambient reflections off the street, making the image appear almost monochromatic.

Oh, what the heck. Might as well go full out. I captured the end of the video sound track from my phone and played with it a little bit. I doubted anyone would recognize the sound for what it was, and if any questions arose, I could claim that it was a growl of a big cat I found on a wildlife video. The thought of Azzuri as a big cat made me smile. The image seemed appropriate. Not wasting any time, I used the office phone to call myself.

"Gwrrraaaahrrr!"

My cell phone just had an orgasm. If lots of people called me, I'd have one, too. Hands free.

On a more serious note, I really had to return all those items I stole. Having become intimate with their owner in a virtual, roundabout sort of way, it no longer seemed acceptable for me to keep them. Now, I had been known to occasionally return an item, but knowing the guy was in town made it slightly tricky. First I called Reyna, who naturally couldn't pick up, so I left a message.

I worked for maybe ten minutes, rehearsing my presentation for Mr. Schiffer of Black, White, and Blue, LLC, when my phone roared.

"Gwrrraaaahrrr!"

I jolted. The primal roar hadn't lost its original effect on me. Wiggling in my seat, I picked up. "Reyna!"

"Hi, Wyatt." A slight pause followed. "Hey, are you alright?"

Everyone was suddenly interested in my well-being. "Yeah, why?"

"You sound a bit off, is all. What did you want? I'm finally catching up on all my work, now that Azz-hole isn't breathing down my neck." She paused expectantly.

"Just checking up on you. So he's still out, is he?" I asked to make sure.

"Yep. Wanna pick up a drink after work?"

"Sure," I said, my response utterly automatic. We'd meet at the same place at the same time and have the same drinks and the same bar food—wait. Wait—*wait*!

I couldn't get drunk or even slightly impaired if I had plans to infiltrate Azurri's apartment and get away with it. And I had to do it because, face it, the guy was hot and I felt like we had a connection of sorts, and I felt bad about what I'd done. There was no way to cancel on Reyna now, though; she'd want to know why, and I didn't feel like coming up with a lame excuse.

LATER that night, Reyna was on her third beer while I was on my first. I felt her warm eyes sharpen as she took me in and scrutinized my nondescript black top and the way I had slicked my hair in an effort to make it obey. And, of course, the one and only beer I was still nursing.

"Wyatt. Something isn't right with you. You're not keeping up."

"I'm fine," I lied. In reality, I was scared shitless. Suppose the gorgeous guy was there again, and suppose I didn't have it in me to leave?

"Wyatt, you're doing it again. Hellooo!" She waved her languid hand before my eyes, making her silver bracelets jingle.

I made an effort to pull myself together and chose a diversionary tactic. "So, Reyna, has it occurred to you that you and your boss are just clashing on personality? You could both be nice when you're apart, you know? Some people just aren't meant to work together."

"Dang, Wyatt. You're saying he's as cool as I am? What basis do you have to form that conclusion?"

I did have a basis. I just couldn't share it with her, so I just sat there thinking, my mind whirling like a gerbil wheel. "But you're more effective with him on vacation, right?"

"You're saying I should find another job? I love my job. It's just Azz-hole who's the problem here. You don't know him. He's capricious. Violent, even. His temper is legendary, and he always has to have his way."

Oh boy.

I really didn't need to hear that.

THREE hours later I was ready to head into the night, dressed in my black cargo pants and with my loose, black shirt tucked in. It was best not to be recognized. A lot of times I've cursed my too-short figure, but even I had to admit it was extremely convenient to look androgynous and nondescript. I fluffed up the black hair attached to my usual repairman's cap and said hello to Haus behind the desk.

He lifted his eyes up from his book, his wide mouth giving me a toothy grin. "Long time no see!"

"Yeah.... Whatcha readin'?"

"*The Old Man and the Sea*," he gruffed, as though he wasn't keen on sharing that. "Some people live the life, the rest of us grunts just get to fantasize about it, you know?"

"You bet," I said, nodding. I didn't know. I was living the life right now. The sweet glow of excess adrenaline already made me feel like I was floating two inches above the floor.

"Back to Azurri?"

"Yeah."

"Okay."

Well, that was smooth. I suppressed a breath of relief, signed the guest book, and then took the elevator to the fifth floor. I made it to the flat roof and enjoyed the feeling of being on one of the tallest buildings in the neighborhood while I navigated among the chimneys. For Shadyside, this building was pretty tall, and I thought I could almost feel the Allegheny River to my right and the Monongahela River to my left, merging past the lit-up skyscrapers of the visible downtown area to form the Ohio. It was pretty hot that night, and I regretted the necessity of dressing in long pants and long sleeves. Chafing from sweat already, I pulled my harness and rope from the vent where I had left them. I put Azurri's silver dish and the cash from his freezer into the cargo pockets and descended the wall. I felt that old thrill of hanging over a precipice. Wind whipping up the wall caressed my exposed neck as I moved my feet down the carved toeholds of the façade. Fifth floor and fourth floor, dark. Third floor, also dark.

I landed on the parapet with a light thud. Wind swirled around me again, and I unclipped the line while bent over in a protective crouch. I needed to get in fast, before the weather took me for a very short ride.

I pushed in the half-open casement windows, slid to the carpet, and crouched. The bed was, thankfully, unoccupied. I listened; there were no signs of life. Like a cat, I stretched my limbs, then progressed through the dark apartment. First I'd return the silver candy dish. As I pulled it out of my pocket, the sound of Velcro ripped through the silence of the evening. Damn… that was way too loud for comfort. I pattered over to the dining room table, only to find its surface empty. The boxes were gone from the floor. Where there used to be an expanse of antique-store items, order ruled once again. Only the ruby-eyed, ivory tiger remained.

Shit. Now he would notice.

No help for it, though.

With the gentlest care, trying to be perfectly silent, I reached out to place the antique piece of silverwork onto the gleaming wood next to the tiger, and was about to touch the polished wood when I heard the unmistakable *click* of the slide of a semiautomatic pistol being moved back.

"Stay where you are, punk," a velvet voice rumbled deep right behind me. I stilled in midmotion, my former quiver of excitement drenched by cold fear.

He was here.

Endless seconds ticked by before the tense silence was broken.

"What the fuck're you doing here?" The voice was rough suddenly, and as soon as I finished setting the silver candy dish next to the tiger, a large hand spun me around.

He reached to the wall, keeping the gun trained on me. The overhead light came on, almost blinding me. He wore jeans and a button-down white shirt, and his feet were bare. As he moved toward, me I didn't hear a single footstep; he prowled with a silent and predatory gait.

He threw a left hook. The heavy blow landed on my cheekbone, and I crashed into the table behind me.

"I asked you a question."

"Just putting some stuff back," I said nonchalantly, suppressing the pain, not letting my hands fly to my face; betraying any evidence of pain wouldn't do me any good whatsoever.

"You do that often?" His voice exerted a force of its own. I couldn't keep my eyes off him and let my gaze slide up and down his intimidating form. He exuded confidence. It appeared that my presence was not exactly a surprise.

"How did you know?"

"Shaddap, punk. I'm asking the questions."

"For now," I quipped, right before the gun lashed forward and made unwanted contact with my jaw.

I CAME to, firmly affixed to a dining-room chair. My head felt a bit fuzzy and my jaw and cheek hurt, and stiff, sticky tape was digging into my wrists and ankles, so naturally they hurt too. The man I used to regard as the object of my desire stood across the room, leaning against the doorway in a casual contrapposto, his gun now stuck in his waistband.

"So, talk."

The situation was complicated by the fact that I had the hots for this guy in the worst way possible. I never expected to get beaten up and I've always been able to talk my way out of anything, yet this guy pistol-whipped me as soon as I opened my mouth. It was time to reassess my strategy. It wasn't too late. I didn't see a phone in his hand, so I assumed the police weren't on their way.

I've been operating under the theory that if I was ever caught as a burglar, the best bet would be to seem amateurish and bumbling. Hopefully, the homeowner would let me go. I planned to just talk, talk, talk my way right out the door. Somehow I didn't think Azurri would have been impressed by a lot of jaw flapping, though.

I returned his penetrating gaze with all I had. "I'm sorry?" I lifted my eyes to his, going for the innocent puppy dog look. "Look, I just felt bad for doing some things I shouldn't have. I bungled it, and I came back just so I could return the stuff I took. I am… sorry." My voice grew quiet, and he remained silent, and there was just the hum of the refrigerator from the kitchen nearby.

He looked me up and down with unveiled curiosity. "I've never met a real burglar before." His eyes drifted toward my soft climbing shoes. He examined my black cargo pants, the long-sleeve shirt and the leather gloves, all black. He took two steps and reached his hand for my head, and I tried to dodge his touch, forgetting I was tied to one of his dining room chairs. My overgrown hair tickled my neck as he plucked off the hat with the wig and my skullcap.

Revealed and helpless, I drew myself up as much as my restraints allowed and flashed him a defiant scowl. "What would you like to hear, Azz-hole?"

He straightened some as a suspicious look narrowed his eyes. "Only my employees call me that, punk."

"Your employees are right regarding your temperament. Although, I guess I deserved it this time."

He arched his eyebrow. "Oh yeah?" He frowned, pulling a cell phone out of his pocket and aiming it my way. "Say 'cheese'!"

And dammit if I didn't grin my best, bruised-and-battered smile as he took my picture.

"I found this in your pocket," he said, picking up a plastic bag full of cash.

I nodded. "Yeah. You have to find a better place to hide that. At least get a fake frozen dinner box or something."

"Shaddap," he said, but he sounded somehow deflated, as though the bite was all gone from his bark. He pulled the money out and counted it. Not a dollar was missing. "Any other clever security suggestion, Burglar-dude?" he asked, his voice dripping with sarcasm.

I paused thoughtfully. "Yeah, actually."

He looked at me in expectant silence.

"First, talk to Haus downstairs. He's easily distracted from screening visitors."

"I've already done that. Who do you think called me, letting me know you were finally on your way?"

Oh. "Second, that safe of yours."

His eyes bulged.

"Too obvious. Your taste in art is exquisite, yet you put such a piece of fake junk up there? In such a prominent location? A family photo would've been better. At least that's genuine."

He took few quick steps to the wall and tugged on the frame of the painting and let it swing open. He dialed the safe open, shielding his hand from my sight. Like I needed to know the combination. The heavy metal door opened and an automatic light came on inside. He peered at the contents. "Nothing seems to be missing."

"Haven't tried it yet. Safecracking takes more time, you know. Although this one looked about medium difficulty, at best."

He spun at me, his face darkening with rage. "You impudent asshole!" He raised a fist as though he really wanted to slug me, but stopped himself as though he had just remembered I was still tied to his chair. Some kind of a misplaced chivalrous impulse must have taken over at that moment, because he cursed and pulled back. It was good to burgle a true gentleman. Lucky, even.

I watched him seethe, sucking down deep breaths as I tried to regain control. "Hey!" I cried out. "I would've returned it. I didn't have to come back, y'know. You don't have to hit a guy while he's tied to your chair, Azz-hole!"

He came so close, our noses almost touched. "I didn't hit you, now, did I." He fixed me with a hard, penetrating look. I returned his stare. His irises were impossibly blue. You could get lost in eyes like that. They looked like swirling galaxies, pulling me right in.

Without really wanting to, my glare turned into a soft puppy-dog stare again. Some indescribable quality of his gaze was riveting; the color changed from a deep cobalt blue to the palest of sapphire, with tiny little sparks of silver in between. I felt like I was drowning—I had to look away. I examined his straight nose instead and then continued farther down until I stopped at his thin, pink lips. They were pressed together in anger right then, but I had seen them smile before and knew they could become generous and pliable, given just the right incentive…. I swallowed and fought not to look away, my face flushing.

"I see." His voice was but a whisper. Then he ripped the tape off my limbs. "Get out and don't come back. You're lucky I'm feeling too fucking depressed to do anything about you."

He didn't have to ask twice. I walked to the bedroom as fast as dignity permitted and gave the empty bed but a quick glance. I stuck my head out the window; the wind had picked up, and rain threatened.

"Mind if I use your front door?" I asked.

"Sure do. You made it down, I'd like to see you make it up."

"You won't push me?"

"No, asshole," he said, and his gravelly voice sent an inexplicable flush of heat through my body. "I wanna see you climb."

I positioned myself on the ledge and caught the swaying rope. I clipped it to my harness like I was taught long ago and looked at the tall-and-gorgeous man who just stood there, watching my every move with visible fascination.

"Hey, Jack."

He jerked his head up, not expecting to hear his given name.

"I could offer to make amends. Buy you a drink, you know?"

He scowled. "Get outta my place."

I nodded, allowing the disappointment to show in my face. "Bye, then."

My rubber soles gripped the moist façade with just enough friction and, with gloves on my hands, I could grasp the rope securely as I climbed my way up, enjoying the flex of my biceps and the push of my muscular legs. As I got above his window, I froze in midmotion, chancing a look down. There he was, leaning out and looking up, as though he was curious to see what I'd do next. His eyes betrayed an excited gleam, and his lips were stretched in a hint of a grin. He liked to watch me climb.

Poor guy, his life was boring. All he needed was a bit of excitement. Like me.

THE alarm was kind of harsh the next day, blaring music right next to my ear. I slapped it and rolled out of bed. No sense delaying the inevitable. I showered and dressed in my crispest monogrammed dress shirt, with cuff links gleaming as they peeked from underneath my dark blue business suit. I decided against a red tie—the color was too loud for the way I felt after such a disaster of a night. I sifted through the collection of neckwear my sister bestowed upon me over the years, finally selecting one with an Escher fish pattern on it. Its shade of blue reminded me of a pair of blue eyes I couldn't quite erase from my mind. He'd looked so intense—not at all mellow like after... you know.... Dangerous, somehow. Yet inexplicably attractive.

"WHAT happened to your face, Mr. Gaudens?" Pillory looked me over. The bruised cheek and black eye were on one side of my face, and on the other side, my jaw sported a developing bruise topped by scratches from being gun-whipped.

"I fell off my bike," I said as I let embarrassment tinge my voice. "I can be such a klutz!"

"You'll have to make your apologies to your client. Mr. Schiffer will be here in an hour. Are you prepared?"

I nodded. "For sure! I think we can do them a lot of good, Mr. Pillory. We can control the cost by targeting the campaign to their next strategic growth areas—it's just a matter of how far he'll want to take it."

Pillory gave me one of his calm looks and curved his lips in a slight gesture that passed for an encouraging smile. Then again, Pillory never showed much. "Very well, then."

I was straightening my desk, getting the laptop ready to project my presentation onto the small screen in my office, and generally fussing before the new prospect arrived when I heard my cell phone have an orgasm in my pocket. I flushed at the memory of having seen Jack's deep blue eyes in person as I checked the caller ID. "Hey, Reyna. I have ten minutes. What's up?" It must have been important— we called only right before lunch or the end of work. Both of us had our hands full.

"That fucking asshole fired my ass, Wyatt. And it's tied to you somehow."

"What?" I couldn't believe my ears.

"He came to work today, early from his vacation. He showed a picture of this guy around, asking if anyone knew him. So I said yes, and since I was the only one to recognize you, he told me I can pack up my things."

My heart stilled. Never had I expected to drag Reyna into my extracurricular obsession.

"Hey, Wyatt. You alright? You looked like you had a bruised cheek in that picture."

Guilt suffused me. My best friend got fired on my account, and now she was concerned over my welfare. "I ran into him, kind of. We exchanged unkind words... sort of. I called him what you generally call him and it came to blows, and... well... he took my picture. He said only his employees call him that, and I said his employee was right about his temperament. Shit, Reyna. I'm so sorry. I had no idea this would happen."

I heard heavy breathing for awhile, expecting Reyna to explode.

"He hit you?" I heard her hiss.

"Well... I did provoke him, y'know."

"What a jerk. Really, now. How many grown men do you know get in fights over trivial things?"

How many grown men do you know burgle such men's apartments?

I took a deep breath, but before I could speak, her ringing voice sounded again. "Let's meet for drinks tonight. Your treat, you jerk, since you're still employed. And I'll expect you to help me update my resume."

JUST as I hung up, Frank Yamada, my assistant, stuck his head into my office, his soft, brown eyes wide with excitement. "Your appointment has arrived, Mr. Gaudens! Mr. Schiffer felt ill, though. He sent a substitute."

He flashed me a nervous smile. He was slight, shy, and always nervous, a disaster in the making. It was a wonder he could function in his position without really screwing up.

I walked to the reception area, putting on my best professional face. Pillory was already waiting with our guest. He stood with his back to me, letting my eyes feast on the way his sharp suit enhanced his shoulders.

"Mr. Schiffer is ill with the flu, but he sent a substitute," Pillory said. At that point, the man turned. I froze in place and words left me entirely as I recognized him. No wonder his shoulders looked so bloody enticing.

"Mr. Jack Azurri, please allow me to introduce our account manager, Mr. Wyatt Gaudens. He's been instructed to take good care of you and your needs."

I shook hands with Azurri. The pale, shocked expression on his face was soon replaced by a full-out grin.

"I'm sure I will find Mr. Gaudens's service most satisfactory."

CHAPTER
THREE

I DIDN'T expect Azzuri's hand to feel so warm. His grip was strong; he squeezed just a bit to let me know he had extra in reserve as I did my best to match him. He eased off with a knowing smile, his eyebrow arched and a grin still plastered to his face.

"It's so nice to meet you, Mr. Gaudens," he said as though we met for the first time ever, yet he still reminded me of a kid who had found the biggest Easter egg. He clasped my shoulder while still squeezing my right hand in his warm, generous hand, almost engulfing it. "I am sure we will work very well together."

I tried to catch my boss's eye. I had hoped he would intercede somehow instead of just standing there being all professional and observant. When I extricated myself from Azurri's grip, I noticed his warm scent now clung to my shoulder, and I suppressed a shiver. Yes, he was very, very attractive. My job, however, was to sell his company our marketing services. Our eyes met, and I felt his gaze drop to the swollen bruises on my face. A twinkle of humor receded as he touched one of them with his fingertips.

"An accident?" he inquired.

"Mr. Gaudens had a mishap on his bicycle," Pillory chimed in, finally taking pity on me.

"Right… right! I can be very clumsy at times." I pulled my right hand out of his enveloping grasp. "If you'd care to follow me, Mr. Azurri." I only hoped my voice was cool and collected, but there was no guarantee—his lingering warmth made me feel all mushy inside, and it took all the rigid effort I could muster to present a calm expression. I spun on my heel and preceded him to my office. Yamada trailed behind us with an eager, helpful expression on his face. Usually I'd chase him away, but I figured with Yamada around as a witness, my new client was less likely to bring up uncomfortable topics.

Under usual circumstances, these presentations were routine: find out what they wanted, show them your plan, discuss a mutual course of action, figure out how much they were willing to spend. No problem, right? Yet the familiarity and comfort of the routine process eluded me today. For one, I had the hardest time just making eye contact. It was in my best interest to stay away from those bewitching, impossibly blue eyes. I felt Azurri brush against me as he settled into the client chair; his spicy personal scent assaulted my senses, and suddenly I forgot where I was.

Shit. What am I doing, again?

"Um, sorry…. Here we go." I tried to hum in a reassuring way, alarmed to find my voice quavering the slightest bit. I shot a glare at the man who bored holes into me with his amused gaze. All of a sudden I had to get away from him—just for a little while. I needed to buy a bit of time to compose myself. Yamada raised his eyebrows, silently asking if I needed any help. I nodded at Yamada and reached into my right pocket for the flash drive that contained my presentation. It wasn't there. Flummoxed, I proceeded to check all my pockets, feeling like an idiot while items accumulated in a small pile on my desk. Finally, a familiar, silver flash drive appeared along with two pens, a few business cards, and a packet of Orbit gum.

"Can I offer you something to drink? Coffee? Tea?" *Or me?* My voice sounded only a bit steadier than before.

"Coffee would be great. Black, three sugars."

I nodded at Yamada. "Please give Mr. Azurri a copy of the presentation, would you? I'll go get his coffee."

Breathe.

I kept telling myself to breathe like it was a sacred mantra, inhaling deeply and exhaling very, very slowly, repeating the action over and over while I assembled the tray with our white, gold-rimmed client coffee cup on top of its fussy saucer, and a small bowl of honey-roasted nuts.

Then I spilled the coffee and had to clean it up and start all over again, which was why I took so long getting back.

Yamada was walking down the hall. His whole body language betrayed agitation. I was late, and that just wasn't done—he'd come to fetch me.

"Oh, there you are, Wyatt! I was getting worried." He gave me an assessing look. "You sure look like you need some help today. I got your laptop prepped and hooked up. You're ready to go!"

"Er… thank you, Frank." I lengthened my stride as much as the coffee tray allowed in an effort to get there sooner and take control of the situation. I worked best alone, and Yamada's helpful demeanor filled me with a sense of foreboding.

I pushed the door open with my shined shoe as I balanced on the other foot and maneuvered the coffee tray inside.

"Here you go…." My voice died in my throat. My laptop was prepped, alright. Hooked up to the projector with the silver flash drive already in the USB port. My newest client sat stiff and motionless, his eyes riveted to the projector screen. The sound was turned very low, but even so, both he and I could hear the unmistakable sounds of pleasure from the man in the video. The eerie lighting showed him in stark, almost baroque light-and-shadow contrast. The image wasn't perfectly centered and the inflated picture blurred the outlines somewhat, but even so, there was no mistaking his identity.

First, I thanked Yamada and shut the door in his face. Then I got in the way of the projector beam, deposited the coffee tray on my desk with haste, and reached to pull the stupid, treacherous flash drive out of my laptop.

"Gwrrraaaahrrr!"

The man on the screen climaxed, the image of his ejaculate projected onto the chest of my pristine shirt. I shot a distressed look at my client. He stared back at me, motionless, his wide grin gone.

I put distance between us by moving behind my desk and ejected the flash drive from the system. My wallpaper came up: bigger than life and absolutely gorgeous, his angelic face in postcoital languor graced the projection screen.

"Sorry...." I cleared my throat, fighting for a semblance of control over my runaway situation. "That was obviously the wrong presentation." Words spilled out of my mouth without the benefit of my brain regulating their content. I pocketed the flash drive and searched my other pocket, fishing out an almost identical device after a bit of effort. When I plugged it in, the relaxed, almost monochromatic face on the projection screen was now partially obscured by a list of files. I clicked on "BWB Proposal"; a slick PowerPoint presentation replaced the unspeakable scene from before.

"You got a hard copy?" I asked, instantly regretting my word choice. "I mean, a printout." Heat crept up my neck and stained my face tomato red.

He looked at me, bereft of words.

His prolonged silence gave me a false sensation of being in charge once again. I picked up the blue-bound portfolio. "All parts of the proposal are in here."

I couldn't say his name.

I just couldn't.

"It has a space for notes, if you want to take notes." God, my words just got up and left. My customary eloquence had disappeared. I just plainly could not summon all those smooth, comforting phrases I'd learned to use in the course of the last two years. I felt totally exposed and brand new, waiting for him to deliver his devastating strike.

His silence was unbearable.

I slid my hand up my face to wipe the dampness off my brow, brushing against the tender flesh he had bruised so easily the night before. The sensation was unexpected. I barely bit back a hiss of pain. Finally, I turned the projector off, stood up, and walked halfway around my desk. I leaned my butt against it as I folded my arms across my chest and stared into his shocked, pale face. "Just... just say something."

He twitched.

"I know you're really mad, and I don't blame you. I'm so sorry you had to see that." I didn't say I was sorry *I* saw that, and I knew right away that he took note of my careful phrasing.

Jack Azurri rose from the client chair. He was somewhat taller than I, broader in the shoulders, and I was already well acquainted with the power of his punch. Cowering would do me little good, and besides, I had a thing against cowering.

I stood up straight and looked him in the eye.

It was his move.

He grasped the sculpted lapels of my suit jacket with his large hands and pulled me in the slightest bit as he peered into my face. His gaze was icy cold and without apparent interest. He looked over the damage he'd done me last night, emotionless. "Sorry about that." His voice was low and without inflection.

"No, you're not."

He looked over me again, and I saw the anger from last night well up again. "Nah… you ain't worth it." He pushed me away hard; there was no time to regain my balance as I stumbled and bounced against the wall with an awkward thud.

I straightened myself up fast, alarmed to see his back in the doorway. "Wait. Don't go. The presentation…." My voice had an edge of raw panic, and that must have caught his attention, because he turned back toward me.

"Oh yeah. Your precious presentation. Good thing I have a hard-copy." He emphasized the last two words, smirking at my apparent discomfort.

"I'm so sorry," I said, and as the words left my mouth, I realized I did, in fact, feel remorse. "So sorry… for everything. Isn't there anything I can do to make up for it?"

I saw him hesitate. He took two steps back inside my office and closed the door. "I don't know," he said, his voice edged with that cold, seething anger. "I don't know what you're good at."

Without thinking, I blurted, "I'm good at a lot of things."

He startled, then paused. "What... what did you say?"

"I'll... I'll do.... Just... don't tell my boss." I gazed at him with entreaty. "Please," I added, my voice a mere whisper. Here I was with the object of my desire, my wildest fantasies, and... his seething anger was aimed at me.

Justifiably so, and it was killing me.

"What are you good at?" His face took on an intrigued expression. "Like, doing the advertising campaign for free?"

"Anything that's mine to give," I said. "I won't steal from my employer."

"Ah, there is honor among thieves," he snarled. "You won't bite the hand that feeds you; anyone else is fair game."

"No. Not anyone." I paused. "You aren't fair game anymore."

"Because?"

I blushed and looked away. Just at that moment, my cell phone went off in my pocket.

"Gwrrraaaahrrr!"

I froze, blood draining from my face.

"What was that?" he asked, his rage toned down by a hint of confusion.

"Gwrrraaaahrrr!"

"Sorry.... Let me get that." To his utter shock, I pulled my cell phone out of my pocket and declined the call, then set it on vibrate.

"Are you for fucking real?" he asked, coming closer to me. "What are you, some psycho stalker?"

I shook my head. "I... I didn't know you'd be home that night...." The oft-repeated word fell off my lips again: "Sorry...."

"I'll make you damn sorry. I'll give you one chance to convince me not to report you immediately."

I considered my options. There was the video; if I put it on YouTube, it might even go viral. That was a weapon of last resort, though, because this guy was hotter than July and I wanted to actually get to know him. Not just his place, not just his stuff and the contents of his safe—I suddenly wanted to erase that awful, mortifying embarrassment I put him through, and there was only one way I could think of doing that. The way he had put his arm around me in the lobby earlier indicated that he didn't, in fact, mind touching me. The way he was touching himself the other night suggested he might even swing my way. There was only one way to find out. I had nothing to lose, and if he stormed out, there was always plausible deniability.

The presidential treatment.

"Please. Won't you sit down?"

Our eyes met. I saw understanding dawn, then a bit of hesitation as he glanced at the closed office door.

It felt like forever before he made up his mind and sat. I approached him from behind, running my hands up his shoulders and into his lush, wavy brown hair. It was gelled in place, but I didn't care if I messed him up. My one and only goal was to make him feel absolutely, positively fabulous, and the only thing I had to go on was the video. Considering what I already knew about what he found pleasurable, I'd make sure he found my company as thrilling and as relaxing as possible.

I rubbed his scalp in gentle circles with my fingertips, progressing outward toward his jaw. "Relax," I whispered by his ear.

He hesitated and then his shoulders loosened just the slightest bit.

"There... not so hard, is it?" I let my breath caress his ear and was gratified to hear him draw a deep breath. My fingers progressed outward, massaging his scalp and letting my nails scratch him the slightest bit.

He leaned into my hands.

Surprised, I leaned around and deposited a small kiss on the edge of his jaw.

"C'mere," he growled, pulling me around. I complied, ready to go through with my penance. "Kneel." I shrugged out of my jacket, folded it, and put it down between his polished shoes. Just when I was ready to kneel, my pride stirred and made me falter.

I've been dreaming of doing just this... have I not?

I've been obsessed with fantasies about this man—and how I'd make him growl with pleasure.

Why hesitate? Seize the moment....

First one knee, then the other hit the soft material, protecting my trousers from the industrial carpeting under his polished shoes. I looked him in the face.

"You know what to do," he said with a challenge in his eyes as though he was daring me to proceed.

His legs felt strong and muscular under the fine wool of his trousers as I ghosted my fingers over his knees and thighs. His eyes were on mine, as still as deep water. He didn't move a muscle, didn't flinch. Suddenly I understood. He seemed determined to prove a true challenge. At that moment I felt a wild, irrational desire to hear those little sounds of ecstasy again. He wore a fine-grain leather belt with a silver buckle, which I unfastened. Then I popped the button and the inner hook of his trousers, and leaned in close enough to grab the zipper pull of his fly with my teeth. As I pulled his zipper open, the lush material slid against my hands and cheeks like a caress, and I shivered as a memory of his closet hit me.

Soft fabric.

Enticing scent.

The hiss and pant of pleasure.

Memories flooded me, and I felt my body respond. My lips felt dry—no wonder, they'd been parted for quite a while now, dried by soft little puffs of air making their way in and out. I licked them. Azurri tensed at that; I basked in the sight of those eyes darkening, his pupils dilating.

I let my fingers slide in to feel his silk boxer shorts, careful not to touch his cock as I freed him and discovered he was already half-erect. Teasing in a game of impromptu seduction, I let my head descend between his legs as I exhaled a puff of moist breath. He stirred, and I looked up. His eyelids slid halfway shut as he watched me with his pink lips slightly parted. I grinned.

"Wyatt." His gravelly voice sent a shiver down my spine.

He eased his fingers into my hair, messing it up as his hand clenched into a fist. I thrilled at the feeling of his grasping hand guiding me as I opened my mouth. The head of his cock was warm and silky against my tongue, and I ran the tip around it in gentle exploration. My scalp stung a bit as his fist tightened, and I felt his legs straighten and relax.

"Wyatt!" His voice, which was a rough growl only moments ago, turned into a soft whisper.

I moaned, barely hearing, lost in the sensation of his silky hardness against my palate, letting my head bob as I slid my tongue up and down his shaft.

"Wyatt Gaudens, what is the meaning of this?" Auguste Bernard Pillory the Third's head was stuck through the open door of my office, his expression shocked, his hand still on the doorknob.

I STOOD before Pillory's desk. He leaned back in his black leather chair, his eyes on my flushed face, an expression of disbelief still etched into his features. His stunned gaze took in my disheveled hair, missing jacket, and a tie that was loosened and slightly askew. "Mr. Gaudens. Words fail me. You've been in my employ for two years now." He paused, studying my sorry person for a while longer, not seeing what he was looking for. "You have a lot of promise. However… your sense of judgment is sadly lacking. This prospective customer could have been one of our biggest clients. Your conduct…." He paused again, and I jumped at my chance.

"Boss, I can explain—"

"Gaudens." His lips thinned. "Your conduct was disastrously unprofessional, to say the least. You wish to explain? Be my guest, but my mind is made up."

"I… I'm in love, boss."

His thin, elegant eyebrows rose. "It is my understanding that you've never met this man before."

"I've never met Mr. Schiffer before. Mr. Azurri and I are... well... our relationship, if you can even call it that, is complicated, and not always easy." That, at least, was the truth.

Pillory swiveled in his posh chair and stared out the window for a while. "You may move your personal belongings out of your office today. I will give you two weeks' severance pay, but don't expect any glowing references. My recommendation will state you are capable, talented, and resourceful, yet sadly immature."

He stood, and I knew it was over. Suddenly it occurred to me that he was beautiful in a way I had never appreciated while he had still been my boss. Midnight black strands escaped from his ponytail, framing his face with those devastating, high cheekbones and changeable eyes, and I could only imagine the toned frame underneath his office attire.

"Is there anything wrong, Mr. Gaudens?"

I sighed. "No.... No, thank you. It's just... I was wondering, now that you fired me, why the hell didn't I fall for you instead."

To my surprise, his lips quirked upward in the slightest hint of a smile. "Because falling for your boss is never a good idea, Mr. Gaudens." He paused before he exited his office and looked me in the eyes, all serious now. "I wish you the best of luck."

"THE bad news is that this is the last round of drinks I can afford," I told Reyna. "Pillory fired my ass."

"No way!" Reyna's eyes widened, her prominent, plucked eyebrows giving her a fierce appearance. "What for?"

"Because Schiffer from BW&B is sick today and your former boss came instead of him. I was supposed to give him a presentation...." My voice trailed off, and I reached for my beer and took a healthy sip.

"No way! He happened to show up a day after he gave you that bruise? What happened, did you two explode at each other or something?"

"You won't believe me."

Reyna took in my miserable countenance with a gaze both protective and incredulous, and her fingers began to twirl a strand of her hair in a gesture of impatient anticipation. A sly grin began to spread slowly across her face. "Try me, you nut!"

"Pillory walked into my office just as I was…." I paused, hesitant to fill the expectant silence. "He walked in just as I was on my knees in front of Azurri, giving him head."

"Fuck!" Reyna's mouth was full of beer as I said this, and that was a mistake on my part—I should have waited for her to swallow. Her beer spray covered my good suit and white work shirt, silk tie and all.

Reyna looked at me in outrage. "That asshole forced you to go down on him in your own office?"

I cast my eyes down at the round bar table, studying the scarred wooden surface.

"You don't have to put up with that kind of shit, Wyatt, let alone be fired for it. I want you to go and—"

"Reyna." I put up my hand, feeling guilty because she was the best fag-hag friend a guy could ever have. "Reyna, I offered."

Her look turned from protective to disapproving. "So what's the good news?" she asked.

"The good news is, you can apply for my old job. Pillory's a pretty nice guy. He never yells, he gives precise instructions, he's pretty good-looking…." I sighed. I'd miss good ol' Pillory.

"So what now? Will you apply for my old job now?" Reyna asked, uncertain.

"No. I thought about it, but no. It's… I want him for myself. As a lover, not as a boss."

"What will you do, then? Job hunt?"

"I'll manage." Reyna might have been my best friend, but not even she knew of some of my more eclectic skills.

CHAPTER
FOUR

TWO margaritas, one with salt, one without. Two beers. Nachos grande.

I wrote the order down in shorthand, looked at my party of four, and smiled. "Coming right up!"

I'm sure the smile didn't go all the way up to my eyes—it was that tired, professional smile waiters got toward the end of the night when their feet hurt and their knees ached and they are thoroughly sick and tired of humanity in general. My body might have been surprisingly beaten down by four consecutive days of waiting tables, but my mind was alert and keen, my ears searching for the right stray bit of somebody else's conversation.

"So I told them we can't afford that—that's crazy. I'd rather save the money for my kids' college."

No use barking up that tree. I moved on.

"Did you call your lawyer? You gotta talk to your lawyer 'bout all this. There's no way he can do that to ya."

A tough mother-daughter conversation was taking place in the corner. I felt bad for the daughter. She nursed her strawberry daiquiri and heavy makeup barely covered a bruise by her eye. There was no way I'd touch her, her mother, or their possessions. If I could relieve her asshole husband of some of his toys, maybe....

Suddenly, a song of profit and adventure rose to my ears from two tables over.

"So we're leaving on the twenty-first, and we'll be in Prague for the ten days it will take to get my eyelids done. And then! Oh, I'm just so excited—we'll swing through Paris. I have some shopping to do. Two weeks altogether."

The aches and pains of the preceding week dissipated as adrenaline surged through my veins. Having deposited the two margaritas, two beers, and nachos grande where they belonged, I reached for a pitcher of water and hovered by the table occupied by two middle-aged couples, waiting for an unobtrusive time to top off their ice water. A well-maintained blonde was holding court, her husband in attendance. I noticed her fifty-dollar manicure and her upscale haircut.

"Where will you shop?"

The question was posed by her brunette lady-friend, who did her best not to show signs of jealousy. Her jewelry was understated by comparison; her fingers didn't drip gold and diamond pavé rings, she didn't wear a Cartier watch, her neck didn't sport a heavy gold necklace, and her ears were decorated with discreet, delicate pearl studs instead of all those multiple hoops. Her jaw was a bit tight, perhaps, but other than that, her decorum didn't slip one bit.

"We'll go to the Galleries Lafayette again. Their styles are so different from what you can get here in the US—so feminine and elegant and so avant-garde...."

I topped their water off and eyed their half-empty plates.

"Are you enjoying your dinner? Is there anything else I can get for you?" My smile was on, and I was unobtrusive, just as they expected. I had to make sure not to serve them too poorly, nor too well. I was shooting for dead average. No sense standing out in the crowd.

The blonde's husband, a thin man with a shiny pate surrounded by still-dark hair, looked at me with apology in his eyes. "No, thank you. Everything is very good."

"Oh, but, honey." The blonde's whine cut through the din of the restaurant's dining room. "I thought you didn't get enough of that guacamole." She lifted her hooded, heavily made-up eyes at me. "Bring us more of that guacamole. And I'll have another martini, with a twist of lemon this time."

I nodded. "Sure. Right up."

I brought them the guacamole and another martini. "Would you care for some dessert and coffee?" I asked. "We have a new specialty...."

The discussion over coffee and dessert always sparked an argument over dietary shoulds and should nots.

"Go ahead, Janet," the brunette said. "You won't have Tres Leches cake in Prague!"

Her name was Janet. That's all I got to find out.

When they were all done, the brunette's husband picked up the tab, which was highly inconvenient because I didn't want to burgle *them*; no, she'd been kind and always said "please" and "thank you." I wanted to burgle her overbearing blonde companion, who probably had a whole treasure-trove of gold jewelry she never even wore anyway. Gold sold for a good bit these days.

However, not all was lost. They left an average tip—no more and no less than I've earned, and now I had the brunette's husband's credit card information. That was enough, really. He wasn't on Facebook, but he was on LinkedIn, where he shared some personal details, from which I learned that his wife's name was Suzanne Gould. Suzanne Gould was on Facebook, however, and she shared some of her interests in the publicly visible profile, so I friended her immediately. I used my faux identity.

Dear Suzanne, we've met at the Library Benefit a few weeks ago and only now I remembered to friend you—we talked about some possible projects for offsetting the government cutbacks. We should talk some more, this is a worthy cause.

Now, having learned Suzanne Gould sat on the public library's steering committee, I deduced that she attended benefits all the time as part of her job. Everyone was talking about the state funding cutbacks, and fundraising was indeed a worthy cause. I loved my library—how else could I set up a hard-to-trace Facebook and LinkedIn account?

She friended me back the next day, using that sort of obscure language people use when they have forgotten who you are but are embarrassed to say so. I grinned and perused her "friends" list. Sure enough, there was a Janet, and her picture indicated she was indeed the blonde I saw at the restaurant.

My parents always taught me to be modest and not to brag, and I took it to heart for the most part. Their wisdom was now apparent to me. Had Janet Barnaby not crowed about that upcoming trip to Europe and had she not posted pictures of a recent landscaping and remodeling project, I would have never known where she lived. As it was, I recognized the street, and I had a street number from above their mailbox by the road; all I had to do was wait a few days.

I HAD the next night off, which was a financial killer for a waiter, because tips are always heavy on Saturdays. I had to see Reyna, though.

"So, have you applied?" I asked, twirling my beer glass in my hands.

"Yeah. He didn't like my red nails. He said they're too long. And the tattoo on my neck wasn't covered up; he said it was unprofessional."

The huge, black banana spider still sat on the nape of her neck. The tattoo was part of Reyna's individual style; she had always been the kind of a girl who would never give a damn what others thought of her appearance, and she aimed to please only herself. If a black, lace-edged camisole revealed her poison-green bra straps and she happened to like it, that's what she would wear. Sporting a bit of ink on her skin was a personal matter, as were her long, red nails. Or so she said. This attitude of supreme confidence, together with her athletic figure and ravishing hair, swept away most of the people she met, her quirky fashion choices notwithstanding. She was like a force of nature, and I'd always been a bit jealous of the way she could wear a garbage bag and nobody would notice because they were so focused on the sparkle in her eyes. I always looked like a pity date by her side—or her little brother. It was virtually impossible to cruise for guys with Reyna around—but I digress.

"And I was good and all. I had a blouse on I totally despise, and my hair was put up in a conservative bun. What else does he want, anyway?"

The image of the good and honorable Auguste Bernard Pillory III, with his old-blood pedigree and old-money backing, popped into my mind, and I found the image of him and Reyna in the same room rather amusing: there was Reyna, doing her level best to wear the clothing that would make her fit in, and there was Pillory, unable to take his eyes off the gigantic spider on the back of her neck.

"Did he look at your resume?"

"Yeah.... He looks a bit cold, your Mr. Pillory. He didn't say anything one way or the other. I think I have a better chance elsewhere." She popped a salted almond into her mouth, raising a groomed eyebrow in my direction. "So... how is it with you?"

I grimaced. Finding a real job was hard enough with a good recommendation, let alone with a tarnished record on account of my extremely poor judgment. "My infatuation cost me dearly, I'm afraid. When I tell my prospective employers that I won't get a good recommendation from Pillory, I get the 'don't call us, we'll call you' treatment."

Reyna sighed. "That's tough. But, hey, think out of the box for a minute, will ya? What is it you're good at?"

Breaking and entering. "Um.... Nothing...."

"Bullshit!" Reyna crowed, ready to give me a professional makeover. "Didn't you say you have prepared analyses of your clients' existing customer base? And you have developed those marketing strategies and stuff?"

"Yeah?"

"You could freelance, you know. You don't have to work for anyone else—you have a computer and a printer, and a phone... and you know the ropes. You could pick up the accounts that are too small for your old firm. Didn't you say Pillory specialized in larger clients with fatter budgets?"

I nodded, twirling my tepid beer some more and noticing my blunt nails and the way they were all broken from rock climbing. How

Reyna managed to climb *and* keep a good manicure, I'd never know. Not that I cared for painting my nails—I was too manly for that—but still, it boggled the mind. I drank some. Her suggestion wasn't so bad, so I drank a bit more, thinking.

"Here," Reyna said. "I'll help you with your business plan. That's what I've been doing a lot of at my old job. I'll e-mail you this blank form.…"

We drank some more beer and ate some stuffed hot peppers and chicken wings. My tongue burned, contaminated with a side order of that awful habanero sauce Reyna favored. I didn't bitch, though, because she had some good ideas. Most people figure Reyna's a slow child because of her bottle-red hair and tattoos, excessive gypsy jewelry, and dragon-lady crimson nails. The fact that she gets flustered when she has to speak in public doesn't help her image, either. She doesn't make a really great first impression, but when it comes to results, she can deliver.

She was doing good by me and I owed her one, and suddenly I realized how I could pay her back. I smiled and chased the potent hot sauce with more beer.

"Okay then. We'll meet tomorrow at eleven at Starbucks and give it a whirl."

TWO days later I was seated in Mr. Pillory's client chair with a gold-rimmed cup of coffee on a tray before me, feeling distinctly aware of the fact that I was the one drinking the coffee and not serving it. Frank Yamada gave me an encouraging smile as he left, closing the door.

Pillory peered at me with his steady, gray gaze. His hair spilled in midnight streams down his shoulders, making his chiseled face seem even paler. "I hope you didn't come with hopes of getting your job back, Mr. Gaudens," he said, his fine-boned hands steepled before him.

I sipped some of the good coffee, set the cup down, and smiled. "No. I know you don't go back on your decisions, Mr. Pillory. However, there are two other issues I'd like to bring up."

His eyebrows rose, beckoning me to continue.

"First, I decided to go freelance. Now I realize you've taught me all I know in this field, and I wouldn't dream of poaching your clients, so I have a proposal. Those smaller companies with a small advertising budget that can't afford you—if you'd refer them to me, I'd greatly appreciate it. In turn, when I run into a client too big for me to handle, I'll refer him or her to you."

At that point I shut up and rested my hands in my lap. Silence was golden, and I knew he wouldn't take me seriously if I weren't at my professional best. I was selling something, and you can't sell if you talk all the time. You have to give them space to think.

One minute doesn't sound like a lot, but when you're sitting in somebody's office, it drags on for eternity. A typical American salesman can't shut up for more than six seconds on average; I was doing pretty well so far.

Eventually I saw him stir.

"Do you have anything worked out, or is this just an idea right now?"

I reached for a small, faux-leather portfolio and pulled out one of those paper folders with pockets. It had my business card in it and a flyer describing the services of WG Guerilla Marketing. I let him look it over. "I also brought my business plan," I said.

He extended his hand, his eyes still on the graphic layout of my promotional materials.

I handed the bound, fifty-page business plan across the table, mentioning in an off-hand manner, "My best friend, Reyna Guajillo, helped me pull this together. I would have just been in the planning stages without her." I saw his eyebrows twitch.

"Reyna Guajillo is your friend?"

"Since our first year in college," I said.

"Why did she apply for a position with me?" Pillory asked, lifting his eyes from my business plan for the first time.

"She got fired by her boss for no reason of her own. Her boss is a real jackass—he yells and throws things... he's a difficult man. Reyna got her best work done when he was on vacation. So anyway, she's determined not to work for someone like that again, and I recommended you."

The compliment might have been veiled, but it was still there, and Pillory's face assumed a peaceful, almost-smiling expression. "Your friend doesn't make the best first impression."

"Yeah. Our first contact in college was a bar fight." Oops, that just slipped out. "She's not like that, you understand—it's just that there's more to her than meets the eye." I saw him nod, leaf through the rest of the thick document, then nod again.

"If this is a sample of Ms. Guajillo's work, maybe I should talk to her again."

ON FRIDAY, I dressed like a landscaper in a loose shirt that concealed my fairly fit figure. I wore a short brown wig and a baseball cap, and with my own hair tucked underneath, it was bloody hot, but there was nothing I could do about the weather. Janet Barnaby thought it suitable to announce to her Facebook friends that she fired their gardening service. My friend Lenny loaned me his truck with his lawn mower and tools, and I went to the Barnabys' residence. Posing as the new victim of her perfectionism wasn't too hard.

I lowered the lift gate of the red pickup truck, attached the steel-grating bridge, and eased the lawn mower down to the street. I mowed the Barnabys' already trim lawn and used the blower to get clippings off the paved walkways, which got me all the way to the doors and windows. The wiring I saw indicated they a security system, but probably only on the first floor. The second floor seemed to be accessible from the pergola over the backyard patio. When people departed for an extended time, they usually left a window cracked open somewhere so the house could breathe. If I could find that window, I could be in and out pretty fast.

REYNA and I met on Saturday again.

"You'll never guess," she said, a wide smile on her strong, pretty face. "Mr. Pillory called me back yesterday. I was trying to call you, but you weren't picking up."

"My phone was off for a while," I said, thinking she must have called while I was casing the Barnaby residence.

"So anyway, he wants me to work there for a month—a probationary period, he called it. If he likes my work, I can stay."

I grinned. "Did he mention anything specific?"

"Well... he said lots of his clients don't think strategically, and it would help to have their plans down in writing. It's not in my wheelhouse, but I could do it, I guess."

"He liked the business plan you did for me."

Her eyes popped wide and her lipsticked mouth gaped. "You went to see him?"

"Yep. He and I will refer clients to one another. He didn't say so, but I think he felt kind of bad about kicking me out. I showed him my materials and mentioned that you helped me with all that. I guess he changed his mind."

"You think?"

"Hard to believe. I didn't think he was capable of rethinking anything once his mind was set."

Reyna got a dreamy look in her eyes as she adjusted her hair, which was tied up in one of her bizarre retro beehives. "In that case, I'll work my butt off. He really seems like such a nice guy...."

I rolled my eyes and gave her an ironic smirk. "Just a reminder, Reyna... I got fired on account of an office romance."

SUNDAY evening was a good time to break into a suburban house; the heat was still oppressive, and the Barnaby neighborhood was humming with straining air-conditioning units. The neighbors were inside, eating dinner and getting ready to watch their favorite TV shows before they had to get ready for the upcoming workweek.

Dusk fell as I parked my bicycle in a copse of trees two blocks away. I wore simple, long black biking tights and a loose, black cotton button-down shirt over my neon-green cycling tee. My concealed waist pouch contained all I needed.

The neighborhood was deserted as I ghosted through the backyard shrubbery. The minutes I spent to reach the Barnaby backyard seemed endless. I jumped up, grabbing one of the beams of the pergola, and walked my feet up the wooden pillar. I hooked my knee around the top beam and hoisted my body up, crouched, and looked around. The neighbors were still inside. There was no traffic in the street. I balanced on a beam and walked to the second-story windows and inspected them. Sure enough, there was no sign of an alarm system—and none of them were unlocked. I sighed. I hated to leave a calling card, but there was no help for it. With gloves on, I pulled an egg of silly putty out of my pouch and I stuck it to the bathroom window. Using a diamond-tip scribing pen, I drew a careful circle around the putty, then pressed in. The windows were double-pane; the first circle fell between the two sheets of glass, leaving me with a blob of silly putty in my hands. I repeated the process on the second pane, producing a tidy opening just big enough for my slender hand. I reached in and up, unlocked the window, and made my way into the house.

The air on the inside felt stuffy. The homeowners must have turned their air conditioning off while they were gone. The bathroom window, just like the rest of the upstairs, didn't show any wiring and I figured it wasn't hooked up to their security system. I drew the blinds and closed the curtains before I clicked the lights on.

The house was amazingly cluttered. It must have been decorated professionally some years ago, but strata of various objects were deposited onto the formerly elegant surfaces over time. Only a few of these objects were of value, but I was fine with that. My job was to find Janet Barnaby's secret hiding place. Almost everyone had a special place where they put their valuables while they were away. I wasn't disappointed. The master bedroom was upstairs. Its closets were full to bursting with predominantly women's clothing. Child-sized access panels connected the bedroom to a number of little crawlspaces. It took me two minutes before I pried the stuck doors open. I found two pieces of luggage the Barnabys chose not to bring along behind the first door. The second door opened onto a cache of round hatboxes. Some of them still had price tags on—she got them on sale at Marshall's, mostly. I looked through their contents with care, trying not to disturb the carefully arranged surface of old gloves and scarves. There were no hats; she apparently used the pretty boxes as storage for her Hermès scarf collection. Each scarf could fetch around three hundred bucks on eBay—but I didn't feel like dealing with the process of selling them and leaving a trail. I was after smaller, denser stuff.

Sure enough, four rectangular shoeboxes on the right side of the crawlspace contained anything but shoes. Just the fact that Janet Barnaby chose to store these particular pieces of jewelry piled in shoeboxes was telling of the fact that she rarely, if ever, wore them. I selected quickly, avoiding unique, easily recognized pieces. Soon, my quart-size Ziploc bag was full of chains and earrings and bangles. Not one of them had stones; her good gemstones would reside in her real jewelry box, which was probably in a safe under the bed. I didn't feel any desire to crack a safe that evening. Satisfied with a pound of gold, I arranged her boxes back the way they were, replaced the crawl space cover, dusted my gloved hands off, and made my exit the way I came.

The next morning, my fence looked at the jewelry I brought in and smirked. "Looks like a good haul for one night," he said.

"Well? How much?"

"Seven thousand," he drawled, pushing his stringy brown hair behind his ear in a nervous gesture.

"C'mon, Slavko. We both know gold's at over fifteen hundred per ounce. This is all good stuff."

"Maybe so, but I have to make my profit, too. You can't take it to a scrap dealer, not unless you want to give them your ID."

We haggled for a bit, and he upped his offer to eight grand, which I accepted with a grudging air but a grateful heart. I deposited half the cash in my bank account and put the other half in my emergency cubbyhole. I figured I'd use some of the cash for building my website. I used a lot of the money to place advertisements in a local business newspaper, and I spent only a bit less on targeted mailings to three hundred local, smaller companies. With a three percent response rate, I was hoping for nine or ten solid leads, which would typically result in two to four paying jobs.

REYNA couldn't meet me for drinks on Saturday, as she managed to screw up some key paperwork for Mr. Pillory. She offered to stay until it was done right, and apparently she really applied herself to the task with great dedication, because she left me sipping my beer by my lonesome self. It frankly sucked. I was almost ready to go home when my phone roared in my pocket.

"Hey, Wyatt! I got it done, but I'm totally bushed. He uses a different filing system from what I'm used to."

"You could have called for help," I said, irritated at losing my drinking buddy to my former boss.

"No way. I gotta learn how to do it right. He won't accept anything less." There was an odd note of dedication in my best friend's voice.

"So you like working for him?" I asked, nostalgic for the good old days of a steady paycheck.

"Oh man. The difference is unimaginable. He's so quiet. He hasn't yelled once. He'll just explain, and if I start to space out, he'll just say 'Ms. Guajillo'! You know? And he came in today and brought me pizza, since I was staying on a weekend."

I frowned. Pillory had never brought me lunch, and I stayed weekends every time I screwed something up, too.

The next Monday, Pillory called to let me know he saw my ad in the paper and that it looked pretty good. "Nice website, Mr. Gaudens," he said in his customary, formal tone. "By the way, I felt very bad about detaining your friend this weekend. As her boyfriend, you must have been very disappointed."

"Reyna doesn't have a boyfriend," I answered, the words spilling out automatically.

"Oh? A girlfriend, then?"

Shit. This was Reyna we were talking about. I really didn't want to screw up her new job for her. There must have been a neutral way to say she broke up with Tim three months ago. I paused. "Reyna is unattached, as far as I know."

"Ah." Somehow, Pillory must have heard what he wanted to hear, because his next words were infused with an unusual level of warmth. "I may have a client for you—new flower shop in Lawrenceville. The owners call it 'The Stamens,' which means absolutely nothing to your average customer." He let out an exasperated sigh. "Let me e-mail you their information. You may use my name."

ON WEDNESDAY, my landline rang. Not many people called my landline, and I had it only so I could hook up the fax machine. Expecting a telemarketer, I picked up. "WG Guerilla Marketing, may I help you?"

I heard somebody breathe on the other side, and then he cleared his throat and said, "Is Gaudens there?"

My arms broke out in goose bumps; the voice was unmistakable. "Speaking."

"I still have that marketing proposal you prepared over two weeks ago. Do you still do that kind of work?"

Silence froze the line for an indeterminate amount of time. "Is… is that you, Mr. Azurri?"

"Yeah."

His deep, gravelly voice made my heart speed up and I had to press my index finger to my nose to contain a sudden sneeze. I leaned back in my computer chair, my other hand limp over my forehead. "H-how may I h-help you?" I could tell my voice was a bit breathy, and I absolutely hated that stupid stutter.

"I need some help with advertising, and I can't show my face at your old company anymore. I called my former assistant, hoping she could arrange for the work, but she now has your job, and she says you're freelancing." His voice was full of disbelief at his ill fortune. "You owe me, Gaudens. And I want that video back."

"Mmm," I hummed, not committing one way or the other. "Do you want me to come to your office?"

"No! Not there. Not ever. Just… meet me at Starbucks, the one off Fifth Avenue." All of my business seemed to be taking place at Starbucks these days. "Half an hour."

I grabbed my laptop and some of my new marketing materials, got out of my jeans and T-shirt, and put on a pair of gray tailored slacks with a black leather belt and monogrammed white dress shirt. I slipped into my uncomfortable yet professional leather dress shoes, and spent a good ten minutes brushing my teeth and tousling my hair so it was shiny and spiked in a carefree, sexy mop, hoping it would suggest the richness of a field of ripe wheat. My heart was beating hard.

This is not a date. This is not a date. This is not a date.

I got there first and ordered an iced grande latte with an extra shot of espresso. I was sucking cold coffee through a green straw when I saw a flash of warm, chestnut hair burst through the door, and there he stood in all his glory.

He wore dress slacks and a white linen shirt with a stand-up collar, no tie. His sleeves were rolled halfway up his sinewy forearms, and his sapphire-blue eyes drilled me with a predatory gaze. The straw stayed in my mouth, frozen. I quickly released it, licked my lips, and stood up, extending my hand.

He took a few steps closer and grasped it, giving it a firm squeeze. "You owe me, Gaudens," he growled, putting on his serious face.

I felt the vibration of his voice all the way down my spine as his powerful hand swallowed my smaller one. His hand was strong and warm, with rough fingertips, the nails too short to dig into my palm. I didn't miss the way his eyes scanned me up and down on the sly, or the way they lit up. My hand felt warm in his, and I thought my knees would buckle. A treacherous blush made its way up my neck and onto my cheeks, and I could only nod.

We stood there and squeezed for a while, locked in an ancient ritual that must have originated with our caveman ancestors. Neither of us was willing to loosen his grip first, and it would have been awkward had I not enjoyed the waves of heat rolling off his body. He smelled good—an image of a dark closet flashed through my mind, and I bit my lip, struggling not to whimper. Then again, he didn't have to hold me with such vehement firmness; I had no intention of going anywhere. My eyes sought his shocking pools of blue and saw the lines of his face were hard, but the assessing warmth in his eyes betrayed more than just a glimmer of interest. I couldn't rip my gaze away.

I tried to find my voice and failed. My knees felt a bit soft, and the distance between us three feet too wide.

CHAPTER FIVE

"You can let go of my hand now," he said.

I realized he loosened his grip a while ago and I had just been standing there in a public coffee shop, holding a strange man's hand for the sake of prolonging contact.

"And stop looking at me like that."

"Like… like what?" I whispered

"Like a kicked puppy. Dammit, I need your help, and this project would have been on track if it weren't for you. You broke it, you fix it." All business now, he settled in the solid, wooden chair and pulled out the blue report folder I had assembled for him over two weeks ago.

"Can I get you something to drink?" I asked. I didn't stutter this time; realizing that, increased my confidence. I even flashed him a little smile.

"No. Last time you got me coffee, it didn't go so well. I'll go get my own. Reread what you wrote while I'm gone." He left, and I hefted the proposal, familiarizing myself with the very real publicity problems of BW&B, LLC.

There was a long line of people cutting out for lunch a bit too early, and while Azurri waited for his dose of caffeine and warm comfort, I rolled his name on my tongue for a while. Good thing he was standing in for Schiffer that day… Azurri and Schiffer.

Azurri and Schiffer.

It rang a bell, somehow.

I woke up my Mac and signed in on the coffee shop's Wi-Fi. Several keystrokes later, their names were entered in my Google search window. I didn't have to wait too long before the results began to pour in. The sheer number of them was overwhelming. I raised my eyebrows, seeing my new client's name mentioned in CNN reports and Wall Street Journal articles.

The derivatives scandal? No way—that just can't be....

Suddenly, the corporate name of Black, White, and Blue, LLC made a lot of sense. No erudite client worth his or her salt would deal with the former partners of the now-defunct Provoid Brothers, whose Mr. Emil Provoid was currently an honored guest of the state penitentiary and whose Kevin Toussey escaped a jail sentence only due to his sudden disability, which included blindness.

I visited the Secretary of State website and looked up Black, White, and Blue. The corporate shell of my newest client was owned by Louis Schiffer, Rick Blanchard, and Jack Azurri. All three were former high-level employees of the now-defunct Provoid Brothers, a company that had managed to lose billions of dollars and totally annihilate the retirement savings of tens of thousands of their clients, including their own employees.

I detected a heat source near my back before a head dropped next to mine and looked at the screen.

"Spying on me, are you?"

His voice resonated deep in his chest, and I suppressed a shiver, steeling myself to not move and not click my browser window shut. "You know, I'd like to live in a world where nobody questions the chicken's motive for crossing the road." I sighed.

He moved across the round table from me and set his coffee down before he settled in his chair. I detected the scent of caramel syrup. "So... now you know why we need help with publicity."

"Yep." That was rather obvious. Provoid was screwed, and good riddance, but the others... they'd lost everything. "So you're starting over?" I asked, tilting my head, flicking the long hair out of my face with a habitual, annoyed toss of my head.

"Yeah." He looked away from me and into his cup, his voice low.

"Does everyone from the old company work for the new one?"

He grimaced. "No. Just the three of us and a few of our former assistants. I don't know how much you remember 'bout that case, but there are some guys we won't have back anyway."

"Risby Haus? I didn't realize he got fired, too." I crooked my eyebrow at him, his doorman's name rolling off my tongue.

"The whole company folded. He isn't suitable to our current business environment, anyway. We're doing this with full-out professionalism. From scratch. It's been going okay. Obviously people in the field know who we are, but they appreciate the effort of a fresh start. You don't make profit without planning out your growth, though. I liked your proposal enough to come back."

I sipped my iced coffee, thinking hard. "I promised Pillory I wouldn't poach his clients."

Azurri leaned forward and put his elbows on his knees. His eyes edged away slightly, focused on a distant point. Was that a hint of blush on his cheekbones? "Thanks to you, Gaudens, I can't show my face in Pillory's office anymore. You totally screwed me over that day."

His statement pushed my defensive button, and I could feel my stubborn chin jut out as I snapped back. "Pillory doesn't care what you do. He fired my butt, not yours."

"What did you tell him, anyway?" he asked in an apprehensive kind of way, but obviously unable to reign in his curiosity.

But boss... I'm in love. My ears reddened at the recollection. "I believe you have no need to know that," I answered, feeling no need to unveil the extent of my infatuation.

He drank some coffee and set the tall cup on the table. "Okay, Gaudens. This is the deal. You know we lost everything and had to start from scratch. You know I can't work with Guajillo, and approaching your former boss is just a bit too embarrassing. So this is what's gonna happen: you'll do the work for free. That way you won't be poaching Pillory's potential clients."

"Free?" I squeaked, fighting to maintain composure.

"Free." He grinned.

"Or else?" I asked. He exuded an aura with a dangerous edge to it; his grin and his unwavering, fathomless gaze suggested that with a guy like him, there often was an "or else."

"You, punk, have a strange hobby some people might be interested in."

"You're just such an asshole." I sighed, shaking my head with incredulous disbelief. "You know I got fired—you played your little part in it—and now you're extorting me to work for your company for free?"

"It is customary not to call one's client bad names." His voice might have been stern, but the thinly veiled tug at the corner of his mouth didn't escape my attention, and an amorous song of hope rose in my heart.

"Since you are not paying, you don't count as a real client," I said, softening my unwavering glare in a coy way that expressed all the regret I could muster. "However...."

One Mississippi, two Mississippi, three Mississippi....

A good ten seconds passed before he broke the silence. "However, what?"

"What's in it for me?" I asked, meeting his eyes straight on, my confidence rising. "There is free, and then there is *free*, you know."

He measured me with a calculating look. "What would you suggest, Gaudens?"

I suppressed a smile and counted to ten once again, slowly. Let him think I'm thinking hard, undecided. "I want access to your clients. Many of them will need advertising services, too."

"Your services, or your special skills?" He frowned.

"One of my rules is this: there must be at least three degrees of separation between me and my mark. That is, if we know the same people, or know people who know the same people as we do, they're off limits." I straightened and gave him my best straight-up look. "I broke that rule with you."

"And surely you regret it terribly," he snarled, his voice dripping with sarcasm.

A smile crept to my face, one I just couldn't hold back. "Actually, no. Had I not broken a slew of my own rules that night, I'd have never met you." Only my reflexes saved my laptop from certain doom as I saw him jerk up in stunned disbelief, spilling his hot, caramel-laden coffee all over the table.

THE spilled coffee had been cleaned up long ago in a flurry of fuss and napkins. We were still totally focused, our third round of coffee barely touched and safely stationed on the window ledge next to us. My butt hurt, hips constrained by my fitted trousers and stuck on the hard, wooden chair, but I dismissed the physical discomfort and trained my eyes on the screen once more. Azurri checked off another edit on the blue-bound hard copy.

"Now about the educational seminars—you wanted to tailor the presentation to your audience, right?" My fingers were flying, inserting sentences and marking changes.

"Yeah. Small businesses investing their profit—that would be those hotel functions. Then, private investors—Blanchard wanted to teach those at a local community college." Rick Blanchard was one of the original colleagues and had some good ideas.

"How about an investment club?"

He shook his head, the slicked-back chestnut hair slipping down the side of his neck. "No, too long-term. I need a teaser. Educate them, get to know them, but a shorter lead time."

"Okay." I made my corrections and glanced at the paper next to me; he'd made it bleed red ink.

It occurred to me that he was easy to work with. Doing all this work for free was a penance of sorts; I owed him something, anyway, and if he shared his leads with me, maybe I could do a few seminars on advertising for small businesses—

"Grrraahwrrr!"

The sound brought a slight, unconscious smile to my face instead of the former acute embarrassment. I saved the document and reached for my phone. "Sorry.... Let's see if I need to answer—"

"Grraahwrrr!"

It was Reyna. "I'll call her back later."

Azurri loomed over me. His hand captured my wrist, and as I stood up, I noticed the faintest, most adorable flush of embarrassment making its way up his neck. "Let's take care of that ring tone right now, shall we?" He pried my cell phone out of my hand and started to browse through my settings.

"No wait, wait.... Wait! Don't delete anything!" I was alarmed to hear the tinge of panic in my voice.

"Why not?"

"I like it." The words tumbled out of my mouth unchecked, and I turned a brilliant red, as though a tropical sun was beating down on my face.

He glanced at me and paused, noting my flustered state. "It's embarrassing." His voice was muted by a dry swallow.

"It's from a nature video. You know, big cats." I felt myself flounder in search of a feasible story. "Really big cats. I found it on the Internet. I love 'em... and besides, if you erase it, I'll just install it again."

He fought hard not to let a grin shine through. "You're dragging me through hell, Gaudens. Here, done. All gone. You get a traditional ring tone, like an old phone."

"Like in *The Matrix*?"

"Suuure, *The Matrix*. And I added my cell number." He handed me my phone back. "I want you to follow these notes and redo that proposal, and I want you to deliver it to me in person as soon as it's finished. I'll be home tonight—and I want you to call before you come in. Understood?"

I leaned back a bit, savoring the view: he was tall and handsome with his broad shoulders and narrow hips. Even though he tried to maintain a fierce glowering expression, there was an undercurrent of boyish vulnerability, and part of me just lit up at the sight. I had never found his type interesting before, but to my surprise, he looked so hot when he tried to be all bossy like that. Something must have shown in my eyes.

"Stop that," he snapped, looking away from my face, his voice a restrained hiss. "I'm serious. This project is...." He met my eyes again, and sighed. "I just want you to act normal when you come in."

"Oh yes. Normal… yes, of course. Don't worry, I will."

I PICKED up some take-out Chinese food for dinner on my way home. My back was stiff from the hard chairs and I felt jittery from all that extra caffeine. Once Azurri wasn't distracting me by breathing right next to me and almost down my neck, and once I stripped the tight business clothes and slipped into a pair of track pants and a muscle shirt, I got most of the project outlined the way he wanted it. I took a break to shower and eat and do another edit on the document, making sure the spell-check and the grammar-check weren't flagging any stupid mistakes. I recalculated the numbers again, just to make sure. Once I printed the document, I put it back in its blue presentation folder.

But damn, did I ever feel sore after sitting for so long. I'd been busting my butt, and for what? I was being blackmailed into doing my best work ever for free, by a man who wanted me to "act normal."

Booorrring!

I yawned and stretched my hamstrings.

The thought of being planted in his chair, still once again and waiting for his verdict on my work, well… it didn't sit well with me.

What's normal, anyway? Normal for me, or normal for his secretary?

I snorted at the thought of his current executive assistant—I imagined a fine young woman of exceeding capability, normalcy, and breeding—rappelling down his building, hoping to enter his bedroom window. That sure wouldn't be normal for her, would it?

No.

I shouldn't.

I really, really shouldn't do this.

Yet it was just too funny—hilarious even—and I had always been pretty bad when it came to laughing at my own jokes. I changed into my black cargo pants and a long-sleeved Under Armour shirt. Once I put on my soft-soled climbing shoes, I slipped the completed report into my backpack and set out on foot. This time I didn't have to worry about being spotted. This time I was invited to use the front door, and I didn't even have to cover my blond hair to create a disguise. In fact, a glimpse in the mirror revealed I looked like an action movie stunt double, and that thought alone made me grin with delight.

I just want you to act normal when you come in.

Sure, Mr. Azurri.

RISBY HAUS, former director of Provoid Brother's collection's department, was manning the front desk, his lanky figure slouching in a too-small rotating chair as he read his book. He paid no heed to the security monitors before him.

"Hey, what'cha readin' this time?" I asked him, my voice conversational.

He straightened right up when he saw me and his eyebrows rose in surprise. "You again?"

"Yep. Same customer."

He picked up the phone, not sparing me another glance. "It's the front desk… yeah… this guy's here…?" He cocked an eyebrow at me.

"Wyatt Gaudens," I said. He scowled into the set and his voice sounded biting and sarcastic.

"Wyatt Gaudens, he says his name is this time around. He says he's here to see you." He frowned into the phone, nodded, and hung up. "Sign in here," he said. "Oh, and I'm reading *War and Peace*."

"Really?" I asked, shocked. "How is it?"

"The translation sucks," he groaned the words. "I can tell where the syntax is all wrong. Everybody's depressed because of those long

Russian winters, and everybody's bitchin' 'bout it. I may just skip ahead and read the ending first."

"Okay," I said. I've never even picked up a Russian book, so I really had no opinion, although if you asked me about the latest issue of the Locksmith Catalogue. I could tell you exactly what new, pickproof series of locks and bolts Schloss was selling at the time. Admittedly, that's because I already bought one and took it apart for practice. From the look on Risby's face, it must have been a lot harder to take apart *War and Peace*.

I TOOK the elevator all the way up and stepped out on the roof. The air hung thick with moisture after a storm had swept through earlier, and the surface felt a bit slick. The darkness was thin, diluted by the streetlights below, as I rubbed my foot against the edge of the parapet, reevaluating my plan. A bit riskier, perhaps, but I recalled the thrilled look on Azurri's face as he watched me climb up to the roof last time around, and I knew I wanted to see that dizzying expression again. The rope was slightly damp from having been stored in the vent, but was neither wet nor slippery, and that did it. Instead of using my harness, I wrapped the climbing rope around my waist and between my legs and back again and self-harnessed with my own climbing line. I've always thought it was a pretty slick trick and looked sexy to boot, and I was only going down three stories, which was peanuts compared to my other climbs. Once again I leaned my back straight out above the street. A damp rope won't slip through the loops of the harness as fast, so the rate of descent is a lot easier to control than with a dry line.

While I was self-harnessing, the clouds looked a bit low in the sky, but the weather still was good. I hung my butt off the edge and started rappelling, walking my feet down the carved decorations of the building.

It started to rain halfway down.

My grippy rubber soles stuck to the wet stone just fine, and I was grateful to be able to hold onto all that ornamented masonry, because without it I'd be swinging by the side of the building like a pendulum.

A gust of wind forced me to bend my knees and wait for the air currents to settle; my rope was digging into my legs right behind my butt cheeks, almost too close to where it didn't belong.

I felt like an idiot, not wearing a harness because I thought it didn't look as cool. Then again, I was acting exactly according to Azzuri's instructions: I acted normal.

Normal for me, that is.

The parapet of his bedroom window couldn't have come fast enough. I dropped down onto it, letting my body settle into a gentle crouch. The sticky rubber of my shoes was gripping the wet stone for all they were worth. I held both ends of the rope with my left hand while I extricated my phone from the side cargo pocket with my right. I found his number and pressed the green button.

"Yeah." There was a hint of impatience in his voice.

"Wyatt Gaudens here. Would you care to open up for me? My hands are full."

"Took you long enough," he groused. Another light went on somewhere within the dimly lit apartment, and I heard him open the door. "Where the hell are you, Gaudens?" He bellowed so loud, I almost dropped my phone to the sidewalk below.

"On your window ledge. Where else?" My casual tone was getting harder and harder to pull off with sheets of rain driving right into my back.

"You're crazy! You've gotta be kiddin' me!"

I peered through the rain-slicked window as the pristine surface of his armoire was illuminated by a small lamp clicking on; its light was soft and yellow. Intimate.

I shivered, and it wasn't just because of the rain and the wind.

A shadowy figure approached my perch; a long arm thrust the sheer curtains aside. I stood up straight, cocking my hip just a bit and pretending for all I was worth to be just leaning against a wall somewhere. I saw his eyes run over my wet, dark figure. Grinning, I put my phone back inside my sodden pocket. "Open up, will ya?" I yelled, the wind ripping the words from my mouth.

Small, round objects began to pelt the back of my head and shoulders.

Hail drummed against Azurri's window; a flash of bright blue lightning reflected from the vitreous surface and a crack followed on its heels, the thunderclap sharp and deafening.

He turned the latch and flung the tall casement window open, letting the weather inside. "Hurry up, dammit," he said, alarmed.

The sodden rope of my harness got too swollen with water for its own good; it wouldn't slide anymore. It was stuck.

I was stuck, too.

I tried to loosen it with my nails, but my leather gloves, which were soaked and plastered to my hands, got in the way.

"Here, gimme that." He stepped up and grabbed the rope with long, strong fingers, trying to loosen the stubborn loop. A gust of wind shook the window next to him. "Hold my shoulder, Gaudens!"

I reached out and grasped the warm fabric of his dress shirt. His hands skimmed the surface of my pants between my legs briefly, loosening the wet, stuck rope, and then I was free, leaving the rappel line swaying in the wind as he pulled me inside.

The noise of the storm was cut short as he closed the window and drew the sheers. Then he turned and looked at my soaked, dripping person and stepped close enough to grab my shoulders and shake me hard. "What the fuck're you thinking, climbing in weather like that?"

Wait, he cared?

I shrugged. "It wasn't raining when I started climbing. Hey… sorry about the mess. I didn't really want to do that to you."

"I don't give a shit about the mess. Why the hell did ya do it, anyway?"

I summoned the last bit of spunk left in me, met his eyes, and smiled. "You told me to act normal, so I used my usual entrance, y'know?"

NOT much later, hot water rained on my head and shoulders. I had stopped shivering from the cold some time ago, and I was obviously clean—hiding in the shower was nothing but a stalling tactic. The saner part of me cringed at my undignified position. Soaking wet, on a window parapet, unable to untie my own water-sodden rope harness. Being pelted by hail surely didn't help.

Way to go, Gaudens.

The nutty part of me—most likely the part I inherited from my estranged and eccentric father—cackled at being in the same apartment with the tall, handsome, and entirely enticing Jack Azurri. My nutty part was still trying to salvage the situation. I leaned against the moss-green tile wall of the old-fashioned bath enclosure in an effort to get a better sense of my current strategic position.

When he grabbed my arms, our faces were just inches apart.

He shook me while frustrated and concerned.

He yelled at me in a loud, scared voice.

He shoved me into the bathroom, being a bit gentler than I probably deserved.

He tossed a clean guest towel after me, followed by a curse.

He tossed his clean workout clothes after me, sans instructions.

He slammed the door shut.

Temperamental bastard, I thought. I wished he hadn't yelled so much, because then I'd be better able to absorb the content of what he was trying to say. Like, I really wanted to know whether he was yelling over the sodden carpet—my late mother would have—or whether his outburst was a show of concern over my personal safety—my father tended to act like that. My heart sped up at the thought of the second option, but I had no way to be sure.

Once I got out of the shower, I toweled my hair dry, bending over and letting it hang upside down. Then I toweled the rest of me and inspected the garments lent me by my volatile host. His sweatpants were gray and washed into ageless softness; his T-shirt was one of those clingy black microfiber ones supposed to control your body temperature. White cotton socks. It seemed I'd have to make do without the dignity of underwear.

I hung the towel over the shower rail, opened the door, and padded out to the living room.

"Took you long enough, Gaudens." Azurri sat on the sofa, watching the evening news. "You still cold?"

I shrugged. "It's okay."

He glanced over me, presumably to assess my overall condition, but I saw his eyes darken as his gaze lingered, examining the way the tight thermal tee hugged my torso and the sweats barely hung onto my hips. "You sure?" He drawled, his voice velvety soft and deep.

"I'm fine, really. Did you pull the report out of my backpack?"

"Haven't touched your stuff." He nodded toward the foyer coat rack, where my black, rip-stop nylon backpack occupied a place of honor, dripping onto the jackets. I took it down and opened it, half expecting it to be full of hail.

It wasn't. The report was snug in its plastic cover, with just the edges of the paper wet.

"Here. It will need to dry a bit. I have a backup copy on my phone—I'd e-mail it to you, but I don't know how wet my phone got." I nodded at my cell, which sat on top of his glass coffee table.

Azurri picked up his phone and pushed two buttons. "Let's see if it works, then."

"Grrraahwrrr!"

Our eyes met; a motionless eternity passed. The lull before the storm.

We collided in midair with our arms extended toward my roaring phone. Our shoulders crashed as we landed on the dark blue living room carpet, the roaring cell phone still a whole two feet away. I scrambled for it, only to feel Azurri's hand clench around my forearm and yank me off balance. As I fell, I grabbed him tight to take him down with me.

"Oooof." That was me, with air forcibly expelled out of my lungs.

"Grrraahwrrr!"

"Dammit, I'll crush that fuckin' phone of yours!" Azurri's weight, warm and comforting, pressed me into the carpet, and I felt absolutely no desire to move away. My tight, tired body melted into boneless lassitude from the contact, and my face froze as I became self-conscious over my reaction. Azurri reached his long arm above us and clenched the spasming, orgasming electronic device and shut it off. I felt his bent leg, warm and solid across my thighs, his chest lightly touching mine. Azurri was bigger and seemed stronger, but I didn't mind because I liked where this was going.

Full of mischief, I struggled to reach for my phone, successfully provoking him to trap both my wrists in one of his hands, pinning me to the ground. His face hung above mine, the tendrils of his brown hair almost touching my face. Our breath mingled and our eyes met, but it wasn't one of those longing gazes of sudden recognition where both parties feel unspeakable lust for one another. He merely looked pissed off. I gave him my puppy dog eyes and felt his grip on my wrists tighten. Jack Azurri seemed inexplicably immune to my Power of Cute.

"Alright, Gaudens," he said, breathing hard. "Tell me what will keep you from using that particular sound as your ring tone."

I was breathing hard too, albeit for a different reason. "For your information, Azurri, this ringtone is only for you. Not like before, for Reyna and all the other people who call me. You alone. See? You ought to feel good about that."

"Is that so?" He exhaled, letting his stranglehold on my hands loosen a little. I didn't make any attempt to move away from the tingling contact. "I'm not talking about having an exclusive ringtone. I wanna know what can I do to make you just delete it."

Moments passed while I luxuriated under the delicious pressure exerted by his warm and muscular body. As he held me down like that, I felt my nether regions stir, and it took all the control I had not to arch into him. I was tempted to shift and see if, perhaps, he felt the same. My breath became shallow and my face flushed a bit at the thought. However, despite these challenging circumstances, I considered his request.

"Problem is, I really love the sound of that ringtone." I felt him go rigid over me. "If you'd… if you would perhaps find a way that I could hear that sort of a totally addictive, animalistic, wild-cat growl in real life, then maybe—and I'm not making a promise, mind you—but maybe I'd have no need to keep a recording of it."

He pressed into me ever so slightly while keeping himself from crushing me.

I tried to lift my hips, but my legs were pinned with his and the only solid contact I had was our chests. My hips wiggled a bit, searching for something solid, but his hips canted to the side. Frustration was the only fruit of my labors. I scowled at him. "You're a tease, Azurri."

"Yeah, I am." The words ghosted over my lips as he came closer to me; the moist weight of his breath almost made me flutter my eyelids shut, except he finally settled his body right over mine, legs and hips and all. I relaxed into it, allowing a small, pleasured whine to escape.

He let go of my arms and stroked my wrists with his long fingers before he slid his hands all the way to my shoulders. Then he folded his arms on top of my chest, allowing his fingers to skim and drape over the planes and ridges of my body as though by accident. He gazed at me down his perfect, straight nose with the slightest hint of a smile, reminiscent of a big cat.

"Would you care for a drink? I could use a martini just about now."

"Okay." I breathed, never having had a martini before.

CHAPTER
SIX

I LEANED my butt against the dishwasher and watched Azurri fix our third drink. He measured out five small glass jiggers of Blue Sapphire Bombay gin and the last dregs of Cinzano White Vermouth into a large plastic cup, added a handful of ice cubes, and stirred it for a while. Then he poured half into my glass and the other half into his, straining the ice through his fingers. He grabbed the lemon again and removed two whisper-thin strips of lemon peel with a paring knife; he twisted them over the clear liquid, then dropped them in.

I couldn't decide what to ogle first—either his shapely butt or his broad shoulders—but I was soon captivated by the focused frown between his eyebrows. I studied his face, making note of every detail of his aquiline nose, soft lips, and strong chin. He had wide, well-muscled shoulders and strong arms that ended in skilled hands; their every movement was deliberate. He prepared the drinks like an act of artistic expression. The fingers of his right hand were still dripping with the liquid as he handed me mine; I took it from him and set it down.

"Well, go ahead, taste it! This gin's different." He sounded eager to have me try.

I had an appetite for something else entirely. I grasped his wrist. Not bothering to meet his eyes, I bent and wrapped my tongue around his fingertips and licked the drying martini off his skin.

Lemon. Juniper. Alcohol.

My palate demanded more. I wrapped my lips around his fingers and sucked them in, using my tongue to explore their underside, tasting, caressing.

The bitters of vermouth. A hint of salt.

Salt? Jack's salt.

The sound of glass crashing onto the tile floor made me stop and open my eyes. Azurri stood still and breathless and his eyes were shut. I eased his fingers out of my mouth, drawing my tongue along their undersides, enjoying its slither over the pads of his calloused fingertips. A low moan rumbled deep in his chest, escaping his throat as a breathy sigh. Slowly, as though it took a great deal of effort, he forced his eyelids apart to reveal confused, impossibly blue eyes.

"Look… look what you made me do," he rasped. "That was the last of the vermouth."

"Sorry." I felt a blush rise up my neck. "I'll clean it up."

"You'll do nothing of the sort. You're barefoot. Sit up on the dishwasher and stay put."

I did as he said, sipping a bit of the freshly made drink. The Bombay gin was a lot smoother than the Beefeater; the lemon a fine counterpoint to the sublime balance of juniper and bitters—although, truth be told, fine distinctions were becoming difficult to discern because I was on my third drink. Suddenly I felt a bit off balance and the floor tilted fifteen degrees to the right. Acting with smooth deliberation, I set the glass down and grasped the edge of the counter to right myself. Now I knew what a martini was and what went into it, but still—wow.

Azurri returned with a broom and a pan and threw the broken glass in the garbage; then he ran a handful of wet paper towels over the white tile, picking up the smallest shards. He washed his hands at the sink and looked at me just sitting there. Watching him. "Drink your martini," he growled.

Not unless you want it back later.

"I'm waiting to share with you." My enunciation was careful. It wouldn't do to slur.

He wiped his wet hands against his dress trousers. Our eyes met; the arctic ice of his irate glare was long gone, replaced by the soft warmth of a tropical ocean, liquid and caressing. He came closer—way too close—and snaked his long arm around my waist. "The floor's wet, and I don't want you to mess up my socks. Here, hop a ride."

I didn't want him to carry me like a groom might carry a bride—that position was way too loaded with unintended meaning.

Being tossed into a fireman's carry was out of the question—that would make me hurl.

I reached for the last martini with my right hand and wrapped my left around his neck. I saw only one option left, and I took it, feeling brazen and shameless. My face burned as I wrapped my legs around his waist. He pressed our chests together, hoisting me under my rear, and transported us to the living room.

I would have thought I would have enjoyed this sort of a thing. After all, I had been lusting after this fine specimen of manhood for weeks. So why did I feel this sudden sense of ambivalence wash over me? Every step he took made me rub my stirring groin against his belly; the sensation had me turn all warm and gooey inside. Yet I couldn't make myself just lean into it. The tables must have turned while I wasn't looking. The control I enjoyed so much during my invasions and burglaries had dissipated with my landing on Azurri's windowsill, soaked to the bone and stuck in my rope harness. Once I had allowed him to untie me; warm me up in his shower; clothe me in his soft clothes; indulge me in a drink made by his own hand... dammit, where did my sense of control go?

I had to get the upper hand again.

His butt sank into the soft leather sofa as I let go with my legs and straddled him. I sat safely on his knees: close, but not too close. His eyes were darkened with heavy-lidded heat and his hands felt steady and warm on my hips.

"Gaudens." His voice broke the silence as he tightened his hands on my waist.

I met his gaze as I lifted the drink to my lips. Taking an overlarge sip of the strong, burning liquid, I touched my lips against his and curled my tongue into a straw, letting the scorching liquid invade his mouth. His eyes widened as he drew a sharp inhale, the air current irritating the tender tissues of both of our mouths by evaporating the alcohol too fast.

"Fuck, Gaudens...."

I shut his mouth with a kiss, my tongue skimming the bottom of his lip, enjoying the edge of his stubble.

He groaned.

The sound was as intoxicating as the taste.

He responded, engaging in gentle play; his tongue swept the inside of my upper lip, and I moaned, relishing in how sensitive that place can be. Jack's strong, able arms pulled me into him, his undeniable hard-on, imprisoned yet rampant, rubbing against mine through layers of fabric.

There was no hiding it now; I felt a blush coming on again and fought to make it go away.

I'm in charge—it's okay.

I'm in charge—it's okay.

I'm in charge—it's okay.

My control-freak mantra worked its magic. I felt my embarrassment drain away as I rocked my hips, grinding into Azurri's washboard abs. Our fingers brushed as he removed the glass from my hand; the silence of the room was broken by a soft clink as the crystal bottom met the polished wood surface of the side table. Driving rain susurrated against the windowpanes, accompanied by our breathy gasps of pleasure. His hands warmed my skin, skimming my waist, my back. Daring and brave, he ventured to explore under my tight shirt. I shivered at the touch, taking in every nuance of his caress. Tongues met and parted again. I felt him slide out a bit so his hips could reach mine as he arched into the pleasure of our contact, and that familiar, thrilling heat began to spread from my center down, and I knew it was moments from blooming into a hot, wanton ache of desire.

I slid my hand down his chest in a slow, exploratory caress. I slowly mapped his defined contours through the fabric of his shirt. Bent on removing some of the layers of fabric between us, I found the cool metal of his belt buckle. My fingers felt slow and clumsy after all that alcohol, and it took some fussing before it came undone; Azurri's delicate sucks on my collarbone sure didn't help my coordination any. The button finally gave, the zipper fell open, and my hand slid under the silk boxers.

Oh yeah.

The hot, hard, satin-smooth shaft caressed my fingers as Azurri gasped, turning his breath into a growl. "We... we have some unfinished business... Gaudens."

I've always loved the smooth, silky hardness of cock in my mouth. I don't quite know how I got down there; I could never quite recall the exact sensation of the delicate and soft skin—its tender caress along my neck and my lips, avoiding the fine sandpaper of my late-night cheek—until I encountered it once again. It always came as a pleasant shock that I could play with something so smooth and hard and hot; a toy so fabulously responsive.

"Move your pants down," I said as I grabbed his knees to keep from swaying like a martini-soaked rope in the breeze. He wiggled, pushing his trousers and boxers down to his ankles. I had full access. I smiled.

I caressed his thighs and parted his knees, enjoying the feel of his heated skin, reveling in the conflict between tightening and relaxing that now warred within my prey. His shirt was in the way, and I undid the buttons from the bottom up and pushed it to the sides to better see him in his glory. I flickered my gaze up to his face, and our eyes met. His lids were almost closed, yet he struggled to keep his eyes on me. When I saw him bite his lower lip, I smiled in satisfaction. His chest was all firm planes and ridges, with just a bit of hair swirled in its natural growth pattern. It then thinned to an arrow-shaped line that pointed down, traversing abs you could do your laundry on, and then further down, following the hair pattern to its nexus.

There it was, nested in a thatch of brown curls: his cock.

The generous shaft rose toward me, and its smooth, swollen head was circled by a sensitive ridge. It sat there, enticing and challenging at the same time. I eyed it with a mixture of greed and apprehension.

"Hey... anybody home?" Jack whispered in a husky voice, while "Little Jack" just about strained in my direction like a moisture-and-heat-seeking missile.

"Just admiring the view," I said as I licked my lips. Then I anchored my hands against his hips and leaned in, letting him feel the heat of my moist breath first.

"Gaudens!"

"Hmmm." Not to be distracted by his insistence, I leaned in some more, stroking the side of my neck on his silken hardness. He gasped and I purred and did it again, eager to hear the sounds of his pleasure.

His tip felt so soft against my parted lips; he bucked a little, recklessly seeking contact. I had planned to toy with him—to use my tongue sparingly, barely touching at first—but his action brought a scent of his previously hidden parts to my nose.

I loved the spicy, musky smell of sex as much as I loved the smooth hardness of cock.

Oh, fuck it. I just want....

I wrapped my lips around him and descended without hesitation. My nose was buried in those lush curls within a second. I heard him cry out and did it again and again, just feeling his rigid texture and his need—

My fingers grasped his base and squeezed it tight; he whimpered, trying to thrust—

I deep-throated him and gave a few swallows, massaging his head with the softness of my throat.

Jack exploded. I felt his jizz splatter way past my tonsils and, being as deep as he was, the bitter liquid invaded my sinuses. His powerful, musky scent reminded me that I had had almost three very stiff martinis and the world wasn't as stable as it used to be. I swallowed, then swallowed again. The rest of Jack spurted into unintended passages and was dripping down my nose as my eyes begun tearing up. Having Jack Azurri come out my nose was much like being a victim of pepper spray.

I reached for the tail of his shirt and, half-blind, wiped my nose on it.

"What the… hey." His voice didn't have any more bite and hardly any bark left. "You can't do that to my shirt."

"Sorry…." I lifted my head, finally meeting his dazed, glazed-over eyes. "That's just your come. You came so big, it came out my nose."

His laughter split the air and, for whatever reason, he seemed pleased with himself, as though he did something he ought to be proud of.

"Stuff it! It fucking hurts."

"Oh." He handed me a box of tissues, and I turned to the side and emptied my nose of what didn't belong there.

"Why does it hurt?" he asked.

"I dunno. It's just bitter and it stings—I guess the pH is all wrong for that part of the body, y'know?"

"Sorry," he said, not sounding sorry at all. He had a silly grin on his face, an expression similar to my current laptop wallpaper.

Then it hit me. "Hey, you didn't roar for me!"

"I know," he said. "I held back in hope that you'd give it another try soon."

Bastard.

Then again, this way I'd get to keep my ringtone.

I got up and stumbled into the bathroom, the mixture of alcohol and unexpected chemical attack suddenly causing a chain of reactions in my body. As soon as I managed to slam the door shut, I fell to my knees once again, this time before Jack's toilet bowl.

The contents of my stomach were forcibly expelled. Jack's jizz was all gone, Jack's martinis were all gone, my long-gone dinner was… wasn't there. Well, that explained a lot. I hadn't realized how late it had gotten.

Oh God, never again. I promise.

Never again will I drink on an empty stomach.

I heaved again and again, but nothing came out. If you've never had dry-heaves before, you're lucky; few sensations are as disconcerting as feeling your stomach spasm and contract, trying to expel a vile substance that is, unfortunately, no longer there.

"Gaudens?" There was a knock on the bathroom door. I heaved again. "Are you okay?"

I didn't bother with a reply. What kind of a moron would ask a question like that? However, moments later the bathroom door opened and Azurri came in with a tall glass of ice water.

"Have a sip. Not too much."

I rinsed my mouth and spat into the toilet. My hair was plastered to my clammy forehead and my face felt slick with sweat. Never, to my recollection, had I felt less sexy than at that moment.

I closed my eyes, resting my forehead on my arm. Only vaguely do I remember having felt a smidgeon of gratitude for Jack's caring hands, and for the cool, moist towel on my forehead.

I WOKE up in bed. I could tell even with my eyes closed, and I had no intention of opening them, because I had a mean headache. My eyes didn't want to open and face the world. Searing embarrassment flooded me as I recalled the events of the previous night. I suppressed a groan and forced my eyes open, but the bedroom was fairly dark and heavy rain still drummed on the windowpanes. It must have been early. The best I could do was sneak out of Jack's apartment before he woke up.

At some point I began to think of the tall and handsome man by his first name. Up until very recently, we spat our last names at one another with contempt, foregoing all honorifics: manners, the veneer that made polite society a viable concept, were almost absent in our interactions.

Or were they? Did we, perhaps, merely express our dissonant liking for one another in a coarser, more primitive manner?

Being carried over broken glass.

Cool washcloth on my forehead.

No, Jack wasn't an indifferent cad. He only acted like one.

Returning stolen goods.

Doing work for free.

Likewise, I wasn't a hardened criminal. I was merely an incompetent one.

Slowly, not rustling the crisp, white sheet that covered me, I slid to the ground. The soft, white carpet of Jack's bedroom silenced the light tap of my feet as I landed. Crouched behind the bed, I realized I was dressed in nothing but a pair of Jack's black silk shorts.

I listened.

Nothing.

The rain-darkened sky made it hard to judge the time of the day. With painful stealth I straightened, only to find the other side of Jack's bed hadn't been slept on. A feeling of doom came upon me. He must have cleaned me up and changed me into his own clean underwear, and he was probably still asleep on his own sofa.

I pattered outside his bedroom, the layout of the apartment now so familiar I could have found my way around in absolute darkness. I peered down the hallway and into the large living room. In the relative light of day and undistracted by Jack's presence, I took a look around. The space was still the way I remembered it from my first break-in: half of it was full of boxes and assorted pieces of furniture jumbled all together, the other half was a tidy, modern living area with a leather couch and a large, flat-screen TV. The couch was where I had given Jack one of the best blowjobs in living memory—and I expected to see him there, asleep.

Except he wasn't there. Only a pillow and a blanket betrayed where he had spent the night.

"Jack?"

Not hearing an answer, I walked into the living room as a vague sense of guilt washed over me for having driven him out of his own bed. Then I stopped, utterly flabbergasted to see my wet green rappel line coiled on the glass coffee table. Rainwater still weeped from the woven rope, making a puddle on the gleaming surface. My black clothing, formerly soaking wet, was washed and dried and neatly folded on top of my backpack next to it.

I halted my steps, thinking. It wasn't easy to penetrate the drowsy, sore cobwebs of my mind, but eventually I managed: Jack had gone up to the roof to retrieve my rope in pouring rain. He had washed and dried my clothes. What happened to the garments he lent me the night before? If he'd stripped me out of them, I must have been a real mess.

A white sheet of paper was stuck in the coils of the expensive rope.

Hey Gaudens,

I got your rope. Your climbing harness is still in the vent, and if you fail to use it next time, I'll never want to see you again, you idiot. You could've died, you dimwit. Sorry to make you sick. I'm at work; let me know when you're ready to leave.

Jack

I sat on the sofa, reading and rereading the note, trying to discern extra bits of meaning from between the lines. His upset over the harness was rather unexpected, as was the "sorry" part. Maybe he was just sorry about getting me drunk so fast; no guy will admit to tasting that vile. Although, the alcohol might have something to do with my reaction. The thought of his martini made my gorge rise, and I sat up straight, regaining my composure.

My cell phone told me it was almost eleven. First, I'd shower. Then I'd dress. Then I'd snoop around. Jack was a closed book to me. Judging by his apartment, I'd have to conclude his character was akin to having a case of split personality. Streamlined, modern décor clashed with boxes of tchotchkes and antiques. I wanted to use my nefarious skills not to purloin objects, but rather to acquire information about the object of my infatuation.

Half an hour later I felt a lot more civilized, and I applied my newfound energies to cracking Jack's safe. Now, you might think this was an evil thing to do, but I had a good reason. I wanted to learn more about him, and what a man puts in his safe says a lot about what sort of a man he might be. Resolved to only take a gentle peek, I approached the cheap painting replica in its ornate frame and swung it open, revealing a gray, metal door with one simple dial.

I took a deep breath and released the air, preparing myself. My fingers felt sensitive, itching with anticipation. With a controlled exhale, I took hold of the dial and spun it clockwise. The gears moved with smooth precision. I didn't hear any clicks, didn't see it stop at a convenient point all by itself. Lacking my stethoscope, I leaned my ear against the metal and slowly rotated the dial until I detected the slightest change in sound and resistance. The feeling was miniscule and unquantifiable; I probably only imagined it. Eyes closed, I felt a smile creep to my face as I slowly rotated the dial in the opposite direction. I passed the point of the first stop and waited for the next one—then I rotated the dial clockwise again, waiting for the final destination. It felt pretty good, like a highly sophisticated high school locker. It took me a few tries, but eventually I leaned against the door gently and its spring-loaded mechanism pushed it open. An automatic light came on. The safe wasn't huge but it still had three shelves.

The top shelf had a 9mm Glock on it and a few spare boxes of ammo. I recognized the gun but didn't touch it.

The middle shelf had an accordion folder with papers in it; I pulled it out and rifled through the contents, trying not to disturb anything. Insurance policies, a passport, a lot more cash than in the freezer, several loose family photographs, a birth certificate and a social security card, a car title, a will and a living will, and three death certificates. Eyebrows raised, I gently pulled those out. Helen and Raymond Azurri appeared to have been his parents, and their death occurred on the same day ten years ago. The third one testified to the death of one Celia Azurri—its paper wasn't yellowed like the other two, and was dated to only nine months ago.

Had he been married?

He had said he was too depressed to deal with me the first time around.

Shit.

I replaced everything, taking care to make it the way it was—you don't need to have photographic memory to do that sort of thing, you just need to be observant enough.

The last shelf held a thin cardboard box. Well... I had already gone this far, I might as well see it all. I pulled it out and opened it. Gold and silver gleamed at me, reflecting the dim daylight. Green emeralds twinkled from an ornate necklace, a bracelet, a pair of earrings... it looked real alright, and pretty old. There were some other pieces, mostly women's stuff. The two men's rings that sat there would have fit him, but I'd never seen him wear any jewelry at all. I slid it all back and shut the safe and closed the picture. Then I went to the bathroom and washed my hands and face again, barely able to breathe.

Who was this man? Not a single family photo was to be seen anywhere; his living areas, the ones that didn't look like an antique shop, were rather plain. Impersonal, even. I knew a little about his former work at Provoid Brothers. Once their CEO got carted off to jail for massive fraud, the corporate officers got dragged over hot coals. Some, like Risby Haus and his boss, Kevin Toussey, were barred from work in the industry, while others got another chance. Jack Azurri would have been one of those. His work history didn't tell me much about him as a person, though. I needed to find out more.

I opened and closed his drawers, having learned he preferred silk boxers for underwear. His medicine cabinet revealed a snapshot of a healthy man prone to occasional headaches and an allergy to poison ivy.

I decided to call my best friend, since it was right before I knew she'd go out for lunch. "Hey, Reyna. What can you tell me about your former boss?"

"Uh... why do you wanna know?"

I hesitated. Not even Reyna knew about my shadier activities. "Um, I'm at his place right now, and it's kind of... weird."

"What?" I heard her choke on something and cough. "What are you doing there?"

"I, um... I started something with him, as you know, and it sort of took on a life of its own... so anyway, I stayed the night and he let me sleep in. What I wanna know is, why would he have this simple, masculine furniture right next to boxes full of, you know, knick-knacks?"

"Gimme a second.... You made me spill my tea." I hadn't known Reyna to be a tea drinker, not unless Pillory decided to wean her off coffee. My old boss claimed coffee was evil and smelled up the whole lunchroom. "Okay, then. I joined Provoid Brothers as a temp. Azurri was on some kind of a family-related leave back then. I rearranged his files, and when he got back, it really pissed him off."

"What was the leave about?"

"He never said, but wait. I'll ask—they did go to school together, after all...." I heard steps going down the hallway, then a knock on the door. "Hey Auguste, a question for you...."

I tuned out anything Reyna was asking my former boss, too stunned by the fact that my best friend would be on first-name basis with the cool, reserved man. Pillory—or preferably, Mr. Pillory—never let anyone call him by his first name before. Interesting....

There was a bit of a back-and-forth on the other side, and then Reyna said, "Okay, here he is."

"Mr. Gaudens," the familiar, smooth voice intoned. "Why are you snooping on Mr. Azurri?"

"Oh... um... hello, Mr. Pillory. I am not exactly snooping. It just occurred to me that his apartment looks... disjointed, you know? So I wanted to know if something had happened in his recent past... just so I don't step in it."

There was a prolonged silence before I heard the familiar baritone again. "His sister died. It was in the papers. Does that satisfy your curiosity?"

"Yes, and no. Thank you though."

Silence stretched for a few beats. "If you would care to stop by the office, I might have a client for you. A small bakery—we're too big for them."

I felt relief wash over me—relief and gratitude. "Ah... thank you. Thank you very much."

"I take it you're keeping to our deal, then? You didn't poach BW&B from me?"

I swallowed, my throat suddenly dry. "Due to my actions—which I do not regret, by the way—Mr. Azurri is too embarrassed to set his foot inside your offices ever again. He… he sort of… strong-armed me into doing the work for free. So, technically, it's not poaching since I'm not getting paid."

"Gaudens." His voice said it all.

"Had you not barged in like that, he'd have stayed, and I'd have stayed, and you wouldn't have to put up with Reyna."

"Mr. Gaudens, you will be pleased to know that your friend is more than an adequate replacement for you."

I heard Reyna's suppressed snickers in the background and Pillory hung up on me. When I worked for Pillory, he'd never have let me snicker while he was on the phone.

There was no use delaying the inevitable. I called Jack next. "Hey, it's Wyatt."

There was a prolonged silence on the other end before Jack replied. "How are you feeling… Gaudens?"

"A lot better than last night. I wanted to apologize… for everything. And I wanted to thank you."

"Are you still at my place?"

"Yeah."

"When did you wake up?"

"Two hours ago."

There was a pregnant pause. "*Two hours?*"

I moved the phone away from my ear. "Yeah."

"What did you take?" Exasperation warred with curiosity as he contained himself, giving me enough space to formulate an answer.

"You mean except for your black silk boxers?"

Another pause. "You kept my underwear."

"Yeah…." My voice got kind of breathy there, and I felt a blush rise to my face again.

"Is there anything, *anything* at all, you'd like to confess while I'm still speechless and in a fairly good mood?" His voice was a sensuous purr, affecting my sense of reason.

Maybe. I had a lot to confess. I didn't know how he'd take it, though. He'd probably just break up with me, but we were not officially together in any capacity, and even if we were, that was likely going to happen from the very beginning anyway.

Okay, here goes. "Ibrokeintoyoursafe."

"Huh... go again?"

"I broke into your safe. Just to see if it was hard, you know... it wasn't. But then I got curious and wanted to see what was there...."

"Go on." His voice was measured, as cold as the rain the night before.

"I'm so sorry about your sister, Jack."

"You fucking snoop." His voice was incredulous.

"I wanted to find out more about you."

"What the hell for?"

"'Cause... 'cause I'm fatally attracted to you. Moth to flame, Jack. Nothing else seemed to matter at the time."

He was quiet for a bit and all I could hear was breathing. "Has it occurred to you, Gaudens, that you might have a bit of a problem?"

"I know I have a problem, Jack. You're not the problem, though. You're the vacation from my problem."

"Stay where you are. We need to talk about this in person."

Yeah, right. My death wish didn't extend that far. "I can't. I called Pillory and he's expecting me. He has a client for me."

"You told him about poaching me off?"

"I told him about working for you for free and explained it wasn't poaching."

"What'd he say?"

"He wants to take me apart personally.... If you'd like to see me in person, take a number and hope I don't come back to you in pieces."

I heard him cackle. "Alright then. I'll catch up with you later. Probably when you least expect it."

CHAPTER SEVEN

REYNA sat across from me, handling her dinner with unusual restraint. Our past and long-lasting acquaintance led me to expect her to treat everything—with the possible exception of soup—as finger food. She would normally have disposed of her crab cake with unbridled enthusiasm, picking it up in her long, manicured fingernails. Now she was cutting it up with a fork and knife. I watched her handle the utensils with awkward determination, chasing down the last lump of crabmeat.

"These are the best effin' crab cakes I've ever had, Wyatt." She said *effin'* instead of using her ubiquitous f-word. My curiosity was piqued.

"Reyna. Why aren't you eating with your fingers like always?"

She was silent for a while as she continued chasing the tidbit across her plate. "We all had this client appreciation banquet. Did he do that when you worked for Mr. Pillory?"

I nodded. "Yeah. An annual shindig to encourage existing clients to give us referrals to their friends and colleagues."

She gave up in frustration, picked up the desired morsel with her long red nails, and popped it into her plump mouth. "I felt like such a redneck cow, y'know? I sat right across from him and… I dunno, he's just so *refined.* It's like everything he does, every single motion, has a purpose. It's… perfect." Her brown eyes acquired a dreamy expression as she leaned against the back of her barstool.

"What's perfect?" I asked, trying not to show my irritation.

"He is...." She took a swig of her beer straight out of the bottle and flipped hair over her shoulder, letting her spider tattoo peek from under her ear. "Every single thing he does is *just so*. And he looks perfect, too. His hair is just shoulder-length and smooth and shiny—and he smells like fresh air, didya know? He had to lean over me to take a look at my screen today, and his hair fell forward and brushed my cheek...."

My irritation gave over to amusement as Reyna slumped in her stool, her head thrown back in abandon, her eyes rolling back. My snicker gave me away—she sat up and pierced me with a defensive look.

"Well, for your information, he says I have a lot of potential. He says I'll get to interact with clients pretty soon, so I have to make sure I'm up to the task and take care of those 'rough edges' my grandma has been complaining about as long as I can remember."

She hadn't mentioned who "he" was in her diatribe, and there was no need. My best friend was crushing on my former boss, and if she said another "He says...," I was going to explode.

My frustration level knew no bounds. Here we were, on Friday night, having our customary drinks and a small dinner in order to unwind and bitch about life—but Reyna was wasting our night out singing praises to my former boss, Cold Fish Pillory. Meanwhile, I'd been sweating out the remainder of this week without a single contact from her former boss and sex-idol extraordinaire, Jack Azurri.

I'll catch up with you. When you least expect it.

I sighed and drank my Sierra Nevada Pale Ale, its heady hops filling my nose with a citrusy bouquet. I loved beer. I knew beer. It was familiar and refreshing and relaxing—and a lot more predictable than, say, a martini. In moderation, of course. A climber my size can't have too many indulgent dinners or beers every week without having to haul all those extra beers and chips up the rockface.

Reyna honed in on my change of mood, redirecting her focus onto her own former boss. "So what are you gonna do about him?" she asked before she maneuvered a fork full of french fries into her plump mouth. "I mean, won't you try to find out if he's still interested?"

"He's pissed about the safe." Oops, that slipped out all by itself.

"What safe?"

Now, the bad news is, the cat was out of the bag. The good news was, there were many cats in my bag and only one escaped. "He has a safe at his place, and I snooped."

"He left it open?" Reyna frowned.

"No. I cracked it open! Of course he won't be leaving his safe open."

"You did?" Reyna squealed, amazed. Her cinnamon eyes lit up with the excitement of adventure. "Super! When did you learn how to do that?"

"I was born knowing," I said in a flat, nonchalant voice.

She rolled her eyes and pulled on her beer again. "So… what was in it?" Her eyes shone with eagerness—after all, Azurri was the asshole who fired her, and she wanted some dirt.

"I can't tell you that. Nothing bad, though. It's just, I snooped and he's probably giving me the cold shoulder, being pissed and all."

"You didn't take anything, did you?" The words spilled out of her mouth fast, and it occurred to me that my friend probably knew me a lot better than I gave her credit for. I saw her frown again, reaching for her overpriced Czechvar lager.

"Nothing except the black silk boxer shorts he put on me the night before." I grinned.

"Oh, tell!"

My secret was just too juicy to bear. After all, how often does one get as thoroughly embarrassed as I have? Resigned, I gestured for our second round, and the story spilled out of me like beans out of a broken bag. It seemed prudent to edit the facts a bit as I went along, seeing no need to enlighten my best friend about my addiction to outright burglary. I told her just the good parts.

She sat there transfixed, her expression incredulous. Crimson rivulets of hair spilled down her shoulders, the way "he" liked it—as indicated by an offhand comment he probably didn't even remember making—as she leaned back, wide-eyed and motionless. "You used your mountain-climbing skills to break into his bedroom to deliver a report." It wasn't a question. Her eyes shone as she hung on my every word.

"Yeah."

"Why?"

"Let's not go there. Anyway...." I continued with my sordid tale of embarrassment and high adventure. By the end of it all, Reyna was leaning forward on her high stool with her elbows planted on the table's scarred wooden surface and her eyes ready to pop out of her head. I finished my story of waking up all alone and finding my laundry done and rope retrieved—and the last phone call to Azurri, including his incensed reaction to my lack of restraint and spying.

"So that's what happened," I ended in a measured tone, then finished my beer.

She set her bottle down with a clank and burst out laughing. Tears of mirth flowed down her high-boned cheeks. "Shit, Wyatt. I would've died."

"I almost did—especially when I woke up wearing nothing but his underwear."

Reyna finished her second beer. "My question stands, Wyatt. What next?"

I'D GONE to see Pillory early the following week and, true to his word, once he raked me over hot coals for "poaching" BW&B from him, he said he had a client for me. The new business owner, Mr. Novack, had been trying to expand his Oakland bakery by diversifying into light lunch items aimed at college students and office workers. His latest novelty, trendy Parisian crepes, were slathered with Nutella and garnished with sliced strawberries. Almost as soon as we shook hands, he served me one to taste-test the product, and I agreed they were positively addictive. He fed me several more samples to convince me of their virtue, and we proceeded to formulate an advertising strategy.

Mr. Novack was kind enough to send me home with a whole plateful of crepes. Now, after the extra beer with Reyna a few days before and a plateful of crepes at the bakery, there was no way I was keeping this loaded calorie-bomb to myself, no matter how sinfully delicious it tasted. I needed to share them around to stay at my optimum climbing weight—it was the only way, because throwing them out was out of the question. That would have been a sin. I called Jack as I walked home.

"Yeah," he said, answering his phone.

"You home?"

"No. Stayin' late. There's a big push. We have some regulatory requirements we need to fulfill." His voice was an irritated growl.

"Sorry about that. I'll call later."

He hung up on me. Again.

It was rather obvious Jack was in full-blown work mode, but I still didn't like being ignored with such high-handed arrogance. Reyna wouldn't have done that, not even if she were snowed under with paperwork. Pillory? Well, that depended on the circumstances. Pillory was good about returning calls, unlike Jack. I had to get the handsome menace's attention again... somehow.

THE bakery in Oakland wasn't too far from Jack's apartment building in Shadyside. Half an hour later I was in without the usual fuss and drama. Why hang off a building with a plateful of crepes when you can pick the locks?

I locked up after myself, put the crepes in his half-empty refrigerator, and put a big sign on the fridge itself: *Heat to room temperature before serving.* I stood there, debating whether to sign it or not. If I signed it, I would sound needy. If I didn't, he might not even notice.

Instead, I wandered into Jack's bedroom and unlocked his window for next time. The room was meticulously clean and his bathroom still emanated a faint hint of Jack's aftershave. I walked in and inhaled, keeping at bay my memories of having prayed to the porcelain goddess there on the floor. Yep, the air smelled almost like him. Not quite, though. It lacked that undertone of musk I found so compelling.

Now I was at war with myself—I wasn't much into perfumes, and I've certainly never tried men's aftershave. If you're a burglar, you need to keep a low profile, and I've heard of a guy who was caught based on his powerful scent trail. I liked the stuff all right, in moderation, but I've never been brave enough to apply much scent to my body. The idea of smelling like Jack was drawing me in, though, and I found my resolve softening. Maybe just this one time....

I watched my disembodied right hand reach out toward the mirror-covered cabinet above the sink and open the door. Slender fingers grasped a small blue vial and spritzed just a bit on my hands and patted my cheeks, just as I've seen other men do in television commercials. The scent hit my nostrils with unexpected force and I woke up to the consequences of my actions.

Damn.

I had had plans for that night—there was this coin collector who kept his collection in an off-brand safe, and he was going to be at a dinner party tonight—but now I reeked to high heaven. I couldn't go out smelling like this, and not even a shower would entirely fix it—the scent just had to wear off all by itself. The coin job had already been blown. Jack was unavailable, and the only activity available left was honest work: I'd spend the night compiling advertisement campaign proposals.

A wave of ennui washed over me. My life was just so... boring.

I sighed, feeling sorry for myself, when my eyes fell onto Jack's perfectly made bed. I kicked my shoes off and dove onto the tight bed cover.

So comfortable. Not too hard and not too soft, but just right.

I fished a pillow from underneath the bedspread and mugged it for comfort, and to my utter delight and amazement, this particular pillow smelled exactly like the man of my dreams.

Oh God.

I buried my nose into it and inhaled, and there it was. The musky, warm, comforting smell of Jack, with an edge of unidentifiable danger to it, plus my fresh application of his aftershave. My eyes rolled in my head as I rocked my hips into his bedding, breathing deeply. That man smelled like pure heaven.

I WOKE up, alarmed that I'd actually fallen asleep. Two hours had passed. Two hours! I had to get out of there. I leapt off the bed and looked around, and I noticed Jack's closet was cracked open. I had fond memories of that closet, so of course I opened the door farther. His dark, soft suits met my eye… and my nose… and my hands. I heard a moan cut through the silence of Jack's apartment—it must have been me. The closet was orderly and there was a dirty laundry hamper on the floor, right by my feet. It was half-full and….

Oh God.

I was torn, my pride and self-esteem at war with the promise of the delights below. The promise of sensual stimulus won: I just loved the smell of Jack's dirty laundry. It had the musk and the cologne, sure, and that mysterious edge of danger, but it also had clean workout sweat, and the whole mess had had a chance to ripen for two or three days, and its odor wafted up right to my quivering nostrils. Before I knew it, the hamper was spilled on the floor before me and his black silk shorts were there, among his workout clothes, shirts, and undershirts.

I touched the garments with reverence, feeling the fine fabric just as my other parts roused with heat. It was so tempting to purloin another pair of those sensuous silk shorts, but they were expensive, and besides, I already had a pair from last time. He'd need his dress shirt, and it would be too big on me anyway… I was piling the clothes back into their receptacle when my eyes fell upon an old, ratty T-shirt. It was light blue and looked torn and abused; the silhouette of Mt. Whitney was almost washed off its front. The thing was a wreck; he'd never miss it. I lifted it up; it reeked of Jack. Before I knew it, it was rolled up and stuffed inside the waistband of my jeans, the laundry was back in the closet, and I was out the door. He'd be home any minute. I only wanted to remind him of my existence—letting him walk in on me while I was huffing his laundry pile would have been a severe overkill.

SATURDAY afternoon had come and gone, rolling into evening, and I still hadn't heard from that infuriating, obstinate man. I didn't want to go out, didn't want to watch a movie or hang out online; I wanted Jack, and nothing else would do.

Pathetic.

"Hey, Wyatt." Reyna called me later that night. "I got the most unusual phone call."

"Yeah?" I was parading around my small apartment in a pair of black silk shorts and a ratty, light-blue T-shirt at least a size too large. With the phone stuck to my ear, I continued straightening up those odds-and-ends that tend to accumulate over a period of several days.

"Yeah. Azurri called. He wanted to ask some personal questions about you."

"Oh yeah?" I perked up immediately. "Like what?"

"I can't tell you that." She giggled. "Oh, nothing harmful, don't worry too much. It's just, if I told him about you, he'd tell me about Auguste. They went to school together."

My heart sank. "Reyna! Did you sell me out?"

"No, you pathetic goofball, I'm giving you a heads-up. Why'd he ask about you if he lost interest, right?"

We talked some more, me trying to pull critical information out of Reyna, her working hard not to let anything slip. She succeeded; I failed.

Resigned to my fate of earning my living through honest work, I poured myself a tall glass of beer, and once its head settled, I navigated it over to the coffee table, where I left my laptop. I settled on the sofa and got to work. The Novack proposal was beginning to look good. He wanted to target novelty seekers and the lunch crowd. For his crepes, he'd do best to advertise with the Francophiles in the area. Over the next two hours I compiled an exhaustive list of French teachers, as well as local schools and translation agencies, and I was about to get started on travel agencies when my ears picked up suspicious noises from my front door.

Somebody was trying to pick my lock.

That bastard.

Karma was out to get me in this life instead of the next. Payback was imminent. I tiptoed to the door, grabbed my old baseball bat off the coat rack, and listened to the burglar's effort from the other side. I snickered—what a bumbler. Really, my locks were pretty average. I saw no need to draw attention to myself by indulging in high-tech security. A peek out my peephole didn't show anything, since whoever was trying to burgle me was either bent over or kneeling on the floor. I was just about to call them on their incompetence and laugh in their face when I heard the tumblers align and fall in place, and the door swung open.

I jumped back, the baseball bat at the ready on my shoulder. I crouched behind the opened door, waiting to see who it was so I could whack them a good one for their trouble.

Tall, brown hair…. "Jack?" My voice rose, and he turned, startled.

His eyes widened at the sight of the weapon. Then I saw him relax and push the bat down with his long arm. "Hey, Gaudens. Should I also greet you with a baseball bat?"

I cleared my throat. "As I recall, you greeted me with a gun and tied me to a chair."

"I guess turn-about is fair play." He shrugged, sauntered over to the dining nook right off the kitchen, and set a brown paper bag on the table.

I shut the door behind him, turned the lock, and hung the baseball bat back in its place on the coat rack. "Why… why didn't you call first?" Being fair-minded, I didn't ask him why he didn't knock.

"Why should I call?" he asked. "You never do."

"Actually I always call before I break in, to make sure nobody's there. Then I knock for good measure. That one time you were asleep. Your phone must have been turned off."

He glanced at the laptop on the coffee table. "You busy?"

"Yeah. Well… sort of. I can finish later."

He moved to my side and perched on the sofa's padded arm rest while I sat down to save my document. He leaned and slid his hands down my arms, holding me in place as he peered at the screen.

"Hey, that's private client information!" If there's anything I absolutely hate, it's people peeking at my screen over my shoulder.

"Novack's Bakery. I see he's marketing crepes." He pushed my shoulder until I toppled onto the sofa cushion and almost ended up facedown. I heard the laptop close. The warm, delicious smell of Jack enveloped me as he pressed himself into my back, keeping my arms pinned in his generous embrace and his legs on top of mine. "I wonder if he delivers," he purred. "I wonder if he leaves the samples of his newest product line in people's refrigerators."

I felt his nose burrow through the strands of my hair, his moist exhalation tickling my ear. His voice, smooth and seductive, rumbled a low note right next to me, and I shivered, feeling the inner warmth in my lower back, resisting a sudden urge to press up and into him.

"I wonder if he sleeps in other people's beds."

I forgot to make his bed…. A sense of doom washed over me.

"I wonder if he steals their favorite workout shirts."

Well, fuck.

Sharp teeth nipped my shoulder, grabbing the fabric of his light blue T-shirt, and tugged. "I wonder if he is Goldilocks. Hmmm?"

The purr was back at my ear, and I whimpered, my respiration rate increasing.

"What am I going to do with you, Gaudens?"

I could suggest something….

The pressure increased and my nose got pushed into the sofa cushion. I couldn't breathe; my face was stuck and I was pinned and there was no air left in my lungs. I started flailing about.

"What's gotten into you all of a sudden?" I heard him ask, easing off but not letting go.

I jerked my head up, drawing in a frantic gasp of air, relieved. "Couldn't breathe."

"Oh. Sorry." He let go of me and flipped me onto my back, then lay on top of me again. "Better?"

"Yeah. Although there's a *deja-vu* quality to it." There he was once again, his chin propped on folded arms, comfortable in his repose on my chest while I struggled for breath.

"So," he said, his tone conversational. "Explain the shirt to me."

He got me there. I would have been smarter to steal one of his Armani suits and fence it on the street. You'd be amazed what you can actually sell it for, if you know where to go, but I had to go for a ratty old shirt—hell, I had several shirts just like that myself. "I didn't think you'd miss it." I sighed. "It's so old."

"That's precisely why I'd miss it. And it's not something a few crepes is gonna fix, either, Gaudens." The way he said my name—that hurt. I had called him by his first name, failing to elicit a reaction of any kind. "What the fuck do you think you're doing?"

I looked at him, right on top of me but thousands of miles out of reach.

This guy.

This guy was just, so… so….

Special didn't even begin to cover it. Despair at never finding a place in his heart suddenly overcame my desire for him, and I had to spend a moment fighting the dark feeling down. So I borrowed his T-shirt. So what? I'd have given it back… eventually.

I squinted my eyes and clenched my jaw. I still knew a few good moves from years ago, back when I took wrestling and was still welcome at home. I employed a twist, and Jack flew off me. The coffee table was shoved to the side when Jack fell against it, and my laptop slid along its surface and teetered off the edge of it. I was now straddling Jack with my hands on his shoulders, an inexplicable feeling of anger welling within me as I resisted getting sucked into that bewitching blue gaze. "So what. What's so special about this one, Azurri?" I retorted, putting an obnoxious amount of emphasis on his last name.

He returned my stare with nary a waver. "That's the last thing my sister gave me before she died."

Oh... shit.

Gingerly, I let go of his shoulders, shy all of a sudden. I started to get up, but long arms surprised me and I was pulled down into a tight hug. "I'm so sorry." My voice was very small. Barely audible.

He sighed and rolled his head sideways, avoiding my eyes.

"Really, I am. I have a whole bunch of washed-out, ratty T-shirts with mountains on them. So I figured... doesn't everyone? There is no way I would notice one of them missing."

He blinked hard, still not looking at me. "You do?"

"Yeah. I always get one after I summit a new peak...." A sudden realization hit me like a cement truck. The washed-out pattern on the T-shirt seemed familiar. "Jack. Did she... did your sister climb?"

He nodded, his jaw locked and tight. I picked up his hand, brought it to my lips, and brushed his smooth, office-pampered knuckles with a soft caress. Then I flipped his hand over, satisfied that my memory served me right. He had rough fingers—especially the fingertips.

The rest of his hands were smooth, like he had never had to do much physical labor—except for his fingers with their short, blunt nails. Only climbers and guitar players kept their nails as short as that: if you climbed rocks, you needed a good grip, and a nail that was too long was more than just an inconvenience—it was a liability. You break a long nail while you climb—and with my luck, it would hurt like a bitch—then you can't grip the rock well anymore, and boom, you fall. I examined his climbing calluses and beat-up fingernails.

Not overthinking it much, I succumbed to a sudden urge to kiss his roughened fingers one by one. First one hand, then the other; finally our gazes locked. His eyes shone with unshed tears as he took a deep breath to steady himself, and once again I was taken by the almost iridescent quality of his irises. I lay down next to him on the carpet, draped my arm over his chest and slung my leg over his thigh, and pressed my face into his shoulder. Time passed and his breathing leveled out again.

When I didn't need to pretend I could not see the tears because they had finally dried, I stirred next to him. "Would you like to tell me what happened?"

WE SAT at the dining room table, facing one another, our legs carefully retracted under our respective chairs. I scooped up another helping of jasmine rice and saag paneer—a creamy-smooth spinach dish redolent of coriander—using a piece of flat naan bread, all buttery and supple in my hand. The fragrant spices tickled my nostrils as I ate.

"This is so good," I said, heaping another forkful of rice onto a bite-sized piece of flat bread and topping it off with the green spinach goo. A piece of soft, white cheese peeked through the green, and again I inhaled the aroma of Indian spices before leaning over the plate to eat the overstuffed morsel.

Thank you, Reyna, for remembering my favorite food ever.

"How did you know what I'd like?" I asked him, hiding a smile, playing coy.

"I have my ways," he said, not quite smirking, watching me eat with undisguised satisfaction. His smile was like a ray of sunshine that broke through the clouds, and I welcomed it while being aware that the heavy mood from before hadn't quite lifted yet. I observed him carefully from underneath my eyelashes. He sat up straight and strong, his fork toying with a shrimp in the mild and creamy tikka masala sauce, orange with saffron and tomato. His rice was mostly untouched. Soon, the frown mark between his sharp, angled eyebrows reappeared and his jaw tightened again, setting his mouth in a straight line.

Time to try another tack. "Tell me about Celia and her climbing."

He reached for his beer and sucked some down. "Celia was all I had left of my family. My older sister—a bit overbearing, but she meant well, you know? Her only focus was climbing, really. She wanted to go pro and live off endorsements and write articles for climbing magazines, but the field's just too competitive. Everyone wants to do that."

I nodded. "Yeah." She'd been chasing the ultimate rock-bum's dream.

"The shirt you're wearing is one of two she bought in a small Sierra Nevada gift shop right after she climbed Mt. Whitney. She was eighteen then. It was her first big solo climb. She did a route graded as 5.4 III. Does that mean anything to you?"

"If you fall, you die. You better have a partner and good gear. Takes experience, expect half a day to get up."

"Okay. She did it without a partner, and that's pretty good, even though it's rated at 'intermediate lead, beginner follow.' Whatever... I haven't made it to that level yet. Just, she gave me the shirt 'cause she bought it way too big and she was clearing some old things out. She was so happy and so proud, way back then. She climbed that, and much later, she even did El Capitan and all kinds of other nasty, notorious faces, and a few years back, she started to solo all of it. With safety gear, you understand, but still, climbing alone is risky, and I always worried about her. She was chasing her goal a bit too hard, I thought, so I got her an accounting job with Provoid Brothers. That's what she went to school for."

I quirked up my eyebrows with interest. The news articles had made a big deal out of several deaths in the accounting department of Provoid Brothers before the company went under. Three accidents, two suicides.

He saw my reaction and nodded. "Yeah. Well, not too long after she started working there—just part time so she could take long weekends and climb—she and Risby Haus got together. He was the VP of our collections department, reporting to the VP of Operations, so he was pretty high up the ladder." Jack paused and took a drink of beer. He looked like he was going to say more but then thought better of it, and continued. "They'd go out climbing on the weekends. He'd never done it before, so she was teaching him. I hardly saw any of her when she was going out with Haus." Jack drained the rest of his beer, and I got up, walked to the kitchen, and got us two more cold bottles. He accepted his drink with a nod, twisting the cap off with a firm, angry gesture.

"Just about when things were starting to go to shit at Provoid Brothers—it had been a total media circus, mind you—they went on a level 5.3 climb off in West Virginia. It was an easy weekend trip. The wall wasn't too tall or too hard. She could have free-climbed it if she wanted to."

I frowned. "Wait, you mean—"

"Yeah. Like with no safety gear at all. She was pretty confident. I know it's not good practice, but she and her buddies did that at times, just for the thrill of it."

"Did she have a death wish?" My voice was quiet and serious as I asked.

"No. No, she seemed happy. Real happy. Young, in love… she had so much to live for, you know?" He turned his head and studied the curtains to the living room balcony for a good long while.

I gave him some time; when he turned his gaze back to his beer bottle, I prodded again. "So. What happened?"

"She was the lead climber, and Haus was supposed to be belaying her. Except she fell—just three feet before she reached the top, too. She died at the scene. Three hundred and eighty feet is pretty high up when you crash on the rocks below."

"A third of that is plenty enough of a fall to kill you," I commented.

"Yeah…. I drove out to see it. There were ledges and stuff—lots of places with good cover. She fell off the one and only possible place where there was nothing to catch her on the way down."

"And Haus?"

"He made it to the top on his own and walked down the easy side of the mountain. There's no cell signal out there. No witnesses. There's no way to tell what really happened."

I took a sip of my beer, shoving my food aside. To climb with someone was to put your life in his or her hands—especially if you climbed the lead. "So he was belaying her—and when she fell, he didn't arrest the fall?"

Jack's face was still, as still as though carved of stone. "He said the rope just slipped between his fingers. He didn't know what went wrong. He seemed really broken up over it, too." Jack was staring at the table, a furrow between his eyebrows, flipping the beer cap in his fingers. Up and down, up and down.

"Do you know what type of a belaying device she was using?" I asked. That would have made a difference, especially if a beginner panicked.

"It's there somewhere. In her things, y'know." He waved his hand around as though we were at his place, surrounded by countless boxes of Celia's things. "I started climbing two months after she passed, just to see if I could figure out what might have gone wrong. Never had the time to dig into it, though. I've been working crazy hours since we got our little company launched.... You have no idea what that's like. There're nights I sleep at the office and shower at the gym across the street...." He let his voice drift off, suddenly looking worse for the wear.

"What did the police say?"

"An accident. While doing an extreme sport, they said. As though she'd been asking for it." Anger seethed under the surface of his tight, controlled expression.

"So her gear's in one of those boxes?"

"Yeah. It's all her stuff. I don't know what to do with it."

A change of topic was in order. "You still climb, Jack?"

"I try. When I have the time—you know, to figure out what happened—but I'm just a rank beginner."

Slowly I pushed my chair away from the table. I met his gaze and held it as I grasped the bottom hem of the venerable old T-shirt and eased it over my shoulders, revealing my hard-earned abs.

"Gaudens... what the hell you think you're doin'?"

My face was now hidden by his shirt, so I could allow myself a self-satisfied smirk as I flexed my toned midsection just a bit. I wiggled some, pulling the sleeves over my arms before I let the garment fall off my arms. I shook it, turned it right side out, and folded it. "Here. I'm giving it back."

Jack outstretched his hand and accepted the small, still-warm bundle. As I headed for my bedroom to put something else on, I heard a broken, ragged moan escape him. I spun around.

Jack sat at my dining room table with his face buried in the shirt I just removed. Whether he was reacting to his memory of Celia or my scent, his unintended sound was like a siren's call and, heedless of the rocks I was about to be dashed upon, I followed it, unwilling to stop myself.

I flattened my palms across his shoulders from behind; his warmth radiated in ample and generous waves as I detected a hint of his defined deltoids under the scratchy linen of his white shirt. "You okay?" I whispered, stroking my fingers from his shoulder points all the way up his corded neck, bumping over the stand-up collar in my way.

He gave a slight shiver and leaned back into me. After placing the blue T-shirt on the table before him, he raised his hands to touch mine. His fingers stroked my forearms, traveling all the way up to my shoulders, and I leaned into his touch, wrapping my arms around his neck.

"Hey…," I whispered right by his ear, letting my warm, moist breath tickle the sensitive tissue. "Can I take some of this away, at least for a little while?"

He stood and turned, every movement slow and deliberate. He pushed the chair to the side as he did that, and our eyes met as he turned. I wasn't asking him for a lifelong commitment, but he wavered nevertheless before he let his hands travel from my shoulders on down to my abs, my waist, my back…. He explored my curves with those large, strong hands, his roughened finger pads an exclamation mark in the wake of his hot, heavy touch. His hesitant fingers skimmed my back, tracing fire trails to my sides. I gasped as his gentle touch traced my dips and planes. When he brushed my nipple, my knees almost buckled. "Hug?" he said, his mouth on my neck.

I drew him in and molded my body against his. A few moments later, my eyes closed with pleasure at the sensation of his fingers running through my shaggy mop. He breathed into my loose, blond hair, and whispered one word so quietly, I didn't think it was meant for my ears at all:

"Goldilocks…."

CHAPTER EIGHT

WE STOOD facing one another in an uneasy détente. His hands were setting my skin aflame with desire, and for the first time, I thought perhaps taking my shirt off in front of Jack gave me more than I had bargained for. His fingers traced my heaving ribs, his thumbs running up my sternum as his fingers caressed my skin.

His faint whisper was still on my mind:

Goldilocks....

Here was the man of my dreams, tall and handsome and just a bit over the line of dangerous, and he dared to compare me to a *little girl*. My hackles raised immediately. "No girly nicknames."

"Your hair is so rich and gold, like the sweetest honey any bear would love to taste. You break into houses and make yourself comfortable. You're cute. It suits you."

I elbowed him and was surprised when he oomphed and bent over with his hands on his solar plexus. I must have hit him dead on.

"Gaudens... you asshole.... That was a sneaky thing to do."

"You started it," I said, even though I felt bad.

"Okay, then. I should be going home. I don't need this kind of crap from yet another ungrateful malcontent today." He grabbed his blue T-shirt off the table and headed for the door. The man of my dreams was about to put his shoes on and step out of my apartment, out of my life. Getting him here to begin with took me almost a week, and now I'd blown it.

Damn.

"I'd like you to stay...."

He stopped.

"I'm so sorry. Please stay? That landed in a bad place and way harder than I intended. I didn't mean it to hurt... not so much, anyway."

He turned around and eyed me up and down as I stood there with my thumbs hooked over the waistband of his black silk shorts. He didn't say anything, so I continued.

"I'm sorry I couldn't take you down as deep as I wanted to. You're... you're just a little too well-endowed for that sort of a thing... you know?"

His eyes darkened and I saw him suck in a breath; he was focused on my lips as I spoke.

"I just loved sliding my tongue down like that, though. You were so incredibly smooth... and hard... and hot...."

"Gaudens." He mangled my name into a promising growl as he closed the distance between us, discarding the precious T-shirt in passing. He slid his large, warm hands up my sides, and I sagged with relief that he wasn't walking out. He pushed my shoulders into the wall behind me and leaned in to capture my lips with his own, and I felt like melting at his touch, feeling both possessive and insecure. Our kiss was simple; not a lot of tongue. It was a makeup kiss, and we both knew it. "I'll stay if you want me to." He exhaled, sharing his breath with me. I felt his back through that fine, tailored linen; the strong erectors, the defined deltoids.

Twist my arm.

"Only if you really want to." My voice was muffled by his shirt as I inhaled, savoring the scent of his left armpit. Oh God, that man.... A heady scent of spice and musk flooded my senses, almost making me faint with want. Burrowing my nose in there would have been too undignified, so I settled for dizzying, deep breaths.

"You okay? Are you hyperventilating?"

Heat flooded my face as I looked up, barely able to focus on Jack's face. "I… I just love the way you smell. You're like catnip—and I'm the cat."

His eyes widened in sudden understanding. "Is that why…." He nipped at my neck. "The hamper in my room…."

"And the aftershave in your bathroom," I admitted, melting into him, my knee brushing his powerful thighs. "And your pillow…."

"Fuck." His eyes glazed over with lust as his fingers flew over his buttons, ripping his shirt off. "Smell this." He thrust the warm, white garment into my hands and, shameless and greedy, I grasped it and buried my face in it. It held a record of Jack's day: his trials and tribulations and physical exertion, his cooking….

"Cinnamon?" I asked, surprised.

"Yeah…," he said. "I spilled some at breakfast. You can still tell?" He took his shirt back and took in a deep breath, then shrugged. "I can't smell it anymore." He leaned in, and my knee slid between his thighs again as he wedged his leg between mine. We pressed into one another, and I felt his heat.

"You're overdressed." My voice was breathy in an undignified sort of way as I fumbled with his belt buckle and pants button, then slid his zipper down with care.

He let his pants fall and stepped out of them, and there we were, wearing identical black underwear. He ground into my hip as I pressed in, arching my back. "You want this, Gaudens?"

Gaudens.

"Mmm. Feels good, Azurri." And right then and there, as we stood there, rolling against one another, I came to a firm decision. He wouldn't get any until he called me by my first name. The problem was, I felt awkward just asking him to do that. I felt as though he should arrive at that conclusion by his own, lone self. I didn't want to give him remote-control commands and have him do as I said just so he could get me on my back. I wanted him to throw me down and nail me into the nearest horizontal surface and say my name. Scream my name. Not my father's name. My name.

Wyatt.

The name my mother gave me eight years before she died.

"THERE'S condoms by the bed," I said, leaning into Jack, pushing him back a gentle step.

He followed me into the bedroom. "Shower first?" he asked. He slipped his shorts off, and I took stock of what I saw. He was top-to-bottom gorgeous, and so hard it must have hurt. That would never do.

"Shower later," I decided.

He picked me up and dumped me onto my queen-size bed. The look in his eyes was feral, and I returned it with a sly grin.

I sat up halfway; he came in, not expecting me to grab his knees and pull. He landed on his back, just as I planned. I landed on top of him, just as I wanted to. I pinned his legs with mine and anchored his wrists. "Jack...." I panted, raining kisses onto his exposed clavicle. "Would you like the top or the bottom?"

I felt him freeze under me. "What do you mean?"

"Which way do you like it better?"

Instead of answering, he did a fabulous sit-up, dislodging me. "Top, of course."

"How come?" I worked hard to keep my voice level.

"Because I'm bigger and stronger," he whispered by my ear, raising a rash of goose bumps down my body. He tried to flip me.

"But I'm faster and sneakier," I hissed, avoiding the move and trying for a pin. It would've worked if he hadn't bridged and hooked his leg around mine. My leverage gone, I extricated my leg and rolled away, flashing him a *Chase me!* kind of look.

"Not bad," he allowed. "Where did you learn how to wrestle?"

"High school. You?"

"Same. Later I got into tennis."

"Oh." I got off the bed and stood up, all serious and solemn, looking at him with what I hoped he thought was newfound awe.

"What? It's just tennis. It's not a big deal, Gaudens."

"You've spent your college years hitting balls...." I covered my crotch in a protective gesture.

He howled in laughter at the horrible pun, dissolving on top of my bed, his wavy hair a fuzzy halo against the pillows.

I pounced on him in his moment of weakness and pinned him good, locking my legs around his torso and capturing his extended arm.

He could barely speak for laughing. "Wyatt... Wyatt you... sneaky... hahaha... shit! I... I can't... hah... believe you'd trick me... haha... like that."

Wyatt.

I could feel my heart melting. He called me—

Faster than a flash he flipped me onto my stomach. Apparently a melting heart went along with a loosening grip that day, because I found myself under him, his hips pressing hard against my butt. Yet I didn't mind; I was putty in his hands.

He could tell right away. "You giving up?" His voice was low and sounded even disappointed.

"No. You've earned the privilege."

"By what, flipping you over?"

"No... I love what you just called me."

I could hear the flies buzzing inside his head. "You liked being called a sneaky shit?" Not surprisingly, he sounded incredulous.

I wiggled and turned under him, then wrapped one arm around his neck and the other around his broad back. "You finally used my first name."

He raised himself on his elbow, his sapphire eyes meeting mine, and apparently he detected the unfeigned sincerity of my statement, because he smiled a wicked, devastating smile that just about blew me away. "Wyatt." His voice was like dark, melting chocolate

Oh, YES! "Yes, Jack."

"Would you like to face me, or would you like to turn over?"

Now, that was a good question. Sex was like ice cream; it came in all kinds of flavors, and almost all of them were delicious. Today, I decided, I'd prefer to face my partner. It'd been quite a while since I actually had a partner to speak of, and Jack was much bigger than Paul was all those years ago—I hoped my body would adapt. On the other hand....

"It's been a while," I admitted. I didn't mean to make it sound so sad and lonely.

Jack leaned over me, cupping my face. "What's the matter, Goldilocks?" His voice was teasing, but his eyes were all business.

"Nothing."

Sue and I broke up right after high school; she was my early heteronormative flirtation. She was so nice, but the chemistry wasn't quite there. I had loved her. Hell, I still do, in a way. She's the sweetest girl I've ever met. And once we broke up, I couldn't get Paul's glimmer of excitement out of my mind. I thought he'd go after her, but he ended up pursuing me instead.

Which was how we ended up on the floor of my room over a year later, him inside me and me biting on his shoulder to keep quiet, just when my father barged in, his disregard for my privacy an unpleasant reminder of reality.

My father and I had a huge row back then, which centered on his deep dislike both of me dating a guy and me bottoming for him; and he especially hated Paul's father, Dr. Hinge, who my father kept blaming for my mother's death. He gave me a choice that night.

I moved out two days later.

"Hey, Wyatt." Jack's lips grazed mine in a tender caress, and his fingers carded through my hair. "If it's too big a deal, we don't have to."

I realized it had been a whole minute—and that is a long time when you're with someone, not saying anything. "Sorry.... Just a bad memory."

"Of being intimate?" He frowned, concerned.

"Of being found out and kicked out of the house on account of having been intimate." I sighed. "It's been five years. Damn!" I turned into him and buried my face in his chest. "Sorry. I'd have thought I'd be over it by now."

He smiled, his lips stretching in a long, sexy grin. "Sounds like your memory needs to be reprogrammed. Sounds like you need to experience some truly awesome ecstasy to keep the old stuff from intruding like that. When you're with me, you're with me one hundred percent. Aren't you, Wyatt?"

I felt like I was arrested by his heated gaze, and all I could do was swallow and nod.

"I want you." His voice was a sexy purr. "I want you the way you are, and I wouldn't change a thing. I want you to take me in your mouth and do your magic for just a little while. Then I want to lie you down so I can do unspeakable things to you." He buried his face into the crook of my neck and inhaled softly. I shivered when his tongue marked a trail all the way to my ear. He bit me at the juncture of neck and shoulder and sucked, making me writhe in scintillating pleasure. "I want you to scream for me." His voice was but a low rumble that sent a rush of urgent pleasure to my groin.

I wanted this man, and I wanted him bad.

They say the brain is our most important erogenous zone, and I guess that's true, because first I had to take a moment and banish old ghosts. Then I moved down, cherishing small, interconnected bits of Jack with my lips, my hands, my tongue. When I settled between his splayed legs, I took time to stroke the soft insides of his thighs. The pits in the back of his knees were ticklish when I tongued them, which almost earned me an accidental broken nose.

"Sorry!" Jack shrieked in a paroxysm of helpless laughter. "It's just so…. Oh…. Oh…."

Hearing him settle down as I touched the very tip of my tongue to the base of his cock was immensely satisfying. So was hearing him laugh, and I realized I would do almost anything to keep him from slipping back into that earlier, darker mood. I wanted to please him, satisfy him, love him. I wanted to keep him. The desire felt premature, however, and I pushed it out of my mind and focused on the nest of brown curls under my nose.

His pubic hair was soft and wiry at the same time, and it held his musky scent and the residual top notes of body wash. I buried my nose and inhaled him. The scent felt warm and had colors, as though my senses threatened to merge. I licked the crease of his thigh, avoiding his hairy balls—you can't really suck on a hairy object with good results—and I directed the tip of my tongue to the sensitive and perfectly smooth cock that awaited me.

I licked him all the way up and kissed the tip, and when I glanced to Jack's face, I saw him watching me. His expression spoke of turned-on pleasure and lust and sheer amazement.

I sucked him down gently, barely touching, and he rose into me in a slow, gentle arch. He was smooth and hard and hot in every way, and when he plunged his fingers into my hair and fisted it, I moaned in appreciation. He worked hard not to thrust—too hard—so I slid my finger into my mouth, right next to his cock, to gather a bit of moisture. Then I worked my hand under his balls and let the knuckle of my thumb rub against his taint as I reached my finger farther in. I must have rubbed against something good even flying blind, because he thrust and panted, and his grip tightened on my hair as I slid my lips up and down his shaft. I felt his balls tighten and he froze.

"Slow… slow down, will ya?" He let go of my hair and just lay there, taking deep, calming breaths.

I let his cock slip out of my mouth and looked up. "What's wrong?" I asked in a voice that was much too innocent and perhaps a bit smug. Unraveling Jack had proved to be a singular pleasure.

"If you don't want me to blow, you'll stop right now," he said. His eyes were closed and his eyebrows were drawn together in concentration.

I moved my hands up his sides. "Okay," I said. "Whenever you're ready."

I heard a click of a lube bottle. I let him roll me to my side and spoon me from behind, resting his arm under my neck in a possessive embrace. His hard heat, still tacky from my spit, dried against my lower back as he slid his hand down my side, bypassing my throbbing dick and lifting my leg for access, reaching me from behind. He slid a slicked finger up and down my cleft and circled around my hole with a teasing, delicate touch.

A moan escaped me and I heard him chuckle in response.

His finger dipped lower as he breached me.

I hissed in surprise.

"You okay?"

"Yeah… oh!… *Oh!*"

He tried to say my name, but his voice became incoherent as he pressed his hard length against me, his fingers now doing their magic down under. I felt the heat build down in my center and radiate through my shoulders, my nipples, my thighs. My cock, untouched, stood at attention. His desire fanned the flames of mine, and when I thought I couldn't take it any longer, he pulled his hand out and stroked his palm up my shaft.

I gasped, arched into him in a needy invitation and, in not too long, he rolled me onto my back. "Condom," I gasped.

"Oh…. Yeah, right…." With a sheepish smile, he reached over to my nightstand, grabbed a packet, and ripped it open. I heard him snap the rubber on.

His knees eased mine far apart, and I wrapped my legs around his waist, and dammit if I didn't think of Paul just then and how Paul used to do this part differently. I banished my ex out of my mind. I was determined to be eager with anticipation if it killed me. Mindful of the present, I focused on the feeling of the cold, wet head about to enter me, trying to relax and push against him, and next thing I knew, he was buried inside me. He ground his hips into me. I gasped, and he smiled. His face was close to mine with his elbows by my head. He gave another thrust, gentle and slow.

The door wasn't shoved open.

Nobody walked in on us.

Yet.

"Relax, Wyatt…," Jack whispered.

A sudden desire to escape washed over me, and my eyes must have given me away, because he buried his fingers in my hair and kissed me. Then he began to move in deep, slow strokes. I felt his fingers caress a circle around my ear. My apprehension was a thing of the past as I was approaching overload. The amazing, delicious fullness of our joining, the sensuous touch of our tongues, the way he drove deeper and harder with every thrust. His weight became almost too much—I whimpered—and then I felt it. A bright brush of pleasure.

"More!" I didn't ask, I commanded. I heard Jack grunt as he thrust again, hitting that same spot, and I let out a low moan, squeezing my eyes shut against all the sensations I felt flooding me.

One hundred percent.

With Jack.

One hundred percent.

I grabbed his arms, anchored on the ridges of his triceps; he came down for a kiss and my leaking cock brushed his abs again. "Jack... please.... I'm gonna... Oh!"

He grunted, pulled out of me, and squeezed around the base of my cock with his fingers.

"Jack!" I panted. I needed to come, and he wasn't letting me. "Please!"

"Shh." He kissed my forehead. "Turn over."

I did. I heard another squirt of the lube bottle, and then Jack took me from behind. He buried himself to the hilt, hard and fast, making me see lightning with almost every stroke. And when I didn't think it could get any better, he wrapped his lubed fingers over my cock and gave it a few pumps. I bit back a scream as I fell over the precipice with my eyes rolled back in my head and the delicious stretch-and-fill of Jack's cock up my ass reminding me that I was here, alive, and the past was only a distant memory.

He panted, then held his breath and went rigid. "Gwrrraaaahrrr!" He thrust hard as his pleasure crested and I got to hear that awesome, big cat roar once again.

He collapsed on top of me, and I was sandwiched beneath the comforting weight of Jack. We were still joined, and a puddle of jism was cooling under me. Life was good.

There was only the two of us now.

WE SHOWERED separately and slipped into our black silk undies again.

"Bed?" I asked, hoping he'd stay. He looked undecided. "Please?" I knew no shame. I wanted him next to me, his heat making me too hot, his breath keeping me up with sensuous whispers behind my ear, keeping the black-haired specter of my long-gone lover away.

"You sure?" he asked. Apparently he wasn't the type to stay the whole night. "But I have stuff to do tomorrow...."

"Tomorrow's Sunday," I pointed out.

"Yeah. The weekends are pretty much the only time I can sort through Celia's old things."

I thought fast. I'd give up some of my time if only he'd warm my bed—this would be the first time I let somebody sleep over since Paul married Susan. "I could help for a little bit," I offered. "If we find her climbing gear...."

He exhaled, his shoulders slumping just a little. "Okay, Goldilocks. You get to snoop through my stuff tomorrow if you really want to."

I blushed. It wasn't like that... but he'd never believe me. Relieved, I saw him fix me with that devastating grin as he slipped between my sheets.

"Hey, Wyatt. You're with me. One hundred percent. Right?" There was concern in those dark eyes, their brilliant blue dimmed by the night. I could barely see them in the midnight shadows of the room.

"I'm with you, Jack." My voice seemed to have sealed the situation, and I felt him pull me in and spoon me from behind, his left arm under my neck, his left hand stroking up and down my body absently.

"Hey, Jack."

"What," he growled, almost asleep.

"If you keep toying with me like that, I'll get hot again. So unless you're still interested...."

His hand stilled, pulling me in even closer. "Promises, promises... Goldilocks," he said right before his breath evened out and he fell asleep.

I took a lot longer, unable to banish the thoughts of my father's rage every time he happened to run into me and Paul together, of Paul and Susan at their wedding, of my secret meetings with my brother, Carl, and my sister, DeeDee... I remember having heard the first cars rumble in the streets before I descended into the realm of uneasy dreams.

THERE was an arm under my neck; a knee brushed my thigh, a palm caressed my belly ever so gently. It felt familiar, warm and loving.

Paul....

I felt myself smile as I turned into his chest, the cobwebs of sleep distorting reality as my eyes refused to open. I mumbled something, something sweet. The same hands ran up my back now, and I arched into their touch, sliding my own hands up the smooth chest, the throat, the jaw line—the hair was too short. Coarser, too. Bewildered, I pried my eyes open only to be met with calm eyes the color of deep, tropical seas. I was locked into that intense gaze; the straight nose, the perfect, pink lips. His hair wasn't black, and at the sight of the auburn tones in his brown, messy mop it all rushed back at me, like a torrent.

Not Paul. Jack.

I leaned in and brushed his lips with mine, not exhaling. Morning breath was never a pretty thing. "Jack...." I leaned my forehead into his shoulder, stricken with guilt.

I was with Jack now.

One hundred percent.

"Hey, Goldilocks...." There was a faint trace of hurt in his voice. I kissed that strong, warm shoulder, hoping to make it better. "So who's Paul?"

I felt like bolting into a run and never stopping; I felt like crawling under a rock and never coming out.

"C'mon, Goldilocks. If you'll be confusing me with someone, at least let me know who it is."

I looked up, sensing the tension in his shoulders, the frown mark between his brows. I wanted him to stay. I didn't want him to be driven away like the rest, didn't want him to be just the last in a row of sporadic one-night stands.

"I was not confusing you with anyone last night," I said, my tone pointed and defensive. A moment passed before I broke his patient silence again. "You know how you said I needed to be reprogrammed? Sometimes it takes more than once."

He rolled on top of me, stroking my hair to the side and nipping my ear hard enough for me to take notice. "Who. Is. Paul." Implacable eyes gazed down at me, and behind that tough façade was a world of hurt.

"My first real romantic partner was a girl. Susan Pollack. We dated for seven months. Paul Hinge and the two of us hung out all the time. There were other friends, too, but the three of us were inseparable. So, eventually... Susan and I decided to split up, and I figured Paul would court her, but he went after me instead. It was like... it was like a fog had lifted, you know? That feeling you get when you realize something really profound about yourself?"

I saw Jack close his eyes, then open them again, and nod. "You figured out why it wasn't going so well with Susan. You liked guys."

"I like both.... I like guys a lot more."

"So what happened?"

"So Paul and I dated into college. We... we were really right for one another. We drove each other crazy but managed to make it work, somehow—and there was Susan, and she loved both of us and we both loved her back. It was pretty fucked up, I guess...."

A gentle nuzzle tickled my neck; a kiss followed right after. "So what went wrong?"

"Ahh... my dad. He walked in on me and Paul the summer after our freshman year. We were... you know. And I was under him, and dad.... My dad, he just... he totally freaked out. Paul's dad is a doctor and so is mine—there had been some kind of an issue since my mother died that nobody's allowed to talk about. My dad had always blamed

Paul's dad for my mother's death, and Paul wasn't welcome at our house at all. I lost my family that day. Two days later, I moved in with Paul. The family feud didn't go well… Susan cried, thinking she's losing both of us, so we… we invited her to move in with us, and it was good until we graduated. Then Susan got pregnant and Paul proposed, so…."

"So you moved out," Jack said.

"Yeah."

"And you lost your family… again."

Tears threatened my eyes and I fought hard to push them back.

"Have you dated much, since?" He prompted me.

"I tried…."

"And?"

I rolled to my side and raised myself on my shoulder, meeting Jack's searching gaze as squarely as I could bear it. "You're the first one to… to make me feel like that." I paused, watching my words soak in and make their impact. "The first guy I asked to stay overnight."

The serious look from his eyes didn't dissipate. "You're a mess, Wyatt," he said, rolling onto his back again.

"I know." I stayed where I was. "Is that…. Is that a big problem?"

"I dunno," he said. He fidgeted with his fingers, searching for something to do, and as soon as I put my hand over them, he forced himself to still and took several deep breaths. "I used to smoke," he said in a wry voice. "This is just one of those times when I wish for the distraction of a cigarette, you know?"

"No… I've never smoked," I said. "That's not how I release stress anyhow."

"You break into people's houses instead of smoking," he said, frowning. "How does that tie to your stress, anyway?" He turned to his side and propped himself up on his elbow. "What are you looking for, when you do that?"

The question was fair. He'd let me learn that he had been a smoker; I felt I owed him at least some information, so I forced my thoughts to still and think for a bit. "I love finding out how others live. I get a real kick out of finding out that the couple has kids, or is divorced and living together, or that they had roast beef the night before…. There are family pictures around, usually, and when they are not around, that's indicative of something, too. Like, this person doesn't have anyone—why is that?"

"And you take their stuff?"

"Not always," I said, defensive. "Only if they have a lot and won't miss it, or if they're mean, or something like that."

"And then you give it to the poor," Jack said, his voice dripping with sarcasm.

"Sometimes I do," I said. "Not enough, I guess, and I don't pretend that it justifies what I'm doing. It's just like… I'm looking for something and I can't stop." I turned toward him and our eyes met. "This is a problem, isn't it?"

"Yeah."

I sighed and forced myself to meet his eyes, unwavering. "Is it a deal breaker?"

He leaned in and kissed my forehead. "I don't like thinking in absolute terms like that. I like you—otherwise I wouldn't be here, but, yeah. You need to stop doing that. We can work on that together, you know. After all, reprogramming often takes many, many tries."

I released the breath I didn't know I held as a wave of relief washed over me. "So… so you'll… you won't…?"

"You may have to pursue me some more, convince me that you really, truly want me, Wyatt," he said, his voice teasing. "Now I'm hungry, though. What are our options?"

"Cereal. Grapefruit. Coffee."

He wrinkled his nose. "I've a hankering for pancakes. My treat?"

I nodded, burrowing my face into his shoulder. Pancakes would be swell.

OUR appetites were sated, both carnal and gustatory. Now we sat on the black leather sofa at Jack's place, eyeing the looming pile of cardboard boxes. They all held Celia's stuff. She had inherited the estates of two of their aunties, who were big-time collectors.

"They were crazy old bats, those two," Jack said of his aunts with a certain trace of fondness. "They'd give us the craziest shit for gifts. One year, Celia got a little cigar box full of buttons for Christmas. Just old buttons, you know? They were kind of interesting, in a quaint sort of way, and she just let them sit around, not knowing what to do with them, until she found out they were a trendy collectible. She sold that box of antique buttons for almost two grand."

"Wow."

"Yeah, so I didn't want to call one of those junk dealers—I don't even know what's in here. I don't know anything about this kind of stuff."

"I do."

"You do? Really?"

"Sure. I have a fence…." We both froze for a second, and then I tried again. "I know of a reputable antiques dealer who'll give you a good price. My question is, where do you want to start?"

Jack thought about that for a bit. He slid his hand up my shoulder and to the nape of my neck, twirling my hair in absent play. "I'd love to empty that second bedroom."

"Even if it takes over your living room?"

He nodded. "The climbing gear's likely to be buried in there somewhere, you know."

CHAPTER
NINE

I SNEEZED again. It's amazing how much dust can accumulate on the top of boxes in a period of only nine months, and I said as much.

"This dust's older than that," Jack said, pressing his finger under his nose, bringing his own reaction under control. "These boxes sat at Auntie Xenia's house."

"How long has it been?" The room was now halfway empty.

"Oh, I dunno. Years? Decades?" Jack straightened his back, holding another box in his arms.

I got out of his way and grabbed the next one, then followed him to the living room. It looked like a disaster area.

"Shit, Gaudens. However are we gonna sort this out?"

Gaudens, huh?

"Jack, unless you want me to come up with some offensive, inane nickname for you, you'll refrain from calling me Gaudens."

There. That was direct, yet nonconfrontational. Just stating a fact.

He turned to look at me. "Just 'cause you and your dad aren't on speaking terms doesn't make the name bad."

"Says you."

"Says I."

We stood there, staring at one another like two stubborn mules. Two hours of sweaty work had made me grumpy, and my nose itched and my rear still reminded me of last night's fun and games—as well as of the frolicking this morning—and dammit, I was in a foul mood all of a sudden.

"Look. Just make a suggestion, okay? I have no fucking idea how to sort all this shit." Well, then. Mr. Azurri was all sunshine, just like me.

I leaned against the white wall, thinking. "You got any beer?"

"That your suggestion?" He shot me an incredulous look, crinkles giving his forehead what women called "character lines" when they bitched about the unfairness of life.

I nodded. He disappeared into the kitchen, moments later coming out with two cans of Miller Lite.

Now it was my turn to sigh. I had asked for beer, not piss-water. It was cold, however, and as such formed a fitting substitute for real beer, and I made a note to start educating Jack on the fine points of microbrews. "Thanks." I sighed, popped the tab, and lifted the can in a silent salute. Then I did something I never thought I'd ever do—I actually drank some. It was akin to being stuck out in the back of beyond with just a dagger and three matches, eating grubs and earthworms for subsistence.

Jack seemed entirely pleased with his can of light, tasteless, over-chilled beer, and that old grin reappeared on his face. It was infectious, and I saw no reason to spoil his good mood—I grinned back.

"Okay, then. We need to open the boxes. You'll need a bag for garbage, a box for donations, a box for the stuff you want to keep personally, and a box for stuff you'd like to sell."

"Yeah? Okay!" He opened a sturdy box and dug through it; then he poured it out in the middle of the Copenhagen Blue carpet. A partially knit afghan slithered out, followed by a merry chase of bright-colored balls of yarn. Then there was a tablecloth and a bunch of placemats and other fabric items and a white, embroidered cooking apron.

"Girl shit." He grimaced. "Let me get the garbage bags." He disappeared into the kitchen again.

I was drawn to that apron, though. I picked it up, fingered the fine cotton, and examined the careful, geometric cross-stitched patterns and filigree open work. It didn't look too fluffy—no flowers or birds—yet it was delicate and expertly made. A good antique store could sell it for fifty bucks, easy. Not having much patience of my own, I've always been drawn to the intricacy of needlework and had even tried the odd cross-stitch back when Paul and I were an item. Not that I'd use this apron, but my sister would go absolutely gaga over it. She is only three inches shorter than I am. Wanting to know if it would even fit, I slipped the apron over my neck and tied the ties behind my back in a bow. A bit short on me, possibly perfect for DeeDee.

"We're keeping the apron," a husky voice drawled behind me.

I spun around. "I was just checking the size," I said, my tone of voice somewhat defensive.

"Sure you were." Jack said, his predatory eye sizing me up in the delicate, embroidered garment. "My grandma made it for Auntie Xenia ages ago, but Auntie never wore it. It was too nice to get dirty, she said. It just sat there in a drawer until it was transferred to this box." He paused, his eyes suddenly thoughtful. "What do you think of it?"

"I think you could get ten or twenty bucks for it and a store could sell it for fifty or more."

"That's peanuts," he scoffed.

"Sure, but you have got lots of peanuts in here. It all adds up. Besides… if you want to throw it out, can I have it?" I felt uncertain asking—I'd never asked Jack for anything.

His look grew calculating and the silence stretched like a tight string, off-key and filled with apprehension. "If you wear it for me tonight, you can have it or sell it or do whatever you want to do with it."

I groaned. "Jack! First of all, my ass still hurts from earlier, and second, I don't do lacy embroidery. I do black leather."

He was on top of me in a flash, pressing me into the white wall. The dust I had picked up on my hoodie smeared against the wall, decorating it in abstract patterns. "But you look so tasty in that apron,

Goldilocks!" I felt him press his body against mine, trying to pin my hands to the wall.

I narrowed my eyes. "Cut it out, Jack."

He didn't cut it out, so I dropped my weight and slithered under him and out like a snake. He might be bigger and stronger, but I was still the one who was faster and sneakier. I took the apron off and set it aside. "I'll think on that one, but unless you want to put me in some severe discomfort, Loverboy, you'll keep your hands to yourself for now."

His heavy gaze softened—it was as though he pulled his presence back into himself—and he nodded. "All right. Hey… you okay? I didn't realize… you know."

"It's been two years and one month, Jack."

"Two years and one month since your Paul, and counting." I saw his eyes harden and his back stiffen, and he picked up the oversize tablecloth, looking at it. "So what's this, then? Garbage, sell, or give-away?"

TWO more hours and six beers later, we'd sorted through eight boxes. We were also down for the count.

"This shit's tedious," he said, collapsing onto the sofa with a blank stare. "I did three boxes on my own, and it took me weeks. The worst part is deciding what to do with something. If I've seen it before, it makes me think of the old days, and if I've never seen it before, I wonder if it has value of its own."

I nodded, settling next to him with my head against his shoulder. "How about we go for a run, get some lunch on the way back, and do some more later?"

He looked at me. "You run?"

"Yeah. You gotta run if you're a burglar, in case they're chasing you."

He gave me a grin, probably thinking I was kidding. "I used to do twenty miles a week and then all this landed in my lap. I guess it's my turn to throw up on you."

I sprang up, excited. "Loan me some shorts and a T-shirt, will you?" He did, and even clean they still held just that light, indefinable scent I associated with Jack; the fabric felt like a caress against my skin.

He was ready before I was, tying on a pair of ratty sneakers. "Okay, Goldilocks. Let's do it!"

BY THE time we did our three miles, Jack had lost his appetite entirely, and it took forever to cool down and stretch. We staggered out of his elevator, and he just leaned there, propped against his door, staring at me. "Just open the damn door."

"I don't have a key."

"You, of all people, don't need a fucking key."

"I don't have my tools on me. What, you think I carry those around? If I get busted with those tools on me, I'm toast."

"Awww, he's human after all. No superpowers." He tossed me his keys, and I sifted through them, taking my time before I unlocked all three locks.

"Sorry to disappoint. My superpowers don't extend past the bedroom door."

WE SHOWERED our sweat off only to change into our old, dusty clothing.

"So what do you want on your pizza, pepperoni or sausage?"

I lifted my eyes from the box of salt and pepper shakers I was sorting in my search for precious antiques. "Are those the only choices available?"

He shrugged and let a moment pass. "That's all Vito's has to offer."

"Vito's? That little place in the mall?"

"Yeah. I never get any other pizza. Why?"

"I always get Tambellini's. Tambellini's is made all from scratch, and you can get Pizza Hawaiian."

He viewed me with unveiled suspicion. "What's Hawaiian?"

"Ahh…." My tone mellowed out as my taste buds recalled the fine mélange of synchronous flavors. "Onion and ham and green peppers… and pineapple!"

"Pineapple! That's one of those 'kitchen sink' pizzas. Whoever taught you to eat weird combinations like that?"

"Susan." The word just slipped out, asked-for and delivered.

He sighed and fell on his back on the sofa and put his feet up on the armrest. There was no response, so I felt a need to elaborate.

"My *former* girlfriend, who is now the wife of my *former* boyfriend. She loves to cook. For better or worse, since she's highly adventurous and combines the oddest flavors. She can serve you a peanut butter and pickle sandwich on the theory that pickle offsets the flavor and texture of peanut butter, except it's savory instead of sweet. She got this idea from a cool book about a girl bounty hunter she'd been reading."

"Gross."

"That's what I thought until I tasted it. It's quite refreshing in the summer, although I draw the line at peanut-butter-and-potato-chip sandwiches."

He turned his head and looked at my slumped figure. I was sitting propped against his formerly white wall, my butt on the floor. "C'mere." That was not a request.

"Pardon me?" I didn't take commands easily; never have.

"I'm trying to get my latest fling over here for a hug, so c'mere."

I slid up the wall and stretched while taking my dusty hoodie off. Then I sprawled on top of Jack, letting his large hands pull me in and stroke me up and down my back.

"Thanks for helping."

"Sure. It's fun, actually." I smiled, enjoying his touch. I wanted to say I really enjoyed spending time with him, but it felt unnecessarily sappy. No need to expose myself and make myself vulnerable.

"Tell you what. We can order from Tambellini's, but we get a pizza that's half Hawaiian, half pepperoni."

"Okay." I edged higher up his chest and let my lips brush his, sharing his breath, breathing his scent. I felt myself press my middle into his, reacting to his proximity.

"Wyatt."

"Yeah."

"Are you trying to start something?"

A faint blush threatened my cheeks as I shifted my hips, eliminating the contact between us. "No. Sorry."

"Nothing to be sorry about." He reached up and captured my earlobe in his lips. I whined as he sucked on it and then let it go. "Pizza," he said, his voice strong and determined. "We were negotiating pizza. I'll work on your reprogramming later."

NINE thirty rolled around, and I felt a sudden need to be in my own space. We had sorted a good third of all the crap in Jack's spare bedroom; there was even some furniture, which now occupied most of his living room. His clean, civilized area was diminished to half the blue carpet, and his expression was pained as he surveyed the scene.

"This is a clusterfuck, Gaudens. Just a clusterfuck. What am I gonna do with all this?"

I chose to overlook his use of my last name. "Don't you have any storage space in the building?"

"Yeah, but I have my own stuff in there. And it's tidy. If I jam all these things in there, I'll never find anything."

I surveyed the scene, tapping my tired brain for all those little tricks DeeDee tried to drill into us during spring cleaning. Oh, right.

"Well, that whole side is garbage, so we can take that downstairs right now."

Without a word, Jack grabbed two bags in each hand and headed out the door; I took hold of the other three and followed in his wake. We squished into the small, antiquated elevator. He didn't say a thing until the bags were in the dumpster outside the basement door. Then he looked at me and said, "Now what?"

I thought hard. "Can you share your storage with those things you actually want to keep?"

"If I do that, I'll keep too much and it'll take over."

"So… find a place in a separate room, then."

Back in the apartment, he took a large box of keepsake items and shoved it under the dining room table.

"Now for the giveaways. If we load your car, we can take half of this stuff to Goodwill right now and you can drop me off at home."

"And if we do two trips to Goodwill and drop it off by their back door, it will all be gone outta my living room except for the stuff to sell, and then I can vacuum my rug, and then I can drop you off at home. Or you can stay the night and I can drop you off in the morning."

I leaned into him, wrapping my arms around his waist. "This is all moving too fast, Jack. I really want to sleep at home tonight."

I felt his lips brush the top of my head as he nuzzled my hair. "Okay, Goldilocks."

"I'll give you the second trip to Goodwill, Loverboy. Oh, and make a list of your donated items for a tax write-off next year. It adds up."

"Whatever." He stacked two boxes on top of one another and lifted them and headed out the door again, and I followed his example. This time we exited the building through the lobby.

The doorman presented his familiar silhouette, his tall, lanky form bent over a book. He reminded me of a preying mantis.

"Hey, whatcha readin' now?" I asked him on the way back. "Some fancy literature again?"

Risby Haus lifted his head and fixed me with a blank gaze. "You again!"

"Yeah, him again. Get used to seeing him around." Jack grabbed me by the arm and pulled me into the elevator.

"Hey, Loverboy. I don't care for being hauled around like that. What was that all about?"

"You're talking to the man who probably killed my sister." His eyes were as cold as blued steel.

"That's right. You want me to help you find out what happened, don't you?"

"Huh."

"Didn't you notice what he was reading?"

"No. Why should I?"

"He had a climbing supply catalog on his desk."

Our eyes met. Not letting go of my gaze, Jack grabbed the front of my dusty T-shirt and pulled me in. "You better keep your distance from that bastard. I don't think he's good company." His voice was gruff, but his eyes spoke of loss and fear.

IT WAS Wednesday already. Jack was snowed under again, and once again, he was surly and uncommunicative. I called Reyna right before lunch. "Hey… it's me, Wyatt. Are we on for Friday?"

There was a pregnant pause—the sound of which I didn't like. Finally she cleared her throat. "Well. As a matter of fact I meant to give you a heads-up on that. Auguste wants me to attend a conference with him this weekend, and our flight leaves on Friday, right before noon. I'm sorry, Wyatt."

Auguste.

My thoughts wandered back to my former boss. His quiet demeanor, his commanding presence, his lovely, anthracite hair. Much like Paul. You'd never guess Paul to have some wild, erotic tastes behind the closed doors.

"Reyna, is there something you're not telling me?" I couldn't wipe the grin off my face and it showed in my tone, because she began to stutter and sputter and had to clear her throat again.

"W-what makes you think that?"

"Oh, just about everything I know about my former boss? He lets you call him by his first name, he buys you lunch and takes you places—heck, you're so smitten you're even using utensils!"

"But—but—but—"

"I hope you're using protection."

There was silence on the other side.

"Your former boss and I certainly do."

"Wyatt!"

"Have a good time at the conference, Reyna. We should do a double-date when you get back."

"With Azz-hole? No way."

"First of all, don't call him that. Second, he seems to have mellowed some. Can't think of a reason why."

I heard Reyna giggle on the other side of town, and grinned. I knew she'd think about it, then bring it up with Pillory in some not-so-subtle way, and then we'd see. It could be fun. I could pump Pillory for all kinds of dirt on Jack, getting all those embarrassing stories of what stupid pranks he used to pull in college. After what he'd put me through at my old job, I thought I deserved at least that much.

Next, I dialed an often-used number. Izzy was an antique dealer I did business with while handling my "special finds." He had specified that he doesn't accept stolen goods, so I've never told him. With a straight face, I'd say, "Izzy, there was this cool flea market, and guess what I found...." and he'd give me this look, and sigh, and look it over, and decide how much it was worth and whether he was willing to accept it.

"Hey, Izzy, it's Wyatt."

"Wyatt! How have you been?" His voice was slightly nasal, and I could just picture him, with his short hair and an attempt at a beard, with wire-rimmed glasses perched on his nose. He kept his head covered with a fisherman's bucket hat, rejecting the little black yarmulke of his tradition. Izzy Silberman observed Shabbat not as holy, but as one day of the week when he could have peace and quiet without the interruptions from incessant phones, e-mails, and annoying customers.

"I've been great, Izzy. I have a new boyfriend." I bet he winced on the other side, and I grinned.

"You be careful, Wyatt. I take it he's keeping you out of trouble and off the rooftops?"

"Sort of. I actually broke into his place and he caught me. The rest is history."

"Wyatt!" He exclaimed in an appalled voice, full of concern. "Is he a good man?"

"Well… I don't really know him, but I'd like to think so. My good man here is trying to dispose of an estate of his deceased sister and their two aunts, and has boxes of stuff at his place. I'm helping him sort it out, and I was wondering if you'd like to have a look?"

"Aha! Finally you offer me something with provenance. I'll look. How is tomorrow? I can close the shop early."

"He's working. Weekends are just about it, Izzy."

"Hmmm…," I heard him mumble, probably while looking at his calendar. "Saturday after sundown. That's legit, not even my wife can fault me for that, and I'll be able to drive."

"I'll let him know. Pencil it in, okay?"

We chatted some more, and Izzy discovered that my best friend ever, Reyna Guajillo, would be indisposed and I'd be on my own on a Friday night. "Come see us for dinner, Wyatt. Don't bring anything. Debra always cooks extra for Shabbat."

I didn't want to go. If it hadn't been for Izzy's restraining influence over the years, I probably would have been in jail by now. Despite, or perhaps especially because of that, I didn't feel like writhing under his searching gaze. Plus I had other stuff to do.

"Sorry… I just feel like spending some time alone. It's been a while since I've been able to do that. How about we plan for Saturday night, though. I think you'll like Jack. Let me give you his number."

ONCE again, my job waiting tables yielded a potentially profitable lead. I should have ignored it, but old habits are hard to break, and with Jack busy and Reyna out of town, I felt like there was a void within me. My siblings were off to college, my mother had been dead for years, my father and I never talked to one another, and I couldn't really bother Susan and Paul—their baby was a handful, and they barely slept. Plus, seeing them together still felt like rubbing salt into a recently closed wound: not terribly agonizing but not exactly fun either. I just had to find a way to entertain myself.

I scanned the tables under my control as I mentally counted the money I had earned. Two hundred bucks in tips on Wednesday and a bit less than that on Thursday, so my rent was almost covered for the month, but I still didn't have phone and food money—not until Novack paid the second half of his invoice. I did have a modest amount of money sitting in my emergency cash stash right next to my getaway bag, but the rule was, I had to cover my basic expenses every month. If only BW&B had been a paying client… but they weren't. If only I had more clients like Novack… but I didn't. If only I could wait tables every day, I'd be set for cash, but I couldn't get any more hours—people with higher seniority were way ahead of me, with families depending on their income, and the boss knew that.

Friday sure looked like a good day to improve my financial standing by breaking into that lawyer's house while he was at a baseball game.

DRESSED for work, I had my tools in my pocket and a change of clothing and a wig in my bag. My donor lived in a posh, gated subdivision out in Fox Chapel. Those were always fun, because the luxury of a gate and guard gave the residents a false sense of security. Back in the 1980s, the community had been planned with care, sparing no expense to screen the houses from one another by vegetation, privacy fences, and careful positioning. There was no dog; I overheard the owner talk about his plans to acquire one.

After the fiasco where I met Jack in person for the first time, I concluded that being mistaken for a girl might amount to something of advantage, and so dressed appropriately. I wasn't going out in drag—not really—I was dressed only to misinform. When people saw a person in black tights and a pink T-shirt with a floral design, their first assessment was going to be "girl," not "guy in drag." I had to take care not to rip my opaque black tights when I was climbing the neighborhood's six-foot brick wall and avoiding the metal spikes on top. My jump ended in a soft landing due to my sporty black-and-purple slip-on Sketchers girly shoes—and I found myself in a crouch on the other side. I then pulled my baseball cap with an attached brown ponytail over my microfiber cap and sauntered out, just walking, looking for my donor's address. I bet I looked okay; my blond stubble was given a smooth shave before I left, and clip-on earrings lent verisimilitude to my appearance.

I called my donor's landline; nobody picked up. I knocked on the front door and rang the bell; nobody opened. There was still just enough light for me to see the lock without a flashlight. The front lawn was carefully landscaped, with mulch surrounding a large boulder and some short shrubs. There was something familiar about that boulder. Before I reached for my set of picks, I touched its surface.

Laminate. A fake stone....

I glanced up and down the street, and bent down as though to check my shoe while I dug my fingers under the hollow structure. Most people kept a spare key somewhere. This fellow had ordered one of the three fake landscaping boulders available from a home decorating catalog, apparently to disguise his eyesore of a utility vent. It also made a natural hiding place for his spare keys. Sure enough, there was a spare set of keys on the gravel underneath. I pocketed the keys and, still unobserved, I unlocked the door.

Having slipped inside, I drew the curtains and locked the door behind me before I clicked on my small flashlight. The rush of excitement I felt was better than going up and down a roller coaster: I was in, he was out, and I would find out more about him. A quick thought of Jack's disapproval crossed my mind but was soon drowned by the hum of the donor's refrigerator and the particular odor of his house. I lived in the moment—I had broken in and had to stay on my toes or get out. The image of making it out the door and back to the car niggled at me. I could have done that—but I'd gotten so far already, it would be a shame to waste all the effort. I'd just have a look. If the resident was a harmless, pleasant fellow, I'd leave him alone.

The interior was posh but sterile. The owner hadn't been spending a lot of time in his living room. There were no plants; a picture of two older kids sat on the automatic, natural gas fireplace. No wife, though. Divorced, maybe? That would make him another lonely soul, I thought with sympathy. I walked through quickly and checked all the rooms with silent haste, making sure I was truly alone. There was a carved wooden box on his bedroom bureau, and I opened it and rifled through spare change and various receipts, stray cufflinks, and carelessly crumpled money. My fingers skimmed an envelope; it held cash. It felt substantial. Behind the envelope sat a checkbook in its vinyl, leatherlike cover. I pulled it out and checked the register and held back a whistle as the account balance made my eyebrows rise. It must be nice to be king. Further examination of his drawers revealed underwear and socks and folded polo shirts—and a small baggie of white powder atop a mirror, together with an old-fashioned razor blade.

The sympathy I felt before dissipated when I saw the cocaine. So he wasn't a good guy after all. I reached back into the wooden box, took the envelope, and stuffed it in the front of my tights. I was taking the good barrister's drug money, but from the look of it, he had more elsewhere.

Unwilling to push my luck any further, I exited the house, locked up, put the keys where they belonged, and snapped the latex gloves off my hands. As I sauntered down the street, a couple walking a standard poodle bade me good evening.

"Good evening," I replied.

"Are you a friend of Ernie's?" the woman asked.

"Just a casual acquaintance." I smiled.

"I believe he's out tonight," she said.

"Yeah, a ball game."

"Do you want us to give him a message?" The man was looking me up and down. That made me nervous.

I smiled, eager to make my getaway. "Sure. Just tell him Susie stopped by. Although I've already texted him, so he'll know." I nodded at them. "Nice to meet you." Now I had to continue down the road at a regular walking speed and take a turn and cut through another cul-de-sac before I made it to the wall and over it.

Shit. Crap. Oh God.

That had been a close call. With a bit more timing, they could have seen me replace the keys under Ernie's fake stone. I could have gotten busted. Adrenaline coursed through my veins and I felt short of breath.

A bubble of breathless laughter rose out of my throat.

I had gotten away with it.

Again.

Just as I was about to congratulate myself and open my car, my cell phone roared in my skirt zipper pocket. I smiled; there was no need to check the caller ID. "Hi Jack," I said, still slightly out of breath.

"What are you doing?" He sounded curious.

"Nothing good. Why?"

He paused at that, and then he said, "Wanna come over? I did more sorting on my own."

"Okay," I said without even thinking about it. The idea of seeing Jack restored my adrenaline high, and I grinned from ear to ear.

HALF an hour later, he was looking me up and down; my sensible high-tech girlie shoes, black tights with a run down the knee where I snagged the fine knit on the wall despite my best precautions, and that lovely pink T-shirt that drew the eye with its wild flowers, its generous hem hitting me almost as low as a miniskirt. A neutral, green windbreaker covered my top. My long honey-blond hair was in disarray. The strands that were tortured by my microfiber cap only minutes ago were standing up in every direction, charged with static and set in dry sweat. The microfiber cap always did that to me.

"What have you been doing, Gaudens, and why are you wearing earrings?"

Gaudens. He suspected, and he disapproved.

"I told you. Nothing good. You got anything to drink?" Adrenaline was still coursing through my veins.

He took in my flush and dilated pupils and turned into the kitchen. I followed him and watched him fix two martinis; mine with a twist of lemon, his with an olive. He passed me my drink and we touched the triangular glasses in a silent toast.

The first sip always tasted the best; I could feel the soothing liquid fire settling my jarred nerves. I felt like I could breathe again—until he spoke.

"Why?"

I cocked my eyebrow, trying to deflect his question.

He set his drink down on the kitchen counter and stepped close to me, running his hands up and down my torso, over my waist, down my legs. I shivered and a sigh escaped my lips; my eyes threatened to close. His fingers skimmed my belly, halting at the uneven bump inside my tights. Deft fingers slipped in and pulled out a bank envelope.

I tried to reach out, but the long-stemmed martini glass was in my hand and, to my chagrin, my nervous system ground to a halt under Jack's recent touch.

He leaned his firm butt against the other kitchen counter and counted out the money, and then he slipped it back in the envelope and closed it. "I just don't understand this, Gaudens. You just broke into some dude's house and stole over $3000." His lips were pressed together and there was tension in his shoulders; a warning sign, the lull before the storm.

I sipped more of the strong drink, savoring the bite of gin on the tip of my tongue, inhaling the bright essence of lemon oil floating on its surface.

He grabbed my shirt and pulled me in. "Answer me."

Martini sloshed over my wrist as I was stretched to my toes with the two of us standing eye to eye. "C'mon, Jack."

"Why."

"Because I'm running out of money."

"Then get more clients. Get a job. Wait more tables." His eyes were cold, implacable.

I grabbed his hand and yanked it off my shirt. The whole unfairness of his attitude got under my skin; it burned like salt. I gave him my best-ever death glare. "For your information, Azz-hole, I've spent fifty-three hours on that project for BW&B. At an extremely reasonable consulting rate of $80 per hour—which I could easily double, because that's how I've been billed out by Pillory—that's $4240 that I'm not being paid because you decided to extort me. I considered getting a roommate, but it's kind of hard with just one bedroom, you know? Novack paid half upfront, which means I might get to eat this week. He referred another small client, his accountant, who needs to expand. Those projects have a long lead time, and it will be at least three weeks before I see any money out of it. I'm doing a lot of work on my own, for free. No secretaries, no support. Nothing. And you dare to tell me how to spend my time? And even if I could get more hours, do you really think I went to school just to wait tables full time?"

He didn't even pause to think. "My heart bleeds piss-water, Gaudens. I did some things I shouldn't have, and I got my second chance. All three of us did, at the firm. We're doing it all legit now. I got off easy—I'm on probation. We all are. And here you're risking everything for a few lousy bucks. Do you really think I want my boyfriend to go to jail?" His eyes ignited with anger. "Do you realize I'm violating my probation by consorting with a felon? That's you, sweetheart. By not turning you in like I ought to, I'm aiding and abetting. You're screwing up your life and taking me down with you. And for what? Money?" He spat the last word with contempt.

I didn't have a good response to that, so I kept my mouth shut on the theory that silence never did any harm. He stared at me, his gaze pinning me in place, and as much as I wanted to, I didn't see a way out. I wasn't going to apologize. I'd have to think over the fact that he might be getting hurt here, but it was hard to do right then and there, since he was in lecture mode. I hated lecture mode. It turned him from an awesome, sexy guy into a pompous ass. I focused on the mechanics of my breathing.

Damn... keeping mum was hard.

"I bet your father would really disapprove."

I set my jaw. Of course he would. "He already knows I'm no good. What of it?"

"I bet your mother would be really proud of your safe-cracking skills."

I blanched and swallowed, then I huffed to cover it all up. "Keep my dead mother out of it, Jack."

He took the glass out of my hand and set it on the counter and eased closer to me, his thighs barely brushing mine, the wall of his chest looming over me. I strained to hear his strangled whisper. "You're doing it for all the wrong reasons, and one of them is a nice adrenaline high."

This made me lift my eyes again, a slight quirk tugging at my lips.

Finally.

Finally he understood.

"Yeah," I said, growing a full-out smile. "I never know if I'll make it in, and I never know if I'll make it out. I never know what I'll find. It's so… unpredictable. I almost got caught today—the neighbors were walking their dog." The grin on my face was victorious.

He leaned over me, looming. His breath broke against my skin as he spoke. "You want unpredictable? You want adrenaline?" His handsome features were suddenly marred by scorn and I could see his fury build up beneath that controlled mask. "Do you?" he shouted. He reached out to grab my biceps, stopping short. He willed himself to step away, breathing hard. Four paces took him into his dining room; he reached inside a cupboard full of paperwork and pulled out a stack of documents. "You want excitement? Here is some excitement for you. Here, this will give you some adrenaline!" He flung the lightly rolled papers at my face; I felt the wind of their passing against my cheeks. The sharp sound of crisp paper impacting the cabinets by my face broke the silence like a whip crack.

Pages fluttered to my feet.

"Page four, paragraph two. Fifteen year probation. Page six, community service, five hundred hours. Page seven, conditions of probation. Paragraph three—no association with known felons." He cited all this by heart.

I had never known.

"You wanna be a felon? You don't talk about what you do. Felons who talk about the thrill they get out of what they do are known as inmates." His breathing was still heavy, but he stilled for a bit, except in my peripheral vision I still saw his fists open and close, open and close.

My breathing was heavy as well—I also felt an adrenaline rush, but this time it wasn't accompanied by that familiar sense of control over a dangerous situation. There was a dissonance to it, and I wanted to hide away from it, make it go away. But as bad as it felt, and despite the discord and upset and anger, I felt almost whole again. I could... I could *feel* again.

I felt alive.

I stood straight, willing my slump away. My heated gaze sought out Jack's enraged one. "Jack." I reached out. There was nothing I wanted to do more at that moment than stroke his cheek, trace his jawline, pull his neck in for the deepest of kisses.

"You want this?" He growled.

"I want you." The chase after this man and the extent of my actions flashed through my mind, and all of a sudden, I knew there was nothing I wouldn't attempt to keep him from shoving me out his door and out of his life.

"If you want me, you'll return this. If not—"

"Don't say it...." There was a pleading note in my voice. He was annoying, exasperating, arrogant. He also had his soft and entirely sweet, even vulnerable side that made me weak in the knees after I got to see a glimpse of it last week. Aside from which, he was hot enough to melt cheese just by staring at it. I shook my head as if to dislodge the cobwebs clouding my mind.

I wanted him in my life. So much. "Okay. Okay I'll do it."

His eyebrows quirked up. "You will? Why?"

"For you."

MY HEART beat fast as I jumped off the wall again and landed in the grass with a soft thud. The cash envelope was in my jacket pocket; I walked to my donor's house and looked around. Nobody was out, and lights were on behind people's curtained windows. The Pirates game wasn't over yet, either, and to everyone's shocked delight, the home team was beating the Cincinnati Reds by a landslide; I had at least half an hour. I bent over and retrieved the keys from under the fake rock. It occurred to me perhaps I could just leave the money with the keys under there, but I have my pride and like to see a job well done. In this case, that would mean going up to the guy's bedroom and replacing the envelope exactly where it belonged.

I unlocked the door and, keys in my hand, I walked up the soft, carpeted stairs. There, second door to the right was his bedroom. I opened the door slowly, peeking in.

Nobody there.

I retrieved the cash envelope from my jacket pocket and was opening the carved wooden box when the closet door burst open and out spilled a bald guy wearing Bermuda shorts and a Cincinnati Reds baseball shirt. There was a gun in his hand. "You picked the wrong house, you little twerp."

I froze, stunned that he didn't recognize me as a young, adorable, and harmless female. Then I remembered the purpose of my mission. "I'm returning something that belongs to you." I placed the envelope on the bureau and edged toward the door.

"You asshole! The Markovs told me somebody was prowling around here!" He aimed at me and pulled the trigger. The sound of the gunshot filled the bedroom with a deafening boom, and we both froze in the silence that followed. He looked stunned, which is exactly how I felt.

I looked down my body just to make sure, but there was no blood. He missed me. From the way his startled expression changed into one of determined anger, it was too late to try to talk my way out of this one. I turned to flee, but I tripped and had to reach out to grab the door jam. Right next to my hand was one very destroyed light switch, which told me the shot didn't miss me by much. I was out that door and down the short hallway like greased lightning; another shot sounded, then another. As I ran down the stairs, my foot slipped on the carpet and I fell on my side and slid down like a kid. That probably saved my life, since just as I did, I felt a slug whiz through the top of my cap. He'd fired four shots.

Two more and I'm safe.

If only. In my panic and confusion, I headed for the kitchen instead of the front door; Ernie charged after me, spewing obscenities and pulling the trigger. I ran through his galley kitchen; another shot took out his microwave. Like a raging bull, Ernie was capable of achieving surprising speed. I ducked around the corner and heard a shot shatter a case full of tchotchkes I'd noticed earlier.

Six! He fired his six shots!

It felt like forever before I ripped the front door open. "Your keys!" I yelled at him, throwing the ring of keys in his direction.

I shouldn't have stopped to return his keys.

Ernie wasn't shooting a revolver.

Another round was discharged and I felt something sting my butt, but I didn't stop to investigate as I poured out the door and hustled through the neighboring cul-de-sac to reach the wall. And the wall was there all right, nice and tall, and I jumped—and fell right back down. Straight on my butt. It hurt more than usual, but I didn't care. I had all that adrenaline pumping through my system, so I tried again. No luck. My jumping muscles took an unexpected vacation.

I ran to the front gate where the guard sat, reading magazines and listening to the radio. He lifted his head, surprised to see me run past his little booth. That's when I realized Ernie was no longer pursuing me. A police siren sounded from afar.

Fuck.

Nobody was out on the street; the wall sheltered me from the prying eyes of the privileged denizens of that particular gated community. I ripped off my hat with its attached hair along with my microfiber cap, and ran my fingers through my hair in an effort to smooth it down. I took off my green windbreaker, revealing the pink floral tee underneath. After removing my lock picks from my pockets, I ripped my latex gloves off; then I rolled the whole mess together and carried the small bundle while taking a leisurely stroll toward my car. I had to go slow anyway; the adrenaline I was so fond of was starting to wear off, and I had to focus so my limp didn't show.

Finally, my car. Nondescript and modest, it would blend into most neighborhoods. I beeped it open and slid behind the wheel just as the police cruiser sped past me with sirens blaring and lights flashing.

Only when I settled into the driver's seat did I realize why my butt hurt so much. That jerk shot me in the ass.

I'D NEVER been shot before, so I didn't know quite what to expect, but I knew I couldn't afford to stick around that particular neighborhood. The damage was done to my left butt cheek, which was fortunate, because I was able to shift my weight onto my right hip and operate the controls of my modest, automatic transmission vehicle with the tiptoe of my right foot.

My butt throbbed. It hurt like the devil. As the happy chemicals started to leave my system, I felt the pain like a red fog, covering my eyes and impairing my functions. What had been a mere sting in the beginning had bloomed into a raging, burning hotspot on an otherwise delicate area, and to make it even worse, my hands began to tremble.

Sometimes, when the adrenaline wears off, I get the shakes. I used to get them all the time at first, but as I got used to breaking and entering, I just got the fun adrenaline high. Being chased and shot at took my experience to an entirely new level. Ernie had brought me to a new pinnacle of ecstasy; he plain tapped me out.

I navigated the main street toward Route 28 and headed for the city, crossing the 40th Street Bridge toward my apartment in Bloomfield.

Waste of effort.

Controlling my shakes kept my attention on driving and away from my injury, and from the way I felt light-headed, and also from my stomach, which kept doing nasty flip-flops on me. The traffic around me seemed to have sped up and, pretending I had mechanical trouble, I clicked on my hazard lights. City drivers were fast and focused; I didn't want to become their speed bump.

Somehow—and I don't quite know how I managed—I made it to my street. There was no parking available, so I pulled up to the fire hydrant. I'd get a ticket… but now I had bigger fish to fry.

Once I turned the engine off, my system started to shut down. My hands stopped shaking, and that was good, but my body wouldn't do as I requested, and that was definitely a big minus in my book. I just couldn't get my bloody ass out of that car.

Bloody ass.

After some fumbling, I managed to turn the dome light on, and I looked down and behind myself. I was sitting in a pool of blood, and it had soaked into the gray fabric upholstery of my car and dripped onto the carpet. I unlocked the car door and reached for my cell phone. Last thing I remember doing was hitting the redial button. The phone rang and rang.

"Yo, Wyatt. It's almost midnight." Jack's voice was fuzzy with sleep.

"Jack…." Panic seized me. I forgot where I was and why. "Jack!"

"What? Hey… Wyatt?"

"I've been shot."

I heard him draw a breath, and his voice dropped down to his no-nonsense register. I would have gotten flushed just from hearing it if I had enough blood to spare.

"Where are you, Wyatt?"

"In front of my building. The car… the car."

"Stay there!"

"Jack…." I heard him click the phone shut as I drifted off and darkness claimed me.

CHAPTER TEN

BRIGHT light woke me up. It was right in my eyes, its white luminosity burning straight through my closed eyelids. The air had an odd smell. My hands felt cold and my forehead burned, and I tried to turn over and escape that awful brightness, but I couldn't. I was stuck, lying on my back, and my parched tongue was glued to the roof of my mouth.

"I'm almost done here, Mr. Gaudens," a calm voice said, all business. It was a man's voice.

"Dr. Hinge, what was the duration of the patient's anesthesia?"

I heard a familiar voice give a reply, and I felt a profound sense of disorientation wash over me.

Why was Paul here?

Where was Jack?

Had Jack been just a dream?

I tried to call Paul's name, but no sound left my dry lips. They discussed my dosage and how much I weighed and how the same dosage would have affected a female of equivalent mass; I felt cool hands touch me, taking my blood pressure and reporting the numbers.

"Stay with the patient until he is fully conscious, Dr. Hinge."

"Yes, Dr. Brungo." Then there was the sound of receding footsteps, and that awful, bright light was clicked off.

"Open your eyes, Gaudens. I know you can."

I did. "...."

An electrical motor whirred as my bed moved to a slightly inclined position. Cool, gentle hands lifted a cup of water to my parched lips, and I drank, grateful for its soothing comfort.

"You'll feel like your mouth is cotton-dry and you'll be thirsty until tomorrow. It's a common side effect of general anesthesia." Paul looked like he almost always had, composed and calm. He wore a white coat and a nametag; a stethoscope was draped around his neck.

"Paul...." My croak was barely audible.

I felt my hand on his and I squeezed it lightly; the man that had once been the love of my life was, inexplicably, by my side. "Thank you," I said. "What happened?"

"A guy brought you in with a gunshot wound in your butt and significant blood loss. The slug lodged in your pelvis, but it didn't crack the bone. I had the pleasure of removing it personally."

"You're a doctor already?" My voice sounded faint to me, my head still fuzzy, my mind not quite absorbing what was going on around me.

"No, they just call us that. I'm just a lowly med school intern, but I get to learn on people like you. You'll be as good as new. You got a transfusion, and we did some diagnostics to check your organs for internal bleeding. We'll send you home pretty soon with some painkillers. You'll want to take it easy, okay?"

I nodded, feeling the medical details slip past me as I was trying to level with the fact that Paul was here. With me, touching my hand. My mind wandered even further; did I still love him, or not? My chest was cosseted in a warm, slightly fuzzy feeling when I looked at him.

One hundred percent.

"The guy who brought me in—what did he look like?" The sound of my own voice startled me.

"He's downstairs, waiting. They wouldn't let him in because he's not related. Tall, brown hair, irate, doesn't look like a punk." Paul looked at me, questions in his bespectacled, intelligent eyes.

"Yeah. I'd like to see him."

"Okay, then." He took a deep breath and picked up the phone.

Not five minutes later, the door burst open, its frame filled by one Jack Azurri. He looked awful. His hair was wild, his eyes were feral, and his jeans and button-down shirt were covered in dried blood.

"Where is he?" His voice was a rasp of pain, and I shuddered with guilt. I knew he'd been angry with me before, but now—

"Mr. Azurri… Mr. Gaudens just regained consciousness. He may not be entirely lucid yet."

"I can talk—I'm here." To my own ears, my voice still sounded as though it was coming from a metal watering can. "Paul. More water, please." I rasped.

I heard him pour some from the pitcher. He propped my head up with the slender hands I used to know so well and helped me drink. The thirst just would not abate. It was driving me crazy. I drained the cup and thanked him. Then I met Jack's eyes.

"Jack. Allow me to introduce Dr. Paul Hinge, my former lover and a very good friend." Jack blanched, rooted to the ground. "Paul. Allow me to introduce Mr. Jack Azurri… my boyfriend." I forced a faint smile, lifting my gaze to Jack's distressed face. "Jack…."

I reached my arm out to him, much like it had the night before, searching for his hand, or his face, or for at least a sign of anything he was willing to give.

Or forgive.

"Pleasure to meet you, Mr. Azurri," Paul said, nodding curtly. "I'm glad Wyatt has someone by his side." I saw Paul look at Jack and through him, taking his measure. He pushed his glasses up his nose in a habitual gesture. "If you need anything, press the call button and the nurse will come. Oh. And now that you're up, the police will want to talk to you. We're obliged to report gunshot injuries." He gave me a faint smile; it was but a little curve of his narrow lips, but it went all the way up to his dark, penetrating eyes. "Later, Gaudens."

Gaudens.

"Gaudens?" Jack echoed my thoughts, coming closer. Gingerly, he sat on the side of my bed and his hands touched mine. They felt different from Paul's. Warmer. The life signs monitor behind me started to beep a little faster.

"I returned that thing, Jack. As you asked me to."

His ashen face showed some pain at that, and the pain was soon followed by a wave of guilt. "Wyatt." He paused, gathering the right words. "I'm so sorry, Wyatt. I should have never... I should have just made another drink for you." He leaned in, letting our foreheads touch as he slid his hand up to my shoulders. He leaned in and buried his face in the tangled mess of blond hair that covered my neck. "I didn't think you were actually going to go there," he whispered. "Are you nuts? Had I only known.... I thought you were going to mail it or something...."

"It didn't even occur to me to mail it. I just... I wanted to fix it. Right away. That's all." The thought of Jack walking out of my life assaulted me unbidden, a low and dastardly ambush of my subconscious mind. My eyes began to itch, my nose began to twitch, and I got that awful feeling like I was going to cry. I hadn't cried since that huge blowout with my dad years ago, and I took considerable pride in having armored my heart with such ruthless efficiency. Before that, the last time I cried was in third grade when a classmate mentioned my mom and she wasn't alive anymore.

I didn't do tears well; in fact, I tended to channel emotions into violence and other antisocial acts.

This is all Jack's fault.

He's a pain in the ass.

Pompous prick.

Doesn't have a clue.

No tears allowed!

"Wyatt...." He straightened up to take a closer look at me.

I sucked it up, balled up my fist, and punched him straight in the jaw. It was a weak, lousy punch from my semireclined position. He just looked at me, straight in the eyes, and then he reached out and hugged me to his chest. My change of position made my posterior wound throb, but being in Jack's embrace like that was worth it, so I didn't say anything.

"I'm so glad you'll be okay, Wyatt. So glad. I'm so sorry."

That did it. Big, fat tears started to roll down my cheeks, and I hid my face in his bloodstained shirt.

"You can punch me again if it will help," he whispered, his hand rubbing small circles on my back.

SOON after that, I went to sleep knowing Jack had gone to his place to take a shower and change, and he was going to stop by in the morning. Trying to sleep in a hospital is generally a miserable experience. After I managed to tune out all those orderlies and nurses walking about and pushing their carts, and after I learned to ignore the ringing of phones from the nurses' station and the beeping of monitors, I finally fell asleep. Then somebody came in and turned the light on so they could take my pulse and measure my blood pressure and temperature, and then I had to work hard to fall asleep all over again. When I saw the skies lighten outside the large, hospital window, I was finally tired enough to get two hours of shut-eye before the doctors started on their morning rounds.

MY EYES stayed glued shut with the rest I craved; the doctors came and went. The orderly brought a breakfast tray and I cussed him out and told him to turn the lights off and close the door, and I went to sleep again.

I felt fingers stroke the hair on my head; a large, warm hand grasped mine. That sure wasn't a doctor or an orderly. My chest swelled with emotion. "Jack," I whispered, incredulous and giddy with happiness. "You're back, Loverboy."

"Wyatt." The hand didn't stop stroking my hair, but his voice—

That voice.

My eyes popped open. Familiar rusty hair was shot with more white than before, and there was stubble on his chin. The wrinkles on his forehead were deeper than I remembered.

"Wyatt. My son."

I wanted to say something, anything, but I couldn't. It was as though the words dribbled out my ear, bypassing my vocal chords. I was lying there on a flimsy hospital pillow with my father sitting next to me, holding my hand and stroking my hair. Aside from running into him by accident at the mall or post office, the last time I saw him we were yelling at one another all the way to my car, parked by the sidewalk, as I loaded up my things, spreading my wings to leave my nest permanently. I was to choose between Paul, the son of the doctor who somehow failed to keep my mother alive, and the rest of my family. Giving me an ultimatum was a sure way to push me in the other direction. That was then, though, and this was now. Dad showed up. Even after swearing his shadow would never darken my doorstep, here he was.

"Dad." I felt a small, uncertain smile tug on the corners of my mouth.

"Your brother Carl called. He got a call from the man who brought you in. He said he got his number from your cell phone."

I didn't yank my hand back. I didn't tell him to get out of my hair. "You came." My voice was fuzzy with sleep.

"Of course I came, Wyatt. You're my boy." There was pain in his voice, and longing.

There was pain in my voice as well. "Dad...."

Being a dysfunctional child of a dysfunctional parent, I'd always sworn I'd be different from my dad. I'd never be wild and emotional like he was. I wouldn't embarrass my kids—heck, I wouldn't even have any. Now we were in this small room together, and he had those awful, emotional tears in his eyes.

I looked away. I didn't want him to see the wetness on my lashes. I could feel the ball of my other hand form into a fist as I struggled to hold it all in.

"You aren't going to slug me, are you? You used to do that when you didn't want to cry."

His words just about finished me off. "I still do that," I sniffled.

He squeezed my hand and let out an uncertain laugh. "Well, you got your temper from me, I suppose."

I turned to face him, tears and all. Our eyes met, and we grinned our maniacal grins at one another. That's when I realized we were almost entirely alike.

THE nurse came in, asking if I'd accept a visitor. I nodded, and Jack entered the room. He looked a lot better than he had several hours earlier; showered and shaved, he exuded power and sex appeal in his dark navy suit and a white dress shirt. His gray and cerulean tie brought out his eyes.

I pressed the switch on the side of my bed so I could sit up some.

"Hey, Wyatt," he said, coming to my side, across the bed from my father. He looked like he wanted to bend down, but stopped himself at the last moment. I wanted him to bend down so I could kiss him, but my dad was there, observing us, his gaze overcast with dark speculation.

"Jack. This is my father, Dr. Hector Gaudens. Dad, this is Mr. Jack Azurri, my… client."

They rose and shook hands over me; it made me feel like I was spread out on a sacrificial altar.

"I understand it was you who brought Wyatt in last night," my father said. "Thank you. And thank you for contacting the family. Carl and DeeDee will visit him later."

Jack sat down on the doctor's stool next to me and eyed my untouched breakfast tray. "You haven't eaten. Dr. Hinge informed me specifically that you get really whiny when you're sick and won't eat or drink enough. You're supposed to keep yourself hydrated, at the very least." He picked up my cup of orange juice and held it out for me. He didn't embarrass me by trying to press it to my lips in front of my father, for which he earned some unintended brownie points.

"Which Dr. Hinge?" my father asked.

"Paul Hinge," Jack replied, his voice not weighed down by years of difficult family history.

"Is that so...." My father's voice was quiet as he looked away, avoiding my eyes as though he was burned.

Yes, Father. Paul. Son of Richard. Live with it.

I accepted a cup and sipped some juice, and before I knew it, it was gone.

"Still thirsty?" Jack asked. I nodded; he topped my glass off from the water pitcher.

"You are Wyatt's client?" my father asked, his voice suspicious. "What kind of services does my son perform for you?"

"He manages an advertising campaign for a company I work for," Jack replied with casual ease. "Speaking of which, the rest of the management team wanted to meet with you next week and discuss some of the salient points you've raised. I'll schedule you later in the week and drive you in—but let me know if you don't feel up to it, alright?"

I nodded.

"Oh, and I need your invoice so you can get paid."

My eyes bugged out. "But I thought—"

"Nonsense," Jack said. "I appreciate your generosity, but this project is too big for you to do just for client referrals. Keep track of your hours, Gaudens."

I wanted to kiss him.

Except my father was there, discomfort rolling off him in waves. I don't know how he knew, but I was pretty sure he could tell Jack and I didn't just work together.

I glanced at Jack, and he gave me a wry smile, took my cup, and topped it off again. Then he took a sip from the place marked by the lip balm the nurse gave me earlier that morning, and gave it back to me.

"See you after work."

Still holding his gaze, I lifted the cup of water to my lips and took another sip as I accepted his indirect kiss.

MY FATHER left soon after that. The realization that I had missed him hit me like a ton of bricks. The old argument still hung in the air, but we chose to ignore it for now, presumably waiting until some point in the future when I would feel well enough to handle his temper tantrums and ear-shattering tirades.

But he had come. Showing up counts—it counts more than anything.

I reclined my bed all the way down and turned onto my stomach again. I did that whenever I was alone; my butt hurt, and it would be many days before I felt comfortable sitting on it.

"Hey, Gaudens." Paul came in just as soon as I managed to settle down. "No, no… don't flip over. You had visitors for too long as it is." He settled down on the doctor's stool. "I'm here to check your dressings." He pulled the sheet down and lifted my hospital gown, then stripped the tape off my skin to peek underneath the gauze.

"How is it?"

"Looks clean," he said, his interest purely professional. "The wound is closing up, no signs of infection. I'll give you some of these high-tech, nonstick wound dressings. You'll need to put a fresh one on after you shower, or every third day. The sutures are self-absorbing, so you won't need to come back for that, but I'll want to see you in a week. Who will be changing your wound dressings—Jack?"

"I'll do it myself," I grumbled. "Jack and I are kind of new together. Just a few weeks."

"You won't be able to reach," he explained patiently, as though to a child. "You'll have to come here every third day and have it done."

"I can't."

"Why not?"

"It'll cost too much. Without insurance, this alone will cost thousands."

"You're not insured?" There was a touch of alarm in his otherwise calm voice.

"Lost my job few weeks ago. The COBRA payments were half as much as my rent. I just simply couldn't afford it."

I felt his cool hands put on some fresh tape and cover me back up. "I'll have one of the administrators give you forms to fill out. That will cut your bill down a great deal. Oh, speaking of forms, there's a detective you need to call about that drive-by shooting."

Drive-by shooting?

"Oh?" I said, not volunteering anything.

"Your boyfriend brought a printout of an article about a shooting in a shopping mall parking lot. Happened last night. Too bad you got caught up in it." His voice was level, not betraying any emotion, but when I turned my head to look at him, his eyes told me a lot more.

"Thanks, Paul. I owe you." I accepted the printout from his hand and propped myself on my elbows so I could read what the hell happened to me and where I was supposed to have been at the time.

"Wyatt."

I looked up at him again.

"You need to find a better hobby."

"You know…?"

"I've always known." He leaned over; I felt his lips brush the top of my hair. "Susan will stop by at your place and bring you some food."

I couldn't swear by it, but I think his expression was positively wicked right after he said that.

MY BROTHER, Carl, and sister, DeeDee, came over in the afternoon since they had no classes on Saturday. They brought me flowers, balloons, and milk chocolates, and fussed over me until Dr. Hinge shooed them out. It occurred to me that it was actually Saturday, and Jack had shown up in a suit. If he had to go into the office, why not wear casuals?

And speak of the devil, there he was. He sauntered into my room, his sexy suit gone. He wore tan chinos and a black polo shirt and looked drop-dead gorgeous.

"You changed."

"Yeah."

"Why did you wear a suit today?"

He sighed and ran his hand through his hair. "I knew your father would be here. Your brother, Carl, he said he'd let him know and warned me he'd come first thing in the morning."

"They just left." My butt was on fire again. "Sorry, but I have to turn over. I stay facing up only for show." I tried to flip over, but the actual process took a while as I tried to avoid agitating my injury.

"You got shot in the ass, Wyatt." There was a thinly disguised thread of humor in Jack's voice."

"No! No, I got shot in the upper leg."

"Care to tell me what happened?"

"How 'bout he tells me what happened first," a voice said from the door. I lifted my head and looked over my shoulder. A tall guy with mocha skin and close-cropped salt-and-pepper hair stood there, his police badge hanging from the chest pocket of his blazer. "Jubal Lupine, detective. We're working on that Pine Creek Mall shooting. That's where Mr. Azurri said you were last night, anyway." He sounded skeptical. "Can you sit up so I can take your statement, Mr. Gaudens?"

"I can't. I just flipped over. My butt's killing me. Push that stool around to where I can see you."

He did and sat next to Jack.

I thought hard about the contents of the article Paul gave me. There had been some kind of a gang dispute in the mall parking lot just when it was about to close. Several weapons were fired, and two of the gangbangers killed one another. Some vehicles got shot up. Obviously I wasn't going to tell the good detective the truth.

"Yeah. I went to the mall."

"What for?"

"I needed to buy some software, except by the time I got there, the mall was about to close and I didn't have enough time to, you know, look at it carefully. So I decided to come back another day, and as I walked to my car, I heard some yelling and shooting. I guess I should have been more alarmed, but it sounded like kids with firecrackers. It was a row or two over, I guess."

"Did you see any of the shooters?" Detective Lupine asked.

I thought about that. Would I have seen them? Hopefully not.

"No. I was thinking of something else anyway."

"So what happened next?"

"I felt something sting my butt. I didn't realize I'd been shot, but it started to hurt on my way home. I didn't see a good place to stop and get help, so I drove home and almost passed out. Then I called my friend, and the rest is history."

"Why didn't you call the police?"

You've gotta be kidding.

"Well… I guess I wasn't thinkin' straight anymore. Once I realized it was my butt, I was just… um… embarrassed, y'know? How many people do you know that have been shot in the rear like this?"

Lupine grinned. "Not many. The guys in the squad room are gonna love hearing about this."

"See? I wanted to avoid just that. An injured guy has no dignity these days."

Lupine's jaw muscles worked some as he fought to keep a straight face. He pulled a business card out of his shirt pocket; I caught a glimpse of his service weapon in a shoulder holster under his arm. "If you think of anything to add, Mr. Gaudens, here's my number."

"Okay," I said, unable to nod.

"Hope your derriere gets well. Hope you have someone to kiss it all better."

I could have sworn he chuckled. What an asshole.

"SO CAN I go yet? It's been two days!" I looked at Dr. Brungo with despair in my eyes. I needed to sleep, and sleep was hard to come by in a hospital. Especially when the ever-mounting costs of a hospital stay haunted me every time I closed my eyes.

"Not yet," the little man said, smiling. "We want to make sure there is no occurrence of ballistic intra-abdominal trauma. That happens fairly often in the case of posterior gluteal penetrative wounds."

My jaw dropped and I felt like an idiot. The good doctor wasn't speaking English anymore.

"Your ultrasound looked pretty good yesterday," he said. "We'll do another one later and then we'll see. You were very lucky, Mr. Gaudens. The weapon was only 9mm, and the round must have had a low-velocity load intended for practice only. There was a bit of a yaw to the projectile, causing some additional damage within your gluteus. On the other hand, the rotation of the projectile probably saved your pelvic bone from being compromised. A few more days here, and you'll be ready for release."

I panicked and tried to sit up. A shot of pain in my rear made me hiss and lie down again.

He looked at me, his big, dark eyes smiling, cajoling. Obviously I wasn't being a patient patient.

"But I'm not insured, Doc. I can't afford a hospital stay. You said it's just soft tissue damage and I'm looking fine—isn't that what you said?" I shot a look of desperate plea toward Paul, who stood behind Dr. Brungo, taking copious notes.

Dr. Brungo glanced at his watch. "Dr. Hinge will explain it to you in laymen's terms, Mr. Gaudens."

I NEVER knew a simple shot in my ass could have caused abdominal injury and hemorrhaging and sepsis and all that kind of stuff. I was lying on my stomach, pissed off and worried. I was supposed to be in the hospital to get better, but it was hard to get better when my mind wouldn't stop fretting. I hate to belabor the obvious, but really, there wasn't much else on my mind. My butt would heal on its own. My bank account, not so much.

"I'd suggest you stay the night, Gaudens," Paul said. "If you get a blood clot wandering through your system, it will cost even more. And that ultrasound is just an extra few hundred bucks—and if you get an all clear on that again, Dr. Brungo will likely let you go."

"You think?" I had my doubts.

"They can't hold you against your will, and I can stop by and help out some. As long as you don't tell on me."

"Tell who? Jack?"

"No. My bosses. I'm just a lowly med student, dude. I don't get to practice medicine yet. If I see anything at all suspicious, I'm driving you back here myself."

I turned my head; he sat on the doctor's stool, a clipboard with notes in his hands. "Okay. Thanks." He was about to leave when I spoke up again. "Paul... how's Susan and the baby?"

"Great. Susan and Michelle are doing great. You'll get to see them later." He pulled a picture of a one-year-old cherub out of his wallet and put it in front of my face. She had a big smile, dark eyes, and fuzzy, golden hair.

My heart just about stopped. "Um... Paul, I hate to bring this up, but did you guys ever do a paternity test?"

He gave me an odd look. "As a matter of fact, yes we did. She is mine, and I can show you the paperwork, if you want...." A thread of cold fear threatened to escape his iron control—I could tell from his voice.

I smiled. She could have been mine, had our three-way Russian Roulette worked out differently. "No, it's all good. The blonde hair threw me for a bit. Your hair is black, and Susan is a blonde, but still, you know?"

"If she were yours, what would you do?" Paul asked, not meeting my eyes.

"Uh, panic, I guess? I'd be a little excited, but you two really work well together, and I'd never want to rock your boat, man."

One hundred percent.

My mind drifted to Jack. I smiled at the picture and then I turned to smile at my old friend and former lover, who had relief written all over his face. "She's beautiful, Paul."

At that moment a huge realization dawned upon me: I was so very, very grateful little Michelle was Paul's and not mine. There were no outstanding obligations out there—other than my medical bill. I was with Jack now, and I was with him all the way.

THE tedium of my hospital routine was broken by a welcome voice.

"Hey... I brought you some real dinner," I heard Jack say from the door, and I had to look over my shoulder to see him. "Dr. Hinge already told me you'll be staying 'til tomorrow."

Never in my life had I been more grateful for the stimulating, delectable fragrance of take-out Indian food. There was chicken korma and rice biryani and naan. Jack set out aluminum containers on my little food table and uncovered the lids. The scent of good nourishment wafted out, dulling the pervasive odor of hospital disinfectant and bland cafeteria cooking.

"Jack, you're the best," I moaned from my unfortunate position.

"And don't you forget it." He helped me turn on to my right hip, tore up some of the buttery flatbread and loaded up the pieces with rice and chicken and creamy yogurt sauce.

"You want me to feed you?" He gave me a lascivious look.

I only grinned, undecided, when his fingers drifted under my nose, bearing a morsel of real food. I shrugged and opened up.

Heaven....

Somebody moaned; I guess it must have been me. It felt decidedly odd to be serviced in such a way. I felt so spoiled and taken care of—all I needed was a bottle of good beer. It would have been too much to ask, of course. My eyes drifted toward the cup of water.

"Thirsty?" Jack asked, and when I nodded, he reached inside his leather jacket and pulled out a glass bottle. He twisted the top open, then got one for himself.

"It's nonalcoholic. Sorry, but I didn't want to mess with your painkillers."

That's how the head nurse found us: eating fragrant Indian food and sipping beer. She raised a god-awful fuss over the whole thing, ranting on about how the odor spoiled the appetites of other patients, who realized their own dinners were hopelessly bland. She almost poured my beer out, until I literally begged her to inspect the label, after which she grudgingly allowed it. "Just as well you're so eager to go home, Mr. Gaudens. You are not what I would call a calm influence on my ward."

Once she left and closed our door—to limit the other patients' exposure to the fragrant top notes of ginger and cardamom—Jack leaned over and asked, "Did the police detective want to know anything else?"

"No, just what you already know."

"How did it go, you think?"

"Went okay, I guess. Shopping malls can be dangerous places nowadays." I smiled at him.

He didn't smile back, but gave me a serious look instead. "Don't go to that shopping mall again, Wyatt." Then he fed me another piece of naan with awesome things on it, and all I could do was chew and roll my eyes.

As soon as I was done eating, he packed the leftovers and rose to leave.

"Going already?" Disappointment rang clear in my voice.

He nodded. "I have that guy, Izzy Silberman, coming over tonight."

By then I had completely forgotten. "Okay. Give him my best."

"And tomorrow I'm picking you up and taking you home."

"Great. I can't wait to sleep in my own bed."

"You're coming to stay at my place until you can move about on your own."

"No, I'm not."

"Yes, you are."

"I want my own bed." My voice sounded petulant and childish, even to me.

"Okay, then. I'll make sure you have it."

He reached into the plastic box containing my personal belongings, and took out my keys. "I could just break in, you know, except I don't think you'd want any wild surprises."

CHAPTER ELEVEN

I HATED getting shot. I hate hospitals and hospital food and hospital regulations against cell phone use, and I hate the way they put you in a wheelchair and take you to the front door as though you couldn't walk by yourself.

"C'mon, Wyatt, let's blow this popsicle stand!" Jack took my crutches and put them in the backseat of his car, and then he opened the passenger door and helped me in.

I was wearing a clean change of clothes he brought me, together with a pair of shoes that didn't have old blood inside them. "I can do it by myself," I grumbled. My butt hurt a lot. It's amazing how much one uses the muscles in the buttocks for walking around, and the injured parts were hard to rest.

"I know. I just want to get out of here." And no wonder—it was Monday already.

He buckled up, gunned his dark-blue Santa Fe, and navigated out of the West Penn hospital complex. I noticed we weren't going to my place.

"You can't make me stay by force." The words just kind of left my mouth without my permission. Inside, I was happy he wanted me to stay. Ecstatic, even. Just… I didn't like the way he assumed he'd make a decision and I'd be okay with it.

"I know. Give it a chance, Wyatt. You'll see."

I rolled my eyes. I didn't want to sleep in the same bed with him all the time. It was awkward. We would both want to do what comes naturally, and doing that with a distressed gluteus wouldn't work. Saying no all the time would be… bad for us, I guess. I also didn't want to share his living room sofa with all those boxes around me, overflowing with the collectibles his sister and their two aunts had accumulated over many decades of yard-sale frenzy. I wanted a nice, quiet, comfortable place.

A place of my own.

BEFORE I knew it, we stood in the hallway outside his apartment. Jack pulled the keys out of his jeans pocket and unlocked the three locks on his door. He held it open for me, and I hobbled in. My goal was to belly flop on the sofa and stay that way for a long, long time. It amazed me how tired I was just from the trip between my hospital bed and his place.

"Before you settle down, Wyatt, I want you to come see something."

I yawned. "Later?"

"Please." Even though the word was polite, the tone was far from patient.

Biting my tongue to stay a surly remark, I limped behind Jack across the blue carpet of his living room, navigating my crutches past the pile of boxes and old furniture that seemed to have grown bigger since I saw it last. We passed the little hallway leading to his bedroom and bathroom, heading toward the room full of Celia's junk.

"Open the door," he whispered by my ear. Feeling him so close to me gave me a rash of goose bumps on that side, all the way down to my knee.

Confused and just a little curious, I suppressed the shiver as I reached for the antique glass doorknob on the dark wooden door. I turned it and pushed. A sudden sense of vertigo seized me, as though I just stepped through a dimensional portal, entering another world. I didn't recognize the room at all.

The junk was gone.

The fluffy, pink floral wallpaper had been replaced with fresh paint. The ceiling was dark blue, almost black, with one wall to match it and the rest a pale bamboo green. Old-fashioned wooden trim gleamed pure white under the ceiling and around the floor, snaking its way around the doorframe and the closet and the tall, stately window. Gentle light filtered through venetian blinds and sheer white curtains. But that wasn't all.

My queen-size bed stood straight in the middle of the room on the brand-new white carpet. It had my own sheets and pillow and comforter on it, and was surrounded by rustic pine furniture I bought at Ikea two years ago. Two lengths of the sheer curtain material were attached to the dark blue wall, framing the top of my bed in that sort of old-fashioned girly treatment, and even though I've never considered myself a girly guy, a forgotten part of me stirred. I was being nurtured, and I liked it.

I didn't know what to say. I didn't know how to feel about all this.

Jack's amazingly sweet gesture was both stunning and intrusive. Keeping in mind he meant well and went into a great deal of effort to make me comfortable, I bit my tongue on the intrusive part.

I kicked my shoes off and shuffled over to my bed, where I did my long-awaited belly flop. The crutches clattered to the ground, but I didn't care; I just grabbed my very own thick, feather-and-down pillow and mugged it, breathing in its comfortable, familiar scent. It smelled like me and my stuff and latex paint residue. He sure accomplished a lot in two days.

"Well?" Jack eyed me from the door. "How do you like your room?" I peeked at him. He was standing there like it felt unnatural. This was his place, after all.

"Come sit with me?" I mumbled into my pillow. He did; the side of my bed dipped under his weight, making me roll just a little. "How did you manage all this?" I asked.

"Well...." His hand ran up and down my back, soothing me. "Your sister told me what colors you like. Izzy Silverstein and his wife came over and helped sort what was left in here and move some of it to the living room pile, and she did the curtains and such; his friend Silvio painted the room the next day, and a few hours later, the carpet was put down. And... well, I took a bit of a risk with the awning over your bed, but since you liked that kitchen apron so much, I thought I'd give it a try. If you hate it, we can take it down."

I swallowed dry, taking it all in. "Keep it. For now, anyway." I let my eyes wander around the room, and my words came back to me. "But... my stuff! You went and got my stuff!" I vaguely remembered him having taken my keys.

"Yeah. Silvio has a pickup truck. I brought your laptop and phone charger and all that. Your toiletries are in the bathroom across the hall."

"I never agreed to move in with you!"

"True." His hands never stopped tracing their hypnotic pattern up and down my back. "You can always move back when you feel better."

"I'm perfectly capable of staying on my own! I'm not a cripple."

"Also true. Although...." His hand stopped over my right shoulder blade. "Your father insisted that you go stay at his house. With his office right next door, he would have been very happy to take care of you."

I groaned. Not with Dad again. Especially not since Carl and DeeDee were off in college, living on campus. As much as I appreciated the truce he and I currently enjoyed, staying at the house in the placid suburbs would have resulted in discussions I wasn't ready to tolerate, let alone embrace.

"I guess staying with you is nicer...." I should have thanked him, but wrapping my mind around all he had done was just too much at the moment. Not to mention the small detail of having been moved into his place without my consent.

"Did you and your dad talk?" he asked.

"Not much. He showed up, though. I didn't expect that."

"You can catch up with him at your own pace." He sighed.

"What? Why do you care about my dad so much?" Irritation tinged my voice; fatigue and pain eroded my patience.

"Well, he's still alive, Wyatt. If my dad were alive, I'd love to talk to him. Sometimes I think of him and Mom… like when something goes well and I'd like to share that, and I can't anymore."

"Like what?" I asked, chastised.

"Like you and what a nut you are." Jack leaned down and kissed the top of my hair much like Paul had. "I'm working from home today. I have to answer some phone calls and check my e-mail. Any special wishes for dinner?"

"Something simple, with flavor in it."

"THERE'S a lot of artwork in the living room pile," Jack said. "Pick anything you want and I'll put it up. Unless there's something you'd like from your apartment?"

"I'd have to go there and look."

And bringing more stuff here sounds kind of… permanent.

"Go take your shower, Wyatt. Paul will stop by on the way from his nightshift at the hospital and show me how to do your rear."

I pushed at his shoulder, failing to rock him back much. "I thought you knew how to do that all by yourself, wiseass."

Jack grinned. "Just a slip of the tongue," he said, his eyes still on me as he ran the tip of his tongue across his top lip. The sight of it stirred me in places I didn't want to think about right now. Not unless I wanted my shower to be cold.

Everything took too long, so by the time I stepped out of the bathroom with just a towel around my waist, Paul was sitting in the dining room with Jack, drinking coffee.

"Hey, Wyatt, where should we do ya?"

I rolled my eyes. "On my bed," I yelled back. The phrasing was, apparently, just another slip of Jack's pointy, agile tongue.

Before I made it to my underwear drawer, the two men filled the doorway to my supposedly private domain.

"How are you doing, Gaudens?" Paul asked, sounding detached in a professional sort of way.

I had to think about that. I was doing a lot better, actually, and said so.

"Good. Lie down on your stomach and I'll show Jack what to do."

That's how I ended up lying down on my already made bed on top a towel, with those two particular guys sitting next to me and discussing my posterior and its well-being. I felt Paul's cool hands apply an antibiotic cream, and Jack's warm ones place the wound dressing in the right place, as directed; both of them taped it down, stroking the adhesive strips down so they stayed.

They were touching me. Simultaneously. All four hands at a time.

I sneezed, the mucous tissues of my sinuses suddenly irritated by excess blood flow.

Oh no. Not now.

This was no time to become aroused. I tried to think of something else. Hospital food, my dad's stubbly chin, my second-grade teacher with her strict glare. Nothing worked; I tried hard to keep my hips still, and I guess I succeeded, at least for the most part. I didn't make a sound. I swear I didn't.

The guys must have noticed my almost-suppressed wiggle anyway.

"You okay, Wyatt?" Jack asked, curiosity overwhelming the concern in his voice.

"Uh-huh." I didn't dare to speak as I tensed up.

His hand stroked my patched-up cheek. "As good as new, right, Dr. Hinge?"

I felt Paul's cool hands leave the surface of my skin rather fast, and the way he cleared his throat told me he had readjusted his rectangular eyeglasses and he was aware of my involuntary reaction.

"I better get going. I want to catch Michelle before my wife takes her to daycare."

"Oh? Does she work?"

"Yeah… started two months ago. Just part time for now. It's good for both of them to get out of the house." I would have raised my eyebrows at that—knowing Susan, that tidbit of information surprised me—except my face was buried in my covers to disguise my tomato-red blush.

"I'll see myself out. Bye, Jack. Bye, Wyatt."

I didn't move or say good-bye.

"Wyatt. What's wrong?"

The hands of two of the most desirable men ever on my butt at the same time. Oh, God.

I sneezed again. "Tissues."

Jack handed me the whole box, and I blew my nose, only to find out I had a nosebleed.

"Look at me." Hesitation gripped me, but he didn't wait; he rolled me over to make sure I was all right, and in doing so, exposed the red tissues pressed against my nose. His expression went from amused to confused to alarmed. "What's the matter?"

"Oh, nothing."

"That's not nothing, Wyatt. You have a nosebleed!"

"Just some extra blood circulation." He watched me get another clean tissue and frowned, thinking hard. I watched the penny drop.

A sudden, hard expression replaced his former smile. "I see."

I reached my hand to his, twining our fingers together. "I am only human, Jack."

He only looked away, the little green monster peering through his brilliant, blue eyes.

"Having you touch me is very erotic." My voice was calm, matter of fact.

"And him?"

"It's not just him, it's both of you together. He's helping. And… he stopped as soon as he realized what was going on."

Jack freed his fingers from my grasp. "What bothers me is that he noticed and I didn't. Obviously you two have years of history, whereas I'm just your newest fling."

I raised myself on my elbow to see him better. "No. Not newest. After him, I had no flings at all. You're the first guy I brought home, the only one. Jack, you yourself said retraining would take time, didn't you?"

He stood up. "I better go take my shower and go to work."

"Okay." He left me alone with a tissue pressed against my nose, reclining on my queen-size bed, cursing my body and the way it had betrayed me.

From that point on, the days just sort of dragged. I went through the motions of getting better while trying to get some work done on my new advertising business. Jack was polite but distant, coming home late and going to sleep early. Three days later, Susan came by and brought little Michelle, along with a wheeled shopping bag full of groceries.

"I figured your boyfriend doesn't have much time to shop and cook, Wy," she said, using my high-school nickname. "Don't worry, I've been taking classes. My food isn't as adventurous as it used to be. What would you like for lunch?"

I thought for a bit. "A peanut butter sandwich."

She smiled, her gray eyes warming. "Do you ever change?"

The question hit my heart. "I hope I do," I said, my voice quiet.

"What's wrong, Wy?"

I only shook my head. What was I supposed to say?

Your husband still turns me on.

My boyfriend is jealous of Paul, even though he feels obliged to accept his help.

The man I've been pursuing isn't interested in me anymore.

And that was, unfortunately, all true. Time had passed since Paul's visit, and Jack had shown no indications of his former, passionate attraction. It had nothing to do with my injury—even right out of the hospital, we flirted and bantered around. Now there was nothing.

Susan left me with lasagna in the freezer and a pot roast in the oven, and fixings for a big salad in the refrigerator. I knew what to pull out and when. I thanked her and said good-bye.

Suddenly I felt useless. Hapless. Incompetent. I had that funny feeling of being a useless moron, even though I knew I wasn't.

There had to be something I could do for Jack. Some way, any way, to make his life easier.

Time to call Reyna.

S HE came during her lunch break and brought two six-packs of Dogfish India Pale Ale. You can tell a true friend by what they know about you, and Reyna knew a lot about me. Especially when it came to relationships, climbing, and beer.

"So you still love Paul, then?" she asked over her take-out Vietnamese chicken sandwich before taking a swig from the long-necked bottle.

"No—not like that. He'll always have a special place in my heart, but… no. Not romantically. But the idea of both of them together, you know?"

"I never knew you were such a kink, Wyatt." My cell phone made its orgasmic roar just as Reyna finished that statement, and she said, "Never mind, I actually did know that."

I picked up. "Hi, Jack. What's up?"

"You have any plans for lunch, Wyatt?"

I felt my heart skip at the sound of his voice. "Reyna's here, and she brought Vietnamese takeout and beer," I said. "Will you join us?"

"No, go catch up with her. How about tomorrow? I could take you out to lunch, and the management team can talk to you about your marketing plan. Would you feel up to that?"

Oh. The bloody marketing plan. I'd forgotten all about work for BW&B. "Yeah. Let's hash out the details tonight."

"Okay then. Later." He hung up. No *have a nice day*, no *Goldilocks*.

I looked at Reyna. "See? All business."

"I wish I could help you, sweetie." She shrugged, looking helpless and confused. "Although, not everyone is affectionate during the workday. Auguste can be a real bitch...."

A wide grin grew on my face. "Oh, pray tell, Reyna! How was the conference? Are you actually unable to sit on that hard chair, or is that just my imagination?" I was rewarded with a blush that matched her vermillion ponytail.

"Shaddap. He says to tell you to stop by when you're able. He might have a small client for you."

REYNA'S visit invigorated me. She had that happy, in-love glow, and I thought back to my old, in-lust-with-Jack feeling and smiled. My current condition and our unresolved need to talk weren't helping much. I just knew I wanted to be with him. The only question was, what could I do so he'd understand and want to be with me?

What was the biggest irritant in Jack's life?

I was lying on my belly with my head propped up by my hands in what I like to call my thinking position. A memory of the safe in the other room flashed before my eyes, and I thought back to one of the three death certificates.

Celia Azurri.

If I could make headway on figuring out what really happened to his sister, Jack would be happier. But how? Scenarios from television dramas flooded my mind; the occasional detective novel I've read flashed me an image of an intrepid sleuth, asking questions about the deceased. None of that helped much. Maybe I shouldn't spend time on Celia. I had work to do... clients to investigate and find out what they wanted for their companies.

Clients to investigate.

Well. Perhaps if I thought of Celia as one of my clients, I'd get to know who she was and what she cared about. Yes! That was it.

ONLY half an hour later, I peered at my laptop screen, using Jack's Wi-Fi. His sister had apparently been well known in the climbing community. Rock climbing websites ran obituaries after she died; so did local papers. She was a young, promising climber who had based her training at the North Face Climbing Gym. She wrote articles for 'zines and blogs; a few were actually published by national climbing and outdoor recreation magazines. She did win the occasional climbing competition and earned two minor corporate sponsorships. It wasn't enough to live on—thus she had felt compelled to take a part-time accounting job at Provoid Brothers.

THERE was no way I could investigate the defunct brokerage, but I could go and have a peek at that climbing gym. My own training was based at Loose Rock, an ominously named gym populated by low-income climbing renegades. Our rag-tag bunch made do with second-hand gear, rebuilt old belay systems ourselves, and headed for outings to nearby West Virginia or upstate New York on the weekends.

My fingers began to itch. A sudden yearning for the texture and smell of rock and chalk washed over me. I could do it. My butt still hurt, but I could go—at least for a little bit. I wouldn't climb high. I could just boulder, moving laterally without a harness. I could do upper-body exercises. I'd be careful.

There was no way I could walk all the way to the subway yet, and I wasn't willing to bring crutches to a climbing gym. Twenty minutes later I was outside the building with my climbing bag over my shoulder, flagging a taxi. I didn't mind spending the money. This project was worth it.

I WORE low-key clothing and a microfiber cap to keep my hair out of my face. My old, broken-in climbing shoes were supple on my feet, their grippy, rubber soles eager to dig into the artificial rockface before me.

"So this is how you switch hands," I let the tall, bald-headed man explain. "Don't go above the painted line—you don't wanna fall farther than that. Once you feel comfortable with bouldering, let me know, and I'll get you equipped with a harness." I nodded. "Don't worry, you'll be fine." He smiled wide, scrunching his eyes, his sun-wrinkles a testament to the amount of time he spent outdoors.

I put my good foot on a foothold, grabbed a handhold, and pushed up. As long as I wasn't using my left leg, I was okay. I let my left instep rest behind my right heel and reached to my right to grasp another beginner-level handhold. And now the left. I let my body swing from left to right, reaching with my right toe, grabbing another rough protrusion.

It worked. I was breathing a bit harder, my core muscles straining to pick up the slack and my shoulders feeling the pleasant, incipient burn of healthy exertion. Whatever discomfort I felt was outbalanced by the glee that suffused me.

I was climbing again.

"What's wrong with your left side?" the guy, Carlos, asked from down below.

I eased myself down, using my one leg and two arms, breathing hard.

Don't jump.

Just... don't.

"I'm nursing an injury in my upper leg," I said. "Shouldn't put too much weight on it yet."

He gave me an assessing look. "You must be a real hot dog to climb with just three paws. Don'tcha fall, hear?" He flashed me a grin of encouragement, turned around, and left.

CARLOS MADDEN was his name, and he had been in town for only two months, just having moved from California. I watched him instruct some midlevel climbers down in the pit. He looked like he knew what he was talking about. I'd have to talk to him later, find out if he knew Celia.

Barely an hour had passed—and I was ready to pass out.

Seriously?

My body was giving up on me once again. I felt an overwhelming sense of fatigue and knew, with sudden urgency, that I had to catch a cab and get back to Jack's place and sleep off my unexpected exertion.

"Don't worry, I'll give you a free pass for next time," Carlos said. Climbing fees were high in the city, and I'd bought a pass for four hours. "Remind me next time. If you're coming off an injury, you must be tired as hell." He spoke like one who'd walked a mile in my shoes.

"Thanks." I breathed. "Hey, did Celia climb in this gym?"

His eyes narrowed. "So I've heard. Yeah. Why?"

"I've read about her online. What happened?"

His brown eyes darkened and his shoulder muscles tensed. "We don't talk to newbies about that sort of a thing. See that glass case?" He pointed to a display on the wall. "That's all you need to know about her."

I glanced over; a collection of news articles, photos, and trophies gleamed and beckoned. I'd have to check it out. "Thanks."

I was sitting on the bench, trying to keep my weight off my throbbing posterior while changing shoes, when a hush fell over the gym. I looked up. An unusually tall man with lank, black hair and the physique of a praying mantis was signing himself in at the desk.

Risby Haus.

The doorman from Jack's building headed for the locker rooms; only then did activity in the gym resume.

"Hey, Carlos. Who's that?" I asked.

He grimaced. "That? This guy's a regular climbing legend. Haven't you heard of the Demon of Santa Teresa?"

"Him?" My eyes must have bugged out at the famous name. "But I thought the Demon retired a few years back."

"Yeah. I know him from out West. He's the only one to have done the Santa Teresa climb solo and free. His height is a real asset."

"Is he good otherwise?" I asked.

Carlos shrugged. "I guess he is a good climber." He hesitated for a bit as he straightened some paperwork. Keeping my mouth shut never did me any harm. I let him fuss until he opened up again. "I wouldn't chase after him for climbing instruction, if I were you. He's slick. Ever since Celia died, he's been climbing better than ever. Even better than when I saw him out West."

"What are you saying?" I asked in an effort to help him get more specific.

He just looked at me. "He's bad luck. Nobody will touch him after that accident. Most people don't even know who he used to be out West, but something like that.... It didn't go over well. We all loved her."

"So you're saying you wouldn't climb with him, because...?"

"Because he's bad luck," Carlo declared. "If you like to stay in one piece, stay away from him." Carlos stopped the flow of words and shook his head. Then he pulled out a few sheets of paper out of a filing cabinet. "You did okay. Lemme give you some recovery exercises for while you're on the mend."

I left the gym with a handful of photocopied handouts. I didn't bother looking at them, keeping an eye on the taxi meter instead. My adventure might have set me back sixty bucks so far, but it was worth every penny.

Risby Haus was no beginner. He was a pro. Somehow, Celia hadn't known that.

I DIDN'T have keys to Jack's apartment. The doorknob locked automatically on the way out, but now I had no way to get in. The reality of my situation struck me as ironic. I had to break into a place where I was now expected to live. Now, I didn't have my burglar picks with me, but there were some tools in my climbing bag, including a thin spring from a self-belay system I had been repairing some time back and a general tool kit full of thin screwdrivers. Suddenly, the challenge of letting myself in felt rather pleasant. I had to work hard and it took bloody forever, but with Jack still at work, I had no intention of calling him and revealing that I'd been up and about.

He's so sweet when he's overprotective.

Huh. The thought flashed through my mind as the lock finally yielded. He was sweet. He was overprotective. That didn't mean I wanted to face his rant and rampage in regards to my personal health and safety. Sometimes, a guy's gotta do what a guy's gotta do.

The door swung open. I let myself in and locked the deadbolts. My rear was sore and throbbing to a point where I could feel every heartbeat in the swollen, irritated flesh. Before I could lie down and rest, I had to wash off chalk dust, rinse off my hard-earned sweat, and put my climbing bag away. I limped out of the foyer and into the living room, only to encounter one highly agitated Jack Azurri.

His back was turned to me, the shoulders tense under his elegant, charcoal pinstripe suit. He was dialing a number.

"Grrraawwwhrrr!"

My cell phone had an orgasm in my pocket.

I froze in place in midstep like the burglar I was.

He wheeled around, staring at me in disbelief.

"Grrraawwwhrrr!"

I fished the offending telephone out of my pocket and answered it. "Yes, Loverboy?" I met his eyes, trying to keep my voice playful.

He shut his phone off. I did the same and hid it in my pocket, trying to gauge his irritation level. His hair was mussed up as though he had been running his hands through it a lot, and his red tie was askew. There were dark shadows under his eyes and his sweet, lush lips were drawn into a tense line.

"Where have you been, Wyatt?"

"Out," I said, turning around to hang my climbing bag in the foyer. The need to hide it had passed.

"What do you mean, out?" His voice was low and commanding as he neared me. "You're supposed to be resting."

I shrugged. "I know. Just... it's lonely here, and I felt restless. I had to look into something, is all."

His eyes ran up and down my body, inspecting it for damage. "No crutches?"

"Don't worry, I took the cab."

He lifted my hand to his face and smelled it. His clean, soft hands ran over my dry fingertips, over my warm palms. "Chalk?"

"Yeah."

"Did you go *climbing*?" He was incredulous.

"Yeah. I'm so tired…."

I felt hands propel me to the sofa. "You're not supposed to do that. You can't even wear a harness yet. You can't put any weight on that leg, Wyatt. Wait 'til I tell Paul."

I settled on my side with my head pillowed on Jack's powerful thigh. "I only bouldered."

"Hnn."

"Have you ever heard of a guy called the Demon of Santa Teresa?" I asked.

Jack rested his palm on my shoulder, searching his thoughts. "Yeah, it rings a bell, actually. I can't place the term, though. What is it?"

"He is a legendary solo climber—he did most of the big peaks out West, and he did many of them solo and free. As in, no safety equipment." I watched Jack's eyebrows rise up to his hairline. "I know, I know… he's nuts. He's just extremely good. I remember some write-ups on him in climbing magazines from a few years ago when he retired."

"So he's not around anymore?" Jack asked.

"Not exactly… I saw him at the North Face. That's where your sister used to train. His real name is Risby Haus."

JACK was pacing the blue carpet, back and forth.

Back and forth.

I was observing him from my leather sofa perch, lying on my stomach with one arm and one leg draped down to the floor.

"So you're saying Haus must have been an expert climber before he and Celia hooked up?"

"Yeah." I yawned. "There's no way he could have gone from a rank newbie to a nickname-only legend in just a year or two."

"I need to be sure." His voice was grim with determination.

"I'll find out for you. No problem." I yawned again, and my stomach growled loud enough for Jack to hear.

He looked at me, melting into the sofa with my hair sticking out in all directions, and his eyes softened to a heated gaze full of want.

"You won't tell on me to Paul?" I asked, dropping the irritating name just to gauge Jack's reaction.

His eyebrow twitched. "Would you care if I did?"

"I don't care what Paul knows or doesn't know. As long as you don't double-team me."

"Okay, Goldilocks. You go take your shower and I'll heat up some leftovers."

Goldilocks.

I smiled. Things were looking up.

BY THE time I was rinsed off and changed into Jack's black silk boxers and a bathrobe, he was out of his suit, looking comfortable in sweat pants and nothing else. I let my eyes run down his unruly hair. The lines of his strong neck continued into the well-muscled shoulders and back.

He was beautiful.

"Ready?" he asked. Dinner was buttered noodles and defrosted green peas and beef braised with onions, dried apricots, and the slightest hint of anchovy.

"Mmm, nice umami underneath all that fruitiness," I commented. "It was pretty inspired to add cardamom, don't you think?"

Jack poked at it some. "It tastes weird."

I chewed some more. "I know what. It needs a tart counterpoint. Had this been Indian food, there would have been the yogurt sauce, right? So… hmm… do you have any balsamic vinegar?"

"Sure, I have a little bottle." He brought it from the kitchen; it was covered with layers of dust.

"How long have you had this?" I asked, slightly amused.

"Tch. Rick Blanchard from the office gave me a bottle of vinegar for Christmas last year as a gag gift."

"Really? Then it better be good, right?"

"I don't know," Jack frowned. "I haven't even opened it."

Now, I do know what balsamic vinegar tastes like, but have never seen it come in a small, square bottle like that. "You better taste it, make sure it's okay," I said, pulling out the cork and sniffing the contents. "Smells great, but you get the first taste."

"I'm not tasting plain vinegar."

"May I, then?" I asked.

He leaned forward, curious. "Go ahead, I dare you, Wyatt."

I smelled the pungent, sweet liquid and watched its viscous body ooze over the stainless steel spoon. When I dipped the tip of my tongue in, a complex bouquet of dried fruit and florals assaulted my senses, and I even sipped a bit off, letting it invade my mouth and bloom into a complex, sweet-and-sour bouquet. My eyes widened in surprised delight. "It's amazing. Here, you try."

He did, not to be outdone, but his expression was a puzzled frown. "This is totally different."

"Isn't it? Wow. Not at all like the big-bottle balsamic I know. Now drizzle a spoonful over your food and taste it again."

He did, and I did, and soon the only sound audible was that of eating and of silverware clicking against his stoneware plates.

"That Susan is a strange duck," Jack commented. "But she sure can cook."

ONCE the plates were put away, I thought I'd pull out my laptop and do a search on our mysterious doorman, but between the day's adventures and the excellent meal, I was bushed. I yawned again.

"Let's get you to bed," Jack said, escorting me to my room so he could change the dressing on my butt cheek. Then after finishing that, he squeezed my shoulder and lingered, as though he wanted to say something or maybe do something, and I lay there motionless, not wanting to do anything that might chase Jack off.

"Good night, Wyatt," he finally sighed and walked away from me. The sight of his alluring physique on his way out only added insult to injury.

IT WAS dark and I was tired, yet I couldn't fall asleep. Why didn't he have any interest in me? Obviously he cared. He was protective. Nurturing, even. He had reminded me to submit my invoice so I could get paid. He turned his junky guest room into a peaceful haven customized to my taste. He'd been jealous.

Jealous.

And hurt.

Both the jealous and the hurt parts were a bit of an epiphany. I realized I had been an idiot, and I also knew this was something I wanted to fix. Right now, if possible. It was close to midnight, and he'd probably be asleep—but we didn't need to get very far. I craved a bit of closeness—a caress—anything. Even a good fight would be better than the polite reserve of the last four days: the cool, courteous manner one displayed to clients and distant acquaintances.

I slipped out of my bed and limped through the darkened apartment. I had broken into it enough times to navigate it blindfolded. Here was my hallway, and the living room and the television and his hallway and his bathroom with a closet next to it, and his bedroom window, still lit up by an ethereal glow of street lamps and neon signs.

I loved that window.

Then there was Jack's king-size bed, and he was in it, sprawled right down the middle. He slept in the nude and was covered with a cotton sheet, and he looked as gorgeous as the first time I ever set my eyes on him.

He was left-handed, so if he wanted to reach for me, he'd want me to be on his right. I shuffled to the right side of his bed and eased myself down, settling my head upon his shoulder. I could tell he had not showered after work; his warm scent carried to my nostrils.

Just a bit of closeness.

My choice of position left me lying on my hurt side, and it ached, but I didn't care. I was in bed with Jack, feeling his warmth, smelling his musk and aftershave.

"Wyatt." His low whisper carried through the darkness as his large, warm left hand ran over my shoulder, pulling me closer.

I hissed in pain.

"Turn the other way."

Carefully, I did. I turned my back to him, letting him drape his arm across my chest as he spooned me from behind. I felt his dry lips nuzzle my neck as he tasted his way up to my shoulder.

I sighed in happy contentment.

Tender lips gave way to sharp teeth; I hissed again as he nipped my trapezius from behind. Right away, he caressed my distended flesh with his tongue.

"Jack!"

"Yeah...."

"Don't start what you can't finish. I still have some technical difficulties on my end."

Jack slid his right arm under me and wrapped it around my neck in a tight, possessive hold as his talented left trailed down my ticklish ribs and tired abs, easing its way under the elastic of those erotic silk boxer shorts.

I gasped.

"There's more than one way to skin a cat, Goldilocks," he whispered.

The evidence of his excitement pressed into my rear, against the small of my back, and I pushed into it, eager to feel more. He eased the boxers off my middle and down to my knees. I felt his blunt tip tease my lower back as he ground into me. I loved feeling his excitement and wanted more, even though having more was a very, very bad idea.

A few more days.... Arrgh!

He sensed my frustration at being unable to lie on my back. "Shhh…," he said, moving further down my legs and pulling my hips farther back. "Can you lift your leg a little?"

I did, and was soon surprised to find him aim his swollen length between my thighs, stroking in and out right under my tender parts, and I could feel its delicate, gentle brushes against me and the occasional blunt hit against my taint. I gave a little moan of pleasure and reached between my legs to caress his cock from the other side.

"Just let go, Jack," I whispered. "I want to feel you… right in my hand."

The friction of his hard, smooth shaft against my hand and my crack felt good in a teasing kind of way, but knowing I brought him pleasure was even better. Telling him to just let go must have loosened something inside him, because I felt him tense and pant. His coiled, wet heat exploded right into my hand.

"Grrraaaahwwrrr!"

Feeling Jack come into my hand in hot, wet pulses brought a satisfied grin to my face. My wound persisted in aching as I forced the distended muscles to work for me, move for me. I knew I'd pay later, but I didn't care. It was definitely worth it.

Jack caught his slick seed in his own hand and slid it down my cock, wet and smooth.

"How's your wound?" he asked breathlessly.

"I… what wound?" I was enveloped by the caring warmth and the sexy scent that was Jack. My breathing quickened and my eyes grew heavy. Soon I felt no pain at all.

"HERE, tissues."

"Thanks."

Before I cleaned the stickiness off my hand, I raised it to my lips with a measure of curiosity. My tongue darted out as I smelled him, and I tasted his essence. Bitter and briny and redolent of strong musk, same as before. I'd get used to it.

My eyes wandered up to his face as I settled on my back, taking advantage of natural anesthesia. I saw his eyes pierce the dim light of his bedroom, watching me. He didn't say anything. I finished tasting him, and he turned my chin toward his face and kissed my lips, letting his tongue plunge in for a secondary sampling of his own flavor.

We broke for air.

"I don't want you stalking Haus around," he said, his voice hoarse and tight.

"I'm being careful."

"No. I lost Celia already. I'm not losing you, too."

I didn't respond. Of course I'd stick my nose into Haus's business. I'd find all I could about Jack's sister's climbing partner. I'd be careful, though. I nuzzled his neck in a tender kiss. "You won't lose me."

Strong, warm arms embraced me and held me tight.

As I drifted off to sleep, it occurred to me Jack had just said something significant, something having to do with the two of us. Fatigue fuzzed the edges of my conscious mind, and for the life of me, I couldn't make the right connections. All I knew was, it was something good.

CHAPTER TWELVE

THE radio roused me before the crack of dawn. I stirred, alarmed at the sudden voices invading my fragile consciousness. An arm let go of my waist and hit something, making the voices shut up.

I turned around, faced with a broad back and well-muscled shoulders. I ran my hand up and down Jack's back, mindless in its exploration of the bumps, the dips, the muscled ridges.

"Mmmm. Harder...."

I smiled, digging my fist into that tight little triangle right between the shoulder blade and his spine.

"Ahhh... is it really tight?" he asked.

"Yeah. Have you been sitting a lot?"

"At the damn computer," he grumbled.

I nestled my chin on his shoulder, comfortable and warm, and poked and stroked and rubbed and kneaded, making his morning a bit nicer.

"Your cheek is getting scratchy," he purred, and I moved my jaw up and down his shoulder with a sigh.

"This is Nina Totenberg, reporting from Washington, DC...."

The radio alarm went off again, and this time Jack only turned the volume down to an acceptable level. He turned toward me. "Arrrrgh. Rise and shine! I'm taking you to work with me today for at least a little while."

I stifled a groan and slid off his mattress. "I'll go shower. How much time do we have?"

"We need to leave by seven-thirty," Jack said. "I usually walk from the parking lot, takes me twenty minutes. Can you handle that, or do you want to take the jitney?"

"It may take me a bit longer than that, but I'd like to walk."

"Okay."

He disappeared into his bathroom, leaving me to the sounds of NPR and the shower running. I walked back to my bedroom, ready to follow his example.

Breakfast was a toasted frozen bagel with a bit of cream cheese and scrambled eggs, water, and coffee. We sat there in our suits and ties, leaning forward as we ate, careful not to land the sticky bits of food on our work clothes and anxious not to spill coffee on the white, ironed shirts.

"Do you always wear that purple tie?" he asked me suddenly.

"No... I do have several, though. Why?"

He shrugged. "Your hair's pale blond, Goldilocks. I'd peg you for an aqua, or green."

"Mmm... you don't like it. What don't you like about it? Remember, I work in advertising. I'm all about noticeable."

"No, no, no. I never said I didn't like it," he backpedaled, panic in his sleepy eyes. "It looks fine. Really. It's just... I think you'd look so nice in the paler blues."

I sighed. Very few men could discuss fashion with any semblance of intelligence, and not even being gay was a guarantee of a good eye for color. "Should I change?"

"Only if you don't like it... but hurry up. We have ten minutes."

WE WALKED out of the elevator, our pace sedate so I didn't have to limp. My ripstop nylon briefcase was slung over my shoulder, containing a few printouts and some homemade business cards, and, of course, my laptop.

Risby Haus sat behind his marble castle wall. We both nodded to him and he nodded back. I caught a smirk on his face—a rather ugly face, actually—and realized that, to him, I was sauntering down the proverbial walk of shame.

Jack glanced at me and our eyes met. "I don't care what that asshole thinks," he muttered. "I slept like a log last night."

I didn't reply as we exited Jack's building. I looked around in an effort to orient myself in the neighborhood. Jack drove from his Shadyside apartment to the Strip District, where we parked. We missed the jitney that ferried commuters from the parking lot to the office buildings downtown. Our walk took almost an hour, but Jack didn't seem to mind. The offices of BW&B were located in the Gulf Tower, a building dating back to the 1920s. It had modern elevators, but the lobby was still decorated with carved marble and lacy brass trim, and there was a mosaic in the middle of the floor. I loved its quaint *film noir* look and said so.

Jack jerked his head up, uprooted from his thoughts. He looked around as though for the first time, and I saw him take in the urns of indoor landscaping and the antique, Art Deco lighting fixtures. It occurred to me that once Jack's mind was on work, he didn't notice much around him at all.

We walked past the reception desk, which was manned by a large black man with a razored, angular hairdo. Jack introduced us. "Mr. Buddy Love, meet Mr. Wyatt Gaudens. Buddy, Wyatt's likely to be in and out of the office. He's an independent contractor—be helpful, all right?"

Buddy Love shook my hand with his enormous paw as his phone rang. He answered it and forwarded the call where it needed to go. "Hi, Wyatt. Let me know if you need anything." He turned to Jack. "You have some faxes on your desk. These two people called right after eight, wanting to talk to you. They're in Europe, so they'll be gone in three hours."

"Thanks, Buddy." Jack took the messages and motioned for me to follow. We walked through a room of regular, gray cubicles like the people at Pillory's agency used to have. Offices with doors were on the other side.

"Come in," he said. His workspace was overflowing with unfiled papers, all piled in discrete groups. He glanced at his watch. "We have a bit of time. Let me get you situated in the conference room. While you get yourself comfortable, I have to get to my office and return these phone calls."

I ended up sitting by the projection screen with my presentation already up there and several paper copies in front of me in a tidy pile, along with my invoice.

AN HOUR later, I was elbow-deep in spirited conversation with Jack's business partners.

"So, you suggest we focus on clients in the same area of business as our current customers?" Louis Schiffer reiterated in his monotone voice as he peered at me over the rim of his metallic glasses. "And finding them will cost how much, exactly?"

I launched into a detailed explanation of my prospective client search process. The meeting continued like that for two and a half hours. Rick Blanchard was as thorough as Schiffer—poking and prodding, looking for problems to come up. My heart leapt at their interest; a thorough client was more likely to succeed.

Schiffer also looked at my invoice. "Hundred and seventy-five an hour? I thought you charged eighty."

"That rate is for small, distressed businesses and for nonprofit organizations," I replied with a straight face. Pillory had given me a run-down on rates and billing two days prior.

The more they invest in you, the more cooperation you'll get, Mr. Gaudens, he said. *It is impossible to deliver good results without their cooperation. Charging them more is actually for their own good.*

"I have some worksheets for you to fill out," I told them, handing out questionnaires all around. "The more information you can provide, the faster I can get your marketing plan off the ground."

All three of them scowled, not having expected to have to work on this personally.

"Of course, I can delve into your old files and retrieve the information myself. It will take me two weeks of full-time effort. It will take your secretaries less than three days." I gave them my winning, hundred-watt smile. Let them do the math.

JACK wanted to escort me home right afterward; I was so tired, I didn't even want to be taken out to lunch.

"There's leftovers," I mumbled. "I'll be fine. I'll take the bus."

"You sure?"

"Positive. Just ride with me down to the lobby."

He stepped into the elevator and pushed a white button with a star. After we descended a few floors, I reached out and pressed the red stop button. The cabin ground to a halt.

"Wyatt?" He had mischief in his eyes.

"I just wanted some privacy, is all." I sank against him, molding my body against his. Warm hands ran up my back, and I looked up only to have my lips possessed in a slow, languorous kiss. I sighed, rising against him as our tongues met in gentle exploration. There was sweetness and lust, along with the thrill of forbidden fruit in a forbidden place.

We broke for air, panting. His cheeks were flushed, his hair was unruly, and his tie was askew. I fixed the tie and mentioned the hair.

His scintillating blue eyes took my measure. "You look like a cat in heat, Wyatt. You're hardly the one to talk." Then he smirked. "Better get going before they send the janitor after us." He pressed the button with the star again, and we descended and parted with a chaste peck on the lips.

THE bus ride took forever, and I spent most of it standing because, let's face it, my butt still hurt and the streets were rough with patched potholes. Never had I been so glad to be home. I shut and locked the door behind me and stumbled to that friendly leather sofa. It beckoned to me. Disregarding my office suit, I kicked off my shoes and sprawled on my right side, letting the tired, sore muscles scream obscenities at me. They were still healing, knitting themselves back together, and here I'd just taken them onto the bus.

My eyes opened half an hour later. Somewhat restored, I resolved to make lunch, eat it, and then think about something constructive to do. After changing into sweats and a T-shirt, I had a leftover meatloaf sandwich and an apple, drank my glass of milk, and proceeded to just think.

Think of what to do next.

Think....

Think....

I felt like Winnie the Pooh, the Bear of Very Little Brain, at that moment. Stuffing was coming out of me, but no good ideas. In cases such as these, my favorite solution involves drawing a spider diagram.

I took a piece of paper from Jack's printer and found a fine-point mechanical pencil. Between sips of cold, refreshing milk, I drew a circle. Inside it, I wrote "me." I drew a line going outside of this circle. I labeled it "Novack" and suddenly a number of mental leaps connecting to the Novack Bakery came to my mind. I wrote them down as branches off that first line. Another line was "The Stamens," a new and high-end floral design shop in Lawrenceville. Unfortunately, Ricky and Theodore didn't know enough to name their shop in a way that would announce their business to the general public—but I could fix that. Next line: "BW&B." Again, a number of items.

"My apartment" sprouted a lonely limb on the thinking tree. I sat there and thought for a while. The question was, what to do with an apartment I didn't live in? It was a small, one-bedroom place, and I still had a good bit of stuff in it. I made a branch, labeling it "de-junk apartment." First I'd clean it up, then I'd see.

And now the biggest item: "Celia." Now, this line was like a full-grown tree when I was done with it, and questions were hanging off the main branches like leaves. I saw a need for a timeline of events, a list of friends and coworkers, a list of fellow climbers.... Later, I'd make a spider diagram all about Celia. For now, though, one thing caught my eye.

"Her climbing gear."

Jack had not mentioned coming across his sister's harness, carabiners and self-belaying devices while remodeling the room for me. Presumably, it was still in the pile of boxes only fifteen feet away from me. I measured the sprawling pile with a baleful eye. There was no help for it.

If I were going to figure out what happened to Celia, I'd have to delve into the innumerable boxes she and her two aunties left behind. Besides, it would be faster if I did that all by myself. Jack's extra set of hands came along with a set of eyes and a lifetime of memories. He'd slow down for every other thing and ponder upon its significance. I didn't have enough time to do that. I had to find that gear, and I had to find it today.

TIME just flew by; I was no longer bored. Engrossed in my task of sorting and evaluating, I didn't even look up when the key slid into the lock.

"Wyatt. What have you done?" His voice wasn't displeased, exactly. Just… he sounded like a parent whose clever charge had built a pyramid out of chairs to reach the sugar bowl and spilled the white stuff all over the floor. There was no real harm, no bodily injury had occurred, but there was a lot of mess to put away.

"Oh, hi, Jack!" I looked up, pleased. It was good to see him at the end of the day. My back was killing me from hunching over boxes and piles. "I'm looking for Celia's climbing gear. And while I was at it, I began to categorize all these items…." I gestured at the organized chaos with theatrical eloquence. I thought my system was obvious. "The garbage is in those old boxes. You'll want to go through that, make sure it doesn't contain anything of personal value. The furniture is right next to it, all piled up. The boxes are labeled, see? Textiles, silver, porcelain, glass, art, jewelry, books…."

He looked around again, this time truly absorbing the magnitude of my accomplishment. "What happened to the huge pile?"

I flashed him a victorious grin. "Just these few boxes are left. The gear's bound to be there somewhere."

"Do you even realize what time it is?" he asked, glancing at his Rolex.

"No...?"

"Pizza time. I don't want any weird stuff by Susan, and neither one of us is going to cook tonight. Or so it seems."

"Yeah... good idea. I'll have whatever you're having!"

I heard him cackle, disappearing into his bedroom as I stretched my back, bending over yet another box full of the flotsam and jetsam of somebody else's life.

THE heartlessly plain pizza was long gone, but we still had the good beer from Reyna.

"It tastes... okay, I guess. It's chewy. Like you're drinking bread." Jack finished his first-ever bottle of Dogfish IPA and set it aside.

"So would you go back to Miller Lite?" I asked, teasing only halfway.

"I'm not so spoiled I'd turn it down," Jack said.

"Give it a few weeks of being spoiled and pampered...." I said, and then I called Izzy before it got too late, and let him know that he could come over the next few days for a truckload of resale goods. There were still several boxes to go, and I dove right in. Hiding under old, beat-up baby quilts were several moldy, crusty-looking stuffed toys.

I grumbled under my breath, digging under. "Is this garbage, Jack?" I shoved a plush Puss in Boots toward him. His felt was riddled with holes and the stitching showed, although the cracked plastic boots were still securely sewn on.

"Puissy!" I heard him cry out behind me, excited. He picked up the gray cat with reverence. "That's what's happened to him! I was afraid he got thrown out by accident. Celia had been threatening me with hiding him in the garbage for quite a while."

I looked at the depressed cat. His whiskers were broken, his tail hung limp—only his eyes laughed at me, frozen in time. "Yours?"

"Yeah...."

"You keeping it?"

"Of course!" Jack shot me a look laden with suspicion. "I'll have you know we went through a lot together, he and I. He's my buddy, my pal. Puissy, meet Wyatt. Wyatt, meet Puissy."

I gave Jack a sideways glance. "So... how did he end up with a name like that?"

"Very funny, Wyatt. Nobody will ever give me a break over his name. It just happens to be short for 'Puissant,' so you can get your mind out of the gutter right now."

"Puissant?"

"It means powerful, mighty, potent, good stuff like that."

"Oh," I said, trying in vain to suppress my giggle. "Potent. I see. Well right now he looks like he's going to fall apart if you look at him with a crooked eye."

"Yeah. I need to find someone who knows how to fix old toys."

I nodded. "You already know someone."

"Who, you?" Jack's eyes filled with hope.

"Actually... I hate to bring him up, but Dr. Hinge has always excelled in the needleworking arts."

"Paul? Really?" I couldn't believe Jack was so worked up over an old toy. I watched him pick up the phone and shoot out a quick text.

Soon, his phone rang. "Paul? It's Jack. Yeah... got a minute?"

I wandered into the kitchen, warmed up a glass of milk in the microwave, and added some chocolate syrup. A sense of jealousy seized me over the stupid toy. I wished it were me who was uncommonly talented in needlework, fantasizing about fixing Puissy, handing the no longer dilapidated cat back to Jack in exchange for his devastating, full-power smile.

Just like Jack felt jealous of Paul's medical skill....

It seemed we were doomed, Jack and I. We were doomed to keep calling Dr. Paul Hinge's number every time one of us got shot or sprained an ankle, every time one of us ripped a zipper or lost a button. He was the go-to guy. He could patch up anything. Despite my irritation, the thought made me smile. By the time I returned to the living room, Jack was off the phone and I shared my analysis of Dr. Paul Hinge in our lives with him.

The patch-up guy.

The cut man.

The seamstress.

He only grinned. "I bet those old baby quilts used to be mine and Celia's, and I bet you'll find a giant white stuffed cockroach in there somewhere.

I did.

He tossed the quilts. He kept the cockroach.

I dug a bit deeper into the box. Under a twisted mass of dusty, brocade curtains ten decades out of fashion, my fingertips slid over the smooth surface of cool metal. Metal covered with chalk dust. A bit of rope... and some plastic buckles. "Jack. Jack, I think we got it."

He dove toward me. The harness that emerged was still attached to a coil of semielastic climbing rope, accompanied by several carabiners and two self-belay devices.

We lifted our heads and looked at each other. Jack was as white as a sheet, his good mood having sublimated like dry ice on a hot day. He swayed a bit from side to side before catching his balance on the arm of the leather sofa.

I edged all the way toward him. My knees pressed into the blue carpet next to his as I hugged him around the waist. He embraced my shoulders with his long arms. His chin fell into my hair, and I heard him struggle for breath. We rocked from side to side together, the way I saw Susan rock little Michelle to sleep. He was squeezing me mighty tight for a while. His head dropped to the side of my head, and I felt his chest expand in his struggle for air, making my cheek and the side of my neck warm and moist.

I didn't turn to look at him; he didn't need me to witness his tears.

Time passed as we sat there, both of us silent and contemplative about what this piece of physical evidence might mean.

"I feel a bit wiped out," Jack said apologetically. "We should probably turn in."

"It's alright. Really. Just… take your shower, and I'll clean up in here."

He just stood there, watching me place assorted objects in their categories.

I sighed and stood up, facing him. "Jack. Go. Now." I used my no-nonsense voice, and to my surprise, it worked. He turned around like an automaton and ambled into his room to shed his dusty clothes. By the time the rest of the boxes were disposed of and I had vacuumed the much-abused carpet, Jack emerged from his room wearing pajamas.

I'd never seen him wear pajamas before.

"I'm having a scotch," he said. "You want any?"

"Yeah. On the rocks." I'd have to skip my pain meds tonight.

Jack selected two cut crystal tumblers from the back of the kitchen cabinet, put ice in them, and poured a good measure of single malt scotch into each. He handed one to me and raised a toast. "To Celia. She was one hell of a broad, an awesome sister, and she deserved better than that."

"To Celia." We sipped, still standing.

Jack hugged my shoulders with his free arm and pulled me in and kissed my temple. "Good night, Wyatt." Then he returned to his room and closed the door.

I showered and slipped into a clean pair of black silk boxers that I "borrowed" from Jack's underwear drawer earlier that day; they threatened to slide off my hips. I pulled on the climbing shirt with the logo of Mt. Whitney Celia had given to Jack, which he let me wear. My window was cracked open and the autumn breeze played with the edges of the curtains. I settled in the middle of my bed and hugged a pillow to my chest. I wanted to sleep—exhaustion deprived me of rational thought—yet I was still unable to stop ruminating on various tasks that might help reveal the truth about how Celia died. I had lists of things to do galloping through my head, complete with my spider diagram visual. The words and phrases spilled off the jagged branches, calling for attention. Schematic diagrams of the GriGri, an assisted braking device Celia had, popped up before my wide-open eyes. Friction coefficients of various types of ropes with their various diameters cluttered the space behind my ears.

I had finished my scotch and wasn't in the mood for another.

I tossed. I turned. I felt too hot; I kicked my sheet and comforter away. Then I became too cold and had to sit up and hunt for them again.

There was a faint knock on my door. "Come in," I said, keeping my voice low.

A tall, dark figure slipped in; the door closed. My mattress dipped under the extra weight and arms enveloped me and held me tight. Jack sighed.

I stroked his shoulder, his arm, his back. He inhaled again and held his breath. I felt his back pop and he sighed in relief. As he molded himself against me, I felt his body transition from a tense mass that resembled hard concrete, to a pliable puddle of goo. I smiled—the fact that Jack was able to relax just because he was with me really stroked my ego.

"I don't know how you do it," he mumbled, burying his face into the crook of my neck. "You popped my back again." Within two minutes, he was asleep.

"Izzy Silverstein will be stopping by. You think you can stay here for him?" Jack asked over a hot cup of coffee, taking me by surprise.

"I had plans."

"You can work from my home office. And you have your laptop."

I shrugged, pouring more cereal. "I was hoping to unkink my back after all that bending yesterday. Maybe get some exercise."

Jack narrowed his eyes and gave me a measuring look. "You're not going climbing, are you?"

I stared at him like a deer caught in headlights, not saying a word.

"You think you'll be okay doing that? How's your butt?"

Slowly, I felt the tension drain from me. "Fine... I don't have to do much. Just get back in shape. There's this guy, Carlos, who might know what was going on last year and all. I need to compile a timeline, and if I go during the day, Haus will be downstairs, working."

Jack ran his long fingers through his playfully disobedient chestnut hair. "Well… call him then so you can coordinate your schedules. If you get too tired climbing, take a cab home. I don't want you passing out on the bus."

A small, well-hidden part of me stirred as he said that. There he was again, all gruff and sweet and concerned.

Sometime later, Jack kissed me good-bye and shut the door on his way out. His absence gave me space to think about the feelings that woke up as a result of his concern. I felt an immediate need to push it all away and bury myself in work, which was a sure signal there was something important going on.

I wanted to push Jack away.

There. It was as simple as that. I wanted him in my life, I yearned to spoil him and make his days more pleasant, yet as soon as Jack showed what could be construed as feelings for me, I was sorely tempted to back off.

As I did the morning dishes and microwaved the last cup of coffee, I realized I was scared shitless. I was afraid because now that I had something of value, I could lose it. If Jack changed his mind and left, I would be utterly devastated, and after my history of personal relationships and their sorry ends, I didn't want to ever feel like that again.

I was afraid I'd do something to drive Jack away. Pushing him away would have been a preemptive strike of sorts, a way to control the emotional fallout. Finding a bit of insight about my own motivations filled me with both relief and apprehension.

Relief, because suddenly I saw why and how the relationships in my life seemed to be falling apart. Once Mom died, I made sure nobody ever left me again. I was the one who always managed to walk out the door.

Apprehension, because even though I was now aware of a thought pattern, I had absolutely no idea how to harness all that insight.

CHAPTER
THIRTEEN

I WOKE up next to Jack. That fact alone was mildly surprising. He was still asleep, his hair a spill of warmth against my pale ivory sheets. He was sprawled as though he owned the bed, which he didn't, pushing me to the side. I shoved back a bit in a bid to reclaim some real estate. My gesture provoked a mild, sleepy grumble. He grabbed the blanket and turned on his side, away from me.

Jack Azurri is a blanket thief.

I guess I deserved my fate, considering I am a real thief and a burglar. What goes around, comes around. The cool morning air felt a bit too brisk with the window having been open overnight; I shivered and rolled out of bed to use the bathroom. Then I returned and spooned Jack from behind, trying to get some coverage under the edge of my dark blue comforter.

"What?" Groaned a sleepy voice.

"Can I have some blanket?"

He flopped the other way, engulfing me under a cozy tent of fabric and sleepy, warm flesh. I burrowed my nose into his shoulder and inhaled his warm, musky scent.

He smells better than after his shower.

My action didn't pass unnoticed.

"Mmm?"

I inhaled again and ran my hand over his modest, pinstriped pajamas.

"Wyatt?" No longer drowsy, he leaned into me, nosing my hair to the side. I felt warm, soft lips on my neck. "What time is it?"

"Early," I groaned. "You almost pushed me off the bed, and then you stole the covers."

"So sorry," he said, not sounding sorry at all. "Maybe I can make it up to you?"

"Maybe." I whispered, hoping my morning breath wasn't too terrible. I felt his hand skim up my bent leg and across my hip, turning me onto my back, exposing me.

His fingers played over the sensitive skin of my inner thigh. "I may be the blanket thief, but you seem to keep taking my underwear, Wyatt." His hand moved the silk around. The tender caress just about ripped an involuntary gasp from my lungs. "Maybe I should take it back." Clever fingers drew a fire trail along the top of the boxers; the tingle of sudden heat surprised a whimper out of me. "What, Wyatt? Were you going to say something?"

I widened my eyes, looking at him, ready to open my mouth. Whatever I was going to say was wiped from my mind as his hand slipped under the sinuous silk and his delicate fingers teased my curls.

"Jack!" Any pretense at dignity went out the window as I gave a needy whine, bucking up into his touch in search of more contact.

He let go of me, divested me of the silk boxer shorts I had stolen from him, and tucked the wad of silk up his sleeve. "Mine," he said, his eyes now alert and full of mischief. He sat up and swung his legs off the bed.

"Jack!" My voice said it all.

"What? I'll be back... eventually." He disappeared into the bathroom and did his business, and when he came out, he was nude and gorgeous; his half-hard alter ego stirred to greet me as he took in the sight of me, sprawled wantonly across my bed, wanting, waiting.

He pounced.

I moved to roll him under me, but he had the advantage of both size and surprise. Once again he was perched on my chest, twirling an overgrown strand of hair, smiling.

"What would you like me to do, Wyatt?"

I startled, not expecting the question. "Ah… anything goes?" I asked.

"Well… almost anything."

"Top you?" My teasing question gave me wiggle room in case I got shot down.

"Not anytime soon," he said, his voice serious. "Pick something else."

Well, then. How about my special "fantasy number two." I flushed at the thought of saying it out loud, my words frozen under his arctic blue gaze.

"Wyatt?" His expression betrayed amusement. He watched me swallow, then sneeze in response to my sudden arousal as I blushed in embarrassment. "Just whisper it," he said, his voice a sensuous rumble as his ear descended to my mouth.

I did.

He sat up, considering. "We have the time, I think, to do this right. I'll do as you ask, as long as you do as I say." The promise of unimaginable pleasure made me nod without even thinking about it.

I WAS lying on the bed with my butt so close to the edge, I thought I'd slide off the towel Jack placed under me. My knees were bent and my feet were planted to the sides, touching the very edge of the mattress.

"I want you to hold your ankles with your hands, Wyatt."

Dubious, I reached for one ankle, then the other. The open air cooled my overheated skin as my knees spread apart, leaving me curiously open and vulnerable. I tried to do a sit-up to peek and see what Jack was planning to do, but with my hands affixed to my ankles, all I saw was the top of his head.

"Just relax. This will feel… different. Just go with it, okay?"

"Okay." I sighed, my sigh turning to a gasp as I felt a warm, wet washcloth cloth on my thighs, then between them. I was being cleansed in a most thorough and intimate manner.

A question was at the tip of my tongue, but before I had a chance to let it loose, I heard an unfamiliar swishing sound. My ears strained where my eyes wouldn't serve. A cool softness touched the inside of my leg, a wet, tickly sensation circling in from the thigh toward my cock.

What the...?

I let go of my ankles so I could sit up and see what he was doing.

Jack stopped. In a moment, his voice broke the pregnant silence. "Wyatt. How much do you trust me?"

I took a moment to think about that. He was there for me when I needed it most; we had pulled through despite our differences. I trusted him. "A lot," I said.

"Well, then!" he said. "Just remember that and keep holding your ankles. You stop, I stop." Jack's mirth was barely contained.

Groaning, I grasped my ankles again and spread my thighs apart, resigned to my awkward position. The moist tickle teased my skin once again, slicking and smothering the sensitive skin around my cock, all over my balls, down to the sensitive taint and going all the way down to my back door.

Keeping still was incredibly hard. I tried not to move as I was becoming increasingly aroused from the intimate touches, despite being a bit intimidated by their strangeness. "What the hell are you doing down there, Jack?"

"I'm using a fine-bristle brush on you," he said, and I could just hear the playful smile on his face.

Brush... bristle brush....

It sounded familiar, like I should have known what was going on, but without the benefit of a line of sight I felt clueless and not just a bit stupid.

A splash of water broke the silence. His hand stroked my inner thigh, holding it steady. "Whatever you feel, don't move."

"'Kay." I'd try.

Then there was a cold sensation, followed by a somewhat familiar tug of the skin—and now the softness and the faint, familiar odor made sense. "Jack... Jack! Are you *shaving* me?"

"Shh... don't move."

Another splash of water. Another tug on the skin; his holding hand changed position and my state of arousal began to wane as I felt the cold steel near my most sensitive parts. "Jack...." My voice held an edge of panic.

"Stay still. It's a good safety razor. I got a fresh blade just for you."

I let out an incoherent sound of mild distress as I held on. My arms and legs were tense as I felt him banish hair from my most private place. Front to back, side to side.

Threatening. It was definitely threatening. Yet intimate. And I trusted him. Very, very slowly I started to feel myself relax.

Then the warm, wet washcloth returned, soft and... and I could *feel* its touch with unprecedented clarity. With my skin bare, I felt the lightest brush of his fingers, the softest breeze of air. I bucked my hips in eager anticipation.

"You can let go, if you want to see." Jack sounded uncommonly pleased with himself.

I stood and looked down to assess the damage. All he left was a tuft of hair surrounding the base. I felt down under; everything was smooth. A small tray next to the bed held a bowl of water, an old-fashioned shaving brush, a bowl of shaving soap, and his razor. "How could you? And why?" I sounded like he threw out my comic books.

"Because, for what you want, I like the hair out of the way. Now, if you *still* want it, you'll lie down, right?" There was a question in his eyes.

I nodded, now hesitant, uncertain as to what other surprises I could expect from him.

"Well then lie down and hold on to your ankles."

No. Not again!

Yet... being at the mercy of Jack Azurri, as scary as it had been at first, hadn't produced any lasting harm, so I assumed my position once again.

Wet, soft warmth assaulted me without warning. I arched, gasping for air once again. His tongue slithered over the shaved parts, lavishing attention on my smooth, sensitive skin.

"You taste so delicious," he purred, lifting me and sliding a pillow under my butt.

Tense with anticipation, I was curious to see what my erotic wish would feel like. Then I felt the firm, wet tongue sweep a soft path down my crack and over the myriad nerve endings that circled my hole. I cried out—I don't remember what—and bucked as much as my hands on my ankles would allow.

"Keep still," Jack said. "You need to relax your shapely ass if you want me down here."

So I did, panting and struggling for every smidgeon of control as his talented tongue drew intricate patterns around my opening, pushing in here and there. I was so hard I knew I could come from this alone. "Jack... I'm so close."

"Mmm." I felt his hand grip my base, not letting me teeter over the edge, his other hand pushing my cheek to the side. His tongue dug in and wiggled, and I thought I'd scream.

"Please, enough!" I wanted him inside me, dammit. "I want you to fuck me!"

The action down under stopped. "You can let go, Wyatt."

I pried my clasped fingers from around my ankles and lifted my legs in an invitation.

"Your bandage fell off."

It's not like I forgot about my half-healed gunshot wound, but whatever Jack was doing felt just too good. "The wound can wait. The condoms are in your room, right?"

"But I can't," he growled as he helped me move up the bed. He worked his hands under my shoulder blades, and slid his cock up my shaved skin. "The condom may as well be on the moon."

"Bareback," I gasped the word.

He looked me straight in the eyes. His pupils were dilated, his eyes were glazed over, and I could see him bite his lip hard enough to turn it white. He leaned his forehead into my neck and groaned. "Oh, Wyatt... thank you, but no. We'll get tested later." He slid his cock up the shaved "vee" of my hip, and I felt his every scorching contour. His belly brushed my cock, and when I gasped, he snaked his hand down and wrapped around it with just the right amount of pressure.

It didn't take long—his urgent, hard thrust slid up and down my skin, and when I squeezed his shoulders, he exploded with a roar. His jizz flooded my belly and dribbled down the bare and sensitive skin of my hip crease. Jack collapsed to the side of me, and when I arched, there was nothing above me but cool morning air. I gave him a minute, and sure enough, he turned to face me again.

His mouth was back on my smooth skin down under. He tasted himself from the platter of my body. He took some of his naturally produced lubricant and slid his hand on my cock. Then he dove back between my legs. "I need your legs up," he said.

I raised them, holding my ankles in the air and unable to think of anything as the sensation of his tongue up my crack threatened the bliss of his hand sliding up and down my shaft. The sensory overload was almost painful in its intensity, and I didn't fight it. I came long and hard, tension draining out of me. My eyes were closed as I kept hold of my ankles in the air, and I felt a wave of relaxing sensation, like warm water flooding my limbs. Then there was sweet darkness, soft and yielding.

"You can let go now," he said, and I could hear a smile in his voice. We lay still in a tangle of spent limbs, recapturing our breath.

Then the alarm went off.

BREAKFAST was a silent affair. We brewed coffee and microwaved enough instant oatmeal with a side of bacon to hold us until lunch. Flushed even after my shower, I'd occasionally glance at Jack over my cup of coffee with cream. My stolen glimpses measured his sculpted, handsome cheekbones, the curvature of his jawline, the firm lips that softened like petals when kissed. He tried to meet my eyes with his, and every time he succeeded, I'd flush and glance away. Just being together like this was magic.

Little did I know it was but the calm before the storm.

CHAPTER FOURTEEN

WE WERE putting our breakfast dishes away, and I still couldn't meet Jack's eyes. We'd woken that morning and made love—I don't know if I can even call it that; he told me what to do and I did it and it felt wonderful, and my pleasure made him surprisingly happy—then we ate a subdued breakfast, and he left for work.

As I walked him to the door, I felt a sense of lingering incompleteness ricochet through my chest. He lifted my chin to kiss me, but our eyes almost met again and I glanced away and flushed, my breath shallow.

"Wyatt." He dropped his briefcase on the tiled floor of his foyer and gently backed me up against the wall.

I felt his legs pin mine. Air got rare again, and I had to turn away, sneezing into the crook of my elbow as the dreaded blush overtook my cheeks. "What are you doing to me?" I croaked, feeling fuzzy and faint.

"Wyatt," he whispered into the crook of my neck as he ran his generous hands up my arms, my shoulders. "Did you not enjoy it?"

I sneezed again at the memory as I felt my cock fill again. Damn.

"There's no shame in enjoying it," he crooned into my hair, his lips skimming the wild, blond strands.

I snaked my arms up his chest and around his neck and pulled him in even tighter. We kissed. "Have a good day, Jack," I said, producing a shy, yet heartfelt, smile. "I know I'm going to." My eyes lifted only to see his back retreat toward the elevator.

Damn.

Yeah, I did enjoy it. That was the problem. I enjoyed it so much, I craved his closeness with such painful intensity—Jack Azurri was like a drug to me. The longing in my chest filled me with fear. It whispered of attachment, entanglement, and loss.

IZZY SILVERSTEIN showed up about two hours later, just as I finished writing an advertisement flyer for Novack's Bakery.

"Wyatt! How have you been?"

I waved him inside, belatedly remembering that he knew his way. "Great. I especially like my room."

"Oh yeah? Show me how it turned out!"

I sighed. Silverstein's always been the nosy sort. I opened the dark wooden door, watching his reaction to the framed 1920s linoleum cut prints on the walls that I finally chose from Jack's stash. I've come to love their straightforward abstraction, figures distorted, in motion and alive.

Silverstein's eyes rested on the unmade bed. Sheets were rolled halfway down, baring the mattress and the comforter hung off the corner, askew. A stray pillow and used tissues littered the floor. An earthy, primal odor hung in the air. "I'm glad your relationship is working out. I suppose this is not a good time to ask you how you're doing?"

I groaned, feeling myself redden again.

"I was inquiring about the unfortunate gunshot, Wyatt," he chortled, his eyes shaded by his ever-present fishing hat.

I addressed the less painful inquiry first. "The wound is fine. It hurts only a little, and I can do most things." There was no need for him to worry about the stabbing, hollow fear in my heart.

He considered me with a sigh. "How about those boxes of goods, then?"

I sighed in relief. "Coffee or tea?"

"Tea, if you please," he answered, and I preceded him into the kitchen, put up a kettle, and had him select from a box of assorted teabags.

Silverstein made quick work of sorting out the items he was willing to resell; he read them off, and I entered them into a spreadsheet. After countless trips to the truck parked by the Dumpster, his pick-up was brimming with goods. He fastened the cargo down with a tarp and a number of bungee cords.

It was two hours before he turned to say good-bye.

"I think he really likes you, Wyatt," he said instead, the look in his eyes serious. "Try not to screw it up."

Grinding my teeth, I forced a smile at his well-meaning vote of very little confidence. He knew so much about me already, it occurred to me I might be able to bum some relationship advice out of him. The engine of his truck was running already, though, and I felt too self-conscious to chase after him. Once he was gone, I brought the boxes of donation items downstairs, where the Am Vet truck would pick them up in the afternoon.

The living room was now officially empty. The same couldn't be said for the four boxes of keepsakes under Jack's dining room table, but that was his headache. Vacuuming was mine. I cleaned the carpet, eyed the room, and repositioned the sofa and the coffee table. Then, of course, I had to vacuum again.

He really likes you. Try not to screw it up.

Not even the loud whine of the vacuum cleaner could silence Silverstein's words in my head.

AFTER the morning's chores, I came to realize my butt felt just about healed. In celebration of this, I walked almost everywhere that day. I marched over to Novack's, where he approved my work, paid me another installment, and gave me a box of assorted cookies. Then I walked over to Pillory's agency. Reyna received me with good cheer and pressed a cup of coffee into my hand; then, of course, I had to produce the box of Novack's cookies, which Reyna began to nibble and Pillory eyed with reserve.

"So how is it going, Mr. Gaudens?" he asked, sitting in his usual ramrod-straight position, his facial expression giving away nothing.

I gave him a brief update on my projects, as though I still worked for him, and he nodded as he listened, inserting an occasional comment. Those comments were solid gold; I made sure to write them down later.

"Why don't you call him Wyatt, Auguste?" Reyna said all of a sudden. "You know him well enough, don't you think?"

Pillory hesitated, freezing in midmotion, seeming suddenly awkward. "Would you mind?" He rose his thin, ebony eyebrows high in his face.

"No, not at all... Auguste."

"Very well then, Wyatt." He sipped some tea, politely ignoring my cup of coffee, which was stinking up his conference room. "Reyna and I were wondering whether you and Jack would like to join us for dinner someday."

I sat up so fast, my coffee almost spilled. "Um... I'd say yes, but I'll have to check with my... with my... friend." The last word was limp and flaccid on my tongue. I shrank into my chair when I realized I didn't feel bold enough to admit to a lover. I thought Jack and I warranted the boyfriend status, but I wasn't sure how he felt about describing us. "Friend" was a happy, generic term, good enough to cover most situations.

Reyna grinned. "Don't forget today's Friday." She nudged me with her elbow, almost making me spill again.

"Oh yeah, you're right! How time flies." I nodded. "Same time, same place?"

Reyna was about to nod back, when Pillory—Auguste, that is— lifted his hand halfway, letting it hover over the teapot.

"What's tonight?"

"Wyatt and I meet with our friends after work on Friday nights. We eat greasy food and drink beer. It's loud and there's music and we haven't done it in a while." Reyna eyed the quiet man with a measure of apprehension. "You wanna come?"

"No, I do not 'wanna' come. I'm perfectly happy at home, with a book."

Reyna laughed irreverently at his peevish tone. "Okay, my misanthropic sunshine," she chirped. "I'll come home smelling of beer and smoke, but I'll be happy to shower for you."

Auguste huffed and looked away, making me wonder what made the two of them click so well. Reyna was loud and vivacious, even brash at times. Auguste had always been the silent type, every action a study in premeditated control. She must have barged right into his protected private space heedless of convention or propriety, and for whatever reason, he must have decided putting up with a woman who was like a wild force of nature was preferable to being alone. There was a lesson there somewhere, but I had yet to figure it out.

Next stop: my place. The elevator took me up to the sixth floor of my older, run-down apartment building, where most tenants were either very young or very old and lived on tight budgets.

Choosing not to use my keys, I picked my locks open just for practice. The door to my pad swung open, and I reeled as the stench of old garbage assaulted my nostrils. I'd been gone for over a week, and my old food leftovers had ripened inside the garbage can, turning it into a fifth-grade science experiment. I tied the bag shut and took it down the hall to the garbage chute.

Gross.

It didn't take me long to realize the scent-containment properties of my old garbage bags had been vastly over-advertised, so I took the kitchen garbage can into the bath tub and filled it with soap and hot water.

A squeaky growl emanated from my belly; it was past lunchtime. Now, normally I'd fix myself a sandwich. Today, with great trepidation, I opened the refrigerator, alert for new, mutated life forms that might launch themselves at me.

I looked inside. Curdled milk, wilted lettuce, two cucumbers in a plastic bag now decaying into their typical primordial ooze. The plain yogurt container looked promising—I opened it only to shut it again, afraid the fuzzy, lacelike mold it harbored on its surface would crawl out and attack me.

The bread was moldy, the cheese was hard, and the two remaining apples smelled gross from everything else. Only the condiments were still good: mayo, ketchup, mustard, hot sauce. Hardly the lunch of champions.

After pulling another kitchen bag from under the sink and decontaminating the offending refrigerator, I opened the cupboards. There was a can of Spam, a bag of marshmallows, two cans of tuna fish, a jar of peanut butter, and several cans of off-brand chicken noodle soup I bought on sale a long time ago. I gave the soup a good second look. If I squinted hard enough, it was the most edible item around.

While the soup was heating in the microwave, I attacked the now empty fridge with a sponge and hot, soapy water.

Never again.

I'll never leave food in the fridge like this.

Revolting.

The freezer happened to contain three leftover waffles; I toasted them just to be able to throw the box away. Having washed my hands, I sat at my little table, eating my chicken soup and cinnamon waffles, staring at a pad of paper. It was time to make a new list of things to buy.

Unless I wanted to throw away perfectly good food again, I'd make sure to buy only that which would last. Canned soups, chili, beans. Crackers. Evaporated milk in a can. Was I nuts? Didn't I intend to *live* here anymore?

The thin, salty soup cooled before me as I inspected my shopping list, having added condoms, shampoo, a fresh razor blade....

A warm, fuzzy feeling washed over me and I wiggled in my chair, blood rushing to all the right places. I felt the delicious wisp of Jack's silk underwear transport me to another time and place. I closed my eyes.

"Grrrawwwwhrrr!"

Oh yes.

Oh yeah, baby.

I strove not to touch myself.

"Grrrawwwwhrrr!"

Yanked out of my happy dream world, I fumbled for my phone and had to wrestle it out of the too-tight pocket. "Jack?"

"Hey, Wyatt… everything okay?" he asked, and a shiver shook the tendrils of sensuous memories off my shoulders at the sound of his voice.

"Ah… yeah. Why?"

"You sound a bit out of it. Where are you?"

"My apartment." The silence stretched a bit after I said that.

"Oh yeah? What's going on?"

"You should've seen my refrigerator. So gross! Agh." I heard him laugh on the other end.

"I'll be home late," he said. "Something's come up at work."

"Yeah, me too—I have a thing tonight," I said, distracted, as we both hung up.

I FELT like a vagrant, lugging my extra-long duffle bag full of clothing, pictures and books, and my grandfather's cuckoo clock. His father brought it from Germany at the end of the World War II; it was a lovely antique and, despite the fact that it usually didn't run, I've always been unreasonably attached to it. Then I had my backpack with my laptop and my gym clothes and climbing gear; I probably looked like I was moving.

Wait! No! I wasn't moving. I still had my own place; I paid the bills and I even watered the cactus. It was just that wild, fuzzy feeling I had, like being wrapped in cotton candy.

Somehow, staying with Jack had become not only acceptable but even desirable. I had the hots for him, took a video of him, had his voice for my ring tone—my own place felt drab and cold, and it had nothing to do with the décor or the temperature.

Maybe I needed to redecorate. Yeah, then I could move back in.

REYNA met me at the Loose Rock climbing gym almost an hour later.

"Early?" I cocked my eye at her with a sly grin.

"Yep! Auguste let me go early 'cause of your mystery here." She nodded at the large, clear plastic bag full of Celia's climbing gear.

We decided to climb first and see who else would show up. My muscles positively sang with joy at the exertion, my hamstrings screamed in pain after having been idle for too long, and the gunshot wound in my ass was but a distant, dull ache. I strapped into my harness for the first time in what felt like forever, and took my time ascending one of the easier routes to the top. Reyna belayed me down; then she took her turn, upping the ante by avoiding the easier and more obvious handholds and footholds.

"Boring." I laughed. "I'll try that route over there." I nodded at the wall and noted the lack of easy routings before I chose my path and stepped up to the wall. I tied myself in.

Reyna anchored herself in first to floor anchor, which in this case was a massive bolt in the floor. Then I handed her the other end of the climbing rope. She ran it through her stitch plate, a simple breaking device she preferred over the GriGri.

"Belay on?" I asked.

"On belay," she replied. I looked up at the nasty piece of work above my head. It had wide spacings, small handholds, and an overhang. I flattened my belly to the wall and started climbing. My fingers felt strong, and my toes were sticking to the wall like glue. In rock climbing, the real power comes from the legs, which is why women can be just as good and just as fast as men in this sport. My legs were fine, and I felt only a twinge of tension in my right glute.

Soon I was under the overhang. It consisted of a negative incline that jutted out at least a foot away from the wall and loomed over my head. There was a way to get on top of it, if I could only reach a foothold to my far right. I dug my fingers in tight and flexed my shoulders to keep steady. It was just a matter of balance. My abs were sucked to the wall. I let my butt hang out momentarily in an effort to use mere friction of my feet against the smooth surface. I smeared my left foot against the wall right before I crunched my lats in an effort to swing far out and catch my right toe on the foothold.

Almost.

Wheee!!!

Free fall—then a tug, then a harder arrest, and I was swinging fifteen feet above the padded floor, breathing hard.

Reyna let me down. "Your glute's still bothering you," she commented. "You'd had no trouble with this section before."

I rubbed my sore butt, then I rubbed my aching hands and fingertips. "Yeah. It'll come back, though."

"Why did that guy shoot you again?" Reyna asked.

I'd never confided in her, uncertain of the reception I'd receive. Not everyone wanted to be best friends with a burglar and a thief.

Then again....

"If I tell you, it goes no further, right?"

She nodded. I looked around the empty gym; we were alone. I got us each a bottle of a vile, blue sports drink out of the vending machine. Bright blue… it reminded me of Jack's eyes and then it didn't seem so bad anymore.

I told her.

"So you're telling me only because you're retiring?" Reyna asked. She had a speculative look in her eyes.

"I haven't mentioned anything about retiring," I said, suddenly peevish.

"Jack doesn't like it."

"Yeah."

"Will you miss it?"

"I hope not."

Reyna downed the rest of the blue liquid. "Too bad. Ever thought of getting a partner?" she asked, her eyes suddenly on me, her question loaded.

"Ever thought of getting a criminal record?" I shot back, sounding too much like Jack.

"We wouldn't have to steal anything. Just think of the prank potential!" Her wistful voice awakened a latent desire deep in my soul. It's been a while since I invaded somebody else's space. I stared at the cold, blue drink and it seemed to stare right back at me, blue and unyielding. The choice between Jack and my B&E adrenaline fix was really no contest, and I was about to tell Reyna that when Tim walked in. He was an old friend of mine, and even though he and Reyna broke up a few months ago, they still manage to play nicely.

"Hi, you two," he said and ran his fingers through his spiky hair. "So, Wyatt, what's the mystery?"

"I'll tell you when everyone's here," I said. As if on command, I heard the front door slam shut, and a small Hispanic guy sauntered in.

"Chico, just the one we're waiting for!" Reyna exclaimed and jumped to her feet, giving both guys a friendly slap on their shoulders. Then she turned to me. "Well?"

CHICO GARCES was almost my height, but slightly narrower in the torso. He wore purple microfiber tights and a black, tight, sleeveless shirt. He earned his sinuous and well-defined muscles years back as a gymnast, and the conditioned gleam of his straight, black hair betrayed his fixation with his appearance. He was the type of guy who would have regular facials, manicures, pedicures, and massages, which he traded in kind for his services as a chiropractor. When we went to parties, we ribbed him over it incessantly, but he would just smile, toss his shiny hair to the side, and offer us another round of his awesome frozen margaritas. Right now, his nails were short and covered with two layers of clear shellac polish. Nails take an awful beating during rock climbing—mine were scraped and chipped constantly, never growing past my fingers' natural length.

I remember having asked him why he even bothered applying nail polish.

"It protects my nails," he said, bending his hands to show his one-week old manicure. "Without those two layers, my hands would look pretty trashed. And only shellac will take this kind of abuse, too. My patients find trashed hands disconcerting." And, truly, one week and three climbing sessions later, his nails looked only a bit scratched up. That was Chico for you, though. He cared about that kind of a thing.

I told them to sit down and set the plastic bag with Celia's climbing gear in the middle of our little circle. They all settled down and listened until I was finished with the story.

"So, the timeline looks like this," I summarized. "She was climbing as a semipro and picked up a part-time job doing accounting for Provoid Brothers. She was okay for maybe half a year. Then all the media started to notice the discrepancies in Provoid Brothers' stock valuation. Somebody from inside the company leaked some information, which pointed to Provoid Brothers' being just a house of cards—financially speaking—and they were hiding it using fraudulent accounting and reporting practices. Three weeks after this, Risby Haus, the VP of Collections, took Celia out on their first date. According to Jack, they got along pretty well, and Celia started to teach Risby rock climbing. All the while not realizing that he is in fact a top-notch, world-class climbing legend who just happens to hide behind his pseudonym, Demon of Santa Teresa."

Tim Nolan, who worked for a regional newspaper, drew a sharp inhale. "Yeah, a guy like that has no business making any mistakes while checking her fall."

I took her gear out piece by piece. I examined each component and passed it to Reyna, who passed it to Chico, who passed it to Tim.

We found nothing wrong with her harness. Its nylon webbing was strong and its buckles were fully functional. The carabiners looked okay—they were simple, oval devices made to screw shut and stay that way. The rope was slightly worn, its sinuous, green coil sitting snakelike in our midst. This very line slipped through Risby Haus's

ZIPPER FALL

belay device, allowing Celia to fall to her death. Next came two belay devices: a yellow GriGri 2, used by Risby to belay Celia, and a scratched-up blue GriGri, which Risby used to belay himself.

"How do you know which is which?" Tim asked.

"I am not sure, but Jack thinks this one was Celia's, because it's older and she was the more experienced climber. And blue was her favorite color. I figure it stands to reason that Risby, the novice, would buy the newest version of the equipment."

"Okay." Tim sounded mollified for a moment, but then his investigative journalist mind engaged again. He sounded downright suspicious. "Were the GriGris theirs?"

"So I'm told. Risby bought his shortly after Celia started to 'teach' him."

"Yet he handled her device for her. How come?" Reyna asked. "Wasn't it just a level 5.3 climb?"

"She was teaching him to belay her while she climbed the lead." I sighed. "From what I've read about the accident at the North Face gym—where they don't really want to talk to me about it, by the way—she usually climbed solo. That's why she had a GriGri to begin with."

We sat in a circle with our legs crossed. The equipment pile was in the middle, and nobody seemed to want to reach out and touch it first. Whether it was because this was somebody else's gear or because the climber was dead, I wasn't sure.

The lull in the conversation gave me some time to think. When securing one another, all we needed was just a simple stitch plate. Climbing on your own, it was advisable to go a little more high-tech, which is why Celia bought her device, and presumably because she used it, Risby decided to use it as well. But high-tech toys tended to break at times, and that's why Tim brought out his toolbox.

"Let's have a look at these babies," he said, breaking the uneasy silence. Tampering was, of course, strictly prohibited by the manufacturer, but we did it anyway. We often found ways to improve gear we bought already used, saving a lot of money. If you and your buddies build something with your own hands and trust it, well... you're good to go.

Tim worked until the metal plate snapped off and showed the mechanism on the inside. The rope was supposed to pass through multiple openings. If it did so slowly, the rope would pass with ease. If it got yanked hard, though, the increased friction made it choke up those little holes, and the rope stopped going through.

"He has a newer model," Tim noted. The anodized metal gleamed yellow and bright. There was really no reason to tamper with it, but we opened it up anyway. Still, no problem presented itself: both devices looked sound. We put them back together.

"Let's try it," Chico said. He stood up, clipped Celia's beat-up GriGri to his harness, and fed the rope through. He climbed up a few feet, took the slack out of his own line, and let go.

There he was, dangling in the air on one of our green, ten-millimeter-thick ropes.

"Worked fine for me," he said, shrugging once he let himself back down. "Now Risby's," he said, repeating the process with equal success.

"Any difference?" Reyna asked.

"Risby's was a bit smoother, but it's newer, and a newer generation, too. I was thinking of buying one like that."

"What about her rope?" I asked.

"Just a rope." Chico shrugged, picking it up and coiling it about his hands. "Used, a bit dirty. Wow!" He reached for his water bottle and squirted his fingers clean. I saw him rub his hands. His eyes widened in dismay. "Why the hell are my nails so dirty all of a sudden?"

I gave him a bemused look. His formerly white, pristine fingers now sported black half-moons under the edge of his nails. "How beautiful, Chico," I teased, unable to resist.

He snorted. "Let me go wash this off. The rope has been used outside, after all."

We played with the rope some, waiting.

"All clean, Princess?" Tim teased.

"Shut up, Tim. It's even worse now." We looked at his hands; a blue stain seeped from under his fingernails over the rough calluses of his finger pads. He looked a mess.

"Heh, that reminds me of the time we were in college, tie-dyeing T-shirts without gloves," Reyna chortled.

There was something important here, something significant. Green rope. All green ropes made by SpiderSilk were between ten and eleven millimeters thick. Thinner ones were red, and the thinnest ones went down to seven to eight millimeters and were yellow.

"Wait... wait, guys. How thick is this rope, really?" Tim always questioned everything. This quality got annoying at times, but it was awfully useful now. His voice was deadpan straight as our thoughts moved in the same direction. His face was as white as a sheet.

"It's green, it should be a ten," I said. I bent over to pick up the coil and walked it over to the wall, where I compared it to one of our own green ropes. "Is it just me, or does Celia's rope look thinner than it should?" I said.

"Tie-dyeing," Reyna forced out next to me. "I'd bet my next week's salary that bastard over-dyed a thin yellow rope with blue dye to make it look green. Out in the field, you'd never notice."

"Not if you think it's your own old line," Chico said, his expression grim. "When I was looking into buying the GriGri 2, like Risby Haus used, I wanted it because it can handle any thickness—but the older model Celia had, well...."

"It can use only the thick rope," Tim finished for him. "Rated ten to eleven millimeters. Thinner ropes will slide right though. That bastard."

We ran a simple test designed to prove whether we were right. Chico used Celia's GriGri and Celia's thin, green-colored rope. We all agreed it was best if Chico were double-belayed, with me holding him on the suspect rope and using Celia's old device, while Reyna did the same thing with her own, reliable ten-millimeter climbing line and simple number-eight plate. The plan was to give Celia's old gear a fair chance. If it failed to work, Reyna would break Chico's fall with the other set of equipment. Both of us were anchored, making use of the ground straps attached to the strong bolts and cemented into the floor itself inches under the rubber padding. I watched Chico's lithe, graceful form climb all the way up to the ceiling.

"Okay, I'm ready." His voice was cool and steady. "I'm letting go on three. One, two, *three!*"

Chico let go of the wall, falling backward, simulating Celia's fall. I did my best to make Celia's older GriGri arrest his fall. He slowed down a little, but not nearly enough. The thin, green-dyed rope slithered right through the belay device as he hurtled toward the ground. As he descended, the thick belay rope kept slipping through Reyna's hands and her stitch plate.

Reyna was letting Chico fall, giving me every chance to arrest his fall with the thin rope and the blue GriGri.

They failed.

Two-thirds of the way down the wall, Reyna lifted the rope up and over in her experienced hands, exerting force, creating friction and slowing Chico's calamitous progress toward the thinly padded floor.

There.

Chico swung on the end of Reyna's rope, having been halted only five feet before he hit the ground. His luminous black hair looked even blacker in contrast with his pale face.

"You okay, Chico?" Tim asked.

The slighter man swallowed a few times before his voice returned. "Yeah."

Once down and back on the ground, he straightened and took a few deep breaths, letting the air out in a long stream. "How far did you let me fall, Reyna?" he asked in a conversational tone.

"Little over twenty feet," Reyna said. "Sorry. Had to give the GriGri a chance."

Chico nodded. "It's okay. The GriGri usually engages within five feet, and it gives a famously hard stop. It definitely flunked the test."

WE WERE all shaken up and starving; a pizza was in order. The natural course of action was to go to Conti's, a joint near the gym where the locals knew us and we knew the menu by heart.

The mood was somber. Now we knew how Celia died; however, the chain of evidence had been broken long ago and there was no way to prove Risby Haus was the murderer.

"I bet he let her climb all the way up." Reyna ruminated over her beer. "I bet he stopped feeding the rope to her, which took her off balance."

"He might have even pulled," I said. "GriGris can have that problem in the hands of less-experienced belayers."

"Which would have given him cover for the accident," Tim murmured, his voice bitter and dark. "Just pull and let her fall until the rope slips out of the device itself. And the thin rope would have done just that."

We ate a lot of pizza and wings and drank a lot of beer. None of us had to drive, so we did some shots. The topic slowly drifted to our own climbing war stories, close calls of bad falls, calamitous close calls....

"Once I hung on a building in a rainstorm," I said, alcohol having loosened my tongue.

"No shit!"

"Yeah." I hiccupped and giggled. "I was delivering a marketing study to Jack, my esteemed client." I hiccupped again.

"What happened?" Chico asked, his eyes glimmering with amusement.

I told the story—only the good parts. Then I did another shot of tequila. "The rest is history. That's how I got together with her brother."

We all spoke of Celia as though we knew her personally. There were people out there who had in fact known her and would have been interested in finding out what happened.

"We have to take this to the North Face," I said. "We... we need to reassure ourselves that we're right." I rubbed my numb cheek, vaguely aware I was slurring my words.

"All the guys at the North Face are stuck-up bitches," Chico said, tossing his head.

"You know them personally?" I challenged. The bald guy, Carlos, had been really nice.

"No, but—"

We spent a little while discussing whether and how to approach the climbers at the North Face, and continued drinking in honor of Celia and speculating on ways to bring Haus to justice. After a while, I kind of got shitfaced.

Chico frowned. "They might not even believe—"

"Grrrawwwrrr!"

Everyone looked toward me, seeking the source of the unusual sound. Reyna's eyes brightened in amusement, and I felt myself redden. My phone had another two orgasms before I managed to extricate it from the bottom of my backpack pocket. They stared at me incredulously, not quite believing their ears. "Heya, Jackie," I said in a jaunty tone. "I missh you."

"Wyatt—are you all right?" He had been asking me that question all day long today.

"You betcha your schweet assh I'm awright!" I slurred some more. Reyna broke into her typical, uncontrollable peals of laughter, and the guys snickered, banging their fists on the table.

"You are drunk."

"Yesssh. I am. But I love you—hic!—anyway." Now I wasn't only slurring, I was hiccupping and saying....

Oh God.

Not that.

Tell me I didn't say that.

"Coming home soon, Wyatt? It's after midnight."

"Oh. I dunno. I'm on the other side of town." Usually, when we climbed late and drank even later, we all crashed over at Chico's place. Chico nodded at me encouragingly. "Chi… Chico lets us crash at his pad when we get—hic!—like thish."

"Who are you with?" Jack asked, and I could just feel the tense set of his shoulders in his voice.

"Our climbing gang," I said, enunciating very, very slowly. "My best friends! Reyna, and Tim, and Chico."

"I'll come get you," Jack said, sober and calm.

I could feel his steely resolution, but I wasn't ready to leave my buddies yet. I wanted to bunk with them and endure their rude farting jokes and pretend the whole thing with Chico falling over twenty feet never happened. In fact, I hadn't seen them in too long, and crashing at Chico's overnight was exactly what I needed. "No. I... I'll stay here tonight.... Hic!"

"What's Chico's address?" Now I could hear the way his jaw muscles worked, all tight and struggling for control.

I sighed. There was nothing for it—I just had to tell him the truth. "Don't worry, Jackie! I jus.... I jus' need shome time with Reyna and the guys. We figured out how your shister—hic!—was killed, and we are all traumatized. Poor Chico, he fell over twenty feet testin' my theory.... We're gettin' sssshitfaced, Jackie!"

"Wyatt...." There was alarm in his voice.

"Don't worrry, Jackie! We're all gettin' sssshitfaced to—hic!—to honor the mem... the mem'ry of your shister. She was one tough broad and an awesome climber."

"Wyatt. Let me talk to Reyna."

"Okay."

I passed the phone to the very amused Reyna. "Hi," Reyna said, and before my head hit the table, I vaguely recall having felt very relieved she didn't call him Azz-hole.

I WOKE up in the middle of the night. I was on the floor on one of the sleeping bags we always used at Chico's place. My head swam a little, and all those chicken wings began to flap around in my stomach.

I bit back a groan. Best get it done and over with.

Very, very slowly I rolled onto my side. Then I eased onto my knees and got up, navigating the small apartment by memory.

The bathroom—here.

I flipped the switch, flinching away from the light. Then I got rid of those pesky chicken wings and pizza and tequila and beer. I rinsed my mouth with water and used some of Chico's mouthwash, cleaned myself up, and pattered slowly to my little spot on the floor.

There was a giant lump there in the dark, right next to where I always slept. I eased my way down, feeling better but still fighting nausea. A familiar scent of aftershave and musk wafted to my nostrils.

"You okay, Wyatt?" Jack whispered.

Here was that question again. If he'd asked me any other questions that day, I had already forgotten—it was all drowned in a barrage of inquiries after my health. A wave of irritation washed over me. Can't a guy have a night out with his friends? "Yeah," I said, settling next to him.

"OK," he said, draping his arm over my torso and pulling me in. Only as I turned to my side, my eyes closing of their own volition, did I realize Jack had brought me my own, favorite pillow.

CHAPTER
FIFTEEN

"Wyatt... Wyatt... Wyatt...."

I batted my hand at the source of the repetitive, disagreeable noise. It had to stop. My body wasn't done sleeping yet. Hung over and dehydrated, with my eyes glued shut and my hair in my eyes like a stringy mop, I turned away and buried my face into my pillow. The rustle of the sleeping bag fabric underneath hurt my ears.

"There are other ways," said another voice, full of mischief.

"I bet I can wake him up pretty fast for you."

"C'mon, guys," a calm baritone intoned. "Another twenty minutes won't hurt anything. So what if he misses breakfast?"

The mention of food roused me some. I inhaled deeper, intrigued by the scent of bacon.

So good....

I felt my stomach growl, but it didn't turn over like it had the night before, and I was grateful for actually wanting to ingest food. Yet the voices around me filled me with morbid curiosity.

What will they do next?

The guys were a bunch of morons, and my best-ever girlfriend Reyna was no better. I kept my eyes shut tight, my breathing even. I felt a hand near me and forced myself to ignore it. I picked up the sound of a zipper opening. It went on and on—then the cool morning air hit my bare legs. I whimpered, wiggling deeper into the still-warm sleeping bag.

Wild hands ripped the cozy covers off me; a deluge of ice-cold water hit my body right after.

I shrieked, trying to strike at targets far out of reach. My face was drenched and my hair dripped water into my sleepy eyes. An errant ice cube slithered under my loose T-shirt and slid down my formerly warm and comfortable back. I was awake alright, surrounded by grinning faces. "You assholes!" I picked the ice cubes off my legs and from around my butt.

Seated in a freezing, sodden mess, I glared at Reyna's vile smile and Tim's easy grin. I met Chico's amused gaze with a petulant scowl. Then there was Jack. He, too, held a large, empty beer glass. The smooth container was still wet, telltale streaks tracking through the condensation on its sides.

"*Et tu, Brute?*" I shot in his direction, mock hurt in my eyes.

"I came to praise Caesar, not to bury him." His devastating grin split his face, bringing a bright twinkle into those impossibly blue eyes. He reached his warm, dry hand down for mine, offering help. I grasped it, pretending to get up—but then pulled him down, moving aside with every consideration for the comfort of his fall.

"Fuck, Wyatt. Now I'm soaked!"

Tim rushed off, presumably to rescue the bacon on the stove and Chico joined him, saying he had to crack the eggs. Only Reyna stood there, looking at us with an incredulous, hurt expression.

"Since when does he get to be Brutus? I thought I was your best friend."

The kitchen was small and the dining room nonexistent; we had to eat in shifts anyway, so I draped the wet sleeping bag over the railing of Chico's small balcony and opted for a quick shower first. My jeans were still dry and so was my workout shirt from the night before. After peeling the wet T-shirt and black silk boxers off my body, I was about to turn the shower on when Jack slipped into the small bathroom. He locked the door and leaned against it.

"We have to talk," he said without ceremony. His tone was serious and all business, and there was an air of urgency about him.

I wrapped my cold, wet body in a large bath towel and leaned my butt against the porcelain sink. "Right now?"

"Damn straight, right now," he growled, his eyes as hard as arctic ice. "Don't fucking ever do this to me again, Wyatt."

"Sorry... but you got me wet first."

His eyes were uncomprehending for a brief moment. He shook his head. "Not that. Just... what you... you did to me last night was...." He grasped for words, finding none.

Three steps spanned the distance between us. He crossed over and grabbed me by the towel draped over my shoulders and pulled me in. Every part of Jack was hard. His chest, his hands, his eyes. Gone was the tender lover who brought sunburn blushes to my face only twenty-four hours ago. Now fear and despair tightened the set of his mouth, and the squint of his eyes. The once-soft, generous lips were pressed together in an angry line; I saw his jaw muscle work hard, striving to retain control.

"Don't fuck with me like this. Don't you ever disappear like this again, only to be tracked down across town, drunk... and...." His nostrils flared as he took a quick, shallow inhale. "Don't fucking just disappear on me." His voice was but a whisper barely audible.

My mind swirled with mixed emotions. The intensity of his gaze set off a swarm of butterflies in my stomach. I've felt this before—a memory of Jack standing over me at Starbucks flashed through my mind—he'd been angry then, angry and sexy as hell. Now, in the tight privacy of the bathroom, he didn't look so pretty anymore.

"Jack...." I strove to placate him. There was a wild, feral edge to the energy he exuded, triggering what was left of my survival instinct. I didn't know why he was like this but obviously I'd played a key role in it. I felt my eyes soften, trying to understand his distress. "Jack, what set you off?"

He pushed me away. "What set me off? What am I supposed to think happened to you when you disappear like that? You could've called, left a note, anything. You still have that wound healing up.

Just…. And then…. *Dammit*." He let go of me, wiped his hand up his face, and ran his fingers through his hair. "Then I call you and you fuck with me."

"I don't remember saying anything objectionable."

"Ask your friends."

"Well, then, I will. After I have my shower." I dropped the towel over the rack and turned the water on and waited until it got just warm enough.

"Wyatt."

The bossy insistence of his voice grated on my nerves, and I turned my back on him as sudden resentment welled within me. I didn't need to check with him on every single thing. He could damn well wait until I was done and dressed before he got to drive his point home all over again. Streams of hot water erased the searing cold of the ice cubes off my skin. My hair was already shampooed and rinsed, and I was about to reach for Chico's conditioner when a draft of cold air hit my back and a chill body, still wet from ice cubes, pressed against me.

"Hey… you're making me cold again."

Jack only shut the shower-stall door and pressed his chest into my back, embracing me. "I thought I'd go where the action is." His voice was so choked, he barely got the words out.

"No action for Brutus. History has declared he hasn't gotten laid since the Caesar incident."

His hand skimmed the contours of my chest, tracing wet, warm fingers up my neck and to my chin, turning my face to the side. He didn't say a thing. His silence was palpable as his tongue traced the sensitive skin from behind my ear down, stopping only at the crook of my neck. Hot lips descended; an insistent arousal ground against the small of my back. Still eerily soundless, he pushed me around and into the corner.

I twisted to turn around; his intent was clearly written in his eyes. "Jack! Are you nuts? We can't do it in here."

"Watch me."

Anger welled up in my chest. "No. You watch me." I turned the shower off and met his eyes. "You are not my mother. I get to spend time with my friends whenever I want to, and I get to come home late, or the next day, if I want to. I've been spending time with this group of people, just like this, for years." I met his frozen, stunned gaze, and softened my tone. "I was not thrilled to see you last night. I've been hoping we could meet each other's friends another time."

His hands slid up the wall by my face and he leaned in and kissed the corner of my mouth, pressing his body against me. "Wyatt."

"I already said no." I evaded him, trying to slip to the side, away from the press of his body and his need. "Jack. I want you to leave this bathroom so I can take my shower."

His eyes hardened, blocking the warring emotions within, and his hands slipped down to my shoulders, squeezing hard. "Don't ever do that to me again, Wyatt." His grip was hard enough to hurt.

"Let go," I said.

"Don't you ever disappear on me."

"Jack, you're hurting me! Let. Go. Of. Me." I was pushed against the walls of a cold shower stall by a bigger, much angrier man. Hitting him where it hurts sounded good about now, and part of my mind was figuring out the best way to twist and plant an elbow in his gut when the panic in my voice got through to him somehow. He shook his head and looked at me—*really* looked at me this time, seeing fear and pain and disbelief—and he let go of my shoulders slowly.

Entirely silent, his face a blank mask of iron control, he turned around and left, closing the glass shower door and then the wooden bathroom door, and only then did I turn the shower on again as my angry tears mingled with the water. I forgot I had been hungry only minutes ago.

THE North Face Climbing Gym was open for business at six in the morning on Saturdays. By the time our group sauntered in, the regulars and early birds were long gone, and the space was full of kids and climbing wannabes. The ubiquitous vending machine that dispensed sports drinks was right next to the bathroom door; the display with Celia's memorial was on the other side. I nodded toward it. "They've done a good job."

With a corner of my eye, refusing to look at him directly, I saw Jack stiffen at the obvious expression of someone else's grief for the sister he'd loved and lost. Chico walked over, avoiding close proximity, still pissed over the two of us having ruined the pleasant morning for everyone else by exchanging cutting remarks, interspersed by icy silence. They skimmed the articles behind the glass, eyeing her trophies.

"Too bad I didn't get to meet her," Chico said. "I guess I run with a different crowd."

"What crowd would that be?" a low baritone intoned from behind us.

I turned around. The bald man was chewing fragrant cinnamon gum. His scrunched eyebrows gave his previously thoughtful look a fierce appearance. "Mmm… Carlos, right?" I asked, retrieving his name from my sore, hung-over brain.

He nodded at me. "Wyatt. From the Loose Rock."

"You know of me?" Confusion must have been written in my eyes. I'd never seen him down there.

"I make it my business to learn about anyone who's interested in Celia's death." His voice was low and menacing.

I didn't see Jack turn, but I felt him, the heat of his body radiating right behind me, and I drew away, because I was still sorting out my feelings regarding that morning's shower incident.

"Then you'd want to know that I'm her brother. Jack Azurri."

A LOT happened in a short period after Jack revealed his identity to the intrepid guardian of the North Face Climbing Gym. There had been a good bit of posturing and those too-tight, long-lasting handshakes, and Jack had to prove that he was, in fact, Celia's next-of-kin.

Soon we were all packed into the cramped little office in the back of the facility. A young, punked-out girl with wild eye makeup took over the front-desk traffic while Carlos poured burned coffee into paper cups, trying his best at hospitality under difficult circumstances.

"She is— Hell. She was the spirit of this place," he said, his shaved head gleaming under the fluorescent lights. "Our trainer, Craggs, he thought she had everything she needed to break through and go pro. She had the visibility, the charisma, everything. Then this one guy showed up, started flirting with her, and she got kinda distracted, y'know? She'd skip workouts to go out partying with him...." He cleared his throat and flashed a loaded look in Jack's direction.

"Yeah. She seemed really happy." The bitterness in Jack's voice exceeded that of the coffee scalding my tongue. "She thought he was 'the one.'"

"He's still around," I mused. "Question is, how to get him to jail."

"To jail?" Carlos's eyebrows rose, his tan forehead scrunched in lines. "For what?"

"Well... it so happens that Chico, here, made a startling discovery regarding the gear she used the day she died." Jack's voice was impassive, controlled. He handed the large plastic bag with Celia's gear over to Carlos. "Go ahead. You tell me. What's wrong with this picture?"

AN HOUR had passed; Craggs was on his way to the gym. So was Jubal Lupine, the detective who wanted me to tell him how I got shot in the rear two weeks prior.

We waited, alone with our thoughts, until Chico stood and stretched his toned arms all the way up, letting his T-shirt ride up and show his pierced navel. "No point just sitting around," he said, not marring his lovely face with a frown. He tossed his hair to the side, shooting a challenging look in Carlos's direction. "Will you at least let us boulder while we wait?"

What transpired next was rather amusing. Carlos's gaze locked with Chico's in a silent struggle. His lips widened in an easy grin. "Sure, you can climb if you're bored. Although... I better go supervise. Gym policy for newbies, you see."

The air was charged as they stared at one another. There was challenge and defiance, and competition so thick you didn't need a rock wall to get high.

"I'll come with you," I announced, eager to get out of the cramped, stuffed little room.

"You don't want to stay with me anymore?" Jack whispered.

"Not this second, no. If I don't feel like sitting next to you, it's your fault." And it was. My shoulders were sore, his grip marks were developing into bruises, and nothing would ease my foul mood like an easy climb with a few stretches afterward.

He pulled me down by my hand and kissed my shoulder lightly. "Sorry, Goldilocks. Got carried away."

"Would you two just get a room?" Tim snarled, unaccustomed to neither Jack nor any public display of affection. Tim, unlike us, was an intensely private sort. He didn't care what we did on our own time, as long as he wasn't personally exposed to it.

ONLY an hour later, the little office was packed even tighter than before. I opted to stand to make room for the proprietor, Craggs. He was a big guy with long, corded muscles and a black ponytail, and his face was as weathered as the rocks he probably climbed on his days off. He was pissed off royally and his anger simmered under a veneer of manners as thin as new-formed ice.

"So you're saying my star climber, the one I've been working with for years, got offed by this upstart who joined the gym not too long ago?"

Jack nodded. "That's the theory right now."

"And he's supposed to be this fabled legend I never got to see in real life? The phenom who did all those magazine interviews years ago?" Craggs fingered the too-thin rope, spitting on his fingers. "Let's see if this stains like Chico said it would." It did. "Fuck." His quiet, measured expletive sliced the air. "And she was so fearless."

"Maybe too fearless," Chico said. "Did she trust others easily?"

"She just hit it off with Risby. They were a natural team. He said he'd never climbed before, and I chose not to say anything. He was catching on awful quick for a newbie, but you notice things. No newbie can hang off his fingers, no matter how strong they are. You gotta get used to that."

"Why didn't you say anything?" Jack let out a low, pained growl.

"I figured she must have noticed, too. She looked so happy, y'know? And... I figured, why be a cock-blocker? If the guy was dumbing down to keep her happy, chasing after her, well... she was more than okay with it, so I let it slide. And then Carlos came on board. He's from out West, had been climbing out there for years, and he recognized him. Risby Haus must have moved east and landed in Pittsburgh some time after he retired from climbing. Now it comes out that he's the Demon of Santa Teresa. *Fuck*!" Craggs whirled and threw his massive fist into the wall. He made a hole in his office wall.

I think we all wanted to do that.

"WE NEED a motive, guys." Detective Lupine got there within half an hour and, his voice patient and calm, tried to instill order in a hornet's nest. "Why'd he kill his girlfriend, again?"

Tim cleared his throat. "She might have been a whistle-blower.... Remember that Provoid Brothers securities scandal?"

Lupine nodded.

"I'm a reporter and was working that story at the time. There were some deaths in their accounting department. I've tried to track down the apparent accidents and suicides this morning, but it's not hard to find someone nowadays. I found one of Celia's friends from work. A senior accountant, Joanne Tovissi. She used to report to the Vice President of Operations—Kevin Toussey was his name, I think. He's the one who didn't end up serving time due to medical reasons. Sudden blindness and some other stuff."

Everybody sat still in expectant silence.

"So where is she?" Lupine asked.

"Joanne Tovissi popped up in a Google search. Her memorial service was held two months ago. She was run down by a speeding car—there was no license plate."

ONCE the furor died and the people stopped shouting over one another in an effort to work through their countless speculations, Jubal Lupine threw a wet blanket on the whole party.

"Unfortunately, this gear will never be admitted into evidence," the detective said with a mournful expression. "Had the police collected it at the time her body was removed, it would have been okay, but the local force sees the occasional climbing accident and has little patience for out-of-towners getting killed on their watch." He sighed. "The only way to nab him is to have him confess."

"I can arrange for that," Craggs growled.

"No you can't. I'm her brother, it's my job." Jack almost rose out of his seat.

"Not like that, you ass—gentlemen." Frustration and poorly concealed amusement warred on Lupine's face as he shot Reyna, the only woman in the room, an apologetic look for his slip of tongue. "It has to be coaxed out of him so it's voluntary. It has to be wiretapped. I can get a warrant for that, but as soon as you lay even the small finger of your left hand on him, if it's part of a police action, you'll get his admission thrown out of court."

"So I can work him over afterward?" Jack asked, his eyes glinting like hard ice.

"I won't comment on that. I'm depending on you guys to not be stupid." He looked around, taking in our determined faces. "I guess that's too much to ask with your bunch, though."

MY BATH water was cooling. I turned on the hot water tap again and slid under, enjoying its soothing warmth on all the parts that ailed me. My mind whirled. Risby would have to be coaxed to 'fess up. This didn't include violence, but it might include being wily. Of all of us, I was the one best suited to do just that. My climbing skills, my looks, and my determination would help me take care of this pesky problem before Jack lost his patience, hunted down the traitorous asshole, and tore him asunder with his own two bare hands. The law took dim view of such acts of personal vendetta—Jack didn't want me in jail for burglary, but by the same token, regardless how I felt about him at the moment, I didn't want him in jail for murder.

A plan began to form in my mind as I swirled my hands through the water, watching the gentle waves travel out, then bounce back to me. I'd need to employ serious safety precautions. My mind followed various avenues of attack, paying special attention to defense. There was a way to make Risby talk. When I watched him climb that one time—and only one time, but still—I thought I'd noticed he seemed to have made an effort to flirt with me. It wasn't anything obvious, just a meeting of the eyes and a quirk of a smile where there didn't have to be one. I wasn't entirely sure yet, but something told me that Risby Haus might swing both ways.

JACK burst through the door, kicked his shoes off, and dumped a shopping bag on the dining room table. "Dinner!"

The clothing and personal items I'd brought in my huge duffel were all organized and stowed away; I was sprawled on my bed wearing Jack's new navy bathrobe, reading a climbing magazine. "Coming...." My lack of excitement for dinner had a lot to do with my general avoidance of conversation with my mercurial lover.

My head was still a bit sore from my hangover, but that had been my own doing.

My boundaries had been violated with the way Jack had approached me in Chico's shower.

My shoulders bore bruised imprints of his hands.

Worst of all, I didn't need to check with my friends to discover what possible words I might have exchanged with Jack the night before. The telephone call was etched into my memory.

In vino veritas.

There is truth in wine. Thinking back to the beginning of our unlikely relationship, I reviewed the milestones of our association one by one. The events were a comedy of errors and a compilation of embarrassments. The last of which was being held captive in a friend's shower, Jack's intent eminently clear. The memory of an angry Jack jumbled my conflicted feelings into a tangled mess—and considering the extent of the measures to which I had stooped in my pursuit of Jack Azurri, the situation had a sense of surreal poetic justice about it. Now he was pursuing me and I had the proverbial tiger by the tail.

Below the waist, I approved of his vigor. Above the waist, I had a hard time reconciling the attentive, generous, and gentle lover who was Jack Azurri with the possessive, primal beast that had tried to lay claim to my person, my schedule, and my independence. He had given me a glimpse of his dark side. His angry side, his violent side. That side was part of him, but I had said I loved him—and I had to make sure my statement held even now, under the light of new revelations of Jack's somewhat volatile nature.

"Hey, Wyatt…." There was a soft knock on my doorjamb. I caught a glimpse of his chestnut hair as he peeked through the open door. "Dinner's getting cold."

"Yeah. I heard." I flipped the magazine face down to mark my page.

Jack's eyes lit with interest. "Hey… we could go climbing together, y'know. I haven't been able to, lately, but… I really miss it." He was asking to enter into my world.

I nodded. "Okay."

I followed him out to the dining room, remaining silent and assessing: Could I love the bad with the good? Could I tolerate his fierce possessiveness along with the fatal attraction, the gentle caring?

My internal alarms screamed "Danger, danger!" as I hurtled through unknown space, lacking a reliable navigation system. Capturing his heart seemed to have come with a lot more complications than just breaking into his house and taking some cash out of his freezer would have done.

The scent of Indian food hit my nostrils. My favorite dishes were set out on the table in an elaborate gesture of apology. Dark saag paneer with its glistening cheese, orange tikka masala with fragrant jasmine rice, buttery naan flatbread. Cardamom and coriander and love.

I stopped in my tracks, motionless in the doorway. There was a candle on the table, its flickering light illuminating a sad supermarket rose in a washed-out mustard jar.

"C'mon, Wyatt." He wrapped his arm around my shoulder, gently leading me to a chair. There were no words, but the apology and regret in Jack's eyes spoke volumes.

Maybe I didn't have to move back into my solitary apartment with no bed.

Maybe I could stay.

CHAPTER
SIXTEEN

I WOKE up once again, restless and tired at the same time. Gray light of the early dawn filtered through the sheer curtains, leaving my room calm and cave-like. Six in the morning on an overcast Sunday, and my mind just would not stop spinning. I'd been like that all night long. It had been hard to fall asleep; yesterday was so busy and confusing, I needed more time to process it all. Usually, that meant just falling asleep and waking up with a clever insight or two.

Not this time. This time, small sounds kept waking me in the middle of the night. The building elevator. Jack tossing and turning two rooms away. Somebody flushing the toilet one floor above us.

My door was closed. Unequipped with a lock. Every time I woke up, I looked at the door, making sure it was still shut. At that time, I didn't know why.

No use trying to force sleep to come. I rolled out of bed and stumbled into the shower. The hot water was a relief. I always followed it with cold water just to wake up. It infused me with extra energy. Washed, shampooed, and exfoliated, I stepped out and reached for a towel.

Jack's towel.

I felt my chest squeeze at the thought as I was drying myself off. Yep, still sore from climbing. A look in the mirror made my stomach tighten; the bruised grip-marks on my shoulders had darkened overnight. The Mark of Jack. I shuddered at the memory of having felt so helpless and weak, and I wondered if that's what women felt like most of the time. As I patted my tender bits dry, a strange sensation brushed the back of my hand.

Stubble?

I bent over to have a look. Sure enough—what had been shaven so smooth on Friday had started growing back. I had a scratchy, two-day beard on my most sensitive parts. I clenched my legs together experimentally; tiny little pricks impaled my tender flesh. Turning toward the full-length mirror on the wall, I tilted my hips to take a better look.

My triangle looked like a dark-blonde hedgehog, the little African kind some people like to keep as pets. I touched the area. The tender skin of my thighs was waiting to tangle with my hedgehog, except the hedgehog was hoping to score first blood.

That asshole.

Pain shot through my back as I straightened from the awkward position, letting me know I overdid my climbing after my enforced rest. Even worse, thanks to Azz-hole, my whole groin now itched with regrowth. I considered my options: I could wait a few days. There had to be some kind of an anti-itch cream for these things. Like a men's aftershave—except just the thought of aftershave down there had me wincing with pain.

How about shaving it again? That option was out, definitely.

I could ask Jack to shave me, but if I did that, he'd see it as a party invitation, and I didn't feel hospitable.

Having decided to just suffer for a day and think about it, I reached for the door to retrieve my clothing from my room. I turned the doorknob—it wouldn't open. Slight panic seized me until I realized I must have automatically locked the bathroom door upon entry.

I never lock the bathroom door.

Absorbed by trying to figure out why I turned the lock without even thinking about it, I wandered out of the bathroom and put on my own underwear. Unlike Jack's silk boxer shorts, the elastic edges of my briefs dug into my groin lines, irritating the growing stubble. I chose to tune it out.

A locked bathroom door. Really?

I unlocked the bathroom door and, still pondering the implications of having locked myself in, I dressed for the day.

When Jack emerged from his lair, with his hair wild and a bathrobe loosely tied around his waist, I had already accomplished much.

"Mmm. Coffee?"

"Yeah," I said. "Want some?"

"After my shower. You're up early, Wyatt."

I nodded. "Yeah... couldn't sleep."

"You okay?"

I shrugged. "Go take your shower." I didn't want to bellyache about my stiff, sore back, my tender parts, and my jumbled thoughts. Having received his official apology over dinner last night, his behavior in the shower was officially forgiven. An apology didn't mean I felt comfortable cozying up to him, though. I felt like I was walking on eggshells, waiting for the volcano to erupt again, spurred by a hitherto unknown transgression on my part.

Jack gave me a long look. "Okay, then."

BY THE time he emerged from his room, refreshed and dressed for the day, my online purchases were finalized and paid for, and our toast and eggs were ready. We ate in tense silence.

"What are your plans for the day?" My question was phrased with care.

"The office." He sighed. "I was supposed to go yesterday, meet with Rick Blanchard, and go over those presentations for next week. We postponed for today. I should be done sometime after lunch. And you?"

"I have some stuff to do at my place. Also, don't forget we're meeting Reyna and Auguste for dinner tonight. Tamari, over in Lawrenceville on Butler Street. Seven o'clock."

Jack groaned. "God. Auguste can be so tiresome. Reyna and I do nothing but argue. Is this really necessary?"

"Reyna's my best friend. Auguste's a valuable business contact, not to mention a mentor of sorts. Yeah. It would be nice if you could join me… but I can go by myself, if it's too much to stomach."

"No. No! I'll join you." He spoke fast, his voice slightly alarmed. "You're buying the drinks, though. You owe me that much."

MY OLD black duffle bag was slung over my shoulder as I entered my one-bedroom apartment. It held my laptop and my grandfather's cuckoo clock and a change of clothes for more than just tonight. I didn't need much. Most of all, I needed some quiet time and space to myself. I needed to think.

The kitchen had been cleaned last time I was here; this time, I vacuumed the empty bedroom, doing my level best to erase the spots in the carpet where my almost-new Ikea furniture used to be. Presently, my furniture sat in Jack's spare bedroom, moved there during my brief stay at the hospital.

Without my consent.

The thought riled me all over again. My mind wandered back, enumerating all the slights Jack had ever committed against my free will. Against my person.

I've been punched.

Pistol-whipped.

Tied up.

Blackmailed.

I lost my job—but he bore only fractional responsibility for that one.

I've been made drunk and got really sick on his… product.

I had his papers thrown in my face.

I was convinced, against my better judgment, to return some rich guy his drug money.

I got shot in the ass—and for that, he bore some fractional responsibility as well.

I was moved to his place without my knowledge.

I had my privates shaved without being given a chance to have a say in the matter.

My well-deserved time out with my lifelong buddies was invaded, by his nagging as well as by his person.

I've been accosted while trying to take a shower alone.

I got punished for hanging out with my friends by harsh words and bruised shoulders, not to mention his looming physical presence.

Of all those things, the last one was the straw that broke the camel's back. As I hunched over my old vacuum, overcoming my nagging back pain to clean the dust bunnies and various crud, a feeling of panic kept invading my mind.

Stuck. Helpless. Wet. Cold. Dominated.

I had accepted his apology, but the alarming, dizzying feeling just wouldn't leave me. I felt like shit, and I didn't know why.

Right before lunch, delivery guys brought several large boxes and a plastic-covered mattress up to my floor. They used the service elevator and moved them through the door with care, making sure they fit.

"Are we takin' yer old stuff?" the foreman asked, his voice gruff.

"I have no old stuff," I replied. My old stuff was at Jack's. Once they left, I began opening the corrugated cardboard, mindful of nasty paper cuts. It was all there, black and shiny and beautiful.

Reyna arrived at noon. "Hey, Wyatt. So... what's the emergency?" She met me with her warm gaze, and I only sighed and looked away.

"Thanks for bringing lunch. What is it?"

"Peruvian chicken, bean salad, and brownies. Oh, and drinks. Diet Coke for me, milk for you. Right?"

"Right." I smiled. "The lunch of champions." We high-fived and took the food to the dining area to eat.

We were halfway done with the juicy, delicately spiced chicken when Reyna leveled a serious look in my direction. "So... spill it."

And I did.

"He *bruised* you?" Furious lines marred Reyna's forehead and her jaw was tight with anger.

"It's not as simple as that. I did tell him to stop, and I did say no, and he did stop... eventually."

"Bullshit," Reyna spat. "Are you dumping him?"

I paused, gathering my thoughts. "No... but I should have kicked him out of the bathroom right away."

"Why haven't you, Wyatt? Had that been Paul, you'd have broken his nose."

A fierce blush rose to my cheeks; it got only worse when Reyna noticed and raised her groomed eyebrows. "Why the fuck do you think, Reyna?"

"I dunno. You have a mouth on you most of the time. You tell me!"

I stabbed a bean with my fork, the violence of my action making it jump out of the take-out plastic container. This was just so hard to verbalize. I felt such shame all of a sudden. It hit me like a hammer. Had I been a kid, I would have cried, but since I was a tough guy, I only took my plate and threw it with all my force against the wall. It fell onto the kitchen's tile floor and shattered with a satisfying, explosive crack. The gnawed bones left a slick of chicken fat on the wall.

Reyna sucked in some air.

I struggled to formulate my thoughts. "It's different for you, I guess. There are rules against treating girls in a certain way. But I'm no girl, and being gay doesn't make me one either. Had it been Paul, I'd have kicked him out because I could, but... if we were boxing, Jack and I would be, what, like six or seven weight classes apart?" I looked her in the eyes, feeling no emotion. "It was fucking humiliating, Reyna. I thought, maybe... maybe I was tempted to just go along with it, y'know? Just go along with it. It's not really okay for a guy to ask for help. Sometimes the best you can do is save face."

She thought for a while, her eyes flat and unyielding. Then she nodded. "Did he apologize?"

I stood and picked up her plate and hurled it, sending it after the first one. It broke in half and slid partway, stuck to the wall by the remaining food; then it detached from the wall like a clumsy stinkbug and fell to the hard floor, shattering into sharp, jagged fragments. I relished the sound. "Yeah...." I sighed, my voice barely audible. "The next day. I did accept his apology—but I still feel angry about it. Being manhandled like that, and his advances, the time and place, intruding on my buddy time like that—I... I just felt so helpless to prevent it or stop it—that's probably the most humiliating thing of all."

Reyna put the remaining food inside the refrigerator, safe out of my reach.

I finished cleaning up the mess I made. The process of restoring order helped me straighten my thoughts. As I stood up, I looked at Reyna, noting the length of her strong, sculpted arms and her height, her air of fierce determination, and I wondered how she would have fared in my situation. "I just... the control factor. It's just too much. Had he tried to do it in the shower just for kink, like with the shaving, it would have been different."

"Shaving?" Reyna's eyebrows rose.

"Ask me later... but it was good. This time, though... he was just so, so, so—"

"He was angry." Reyna stated a fact as though she'd been there.

"Yeah! Furious! I've never seen him like that before."

"I have." Reyna sighed. "Azz-hole has a bit of an anger problem. He usually doesn't lose his cool, but he does blow up at times. Being around him when he's like that definitely requires special fortitude. No secretary lasts past the two months mark. I was the exception because I worked for him while he was taking a lot of personal leave. I'm told he used to be a lot worse, but that's not saying much."

I drank my milk, my mind devoid of thought. The whole affair was bloody depressing. My perfect partner had a Persian flaw the size of Tehran.

Reyna changed the subject. "So what's all this stuff you need help with, Wyatt?"

I surveyed the scene. Over half of the emergency cash from my secret hiding hole in the closet wall was gone, invested in new bedroom furniture. "I'm remodeling, and my back hurts too damn much to be toughing it out and assembling and moving all this stuff by myself. Plus, there's the benefit of your scintillating company."

Ignoring my sarcasm, she walked over and inspected some of the pieces. "Looks like you're finally treating yourself to the good stuff."

"Yeah. I decided I'm worth it."

A place of my own.

"Y'know, I've come to realize I'm probably destined to be by myself in this lifetime," I commented, fingering my new blue, black, and gray area rug rolled up by the wall with its ends poking out of its plastic wrap.

"How do you figure?"

"Well… people leave me. Sometimes, they drive me away. Mom died, Dad kicked me out when he found out about me and Paul, Paul and Susan started a family…." I sighed. A feeling of loss suffused me. Not regret, never that. Just, a small piece of my heart was empty as I allowed myself to feel their absence every so often. "I've done well, not attaching myself. Then Jack shows up. He looks perfect, but… I just don't know. He has that bad-boy aura, and that's very sexy, but only in moderation."

There was that feeling again—the feeling of impending chaos and destruction. My crazy father used to trigger it with his random, unpredictable behavior that occasionally transgressed into the physical. He thought being hypercritical of my every move on a regular basis was a way of showing he cared.

"You still have your sister and your brother." Reyna's voice tried for upbeat and hopeful.

"I can't burden them. They need to grow up, be free. I should be taking care of them, not the other way around."

"You have friends."

I flashed her a small grin. "Yeah. Amen, sister. My friends make my world go 'round."

At five, we hopped into Reyna's car and ran out to a local big-box store that had just about everything. I bought new turquoise and gray bedding with a comforter, and new pillows and towels to match. It all went really well with my white walls and the blue, gray, and black rug by the side of my new queen-size bed. There was a large mirror on the wall that reflected the pristine, white curtains and blue and black valance. It looked about as personal as an airport hotel.

Just as we were next to check out and pay, my eyes fell upon the wall behind the registers. It was covered with affordable, ready-to-hang art. "And I'll have that one," I said, not thinking twice.

I didn't know what possessed me to buy that huge acrylic painting. There was something thrilling about its flame-colored sunset against a powdery blue sky, its stunning display of flamboyant color reflecting in the window glass of tall skyscrapers. The buildings looked soaring and hopeful despite their gray concrete. Colored light reflected in their huge windows. Clouds floated by, their distorted images like watercolors seeping into old paper.

"That's a little tall, Wy. It will never fit above your bureau."

"It will. I'm hanging it sideways."

WE RINSED off quickly, taking turns and changing into the nicer clothing we'd brought with us. I slipped into casual charcoal trousers and a black dress shirt that had never failed me, tousled my hair with a bit of gel, and I was done. Well, actually I spent a lot more time on the hair than I had on getting dressed. Brushing it out, fluffing it up, and making it obey my will felt a lot like putting on war paint before the tribe encountered the white invaders. Only the rest of me was the same as ever: plain and unadorned.

I saw Reyna in her black jeans, a green silk blouse, and a black and red leather jacket.

"The jacket? Really?" I smiled, remembering the time she found it in a thrift store many years ago. It had been love at first sight.

"It has pockets, so I don't have to carry a purse. It's getting colder, too."

She was right—the weather had broken and leaves were beginning to turn. My jacket was at Jack's, but I had another one from years ago. After some rummaging, I found it: an old coat from a vintage store. It was fitted from the waist up, its stand-up collar offsetting my jawline and cheekbones. From the waist down, the coat draped down my legs in a graceful swirl, reaching well below my knee. I never buttoned it all the way down, so it didn't look like a dress. Its dove-grey lining peeked as I moved before the mirror.

"You still have this old thing?" Reyna asked, amazed. "I haven't seen it in years. What a rag."

"You're just jealous." I grinned. "Ready?"

Tamari was twenty minutes on foot from where I lived. We sauntered up in companionable silence, arriving fashionably late, only to see Auguste and Jack standing outside the establishment, immersed in quiet conversation.

"They're talking. You think Jack told him anything?"

Reyna flashed me a surprised look. "Why would he? Giving you bruises isn't something to boast about."

I gave a relieved sigh. "I guess."

Auguste looked odd without his suit and tie, although the white leather jacket fit him fine, forming a canvas to counterbalance his natural pallor and black hair. Jack was dressed up in a beige suit that offset his chestnut hair to an advantage—only his tie picked up the blue of his eyes. He was dressed up as though this was a date and it mattered.

He looked me up and down, his gaze hungry. "Wyatt."

"Hello, Jack." I turned to Pillory and offered my hand. "Good to see you, Auguste."

His solemn eyes warmed as he nodded. "And it's good to see you, Wyatt. Shall we?"

Reyna only nodded in Azurri's direction, receiving a similar curt nod in return. Reyna and Auguste walked between us, brushing their fingertips. They made a good buffer between Jack and myself.

We had some wine with dinner; the food was very good as always. We discussed politics and the business climate, then decided to skip dessert. I was dying for some chocolate cake, but Auguste declared he was paying, and I knew he wasn't a dessert eater, so I didn't order any. So far, so good. No disasters, no horrid clashes of opinion, no spoiled dishes that had to be sent back. I excused myself to go to the restroom and wound my way between the tables to the stainless-steel bead curtain, which separated the entrance to the restroom from the bar area.

The men's room marble floors swirled with designs belying their metamorphic origin; the stalls were made of reclaimed dolomite, and I took a bit longer than usual, seeing how many different fossils I could find on my door. Realizing I'd gotten a bit distracted, I finished up and rushed out.

Auguste sat at the table alone.

I sat down and looked around. "Where are they?"

Auguste trained his gaze at me. "They are outside."

"But they don't smoke!"

"They need to talk." His eyes softened as he looked me over. "Are you feeling well, Wyatt?"

The question surprised me. Rarely, in my two years of employment at his company, had he asked me a direct and personal question. "What do you mean?"

He didn't say anything for a while. Then he averted his eyes in that "this discussion is over" way of his. But it wasn't. "Jack used to have a frightful temper when he was much younger. Did you know that?"

I shook my head, not liking where this might lead.

"If there is anything you'd ever like to discuss, even matters of… a personal nature, please do not hesitate to talk to me. If you have the need, that is."

My eyes widened in shock and heat rose up to my cheeks. "Th-thank you, Auguste." I still felt ill at ease using his given name, but his offer was nothing short of astounding. Sipping my coffee, I tried to disguise my surprise.

"Ah, here they come. The bill is settled. We may leave anytime."

I looked at Reyna's date. Whatever warmth there had been in his face evaporated, leaving him with his customary mask of feigned calm and indifference I'd come to associate with old money.

Reyna sat down next to Auguste and reached for her tea. "It sure has gotten colder out there," she said, warming her hands on the large cup. She smiled, but her smile didn't quite make it all the way up to her eyes. I shot her a questioning look, but she shrugged. "Jack," Reyna said, "I'll be leaving with Auguste. It's been so good to clear the air. I'm sure you and I could easily work together now, as things stand."

Jack nodded his head, clearing his throat. "Yeah." His voice was a bit raspy and not very strong. He turned to me. "I drove to get here. You... would you care for a ride?"

My eyes flashed a quick look at his sapphire blue irises; they gave away nothing. "My place isn't far from here," I mumbled, not eager to be left alone with him. We would probably have to talk then, and it would lead to unpleasantness.

"What a great opportunity for Jack to see our hard work today," Reyna said in a chipper voice, and I felt something kick my shin. I looked at her face and the way she looked radiant with her hair flowing loose the way she thought Auguste liked it, and I knew it had been her.

Something was afoot.

"Sure," I said, turning to Jack again, unease seeping to the very core of my being. "If you wouldn't mind...."

"It would be my pleasure." His tone was formal and polite.

I hardly knew what to make of it.

THE drive over was quiet. He offered to walk me up.

"Hey... come in." There was no use hesitating as I opened the door. He'd find out sooner or later.

"What's all the cardboard?" he asked, surveying my wreck of a living room.

"Those are the boxes the furniture came in. Here, come see!" Plastering an excited grin onto my face, I led him to my new bedroom. The frameless painting did indeed bring life to my private space. My grandfather's old clock hung on the wall beside it, adding just a touch of a connection to the old country. I walked in, inviting him to my inner sanctum.

His eyes took it all in, everything new, shiny, clean. "You don't like living with me." His voice was flat and hollow.

"I've come to realize I really appreciate having my own space," I said evenly, my eyes on the horizontal planes of the sideways city landscape.

"Wyatt...."

I turned my eyes to him.

"Wyatt, I am so sorry. I hadn't realized... I didn't hear you say anything specific at the time."

We both knew what he was talking about.

"Now I get it. Reyna said... Wyatt...." He crossed over to me, grasping my shoulders in his large hands.

I didn't mean to flinch, but the bruises were still tender.

He let go of me. "Is there anything I can do?"

I shrugged. "This is new territory for me, Jack. I... I just need some time. Some space. I want to build my business and see my friends and go climbing. I'll see you around a good bit, I expect."

"And you won't mind that?"

"N-no. I won't mind that at all."

He gave the room a look. "It's nice. I didn't realize you were so spartan in your taste."

"I'm not.... It reminds me of your room." The words just kind of slipped out, and there was no way to take them back.

Jack flashed me a small, diminutive version of his sexy grin. He took a step toward me and slowly took my hand, lifted it to his lips, and brushed his lips against my fingertips. "How are you feeling, Wyatt?"

I shrugged. "I accepted your apology, but... I'm sorry, but my feelings are... unsettled. I am still angry. I'm angry at you, and I'm angry at me."

"Why at yourself?" The warmth of his hand, the sincere curiosity in his voice, all that conspired to make something snap deep inside me.

"Because I'm so weak. So weak, anyone can invade my space in the shower and take what they want, if they're so inclined. And it's so damn hard to say something when things start to go bad. Jack... you were so angry... so angry.... I was afraid you were going to take things a bit further than either of us felt comfortable. You know, punish. Dominate. The whole situation—you pushing me around like that—everything about it felt just so... humiliating." My eyes felt slightly moist and red rage filled me at the memory. To my utter horror, I felt a teardrop escape my eyelids.

I never expressed negative emotions well. They have always been channeled into violence or antisocial behavior. It's not something I am proud of, but at this instant, I thought I needed to settle the score. Banish the fear. Reclaim what was mine. It wasn't the bruises on my shoulders I needed to banish—it was the sense of trust and security I mourned.

"I'm gonna slug you now," I told Jack right before I let my fist fly through the air that divided us. It cracked against Jack's cheek, splitting his upper lip.

He hissed in pain but didn't move. "I deserved that," he said with a curt nod, his words enunciated despite the thin trickle of blood coming down the corner of his mouth. "I'd never do that... I'd never take what you were unwilling to give, but, yeah... I've been an asshole."

He forced an exhale. "I... Wyatt... I think I'll always be alone. I don't play well with others. You know that by now. The people I love just wink out of my life before their time. My parents perished at sea—they hired a charter boat for their wedding anniversary. I was still in college at the time. The boat got caught up in a storm. They were gone, just like that. And then, last year, Celia. She was laughing at some stupid joke one day, then she headed out to the West-by-God for a quick climb, and... gone. Now you—when you disappeared off my radar screen like that, I—I panicked." His eyes shone bright, but his composure held. Jack wasn't the kind of guy who would cry. "My first thought was, another one down. Another one gone."

He stood on the threshold of my new bedroom, looking entirely bereft and alone. Ready to be told to please go, go and never come back. His haunted eyes misted over and he turned, headed for the door. The man I loved.

Leaving.

Another one was leaving me.

"Don't leave." I was behind him in a flash. I wrapped my arms around his waist and buried my face in his shoulder. "I'm staying here tonight. You're welcome to join me."

Jack turned around, letting his arms swallow me in a hungry embrace. We fit so well, he and I.

"There's just one thing...." I looked up at him, already tempted by his soft, passionate lips.

"Anything, Wyatt." His words were gentle.

"I don't feel like doing anything. Probably won't, not until the bruises fade."

"Oh... I'm so very, very, very sorry...." His words were whispered into the crook of my neck as we rocked from side to side, soothing one another. "What do you do to channel your anger?" he asked, finally breaking the long silence.

I shrugged. "I break dishes."

"Break dishes...." I heard his awed whisper by my ear. Somehow, he sounded like he was trying to remember a new phone number.

"Break dishes... break dishes... break dishes...."

CHAPTER SEVENTEEN

AFTER casting my suit jacket over a spare office chair, I unbuttoned the cuffs that restrained the pristine white sleeves of my work shirt and loosened my tie.

"Can't believe it's Thursday already," I yawned at Rick Blanchard. He was young—my age, I guess—and as his white-haired head lifted from the cheat-sheet for his introductory remarks, his pale blue eyes shone with an alien, almost maniacal gleam.

We were long past the introductory dance of two coworkers, where both parties are polite and a bit strained. He had asked his inappropriate questions about my relationship with Jack, presumably getting the lay of the land. I'd already retaliated by mentioning his freaky white hair, and was regaled with the tale of his sight-saving eye surgery that was somehow related to his lack of pigmentation. "It *was* scary," he said. "But better than being blind, right?" All that was just water under the bridge; now we worked like a well-oiled machine.

"The week went by pretty fast," he allowed. "You've been here for only a few days, though."

"I have other clients, too. Suddenly, I got slammed, and there's no way I can tell them to wait."

He chuckled his breathy laugh. "Keep goin' like that, and you'll have to start a regular company."

"I sent two of the bigger ones to Pillory."

He nodded. "A man of his word. Although I always knew you would be."

Rick performed his speech over and over until he sounded natural and not so nervous anymore. When he remembered not to speak to the ceiling or to the floor, we called Jack and his other partner, Louis Schiffer, to be our audience. As I looked around at them, it struck me as interesting that these guys were getting a fresh start in Pittsburgh after their pyramid scheme disaster, while their bosses sat in jail. The one exception to the jail part was Kevin Toussey, who escaped his jail sentence by going blind and living in an assisted living institution. There seemed to have been a connection between Risby Haus and Kevin Toussey, and I suddenly wondered whether the two were in cahoots over Celia's murder.

Rick ran through his PowerPoint presentation without a hitch.

"Not bad, not bad," Schiffer said in his customary monotone, eyes sparkling behind his glasses with attention to detail. Coming from him, it meant "Bloody fantastic! You're such a genius!"

Rick knew that. "I just follow the commands of our marketing queen here."

I could just feel Jack stiffen, but he didn't say anything. He'd been so controlled in the last few days—mellow, even—to the point of absurdly boring. I met his eyes from across the conference table. "Lunch?" he asked.

"Please."

His azure eyes brightened at my response, and he nodded to the others. "Wyatt and I will be out for an hour."

"Aww, Jack, you're excluding me again." Rick's cackle followed us out the door and echoed all the way down to the elevators.

Few days ago, I woke up with those familiar arms around me. The dawn light passed through the sheer curtains, reflected by the large mirror with shy hesitation. The sideways cityscape graced the other wall, emanating its hopeful cheer.

My room, my bed, my clock. My place.

The arms pulled me in some more, reminding me of my dilemma.

My thoughts churned. Allowing Azurri to sleep over had been a mistake, because I had trouble sorting out my jumbled thoughts while he was around. He did behave himself, however, and his restraint was the very picture of contrition. Now, his pleasant warmth kept me comfortable and cocooned as he was spooning me from behind, his arms squeezing me tight. Unbidden, a thought of old, ragged Puissy with its stuffing coming out floated into my consciousness. I've become his comfort item and now basked in his warmth, enjoying the firm press of his body, the firm pillow of his relaxed arm, his breath in my hair. Despite what had transpired between us, I found his warm scent pleasantly arousing. That fact alone imbued my chest with a warm, fluffy feeling, Perhaps there was hope for us still.

The luxurious embrace was shattered by the sound of his cell phone alarm. His arms left me out in the cold; I felt him tuck me in and sneak out of my new bed, then slip into yesterday's clothes. I let him, curious to see what he'd do. My eyes fluttered almost shut. I felt his shadow over me as he leaned to kiss my forehead.

"Gotta go, Wyatt. I have to be in the office by eight."

I reached out from under the warm covers and pulled him down for a kiss. "Okay," I mumbled, feigning sleep. Our lips met; I couldn't pretend anymore and cracked open my eyes. His gaze was guarded, hesitant. I gave his shoulders a reassuring squeeze. "I love you, Jack."

He sank to his knees, burying his face under my chin. "Oh God, Wyatt. I... I... I don't deserve you. I gotta go." His voice was tight and raspy, overcome by emotion, and I was sorry to see him disappear out the door.

The lock clicked shut and I was alone in my space. The spicy scent of Jack was the only reminder that he spent the night.

The elevator came. We stepped into the empty cab. Jack, whom I had known to push through other people's personal boundaries without a wink, stuck his hands behind his back and leaned on them. This was the first time we were alone since Sunday.

I craved his touch.

I had also behaved. I didn't even dare think of casing a place, which of course meant I was in dire need of my adrenaline fix. Hazard is what makes my world interesting, and adrenaline can be obtained in various ways. The threat of being caught is one of them.

I closed the three feet between us and let my arms slide up his shoulders. "Hey, Jack."

His hands stayed behind his back.

I pulled his head toward me and pressed my lips against his in a tender kiss. "What's wrong?"

"Nothing's wrong," he said with a tight smile. "I'm... I'm just working on it, y'know?"

"Working on what?"

"Control."

"I meant what I said." My voice was stern. My expression of love might have been a drunken one, but it was no less genuine for all that.

"I know." His hands finally emerged from their hiding place. With careful hesitation, he slipped them around my back, pulling me in. His chin rested on top of my head for another three floors. "I want to be deserving of those words, Wyatt."

Then the elevator ground to a halt and broke our embrace, standing side by side as several office drones stepped in. I couldn't have described them if my life depended on it.

WHEN we got to the restaurant, he opened the door for me. He pulled the chair out for me. He asked me what I'd like to eat.

I sighed. In his effort to gain better control over his temper, he'd started to treat me like a girl—a fictional female made of spun glass. It was all very courteous, and chivalrous, and Victorian. I decided not to say anything. First, the experience was rather intriguing—nobody had ever treated me like that before. A brief thought of dressing in pink, fluffy dresses to better fill the role crossed my mind—an amusing thought best suppressed. Second, I don't think he'd have stopped if I asked him to. He had a Strategy in mind, one with a capital *S*, and he'd follow it in his quest for personal perfection. I could only hope it was just a short-lived phase and he wouldn't go too overboard.

Twenty minutes later I was playing with my chopsticks, chasing an errant grain of rice. "Craggs called," I said. "He wants me to create a marketing program for his gym. They started losing the women to Zumba."

"What's Zumba?" Jack asked.

"I don't know. Some exercise. These fads are cyclical, though. He needs to up his membership. So we devised this Internet coupon strategy for an almost-free introductory seminar to climbing."

"Oh yeah? How much is he paying?"

"We bartered. The two of us get to climb and rent gear free for a year."

"Is that worth it?"

"Depends on how often we climb. However"—I punctuated with my chopsticks in the air—"he'll ask Risby Haus to teach the seminar. Craggs will feign being sick with the flu, and Carlos will feign having a sprained wrist, so they'll turn to him. He has the expertise. It will stroke his ego just to be asked."

Jack's eyes narrowed in suspicion. "So, what's the catch?"

"I get to participate as a novice climber. That way, it won't be suspicious for him to run into me, considering he sees me at your place a lot." And that way, I would get to flirt with him and get to know him closer—like an undercover 007.

"No."

I waited for him to say more, but he didn't. "It's already been arranged. It's this Saturday, nine to noon. In case you don't realize, this will be highly frustrating for me. I have to play a newbie. It's not like I'll get to climb and have fun at all."

"I don't like it." I saw his hands grip the edge of the table so hard, he crinkled the white tablecloth.

"Carlos will be there, supervising. Afterward, the guys and Reyna and I are meeting at Loose Rock to discuss what I've found and to just hang out. I thought… would you like to come along?"

His eyes bored into me. "I see you have it all planned out. I don't want you to put yourself in harm's way. It won't bring Celia back to life."

"You don't want to see justice done?"

"I do! Of course I do. I've spent sleepless nights, thinking of so many different ways to just kill that unworthy sonovabitch." He took in my expression of concern and understanding. "I won't. Not unless he threatens you."

"You're not the only one, Jack. There's a whole community of climbers out there that loved her. You have no idea the lengths she went through to recruit and train new climbers. To inspire them, see? One climber killing another like that—it violates everything we do. Everything this sport stands for. Letting another guy, or gal, hold the end of that rope while you're up there is a sacred trust. Had he just shot her in some alley, it would have been cleaner. We can't stand for this. We police our own."

Jack's straining jaw muscle couldn't have been any tighter. I observed in quiet fascination as he stood, his nostrils flaring, his eyes wide.

Anything could have happened. Storming out. Shouting. Slamming the table with his fist.

He did none of that. With quiet determination, he extricated the serving platter from underneath his curry bowl and threw it, as hard as he could, against the nearest wall. The eerie silence was broken as the sound of shattered china ran counter to the cacophony of alarmed shouts of waiters and customers alike.

WE TOOK the long way to the office, walking fast, shedding excess adrenaline. It wasn't every day we got thrown out of a restaurant. There was a nip in the air, and I felt my face flush with both weather and excitement.

"So... Jack."

"Uh-huh?"

"How did it feel?"

He stopped and grinned, his sexy, devastating smirk back at full power. He pushed my shoulders against the rough surface of a carved lion that guarded one of the oldest banks in Pittsburgh. The fine weave of my suit jacket's fabric gripped the statue's abrasive sandstone grains, and I felt the delicate fibers snag. "It felt fucking fabulous."

I grinned back, throwing my head back against the cool stone. Inviting him. Soft, demanding lips claimed mine.

Finally!

I gasped in pleasure at our first kiss in many days. He swallowed my whimper as my fingers plunged into his warm, wavy hair.

Don't stop... don't... stop....

We broke for air, laughing like idiots.

"If I don't get any work done today, it's your fault, Gaudens."

"I'm almost done with Rick—I'll be out of your hair soon."

"I don't want you out of my hair."

We left the solid support of the sculpture. We walked side by side, letting our fingers brush all the way back to Jack's office.

MY ROPE spun as I hung in the air, helpless. Bare, muscled legs emerged from my tight Lycra shorts, stretched and bent in a casual display as I arched my torso back, throwing my head back to give Risby Haus a sultry, upside-down grin.

"I don't know how you do it, Risby. That ledge is bloody impossible."

He smirked and belayed me down, nice and slow. "Straighten up. You want to land on your feet."

I did, letting the unfamiliar, rented climbing shoes I wore hit the rubber padding of the North Face Climbing Gym floor. I didn't bring my comfortable and already broken-in gear. A few of the other class attendees made appreciative noises as to the quality of my effort. I only hoped I didn't do too well before I lost my grip and fell off. "Yeah, thanks!" I grinned, noticing Carlos's stunned face in my peripheral vision. "That was my best try so far!"

"Yer doin' okay, kid," Risby said, patting my shoulder, his long-fingered hand resting there just a bit longer than convention demanded. "Next!"

Others took their turns, two of them making it as far as I had. Class was officially over after that, and Carlos appeared with a handful of pamphlets and coupons, encouraging us all to come and try again. It was time to turn in the rented harnesses and climbing shoes and join the others in reentering our regular, mundane lives.

The harness I had on wasn't anywhere as nice as the one I owned. Its too-narrow straps had the unfortunate tendency to get stuck in the buckles. I knew how to remedy the problem, of course, but since the others were struggling with their harnesses, I was determined to flail around and struggle with mine. "Damn... this stupid... thing's.... *stuck*!" I hissed, just loud enough to be overheard, yanking on a strap and tightening it even more.

"Havin' trouble there, Wyatt?"

I scowled at Risby, mostly because it was expected. "I'm stuck."

"Here, lemme help ya." The tall man knelt before me and slid his fingers along the stuck strap. He gave it an experimental tug. "Spread your legs a bit," he said. I watched his face as he said that, and I noticed the way he suppressed a grin. "It's so tight, it doesn't want to let go. I'll need to get some slack."

"Uh... okay." I moved my feet a shoulder's width apart, feeling Risby's fingers slide under the leg straps digging into my thighs. I felt his hand turn in the tight space, his thumb wedged under the offending strap, pulling it forward and gaining enough slack to loosen the buckle with his other hand. He switched hands and repeated the process on the other side; this time, his fingers brushed against my front on the way out. Even knowing he'd probably do that, the drag of his long fingers over my Lycra-covered tender bits startled me; I made a show of biting back a gasp and stumbling forward. I caught myself on his shoulder. He was staring at my navel. My tight shorts left little to the imagination. It was, after all, my job to lead Risby on.

He unfastened the main buckle, letting my harness fall to the ground. He let his eyes pause on my chest before he let our eyes meet, and then he grinned, revealing a set of white, prominent teeth. "You may wanna be careful with those straps."

"Uh-huh." I turned away from him and adjusted my garments.

Carlos busied himself with straightening the rubber mats on the floor, coiling the ropes, wiping excess chalk off the handholds—simply keeping an eye on me.

"Thanks," I mumbled. "I'll go change."

I've been molested in the line of duty.

Actually, truth be told, it didn't feel so bad. Guilt welled up within me at the realization. Jack would be meeting me in two hours, worried sick, and here I was, enjoying the wandering hands of his prime adversary. Just thinking of Jack made me flush with anticipation. I took my time washing my hands and splashing cold water in my face, thinking of how much fun it was to anticipate Jack's presence again and then berating myself for getting attached to Jack so easily.

I walked out into the lobby. Craggs stood behind the counter, poring over some numbers with his punked-out daughter, Rosalie. I didn't nod to him because Risby was waiting for me.

"Hey, Wyatt! How about we grab some lunch?"

I looked surprised at first, then embarrassed, then mournful. "Sorry, not today. I already promised to be somewhere."

"How about dinner, then?" Risby's wide grin looked both inviting and predatory.

"Well...." I let the idea roll around in my head for a while. Perhaps a challenge would deter him. "Do you even know how to cook?"

He shot me a victorious gleam. "Sure as hell I know how to cook! Italian okay?"

I nodded. "I'll need your address," I said, eyes downcast. Quickly I summoned the image of him touching me *there*, in public, and my blush bloomed obediently on my already rosy cheeks.

He wrote the address down for me. "See you at seven, then."

Risby pushed the glass door open and left. As soon as he was gone, Craggs and Carlos were on me like wasps on a fallen pear.

"Are you fuckin' nuts? You're goin' to visit a murderer? And what about yer new boyfriend?" Craggs leaned against the counter, staring down his beaky nose at me.

"Yeah... what about Jack, Wyatt?" Carlos said, his arms crossed over his broad chest.

I twiddled with my backpack straps, so reminiscent of that conveniently tight harness. "It's just dinner, guys. I just needed to know where he lives. It's not like I'm staying the night."

I CALLED Jack on my way to the Loose Rock, letting him know the rumors of my death had been greatly exaggerated. He agreed to meet me at the gym and, furthermore, he agreed to stop and buy sandwiches for lunch.

Not twenty minutes later, we sat in the empty locker room, straddling the bench in the middle, facing one another while digging into our subs and drinking soda. I gave him the full report between bites, omitting nothing.

He held his cool pretty well until I got to the stuck harness part. He growled, looked around, grasped the paper sandwich wrapper, and threw it against the nearest locker. We watched the wadded-up piece of paper fall to the ground. It lacked the satisfying crunch of broken crockery. It was, in fact, gentle and almost silent.

"Shit. What can I break?"

"Not much, around here."

"Wyatt," he growled in my direction.

I got up, picked up our garbage, and disposed of it. Then I fished around in my backpack and produced a flat, square, crinkly package. "I have a problem that needs to be taken care of," I said as I held it toward him. My eyes must have had that darkened, molten chocolate look he said before he loved so much.

He got up and came to me, picked up the condom by the corner of its wrapper, and slid it into his pocket. "Wyatt... Goldilocks...."

It was a week and a day since last time. Our eyes locked.

"Where?" he said in a raspy voice.

"In the gym, under the last top rope." Then I went and locked the front door.

My preparations took me less than two minutes. I walked into the cavernous, brightly lit space where sounds echoed like in a canyon in the wild back-and-beyond.

He was standing there, leaning against the plywood climbing wall and letting his body yield to its artificial contours. The rope hung right in front of him. The sound of my bare feet slapping on the industrial rubber mats enticed him to lift his head. He straightened, eyes wide, lush lips slightly parted.

I lowered my eyelashes and gave him a coy smile, letting the towel around my hips slip as I crossed the floor.

His nostrils flared and his breathing quickened at the sight of my attire, or rather, the lack thereof.

I was clad in nothing but a climbing harness.

"Wyatt." His voice rasped in his throat. He reached for me, and the heat of his hands singed the surface of my skin, leaving trails of desire in its wake.

Our lips met. He pressed my naked body against the rough, fake stone surface, and I felt every grain, every crevasse. My eyes rolled back when our tongues touched and danced. Pleasure pooled in my belly as I grew hard, standing there on suddenly shaky knees.

I gasped a lungful of air. "Here...." I reached for the rope and tied it to my harness. Then I climbed three feet up, pulled on the other end of the rope, and looked at him. "This is how you tie me off." I demonstrated the knot and attached the line to a mooring in the wall. Then I let go. I spun free in the air, suspended not far above the ground. My legs arched, extending the curve of my spine as I drew my head back, my eyes at half-mast, my gaze stroking Jack like a hot caress.

A low sound emanated from his throat as he ripped off his T-shirt and slid out of his jeans.

A sway of the rope and a lazy half-turn; my languid arms stretched toward him, beckoning. Ravel's "Bolero" echoed in my mind.

His black boxers tented over his groin. I felt strong arms under my back, sensuous lips on my abdomen. When he licked a trail all the way to my throat, I gasped.

"You're so… beautiful." The sentiment took me by surprise; the feather touch of his hand up my thigh made the rough chafing of the climbing harness easy to ignore.

I relished the delicious suction on my throat, a grazing of teeth on my clavicle, an ardent kiss. A tender, restrained nip on my shoulder. "Jack."

"Yeah."

"I want you."

"I know," he said with some effort, his wild smile a pale shadow of its former self. Then he parted my knees, holding my buttocks steady from underneath as his lips encountered the already outgrown stubble, and all I could feel was his soft, moist heat anywhere but the place I really wanted it.

His movement echoed the crescendo of the sultry music in my mind, intensifying, building up. He finally licked my erection and I gasped for air, trying not to scream.

"You can be loud—you locked the front door," he said as the cooler air hit my wet, sensitized cock. Then he set my legs over his bare shoulders and, bending over, he did dark magic with his agile tongue and firm lips, purring as I howled in ecstasy, letting the echoes rip through the cavernous space. A slicked finger slid between my cheeks and breached me.

I bucked and shuddered, holding on to the climbing rope with my head cast back and eyes shut. The air of the open space reminded me of our location, and the strap of my climbing harness dug into my bare flesh, but I couldn't care less at the time. My body was eager to welcome Jack, merge with him, have him share in the pleasure I had been enjoying in my pendulous position. "Whenever you're ready," I whispered.

I felt him let go of me. Out of the corner of my eye, I saw a slip of black silk hit the soft ground. Then there was a rip of a wrapper and a hiss as he rolled the slick, double-lubricated condom onto his length.

"Wyatt," he said in a plaintive voice.

I sat up and held the rope that kept me suspended in midair. My feet didn't quite reach the ground. "Push me to the wall." He did, and I held on with my bare hands and bare feet, hiking my left leg to a higher hold, exposing the parts where sun don't shine.

His smooth hands kneaded my cheeks; a spit-slicked finger caressed the soft tissue underneath.

"Hurry," I said in a frustrated tone. "I can't move up here." He toyed with me from behind until my muscles trembled and I had to let go, floating through space on my pendulum like a failed Cirque du Soleil audition. The music in my mind moved into the wailing minor chords; or was it just blood rushing in my ears….

He caught me and stepped between my legs.

Aaaah. Better.

I held the rope with both hands, holding myself parallel to the floor with my head thrown back in abandon as Jack pressed himself inside me. I grabbed his waist with my legs and pulled him in, deep and fast.

He gasped, his legs buckled, and then my world went spinning in wild circles. Overcome by sensation, Jack fell and now was lying below me, the condom still covering his erect length.

Dissonant cymbals crashed.

"This kinky shit's dangerous," he gasped, amusement warring with frustration.

We tried a few things without success until Jack leaned against the climbing wall and anchored his upper back against it, spreading his legs forward and out. Our fingers touched, and he pulled me in as though we were underwater, yet I had no fear of drowning. I was so free, straddling him in midair, climbing the wall by his sides with my feet as he grasped my harness with his strong fingers and pulled me in.

We joined. Our rhythm was smooth and gentle; the slow thrust and even slower drag went on for an eternity, punctuated by moans and whispered endearments that reverberated in the acoustic space only to echo back to us.

The languid clarinets dictated the luxurious pace; the rest of the orchestra followed.

Including us.

"Jack... Jack I'm gonna...." His hips canted as he hit my happy place again. I wrapped my legs around his back and pulled in hard. Wanting him. All of him.

Now.

"Jack!" Tears of frustration leaked out of my eyes. "Please... oh...!"

He let go with one hand, wrapped it around my hard length, and stroked up and down a few times. I spilled and let the sound of my pleasure splash against the hard walls in an echo of loud, urgent moans. I felt my body spasm around Jack, who grabbed my hips tight again and buried himself to the balls several times with impressive force.

Our eyes met.

He gasped, tensed, and almost bit through his lip as he came. He was beautiful that way, too, and I let go of the rope and allowed my body to lean back and relax, holding onto Jack with my feet alone. I enjoyed the view for a few moments, and then I let go of the rope and let my arms and torso arc backward. I was still impaled. My arms were worn out from the effort of holding on.

Only the gentle echoes of an ageless rhythm now. Then silence, followed by the applause of the audience. The music in my mind was over.

Jack unfastened the rope off the mooring in the wall, let me down as smoothly as a feather, and knelt by my side. "Here, let me."

And I let him, rejoicing in the sensation of his caring hands loosening the knots and buckles. I didn't say anything but merely observed him with quiet curiosity.

He handed me my towel and slipped into his shorts. "You will want to shower, Wyatt."

Oh, that. My jizz made a crazy splatter pattern up my chest. I felt a delicious, postcoital flush color my face as a sheen of drying sweat cooled my body. I sat up and he held me close, nuzzling my hair with those magical, thrilling lips.

"Wyatt...." He trailed off, his body tense.

"Yeah?" I mumbled, my face buried against his sculpted chest.

"Wyatt, I— Hell, this is hard." He hit the floor next to us with a tight fist.

"Shh, Jack," I soothed him. "No need to worry."

"No, this is important, dammit! I just wanted to say that I... that I l-l—" His sudden, uncharacteristic stutter was interrupted by a rude howl.

"Hey, you two, get a room!"

A chorus of jeering voices reverberated through the cavernous space, disturbing our languid bliss. The blush on my face intensified as I thought back to how loud we'd been. They showed up over half an hour early: an unheard-of occurrence. But how did they get in?

Wrapped in my towel, I picked up my harness and stood next to Jack. "Now we will walk to the showers like nothing happened," I said and looked at Jack with a sly smile. "You didn't roar for me this time, though."

"Fortunately." Jack grinned. "At least you still have a cell phone ringtone that sounds just like me."

ONCE Jack and I were showered and dressed, all six of us sprawled in the middle of the gym, making good use of the comfortable, padded floor. My head was in Jack's lap, my eyes closed, and I had absolutely no desire to move, not for any reason and not anytime soon.

We weathered our share of knowing smirks and stupid jokes. Jack had been made to stand against the wall where we made love, and Reyna traced his outline with a fat marker.

Tim made some off-color remark about not wanting to be exposed to such depravity, and a debate sprang up about whether his elusive and mysterious Paige would ever swing on a line for *him*.

"Maybe I should get Auguste interested in climbing, since he's gotten me into tennis," Reyna wondered aloud.

"Hey, Reyna," I snapped at the spirited redhead. "How the hell did you get inside? I locked the door on purpose."

Reyna's sparkling eyes slid toward me as she gave me a sly smirk. "Remember telling me about your special hobby? It occurred to me that not needing a key is a useful skill. I've been practicing every day since."

Jack groaned. "The last thing I need is have you get in trouble, too. Wouldn't that just make Auguste happy?"

"Who do you think showed me how?" Reyna challenged. "Whose picks do you think these are?"

I stared at her in amazement. My old, soft-spoken boss, Auguste Bernard Pillory the Third, knew how to pick a lock. "But why?" The question flew out of my mouth.

"He's absent-minded and keeps misplacing his keys." Reyna shrugged. "He finds it's a practical skill."

Tim interrupted, eager to divert us off our tangent. "All right, then. What have you learned about Haus, Wyatt?"

I gave them a somewhat sanitized account.

"So, what's next?" Reyna asked. "You'll go over and—what? Eat his dinner?"

I nodded. "I'll bring a bottle of wine but drink very little. He's cooking Italian." Some of my excitement at Italian food must have shown, because Jack's thigh tensed under me. "My goal is to find where he lives, see how he lives, talk to him about climbing… you know, a fishing expedition. Um… I'm aware it's not the safest thing to do, so I figured I could leave my phone on in my pocket, on speakerphone."

"Your battery will run down," Chico said. "Here, I have something better. I can't tell you where I got this, but we'll be able to follow your every word." He reached into his designer leather satchel and pulled out a Ziploc bag full of police-grade spy gear. "Come over here, Wyatt, so I can wire you for sound."

The die was cast.

I was really going in.

CHAPTER EIGHTEEN

I HAD been equipped by Chico; the tiny microphone with its wire antenna was taped to my solar plexus. Except I didn't like it there. Here I was, the gay Mata Hari of the climbing world, out to make a murderer confess by my cunning alone, and if he as little as skimmed his fingers across by my abs, he'd most likely feel the wire through my shirt. I could wear a sweater over it, disguising the slight bump under my shirt—but that would muffle the sound pickup.

I looked through my clothes again, carding through the outfits hanging in my closet at Jack's place. Risby had enjoyed looking at me as I hung on the line, being belayed down; that was an asset to exploit. I glanced over my button-down shirts; too prim. There was the rugby shirt—too loose.

Then, enter the Purple Menace.

My friends had teased me because its tight knit clashed with almost everything I owned; its V-neck was cut low for a guy shirt, offering a glimpse of my clavicles. It set off my blond hair in a good way, though, and its slinky cut skimmed my defined torso, leaving very little to the imagination. That, my tight gray jeans, a silver-studded belt, and my black, lace-up combat boots—I was ready for action.

I ripped the wire off. It was white, and its microphone looked much like my iPod ear bud. Electronic junk. After some consideration, I took my white iPod earphones and cut one half off, replacing it with the wire with its microphone; just stripping the insulation and twisting the wire together did the job. I covered it with a bit of black electrician's tape. The whole mess was loosely coiled and housed in my armband iPod holder, the kind people wear when they're out jogging. I zipped up my black fleece jacket over it and entered Jack's living room. "Okay, I'm ready, guys!"

The whole gang was there, sitting on the leather sectional sofa and staying away from the beer. We had to be sharp. Jack handed me a bottle of red wine. "It's a cheap blend, but it's drinkable. That asshole doesn't deserve anything better."

"Uh… thanks."

"What are you wearing under that hoodie, Wyatt?" Chico inquired, his eyes glinting with amusement.

"Uh… a shirt."

Reyna gave me a sideways look. "You're not wearing the Purple Menace, are you?"

I didn't answer.

"You are!" Reyna cried, and Chico laughed his pretty laugh, covering his mouth with the back of his hand.

"What's the Purple Menace?" Jack growled.

"Oh, nothing…. It's just an old, athletic knit shirt the fashion police thinks clashes with my hair."

"Oh yeah?" Jack grinned. "Lemme see!"

I wanted to refuse, I really did, but I knew he'd find out eventually. "It's just an old rag, Jack," I prevaricated, stalling for time.

His eyes narrowed. "Wyatt."

Slowly, I unzipped my plain, black hoodie and let it slip off my shoulders.

May as well go for the kill.

Suppressing an evil grin, I jutted one hip out and turned slowly while the thick, black fleece slipped down the slick microfiber of the Purple Menace. My muscles tensed just a bit for the definition in my arms and lats to show; I tossed my head back and let the tip of my tongue wet my lips.

"Woo-hoo, you've got something good there, Jack!" Carlos hooted, clapping his big hands.

Chico squealed at my unabashed display, then allowed a mild frown. "Really, Wyatt, that purple is so *out there* with that vibrant hair of yours." He waved his hand. "But the belt brings it all together. It makes you just too over the top to care."

Reyna just grinned as Tim sighed in resignation at my subtle, somewhat slutty look.

"No." Jack's voice was cold enough to cut ice. "You're not wearing that, Wyatt."

I turned to face him, my eyes sultry from underneath my lashes. "Yeah, babe, I am. But don't worry, I'll be okay. I'm working undercover, not 'under covers.'"

My pun did little to mollify him. "Where's your wire?"

I showed him. Chico nodded and tested it. "We'll be in the car outside, listening in and recording, okay?"

"Yeah." My voice came out scratchy and dry, and suddenly I wanted to swallow. There was no spit. My eyes met the arctic ice in Jack's expression. I was scared. I wanted a hug—just a quick little gesture of reassurance. And, since I was busy acting tough, it wasn't okay to ask.

Next thing I knew, the detached frost was melting away and his arms were around me. "You'll be okay, Wyatt. I got your back. We all do."

There was nothing better than Jack's strong arms around my shoulders and his moist whisper in my hair. He squeezed me tight as I leaned in and buried my face against his chest.

"Aww, Jack, let go. I'll be okay." I put on a good front for everybody's sake. Especially mine. Swiftly I rose up and kissed the corner of his mouth, and then, like a cloudburst, the somber mood broke and we were on our way, pushing out the door, jostling elbows and calling out friendly expletives.

Showtime.

JACK drove in silence. We were all packed into his Santa Fe crossover. Chico sat in the front passenger seat, setting up his equipment. Reyna,

Carlos, and I sat in the back, squeezed onto the bench and foregoing seatbelts. If we crashed, we'd be okay since we were packed sardine-tight. Tim, as much as he was a dear friend to all of us, wasn't enough of a buddy to snuggle on our laps and was all too glad for the contact-free privacy of the open trunk space. He had more space than any of us, and for just a moment, I felt jealous of the little-kid fun he was having back there, watching the passing traffic from any angle he chose.

Jack stopped the car. "This is it, Wyatt. Apartment 503. If anything happens, holler. You have 911 on speed dial, right?"

"No... I have Detective Lupine on speed dial."

Jack's blue eyes looked colorized in the sodium streetlights, and his chestnut hair picked up red overtones. For a moment he reminded me of a comic book super hero. His strong, chiseled features matched the image well. "You told him?"

I thought I heard a hint of relief in his voice. "Seemed prudent." There was that dry feeling again.

"Okay, bail then. Go for it."

I forced a grin as he punched the top of my arm with a soft fist, leaning back over Reyna from the front seat to do so.

"Hey, you're screwing up his audio setup," Chico snarled, fiddling with buttons, his ears covered by full-size earphones.

I leaned forward and punched Jack back. Then I got out of the car with the bottle of wine in my hand.

There was no lobby and no doorman in Risby's apartment building, but there was an elevator. It was gouged, dented, and tagged with graffiti, and even though it didn't inspire confidence, it got me to the fifth floor all too fast. Forcing my feet one in front of the other, I took a turn and found apartment 503 almost right away. Disembodied, I watched my right hand rise and knock on the gray door.

I heard some music, then footsteps, then the sound of locks tumbling open, and it occurred to me that all three were cheap and easy to pick. The door creaked open, and there he was, leaning against the doorframe in lazy repose.

"Hi, Wyatt. Come on in." He didn't quite leer, but I felt his eyes burn holes through that loose hoodie of mine.

"H-hi." I followed him in.

"Wanna hang that up? Oh, wine. Thank you." He took the bottle and inspected the label. "All right, this'll go well with what we're having tonight."

I felt his arm over my shoulders, propelling me ahead, and I stiffened enough for him to feel my discomfort.

His arm slipped off and his unapologetic grin slid back to me. "Right this way." I followed him to a small kitchen corner where he had nothing but a two-burner electrical stove, a college refrigerator, and a sink built into a miniscule countertop, with a wall-mounted cabinet over it all. There was a pot of water boiling on the stove and several little cups and bowls of ingredients chopped to the right size and ready for use.

Risby opened a cabinet and pulled out two stemmed wine glasses. The cork popped as he opened the bottle, and he poured us some. We toasted, our glasses meeting with a clinking sound, and suddenly I had a bad feeling, drinking with someone only to take them down later. It felt unclean. I barely wet my lips, letting my eyes pass over his pocket-sized kitchen in appreciation.

"Wow. And here I thought we'd be having takeout food."

He laughed, his head thrown back, his voice rich with mirth, and it occurred to me Chico wouldn't hear much if I kept my hoodie on. I unzipped, trying to be as casual as I could, and slid the too-warm layer off my shoulders. His laughter was cut short, and I felt his eyes on me.

"Wow, Wyatt. That's some... purple... you've got on."

Not sure whether I imagined the trace of excitement in his voice, I shrugged. "My friends give me flack over this shirt because it clashes with the rest of me. I like it, though."

"Yeah... so do I." He stepped away from the kitchen counter and into the little room. There was a sofa in the middle and no television, but an old boom box played a Pink Floyd CD. The walls were lined with books, and climbing equipment was hanging off the pegs where others would have displayed pictures on the wall. There was a small desk against the single, large window with a clunky laptop on it, a black-and-white laser printer, and some plastic file boxes full of paperwork.

I wondered what was in there. Doormen didn't work out of the house. Bills and personal paperwork should have taken just a fraction of that space.

There was no table and chairs and no doors led elsewhere, aside from the bathroom visible through the open doorway. "Your little kingdom?" I asked.

"Yeah. I'm not as well-off as your buddy Azurri."

I shrugged. "Most people need very little, when it comes down to it." I let my eyes scan his bookshelves. "What are you reading now?"

"Pliny the Elder." My woeful ignorance must have shown on my face, because Risby sighed as he dumped the linguine into the boiling water. He gave it one stir. "Did you go to school?"

"Yeah."

"A good school?"

"Yes." I felt my jaw tighten. College had not been cheap.

"So how come you don't know who Pliny the Elder was?" His tone bordered on mocking, just this side of judgmental.

"I was a premed. Then I switched my major to business and had some catching up to do."

"You still have some catching up to do. In fact, we all do." He stalked over to his bookshelf and pondered the worn spines of his books. Then he pulled out a modest hardcover volume with a picture of an old, stone head on the front. "Here, read this. I think you'll like it, considering your adventurous nature."

I felt a blush rise to my cheeks. "What makes you think I'm adventurous?"

"You went climbing because you got a discount coupon, right? And now you're here. Need I say more?"

I shrugged, checking the book out while he poured some oil into a pan and started tossing in the ingredients. Soon, his little, one-room apartment smelled like a first-class restaurant. I took my wine and settled in the corner of the sofa, cracking the book open. He loaned me a book called *The Conquest of Gaul*, written by Julius Caesar.

IN LESS than an hour, his loaner book was on top of my crumpled hoodie, and my focus was redirected to the food. We sat on the sofa, legs crossed and facing one another, trying not to spill the linguine in fresh tomato sauce into our laps. It was fragrant and balanced, the garlic bringing out the shrimp and the diced vegetables providing a contrast in texture. I bit into something I've never had before. "What are these?"

"Pinola nuts. Essentially, seeds from pine cones."

"Seriously?" I chased another oblong pine nut down with my fork and ate it, focusing on its resinous, slightly sweet flavor.

He watched me, a lazy grin spreading on his face. "You like it?"

"Love it." My mouth was full and I was in heaven.

Which is why I almost choked when he said, "Celia taught me how to make this."

My coughing fit didn't go unnoticed. His gaze sharpened as he reached a long arm down, handing me my glass of water. "Thanks," I said. "You knew her? The chick in the display case at the gym?"

"Yeah...." Pain and regret darkened his gaze.

"I'm sorry," I said, my reaction automatic. "You two were close, I take it."

"She was the only woman who'd ever truly fascinated me."

I swirled more pasta onto the fork and kept eating, plotting my next move. What would I have picked up at the gym, being new like I was supposed to be?

"That bald guy at the gym said her death was your fault," I said, my voice quiet and hesitant. I eyed him over my wine glass.

"Yeah. He's right. Of course it was my fault. If you're belaying someone and they fall and die, there's only one fuckin' person to blame."

I looked at him, my eyes hopeful. "Maybe it was an accident."

He gulped some wine. "You're new at this. You don't get it yet. Have you ever belayed anyone?"

"No," I lied.

"Okay. You'll find that when you stand there, anchored to a tree or to a bolt in the rock, and the other end of someone's line is in your hand, they entrust you with their life. It's… it's very special, and we did that a lot for one another, she and I. And I failed her." His wine was gone, and he topped his glass off, his eyebrows quirking up at me. I shook my head; I'd had barely half a glass and I was still good.

"Did you meet in the gym? Or in college?"

His expression changed from pain to a calculating gaze. "Don't tell me you don't know she was Jack Azurri's sister. Maybe it's because she went to school in England."

I let my glass slip out of my fingers, hit the cheap area rug, and spill. I sat there motionless, slack-jawed, goggle-eyed. "You… you dated his sister?" He kept staring at me, and I kept looking shocked, only letting my eyes drift to my still hand much later, now devoid of its wine glass. I looked down, knowing what I'd find. "Shit! Shit I'm so sorry. It didn't break, though. But I made a mess." I ran my hand through my loose hair as though to cover my embarrassment, and began standing up to get a paper towel.

"Sit." Risby was up before I was and refilled my glass and dropped a folded paper towel on the wet spot and stepped on it. "I have a dark carpet for a reason."

"Thank you. I'm sorry." And I was sorry. This man, this well-read, clever, surprisingly charming man had murdered Celia, and I was sorry because, had he not done that, I would have wanted to be his friend.

THREE hours later I was out of that dingy apartment building and getting back into Jack's car, a bottle of cheap wine replaced by a book I now had to read.

"That was interesting," Chico said. They all heard the recording. We traveled down to the Loose Rock, where detective Jubal Lupine planned to meet us and listen to the conversation.

Jack was silent, his eyes on the road. I didn't feel like talking, either. Risby's admission of guilt had been genuine and unexpected—but a simple, fatal mistake while belaying his girlfriend would hardly hold up in court.

Which is what Jubal Lupine said, too.

"You did a good job, letting him talk like that, but it doesn't get us anything. He feels guilty, as well he should. The thing is, so what? He screwed up and she fell and died. So far, with the thin, dyed rope being inadmissible as evidence, it's still only a tragic accident with no foul play involved. Legally speaking, anyway."

I hung my head. Risby's sad expression was hard to erase. It had seemed so genuine—but then again, my surprise and spilled wine had been calculated to seem genuine as well. "I'd like to go home," I said, leaning against Jack's side. "I'm so tired."

We drove to Jack's apartment in Shadyside and only when he was about to park in the lot three blocks away from where he lived did he break his silence. "Your place or mine?"

"Yours."

He nodded. "Okay."

Once we stepped into his foyer, he hung his jacket, kicked off his shoes, and strode into the kitchen. I was still untying my infernal combat boots when I heard the first plate crash against the wall.

And another, and then a few more.

I edged my way through the living room and the dining room into the modest, functional space. The wall next to the refrigerator was his anvil, and he was the hammer. I watched him heft another plate in his hand and fling it, full force, against that little wall. It was like watching a pitcher warm up before a baseball game.

A large serving platter decorated with a floral pattern was balanced on his fingertips now, and he glanced at it, freezing in place. Pink roses winked from their garlands, gold accents glimmered in the dim light of the faraway hallway light.

He set it down with precious care, and I saw a tremor run up his spine.

Like a flash I was behind him, embracing him from behind. "Jack." My face was buried into his hunched, quivering back. "Jack." I wrapped my arm around him and picked up the oval serving platter. It looked antique. I liked it. When I turned it over, the maker's mark said "Limoges, France."

"Why not break this one, Jack?" My question was calm, factual. I needed data.

He turned slowly, pulling me in, taking the plate out of my hands only to set it down with the greatest of care. "It was Celia's."

I ROLLED off Jack, my breath still heavy. Both of us were sticky with the evidence of our love. Twice in one day we had shared one another's bodies, one another's souls, but the spirit of that sharing couldn't have been more different. Earlier in the gym, hanging off the climbing rope, had been a mutual exploration into the world of kink. It had been happy, loving, adventurous. What we had just shared was my effort to comfort him by impaling myself on his flesh while kissing his pain away.

I showered quickly, cleaning up just enough before I let the bathtub fill with hot water. Then I pulled on Jack's arm and coaxed him in. "Come on. You'll feel better."

His eyes were empty, much as Risby's had been for just a flash of a moment, and I noted the similarity and filed it away. I cajoled Jack into the tub, put on water for tea, stripped his old sheets, and changed the bed. I made sure clean, soft towels were laid out for us when I brought two cups of Sleepytime tea with honey into the bathroom.

"Here, drink this."

"I don't want whiskey," Jack said, his eyes closed.

"It's tea. Chamomile, mostly."

He took it from my hands and hissed at its heat. We both had a sip and set our cups on the bathroom floor to cool. "Join me?"

"Yeah." I stepped into the tub and settled between Jack's bent legs. We barely fit, and the water was now raised almost to the rim. I could hear the overflow drain do its job, letting the excess run away. His arms hugged my chest; I leaned my still-moist head against his shoulders, getting my hair wet all over again. "We don't have to do this, Jack. I thought it would make you feel better, but… I don't know. I hate seeing you like this."

We both knew what "it" was—the belated investigation of Celia's death.

I felt his arms squeeze. We stayed that way for a while, sipping our tea and sharing our distress until the water cooled enough to be uncomfortable. Then we did the same in the fresh, clean bed, with Jack spooning me from behind and holding me tight, his nose nuzzled into the crook of my neck.

"I love you, Wyatt."

I turned in his arms to face him. He was barely visible in the dusky corner of his bed; only the neon lights reflected off the white bedding made his face visible. "I know." I slipped my arms and legs around him, maximizing our area of contact. "I love you too."

"I'll be fine," he said, suddenly gruff. His large hand was rubbing circles into my back. "As long as you're fine, I'll be fine."

I smiled in the dark. "I'll be fine. And tomorrow I'll go buy you some new dishes."

ONLY a week later I walked into the North Face, my regular gear on and Celia's old GriGri belay device in my hand. Risby was thirty feet up the wall, defying both gravity and gym regulations. He wore no harness; nobody stood by to arrest his fall. I leaned back against the opposite wall and watched his long limbs execute their graceful dance of impending doom. He climbed down using a different path, feeling his way. When he was only six feet up from the ground, I raised my voice.

"Yo, Risby!"

He tried to look down, missed his foothold, and slipped; only his strong fingers grasped the handholds. He smeared the ball of his foot against the wall itself in search of something to step on and, realizing how close to the ground he was, he cursed and jumped. "Don't ever do that, Wyatt. Not when someone's free-climbing."

"When I walked in, you were almost all the way up," I said. "What, you have a death wish or something?"

He didn't reply; he just leaned down from his considerable height and kissed my neck.

"Hey!"

"Looked tasty." He shrugged.

"You're as bad as Jack." Oops, that just slipped out.

"You two together?" His eyebrows went all the way up as he shot me an assessing look.

"None of your business."

"Maybe it is. Maybe if you two are together, I don't want to poach. Considering I killed his sister, stealing his boyfriend would be just rubbing salt into the wound."

Now it was my turn to just stand there, not knowing what to say. "I started reading the book," I said instead.

He walked off to the wall and got his water bottle and drank some. "You liked it?" he asked once he wiped his wide lips with the back of his hand.

I shrugged. "History has never been my thing, but this writer is interesting. It must have taken a lot of research to pretend you're an old emperor and write about all those tribes."

The dark gloom lifted off Risby's face. "The emperor actually wrote it himself."

I took a minute to wrap my little thieving mind around that. "No shit?"

"No shit. Gaius Julius Caesar was *the* Caesar. He was the first-ever emperor of a decaying republic, which is why he got killed...."

"I know who he was from Shakespeare."

"Okay. Shakespeare must have read his writings, and writings about him, to get all that history right for the play. Shakespeare is derivative. The book I gave you is a translation of the original, from the horse's mouth."

"Oh." Words failed me, so I turned to action instead. My cover was blown; Risby figured Jack and I were together, and the romance of Mata Hari was a thing of the past. I looked at that wall and walked up to it. I climbed up to the blue line that told us not to go any higher without a harness. Then I went a bit higher, and a bit higher still. I felt comfortable. It wasn't any harder than climbing while being belayed, but there was a serious adrenaline rush knowing you could just fall and get badly hurt.

Not die. Not here. The floors were padded. Maybe a few weeks in the hospital....

"Wyatt." Risby's voice was calm as I approached the ledge. The same ledge I had pretended not to be able to climb last time. "Wyatt. You're doing great, but I need you to start climbing back down."

I kept going up; my belly was sucked to the wall as I grabbed a handhold and swung my right leg over the ledge, gripping a stub of fake rock with my toe. One, two... then I was over on the flat wall again and found a good foothold and two handholds where I could stop and rest.

"Wyatt, I want you to climb to the right, past the ledge. Don't do the ledge on the way down." There was panic in Risby's voice.

I climbed four feet higher, touching the wide, red pipe by the ceiling as I always had when I made it up. The sweet symmetry of what I did to Risby struck me as ironic. He pretended to be the beginner for Celia, and I pretended to be the beginner for Risby only one week ago. The deceit might have unfolded on the very same wall, too.

"To the right, Wyatt."

I did as he said as I glanced to the side, picking the best place to begin my descent.

Going down was five times harder than going up. My focus was so total, so unwavering and complete, that I had to forget about my mission, about Jack and Celia and Risby, and finally, all there was left was the wall and me. I'd climbed down before, but never without a harness. I probably did the best, most intricate climbing of my life that day, using every technique, every trick up my sleeve. My feet hit the floor and I turned around, breathing a bit harder than usual.

Everyone was there. Craggs and his punk daughter Rosalie with her wild hair, Chico and Carlos, Reyna, Jack....

Wait. Why was Jack here?

Before my exhilarated mind even had the chance to come up with the answer to that question, Risby stalked to me and shook me by my shoulders. He was tall and thin, and there was that empty look in his eyes again. His voice was a cold hiss laced with panic. "I told you to get the fuck down. You wanna get killed? You wanna learn from me, you have to listen!" The pain and fear in his eyes was only thinly veiled with anger.

I wanted to take him seriously—except I've developed something of a reaction to people yelling at me of late. "Oh, fuck off, Risby." My retort was automatic; so was his, apparently.

His fist cuffed my cheek so hard I saw stars before I fell to the ground.

WHEN I came to, I saw the uneven face of Craggs, who bent over me, frowning while wiping my forehead with a cool cloth. I didn't know him well and found him a bit scary up close, with his weathered furrows lining his forehead and those feral eyes just drilling me into the rubber floor, making me stay put by his sheer will alone. "Here, drink this."

I took the water bottle from his hand and sat up. My head hurt, but nothing was broken. "What happened?" I croaked.

"World War III happened. Risby hit you, Jack jumped Risby, and they had it out while you were out."

"Is he okay?"

"Who?" Craggs grinned.

"Jack."

"Yeah. A broken nose... could've been worse. He gave Risby a concussion, and now they're being babied by all those friends of yours."

I sat up and, testing my balance, I stood. My head hurt, and a cut on the inside of my lip left a metallic tang in my mouth, and now the small wound was hot and swollen. I padded over to a group of guys hovering over Jack. He sat holding an ice pack over his face; cotton balls kept blood from flowing out of his nose.

I pushed my way through and knelt next to him. "How does it feel?"

He gave me a baleful eye. "Ligh m'nohze 'es broke."

"Can I get you anything?"

He just hissed, looking entirely miserable, and turned to get a sip of water Craggs had provided earlier.

I turned my attention to Risby. He looked a bit dazed, sitting up against the wall further down, and he wasn't attended by my friends; no, he enjoyed the attention of the police.

Well, sort of. Jubal Lupine sat next to him, holding his cup of water and talking to him in a low voice.

"It's his fuckin' fault," Reyna said, nodding at Haus. "Had he not hit you, Azurri here wouldn't have gone ballistic."

"No, it's Wyatt's fault." Tim's voice was calm and analytical. "Had he not free-climbed like an idiot, Haus wouldn't have freaked out at him."

I looked at Jack and he gave me that pissed-off look again, not saying anything. "I got some useful data, though."

The dismissive looks didn't encourage me to share my findings, but the data I received was both intriguing and disturbing. Interesting, because Risby acted as though he really didn't want anyone else to die on his watch again. Disturbing, because maybe he really was innocent—until proven guilty. Yet if it had not been him, then who?

I needed more information, and I knew just how to obtain it. My fingers developed that particular, annoying itch, and despite the adrenaline high I'd gotten off the free-climb, I had to suppress the delicate quiver of anticipation that had always preceded a satisfying breaking-and-entering.

This time, I knew it would be easy.

Risby Haus had cheap locks on his door.

CHAPTER NINETEEN

THE bright, fluorescent tubes of the hallway fixtures shed cold light on the locks before me. I worked the middle one first, as I always had; many people used only the lock attached to their door handle and kept the rest of them as a psychological deterrent—unless they really needed them, the extra locks were just for show. My thin pick slid into the key slit; my sensitive fingers detected the correct lever to press down. I inserted a rigid wire to keep it down and moved to the next internal doohickey, lining it up with the first one. When all three were lined up, I extracted the pick and inserted a hook-like device, grabbing all three lined-up tumblers. Then I pushed them down.

The lock opened with a click, and I felt that old, warm satisfaction flood my veins. I knew Jack would disapprove—more than disapprove, he might even dump me, and for cause—but if we were to find out who killed his sister, we had to find the missing pieces of the puzzle.

I pushed Jack out of my mind as I tried the doorknob—it was unlocked all right, but the door was still being held shut.

"Let me try the top one." I exhaled, straightening up and stretching my shoulders.

"No, let me do it." Reyna was right next to me with Auguste's picks in her hand.

I turned to her; long hair spilled down her shoulders, held back by a white-and-purple sweatband. A white-and-purple top with a prominent V-neck molded to her body. Her size-L sports bra gave her the engineering support she needed; the hem of a bicolor, pleated cheerleader skirt reached only a hand-span under her butt. Knee socks didn't quite cover Reyna's strong, sculpted calves. This wasn't the time to examine my best friend, certainly, but I couldn't help but notice her legs were, for the first time in my memory, entirely hairless. "Did you actually bother to shave?"

Her face reddened. "No. Auguste took me in for a body wax."

Ouch.

The rest of us were all guys, and we had depilated all exposed parts in a manner commensurate with our bravery and pain tolerance, aiming to lend our cheerleader outfits an air of verisimilitude. Chico was unbearably smug, rocking his gaudy little outfit even though he was a guy. Tim was resigned to his fate, having covered up his shoulder tattoo with copious amounts of makeup he bought together with the fake eyelashes. As for myself, I was way past the point of embarrassment. After all, it had been me who explained to everyone that people don't remember faces as much as they remember uniforms… and it would have been unconvincing to meet a team of four plumbers entering the apartment. As the leader of this expedition, I felt responsible for my team members' safety and, biting the bullet, I had been the first one to put on a long, black wig that disguised my hair, along with a bra overstuffed with socks and a ridiculously short cheerleader's miniskirt.

"I wanna pick this lock, Wyatt."

I gave Reyna a stern glare. "You have two minutes. Our disguises won't hold forever."

"They would, had you not been so damn cheap. We should have gotten those soccer uniforms," Tim hissed at me from his lookout down the hallway. A mesh bag full of white and purple pompoms bounced against his bare thighs, and his toned, equestrian legs looked powerful and somewhat hairier than might have been expected from a college cheerleader.

Reyna pushed two tumblers down, but as she was going for the third, her wire slipped and she had to start all over again.

"Reyna, let me do it." Nervous sweat was escaping my cheap wig and pouring down my face. This was no time to experiment.

"Just one more try...." She drew her plucked eyebrows together in concentration, and I heard her draw a deep breath. Seconds ticked by. It felt like half an hour before the tumblers aligned and we all heard the rough click of the mechanism turning as the lock yielded to her efforts. I saw Reyna's grin, giddy and victorious.

While I picked the last lock, my mind pondered the incongruous reality of the four of us in these ridiculous outfits. The used sporting supply store did have soccer uniforms, many of them, but we weren't willing to pay their full price. Soccer gear was in high demand and the store had no reason to put it on sale. The gaudy, awful purple uniform we finally purchased used to belong to the cheerleading squad of a defunct college rugby team and, since it was too atrocious for anyone to wear ever again, we got it for a song. The stretch fabric, together with its sleeveless design, even accommodated the guys' broad shoulders.

The door swung in and we poured into Haus's empty apartment. I closed the door and clicked the main lock shut, then looked at my eager helpers. "When you break into a place, you look in all the rooms to make sure there are no unexpected guests. This place is really small though, and Haus is pulling a double shift tonight, so we should be alright on that account."

We spread out, peeking into the bathroom and behind the shower curtain, inside the closet and under the sofa. The place was so small, there wasn't anywhere to hide.

"Next, we do our tasks. Tim, you have the desk with all those papers. Chico, you and I will go over his climbing stuff. Reyna, you go through the whole place systematically, and if you find anything interesting or unusual—anything at all—let us know."

Reyna's face lit up. "You want me to toss the place."

"No. Not 'toss.' You need to be organized about it.... Here, start by the door and go clockwise from top to bottom. You may find secret hiding places, documents, whatever. Anything that catches your eye. And Tim can take pictures of it all."

"Thank heavens for digital cameras," Tim grumbled, extricating his precious Nikon from its nest of cheerleading pompoms. "I'm here as a journalist. Just in case anybody asks."

CHICO was our climbing expert. We all recognized that, and were happy to let him pore over the neatly coiled ropes and harnesses suspended off hooks on the wall. Some moments passed.

"This is all surprisingly simple," he commented, handling the basic friction plate. Not a single self-belay device polluted the purist ideals of the climber known as the Demon of Santa Teresa. He owned two pairs of climbing shoes, two pairs of Vibram FiveFingers shoes, and a pair of sneakers. There was one old, worn harness, two elastic climbing lines, and one nonelastic rappel line. All of Risby's equipment was made of a green, gray, and brown-speckled weave cordage. Natural camo colors blended such as hunters would have used. None of his ropes bore the color-coding so common to major brands. And his ropes seemed almost new. He hadn't used them much.

"Risby is mostly a free-climber," I reminded our expert. "I guess he doesn't use ropes as much as the rest of us." My tone must have sounded somewhat wistful, for Chico gave me a curious look, his finely sculpted eyebrows arched.

"That's not something to aspire to, Wyatt. Lots of climbers have died doing that sort of a thing."

I shrugged. "Gotta admire his guts, though."

TIM treated every single document in every single file box to at least a cursory glance. "It looks like he was really interested in the exposé of his former employer, the Provoid Brothers," he said, rifling through yet another stack of papers. "He has some of the depositions, even. He took the trouble to obtain a copy of those from the court using a FOIA request."

"FOIA?" I asked.

"Freedom of Information Act. I get a lot of background information that way, but it can be a real pain…. And look—here! This looks like Celia's sworn statement."

We all perked up and crowded around the desk, helping Tim organize the complex paper trail.

"There *was* a whistle-blower. There's also that guy, Kevin Toussey, who directly opposes just about every statement Celia made. Or her boss, Mila Rose."

"Who's Kevin Toussey?" Chico asked.

"He was one of their vice-presidents," Tim said. "He ran Operations—Risby Haus ran the collection department and reported to Kevin Toussey directly. Toussey showed up earlier on in the investigation process, but somehow he managed to escape serving his sentence on medical grounds.... Operations was his job description, but that doesn't say what he really did for the company." Tim's voice was dour. A true emissary for the Pittsburgh Morning Gazette, he didn't like incomplete answers and proceeded to dig for more.

I'D TAKEN it upon myself to examine Risby's personal items. It appeared the sofa in the middle of his room folded out, and that's where he slept. The lamp table right next to it was rife with drawers and shelves, and I opened every single one of them. Removing the small, assorted objects and replacing them with delicate precision was difficult—I didn't want to make it obvious the place had been searched. Many of these objects were of practical use, such as a box of tissues along with condoms and lube. There was a manicure kit and a drawer full of winter gloves. The function of the spare change drawer was rather obvious. There was a stack of magazines, some loose buttons and paper clips, postage stamps, and several pieces of personal correspondence.

An envelope mailed from Alaska caught my eye. There was no return address, but the handwriting was cursive and elegant, harkening to bygone days. It was addressed to Risby Haus at a different address—a home in a much better part of town than his current digs. The date on the stamp was well over one year old. I pulled the piece of hotel stationary out of its envelope.

ZIPPER FALL

Dearest Risby,

How I wish you could be here with me! Alaska simply defies description, and I feel humbled by her majesty and strength. I opted to skip Denali and attempted an ascent of the capricious Mt. Saint Elias instead. To refresh your memory, it's the second-highest peak in Alaska, separating Alaska and Yukon. I figured it would be more accessible, being close to the water, but nothing could be further from the truth.

The weather coming off the gulf has been simply horrid. The locals thought me daft for even attempting the climb, and especially for going solo. A local game guide ended up accompanying me—a Tlingit woman named Lucy, who speaks English, as well as Tlingit and some Aleut. She is small and round, but possesses amazing strength and resilience, and knows the land and the weather better than anyone I've met to date. We decided to follow in the footsteps of the original explorer, Prince Luigi Amadeo di Savoia. If he was able to summit in 1897, with his old technology, we should have been able to do just as well—or so I thought.

Lucy insisted that we carry all this extra gear. We hiked up to the position of their 5th camp (out of 11!) and it wasn't even proper climbing yet when the weather hit. We got snowed in good and proper, huddling in our little pop-up tent on the side of the mountain, wearing every shred of fabric available. Once we got snowed in, the tent got a lot warmer. We had to wait two days for the storm to abate before we could strap on the snowshoes Lucy insisted we bring (in May!) and navigate our way down. We did good, considering my total lack of preparation. Climbing under these climatic conditions....

Celia rambled on and on about various observations, both related to climbing and to Alaska, where you had more grizzly bears per square mile than people, where everyone carried a gun in case they ran into a grizzly, and where the airplane-delivered mail was often the only means of communication between far-flung villages. The tone of her letter reminded me that she spent some time in England.

"That explains why she didn't use e-mail," I said to Chico, who ended up reading the letter with great interest. Celia's other letters were similar: they came from afar, she had missed Risby's company terribly, and the poetry he kept sending her truly warmed her heart.

> *"Truly, my lovely Risby, someday you shall forget who you are and the century you live in, and you'll start speaking in iambic pentameter to your obtuse coworkers...."*

and

> *"I sure hope Toussey dropped all that ridiculous talk of suing me. Nothing I have said up 'til this date has failed to be substantiated by the corporate record. I don't know how these things go in Collections, which is your domain, but Toussey not only keeps a double set of books, he even makes no secret of it."*

Now that was interesting. "Tim... come look at this!"

Tim scuttled over, looking harassed. "I'm busy... what is it?"

"Chico and I found these old letters from Celia, and this one refers to Toussey again."

Tim glanced at the letter, and then he put it on the desk and photographed every page. "I've been taking photos of the files, mostly. There is too much to absorb this fast. What else have you got?"

I fished inside the almost empty drawer. One more envelope—a letter addressed to Celia, yet unsealed. And, in the back of the corner, my fingers felt a curious shape. I teased it out from the dark recesses of Risby's night table and wiped dust off the box covered in red velvet.

"Open it," Reyna whispered over my head.

The tension was unbearable.

Slowly, I eased the spring-loaded lid ajar. A white gold and platinum ring sat in the middle of black satin; a large solitaire diamond sparkled in a simple, elegant setting. "Wow. He spared no expense," I said, barely breathing. The stone itself could have been bartered for a modest suburban house. Nothing I'd ever stolen came even close to its quality.

"How do you know it's not glass?" Reyna asked.

"I know diamonds. The size is good, the clarity is great, it has virtually no color, no gray overtones... it's beautiful. And look at the even, brilliant cut." I closed the box and placed it in the back corner of the drawer.

"What's in the envelope?" I looked up at Tim, who studied the single sheet of paper with a light blush in his face.

"It's a... a marriage proposal. The verse is surprisingly good. It's... it's rather passionate." He passed it around, and we all read the private, expertly crafted words Risby had intended for Jack's deceased sister.

The silence was deafening.

Tim photographed it only for the record. "It still doesn't let him off the hook," he said. "He still could have done it."

"His motive is greatly diminished, if he intended to marry her," I said. "You don't just buy a ring like that without having big plans."

"Is it possible he could have killed her, even though he had loved her?" Reyna speculated. She returned back to the shelf where she had been examining various objects.

"That's exactly what he admitted to doing when I was here last," I reminded her. "Anyway... have you found anything, Reyna?"

The tall woman stood up and stretched, ignoring the fact that her careless action caused her adorable cheerleader outfit to show a great deal of her sculpted midsection. "He's into all kinds of stuff besides climbing. There's books on wilderness survival, music, brewing...."

"Brewing? Like beer?" I perked right up. Beer brewing had been a great experiment of mine some years back. Homebrew had been well worth the effort back before microbrewery beer became both affordable and ubiquitous.

"No... he's using mash, and a copper coil, and he has these thermometers up here...." Reyna pointed to a large plastic tub full of equipment worthy of a medieval alchemist.

I'd seen stuff like that before. "It's a still!" I exclaimed.

"A what?" Chico asked.

"A still. A piece of equipment used to distill whiskey. Or moonshine, hooch... you know, the illegal side of brewing?"

"Oh that. How revolting. I'd never drink that—moonshine can make you go blind if you're not careful. You can even die."

"Yeah. If you don't separate your methanol from your ethanol, you're screwed."

Tim looked at me with curiosity. "You seem to know a lot about it."

"Yeah...." I gave him a sheepish grin. "Someone I know has a still on the roof of his apartment building. Moonshine isn't just for rednecks anymore."

"Whatever, guys. This is irrelevant. Booze doesn't let us know what happened to Celia." Tim was the voice of reason once again, and we bent over our tasks, restoring Haus's humble abode back to its original state. When we were done, Tim photographed the copies of Risby's brewing records. "Just to be thorough," as he put it.

Then we filed out of the apartment, and I locked all three locks. Tim's camera was back in the mesh sack full of white-and-purple pompoms. Our mission may have been accomplished—but unfortunately, it managed to raise even more questions than it had answered.

We were silent on our ride down, lost in our thoughts and our doubts. The ancient, rickety elevator shook and groaned—until it jostled hard and stopped.

"What the heck?" Reyna gasped as the sudden movement tossed her right into Tim.

"We better not be stuck in here in these stupid getups," I groaned. "Who has a cell phone?" I didn't. Girl clothes, especially cheerleading uniforms, were not known for their profusion of pockets. This was one of those times when I had chosen *not* to stuff my iPhone in my sock-stuffed bra.

"Let's use the service telephone," Reyna suggested and removed the panel, which was supposed to hide the simple phone. Except the phone wasn't there; it had been ripped out.

"Here you go," Tim said, fishing in the large net bag full of pompoms. He produced a simple flip-phone. "So, who do we call?"

I peered at the control panel. There was a toll-free number to call in case of an emergency. "Here, this one!" I pointed to the number.

Tim dialed and listened for a while, and then he flipped his phone shut. "The robot voice says the number has been disconnected."

"We can't call Jack," I said, my voice kind of small as the words broke into the thick elevator air. The guys looked at me, all serious, and nodded. We all remembered the scene after Jack and Risby tangled at North Face, and Jack still had the remnants of bruising under his eyes.

"Okay. Carlos's out of town, Craggs would throw a fit, Rosalie only has a learner's permit.... How about Auguste?"

Chico's question stunned Reyna. She flopped against the cold wall of the elevator, her russet eyes wide and incredulous. "A-Au-Auguste? Oh, you have no idea.... When he showed me how to pick locks, he never figured I actually meant to—no. No way."

Tim sighed, rolled his eyes, and dialed a number. "I'd like to report an emergency," he said, cool as a cucumber. He stated his name and location, and all of a sudden, it occurred to me that the pompous jerk called the bloody police on us.

"Act natural. Just, act natural, everyone." My voice was a bit tight, which made it somewhat higher pitched than usual.

"Wyatt, you sound like such a girl," Chico snorted, covering his well-proportioned mouth with his even better-proportioned hand.

"Just act natural, asshole!" My face felt red and hot, my cheap black wig made the back of my neck itch, and I was checking out the elevator for hiding places for my lock picks.

"Reyna… you don't want the police to find those lock picks on you," I said, stashing my own set into the dark recess of the removed elevator control panel.

"They will find it in there, Wyatt," Reyna said. "I can't lose Auguste's tools."

"If you stick it all the way in the corner, yeah, there… maybe they won't. And wipe your fingerprints off."

Reyna followed my example, wiped the picks on the pleats of her skirt, and stashed the small metal set where I told her. Her expression was sullen. "They better be there tomorrow."

"Or not. Relax…. For now, just act natural. We're four chicks and we're cheerleaders and we got stuck in an elevator, and all we need to do is go to the subway and go home. No big deal."

IT HAD been hours and my bladder was full before the elevator began to jostle and creak again, moving us to the lobby with exaggerated care. The door slid open and we stepped out into a small entrance area full of people. The police were there, firefighters were there, and maintenance workers in their navy blue jumpsuit uniforms and yellow leather tool belts swaggered, all tough and masculine, having just fixed a problem.

Flashes of light blinded me as we stepped forth.

"And here they are, the residents who had have been trapped in an elevator for five hours in this Oakland building…."

More flashes. Black, fuzzy microphones appeared before my face.

"Tell us about your ordeal, Miss… Miss… what is your name?"

"Gaudens," I answered, stunned stupid.

"What happened, Miss Gaudens?"

I gave the TV person a vapid smile. "The elevator got stuck."

"Yes, and you and your fellow teammates were stuck in there… for how long?"

"For too long."

"Of course." The ditzy blonde smiled at me.

"Your companions aren't all women, are they?"

"Uh… does it show much?"

WE CONGREGATED in Chico's apartment, where we changed into our ordinary clothing. Once again, we felt normal.

"I can't believe you talked to that woman from Channel 11," Tim said once again. "Which part of 'no comment' don't you understand?"

I shrugged, buttoning my jeans, searching for my cushy socks.

"At least you could have told her we were a singing telegram or something," Reyna quipped, brushing her hair out and then braiding it into a long plait.

Only Chico was unperturbed. "Nobody asked me if I was a guy," he said, sounding very pleased with himself. Nobody cared.

I STOOD at the stove, sautéing chicken the way I saw Jacques Pepin do it in a TV special, with just salt and pepper and rosemary, making the skin nice and crisp on the bottom, when I heard a funny sound from the front door. I smiled, pressing the sliced chicken thighs into the hot pan while the potato gratin baked in the oven. It was so cute of Jack to use lock picks instead of his keys. It seemed I had started a trend.

The door clicked open behind me. I didn't turn around, having just rinsed the green beans and now ready to toss them onto the hot olive oil in the pan. "Hello, Loverboy," I sang out while tossing the beans. I put the pan back onto the burner and topped the softening beans with grated lemon peel, capers, and a minced anchovy.

Light steps approached me from behind.

"Pull a bottle of white wine out of the refrigerator, will you?" I asked as I tossed the green beans some more and flipped the four chicken thighs. It was always good to have leftovers, after all....

"Of course, darling." The amused baritone behind me made me spin around so fast, I almost spilled my beans.

The man wasn't Jack.

I looked up to meet the eyes of the impossibly tall man, his black hair slicked back and a wide, toothy grin meeting my shocked expression with incredible arrogance. "R-Risby?"

CHAPTER TWENTY

"Don't just stand there, Wyatt, your food will burn." Risby took two long steps and stooped to peer inside my fridge, soon extracting a pale green bottle of wine. He fished in his pants pocket and pulled out a Swiss army knife with a corkscrew.

"You'll break the cork using that," I commented while rescuing dinner.

"Why do you say that?"

"Jack and I always break the cork with those cheesy little corkscrews that come in survival knives."

I heard a pop and turned around only to see Risby remove a whole, unblemished cork from the neck of the bottle. "I am more patient than the two of you combined."

"Hmm." I shrugged and bent over to pull the potato gratin out of the oven. The surface was still napalm-hot and bubbly; the edges had begun to brown. I slid the piping hot dish onto the trivet on the table and, not bothering to ask, I reached for an extra plate and utensils to add on the table.

Risby just raised his eyebrow; then he sauntered over to the living room, propped his feet on the glass coffee table, and clicked the television on.

Thoughts were roiling under the surface of my calm.

Did Risby know? How much did he know we knew? How mad would he be if he knew? Did he really not do it? Who was Toussey, really?

My cell phone rang just as Jack's lock picks began to rattle in my lock. I went over to watch my mercurial lover's progress from the other side as I stuck the phone to my ear. "Hey, Reyna!"

Reyna's voice was strident and filled with urgency. She talked for a long time while I nodded into empty air and made all those "Yes, I see" and "Uh-huh" listening noises. Reyna kept talking while I kissed Jack's cheek hello, while I filled three glasses with wine, and while I served Jacques Pepin's chicken au jus with green beans onto three plates—a dish that was, to date, a pinnacle of my masculine culinary accomplishment.

"Okay, Reyna. Thank you. That's… disturbing. No… no, I won't drink anything. Don't worry… and let Auguste and Tim know I thank them for the intel."

I clicked the phone shut, only to see Risby and Jack sitting on opposite ends of my oatmeal-colored sofa, staring at the television.

The Channel 11 news broadcast was down to those regional, juicy tidbits with a bit of humor and local color. Now the funny news of the day revolved around a group of cheerleader drag queens stuck in an elevator. Risby's amused smirk was a direct counterpoint to Jack's appalled glare as the newsreel showed me coming out of the elevator wearing a purple-and-white pleated skirt and a skimpy top, my long, black wig slightly askew. Reyna strutted behind me, looking like sex on wheels with her sultry glare and long crimson hair spilling down her shoulders. Tim Nolan came across as the punk he probably was; serious on the outside, mischievous on the inside, while Chico sauntered out with a toss of his polished, black hair and swaying hips: catwalk time.

"Uh… does it show much?" I asked the reporter while on camera, looking stunned in the arresting glare of all those bright flashbulbs, with strobing emergency lights outside still lighting up the street.

Jack took the remote from Risby's hand and clicked the television off. Then he stood up and faced me, his extra height suddenly more apparent. His eyes were solemn in that kind of stiff, controlled way that always told me he was keeping a tight grip on his short fuse. "Care to explain that, Wyatt?" His level voice betrayed a hint of fear and immediately I was transported to a tough conversation we'd had what seemed like ages ago.

Do you realize that I'm violating my probation by consorting with a known felon? That's you, sweetheart. By not turning you in like I ought to, I'm aiding and abetting. You're screwing up your life and taking me down with you. And for what? A few lousy bucks?

Our big fight—the one right before Ernie shot me in the ass. Jack still had several years of probation left; I'd tried to be good, I really had, but this was different.

"The gang and I had a small mission. Don't worry about it. Here, dinner's on the table."

"Small mission?" Risby spat as he drew himself to a height that towered even Jack's. His face reddened in anger and his eyes narrowed. His tone was nothing short of incredulous. "Then how the hell do you explain these?" He fished inside his plaid shirt pocket with sinewy fingers and eventually and produced several long strands of purple-and-white plastic.

Pom-pom dandruff.

"I don't know. I haven't handled anything like that. What is it?"

"It's part of your cheerleading uniform, just like on TV," he said with a sarcastic bite to his voice. "You and your buddies broke into my place and tossed it. You made an effort not to make a mess, but some things were put back the wrong way, and somebody dropped these under the table. You have a bit of explaining to do."

I sat in a chair, where good food was going cold on the table. Both men stood, one on each side of me, glaring at one another and then at me as though they couldn't decide whom to yell at first. "All right. I'll tell you what went down, but only after dinner. Please sit down."

Jack cleared his throat and his hands gripped the back of his chair so hard I saw his knuckles go white. "I won't sit down to eat or drink with the man who murdered my sister."

I nodded. "I know. I wouldn't expect you to, Jack. Won't you please trust me on this, just this once? What we found—all those things—Risby didn't *murder* Celia. He failed to prevent her death by accident, and her death was engineered, but it was done by a third party. We're still digging for the details in that respect."

I saw Risby's eyes widen; their charcoal gray glistened a bit and he looked away, not meeting my eyes, and not looking at Jack, either.

"Risby, won't you please sit down?" My voice sounded like paper ripping. I hated having to beg these guys. To my surprise, his shoulders slumped upon a forced exhale, and with his head bent, he pulled out the chair to my right and settled upon it with care, as though it might break under him.

"Jack—I swear, there is solid evidence. He didn't do it. Won't you sit down with us?" I met my lover's gaze straight on. There was a barely contained fire behind his impossibly blue eyes, and his shoulders were stiff with suppressed rage—a rage that had been brewing for almost a year now. Grief comes in stages, I'd been told, but those stages rarely come in their preordained sequence and on a schedule. Anger was one of those stages, and it seemed Jack wasn't entirely done with it.

I watched his nostrils widen. Bad sign—my stress level skyrocketed.

His powerful, long-fingered hand picked up his plate with the food on it and hurled it across my whole apartment, right into my front door.

I relaxed, feeling the hint of a smile tease the corners of my mouth.

Risby jumped from his seat, wild and startled. An unshed tear detached from the outside corner of his eye and rolled down, unfelt and forgotten. "What are ya doin'?" he demanded, his voice still clouded over.

I watched Jack look around, his eyes skipping from object to object.

"Hold on," I said quickly, forestalling action on Risby's part. Ducking into the kitchen, I removed a stack of seven dinner plates from the cupboard and placed them on the table before Jack. They were old and smaller than the modern ones he just broke; their baby blue forget-me-not garland decorations had almost washed off, along with the bits of ancient gold trim. Several were chipped; one had a hairline crack that wasn't going to survive the dishwasher anyway.

"What's this?" he said and his voice was so choked up, he was barely able to speak.

"I got these at a thrift store for you. There's more. Go right ahead."

Jack's breathing slowed as he eyed the stack of old, beat-up fancy china being sacrificed to him and his temper. From just the corner of my eye, I saw Risby fix his gaze on a point far, far ahead, not seeing and not reacting, and definitely not laughing out loud as he wanted to do right then.

Risby knew Jack well, it seemed.

Jack hefted one of the old plates. His eyes glazed over; he put it down and sat in his chair with eyes downcast.

"Will you eat now?" I asked.

He nodded.

I took the topmost plate, shoving the remaining six next to Jack in case he had a need for them later. Then I loaded the remaining chicken thigh and beans onto it and placed it before him. I lifted my glass in a toast. "Guys. Here is to strength, to love, and to new beginnings."

They both looked at me with bewildered eyes; on their best behavior, they lifted their wineglasses and we all clinked together and drank.

Then we ate.

I suppressed a smile. It had taken me two days of hard-core hunting before I managed to locate a set of old china even vaguely reminiscent of Celia's old Limoges serving platter. The way to make Jack actually feel his grief, it seemed, was through old china with bits of painted flowers, glistening with wee bits of gold.

When our meal was over, I cleared the table and handed a second bottle of inexpensive Chardonnay to Jack, who opened it with the same absent air with which he had eaten his dinner. With our drinks topped off, he leaned back and ran his hand over his face and through his hair. "Okay, Wy. Spill it."

I needed to let them know what we had found, but I was still synthesizing the information I'd gotten from Reyna less than half an hour ago.

"Let me start at the beginning so we all have the same information. Risby, when Jack and I were going through Celia's old things, we found her climbing gear. It was the same gear she used when she was with you last."

I saw Jack observe Risby with rapt attention. His former colleague and now his doorman looked pained at the reference, but nodded.

"Don't go any further," he said. "You discovered that the rope was too thin."

"Yeah," I said.

There were few beats of silence, and Risby slammed his fist into the table, making the old china and our wineglasses jump. "Fuck! Just, fuck it all. If only I hadn't had a stick up my ass over assisted climbing, I'd have bothered to educate myself on whatever new gear was coming out. And had I bothered to learn what other people were using up there, I'd have known she gave me her updated, better GriGri and kept the old one for herself. And had we switched those, she'd have been okay." Risby's shoulders were tense and his powerful, rock-climber's fingers threatened to snap the stem of his wine glass in two.

"Risby." I attempted to take the glass away from him. He looked at me and then through me with his wild, dark eyes. He stood up, took the top plate from the stack, and sent it soaring through the air. It shattered against my front door with a bright, cheerful sound. Its porcelain pieces clattered onto the tile below, adding to the pile of stoneware shards, green beans, and a cold chicken leg.

We waited for Risby's breathing to even out.

He sat and looked Jack in the eye. "I will never forgive myself. And I don't expect you to forgive me, either."

Jack twirled his glass between his fingers; then he took a diminutive sip and nodded. "Go on."

"That stupid rope. I never use those color-coded ropes. When I do use ropes, which is almost never, I use camo ropes so they don't stand out like a sore thumb. So it didn't occur to me it felt a little thin."

"Where did that rope come from, Risby?"

"Ah...." He took a gulp of wine and eyed the stack of five antique, chipped plates the late Celia would have loved to use. "My former boss, Toussey, he used to climb. He was getting rid of gear he no longer needed. Cleaning house, he said." He spat the words, barely opening his narrow lips.

"And Toussey didn't like whistle-blowers, did he?" I said, my voice breaking the silence.

"No. No, he did not."

"I remember Toussey," Jack said. "A stuck-up jackass. He'd talk a good talk, but his actions.... He did some bad shit to people. I wonder where he is now?" Jack's eyes gleamed with the need to lock onto a new target for his needed revenge.

Risby merely shrugged. "Who cares? Karma's a bitch. It will all catch up with him eventually."

I stood, letting my chair scrape and make a loud noise against the beat-up linoleum floor of my kitchen area. "It already has. Toussey, the former Vice President of Operations of Provoid Brothers, now lives in a nursing home. He's blind. He also seems to have lost a lot of his mental capacity—apparently he liked drinking all kinds of exotic things." I glanced toward Risby. "It seems that he drank some moonshine and it was a bad batch. It almost killed him."

Risby's eyes were drawn to mine like a compass needle to the North Pole.

I betrayed nothing. "Drinking that stuff is risky," I said in an off-handed manner as I turned toward Jack. "Anyway, he tried to kill your sister and frame Risby for it. If we had solid and untainted evidence, we could take it to the police, but we don't. Whatever happened, happened. Toussey paid a heavy price for his greed."

I reached for the last of the wine and divided it equally among our three glasses. Then I raised mine. "I'd like to propose a toast, guys. It's a toast to life, to love, and to moving on."

We didn't touch glasses this time; we only drank.

"And I'd like to say one thing." Jack cleared his throat, his blazing blue eyes burning holes into Risby. "I never knew. We may never have the details, but... shit happens. Celia was deep into a dangerous sport. She knew this could happen; hell, she wrote about things like this happening to other climbers. I... I do not fault you...." He closed his eyes and thought for a while, as if making sure he said what he truly meant. "I no longer fault you for murdering her, 'cause you didn't. I fault you for lying to her just to get laid. Had she known you were as good as you think you are, she'd have never used that type of gear and this situation might have never even happened. And where would the two of you be now? Hawaii?"

"Alaska," Risby said. "She became obsessed with Alaska. Totally fell in love with it. She even bought a claim up there—what, you didn't know? Yeah... a cabin with no electricity, less than two hours away from the nearest village by snow-machine. There's a creek—there used to be gold in those parts. Mostly, the hunting's good and she... ah, never mind. It's all over now." A dark shadow passed over his high brow.

I didn't like it. I didn't like any of it. "I'd like to read more of your poetry, Risby," I blurted out, unwilling to have him hide from what was, what is, and from what will be. "I'd like you to write again—new stories, new material. I'd like to see your work published."

Like Celia encouraged you to publish....

He looked away. "I better get goin'." That thick accent crept into his speech again, a cover-up for his exceptional talent, a camouflage that had allowed the rest of us to pretend that he was an ordinary corporate suit, a common doorman, a beginner climber of limited talent and imagination.

"Okay," I said, getting up to walk him to the door. "Make sure to stop by again. Here, or at Jack's."

A large hand settled on my shoulder; Jack's heat warmed my back. "Yeah. Do come up, Risby. Seriously. You an' I.... Celia would have wanted us to drink together as friends."

The tall poet turned to us and let his hand fall on Jack's shoulder, his strong, climber's fingers giving him a tight squeeze. "Thanks, Jack." Then he turned to me and stroked my hair—the tender gesture took my breath away. "Keep 'im outta trouble, will ya?" His thin, wide lips canted in a crooked grin, and then he was gone. Only the broken plates and cold chicken leg remained, shoved to the side by the door, the green beans forced to lie in parallel as a salute to his passing.

My STARK, black-and-white room felt cold that night even with Jack spooning me from behind. His heat wasn't enough; arctic wind ripped through my soul every time I thought of the haunted look in Risby's eyes.

I turned around to face Jack and slipped my arm over his torso, my leg between his legs, and pulled in tight to maximize contact.

Jack's quiet voice broke the uneasy silence. "He's innocent."

Innocent of murder, yes. But of other things?

I nodded and let him pull me in even tighter. A shiver passed through my body, and his warm hands moved to chase it away. Of course Risby Haus was innocent of murdering Celia. He must have experienced a terrible, desperate panic when he felt Celia's life slip between his fingers along with that too-thin rope as he struggled to arrest her last fall. Perhaps his focus on philosophical purity as a free-climber didn't give him many chances to practice using other types of equipment. Maybe the heat of the moment brought confusion, or perhaps he just plain screwed up. The result was still the same: the woman he loved, the one he had wanted to entice to marry him, fell to her death, and it happened on his watch.

I thought back to those times when I had let Jack down one way or another: embarrassing him, endangering his probation status with my reckless disregard for law and society. My stomach clenched in a sick twist and my eyes watered—suppose I'd killed Jack by accident. Darkness descended upon me as I buried my face into his warm, muscled chest.

"Wyatt... shhh." Jack's hand wandered from my back up to my hair, and he stroked it as though willing the tension in my shoulders away. "Wanna talk about it?"

I shook my head. If he didn't lay off being sweet like that, I might break down and cry, and I definitely didn't want to do that. What an undignified tip-off that would be.

Risby's world was dark with loss and guilt. Guilt over Celia's death. Guilt over Toussey's blindness.

He probably intended to kill him with that bad batch of moonshine. According to Reyna, Tim's friend had analyzed Risby's brewing records. Risby knew how to eliminate methanol from his brew well enough. Yet his record indicated experiments in which he had perfected his control over the precise amount of methanol in his final product; regular, store-bought whiskey has about 7 percent methanol in it, and Risby had been playing with controlling the amounts up to the lethal level. That bad batch had been no accident.

I felt his guilt secondhand, maybe because I was unable to feel bad about it. Knowing Jack and his recent conversion to the way of the law, he would have felt that guilt as well—perhaps because he would have seen himself take justice into his own hands, just like Risby had.

At that moment, I resolved to protect him from that unsavory feeling; I'd shoulder all that guilt and pain. Jack would never know—not unless there was an imminent and unavoidable need. Jack would think his sister's murderer came to his well-earned end by sheer coincidence.

I forced myself to relax, allowing the smallest sigh to escape me.

Jack stroked my neck, playing with my hair and helping me dissolve into a boneless lump of bones.

"Thanks." I whispered, turning and letting him spoon me the way he knew I liked best.

Dim reflections of nighttime traffic traveled all the way to my sixth story windows, gently teasing my sheer curtains and barely making their way inside. The white walls amplified what little light illuminated the eyes gazing at me in the dark. Soft lips descended onto mine in a soft gesture of affection.

"Why can't you sleep, Wyatt...?" he asked.

I tried to answer, but he silenced me with another kiss.

"Hush. Let me take care of you." He soothed my sides with long fingers; a gasp escaped as I felt his rough, dry fingertips slip under my short pajama pants.

"Have you been climbing?" I asked, both surprised and pleased.

He paused to kiss me before he resumed his teasing movement. "Yeah. Gotta keep up with you out there."

I reached to stroke up his neck and into his mussed-up hair.

He captured my wrist and pressed it against the pillow by my head. "Shh. My turn." Hot lips traced a slow, sensuous path down my throat. Jack stopped to spend time at his favorite places, like a pilgrim along a path. Every time he elicited a reaction, I felt his grin against my skin. Every time I tried to reciprocate, he'd press me down and hush me, chiding me for being unable to just lie and receive.

My pajama pants were off and a hot, wet tongue circled around the ticklish point of my hip bone. I plunged my hands into his hair, and this time my action was unopposed.

He moved even lower, making me sigh and gasp, and eventually he made me gasp his name. He curled around me as he gave me one last kiss.

I inhaled, breathing in his scent that mingled with mine, barely able to keep my eyes open. "Thank you, Jack. I didn't even know I needed that." I paused, then yawned. "Now let's see about you."

"It was my pleasure," he whispered, and I heard satisfaction in his voice. "I'll take a rain check. Go to sleep, Wyatt."

Who was I to argue? Pulled in tight, I melted into his embrace and closed my eyes, my last words a sated whisper.

"I love you, Jack."

CHAPTER
TWENTY-ONE

AUTUMN had passed into winter and winter into spring. The weather turned downright hot, leaving me distractible. I yearned for fresh, green leaves on the trees in the city park right outside. I wanted to just kick back and lie down on the edge of the water fountain, willfully endangering my stiff office suit, and watch the white clouds pass overhead as they soared in the sky—its vibrant blue reminding me of the color of Jack's eyes.

Except I couldn't.

"What? What the hell's so urgent right now?" I snapped at Rick Blanchard, dreading another interruption. I'd been rewriting a particular paragraph for two days; I'd even taken to hiding out in Jack's conference room on the theory that my boyfriend's dull office would present fewer distractions than my apartment... or Jack's apartment... or the library... or even Starbucks.

"Jack needs to see you right now."

I looked up to meet Rick's watery eyes with irritation. "I'll never get this done, Rick, and your buddy Louis will rake me over hot coals if I'm late again."

"It's personal. Everyone's there."

Great. Another stupid birthday party.

My hair felt too long and steamy again, hanging over the collar of my shirt and trapping too much heat. I entered Jack's office without knocking, as I always did. There he was, his own collar unbuttoned and tie loose, white sleeves rolled up his well-muscled arms in deference to spring fever. Yet the wild smirk was absent, yielding to an impassive, focused expression.

Louis Schiffer and Rick Blanchard stood by the wall, their eyes trained on Jack's unexpected guest. She sat in the client chair, short and round and unassuming in her Carhartt pants and a short sleeve shirt.

"Wyatt, this is Lucy Baranoff from Alaska. She lives in a small village on a creek right under Mt. Saint Elias…. She was Celia's friend."

I approached her as she stood and extended my hand in greeting. "Uh… nice to meet you," I said.

She didn't shake my hand, and her dark, vaguely Asian eyes didn't rise above my chin. She nodded. "Good to meet you," she said in a soft, almost inaudible voice full of alien gutturals.

That's when it hit me. The guide. Celia's guide she wrote about in her letter—wasn't she Tlingit? So English was one of at least two languages she spoke; thus the light accent.

She sat back down, and I backed away, taking the seat next to her.

"Go on," Jack prodded her.

"Anyhow, as I said," she continued her narrative, her black and shiny hair framing her tan face with high cheekbones and full of sun-wrinkles. "Risby Haus was up our way last fall. He lived at his claim, and it was getting too late in the year to work it. He wanted to go hunting, he said. He had to put some meat in the cache for the winter. And there was wood to split—lots of work to do before winter set in. We all watched him, wondering what he'd do with Celia gone. They had planned to do all this together, to live through their first Alaskan winter up there."

Her soft, lilting voice was spinning a tale with undercurrents of long-set plans thwarted, of great love unfulfilled. Lucy was a good storyteller and we were her rapt audience.

"Risby was obsessed with trying that climb Celia and I had attempted the previous spring. It was fall already and too late in the year to risk the storms coming in off the bay. I told him to wait 'til summer, but he was restless. Then he told me to deliver this package to you if he didn't come back by breakup—that's when the arctic ice begins to thaw and crack. We're past breakup now and… well… he'd left enough money for me to travel on and deliver this, and I've never been Outside before, so… here it is."

Lucy bent down and produced a small package, which had sat under her chair until now. She handed it to Jack.

He pulled a knife out of his pocket and flipped it open, then cut the package's tape. There was a letter inside, addressed to both him and me. Underneath it sat a large Ziploc bag full of old letters; some of them were written in elegant, cursive handwriting, others contained poetry. Then, a small jewelry box covered in red velvet.

I knew that box, and blanched.

Jack opened the letter first and glanced at me for permission. I nodded, and he began to read aloud.

> *Dear Wyatt and Jack,*
>
> *If this letter finds itself in your hands, then I trust Lucy Baranoff is sitting right next to you. Treat her well; she is the last friend who has seen me alive. Be advised that nothing will please her more than a juicy steak and fresh strawberries; however, she will prefer a milkshake to alcohol. Both Celia and I were proud to call her a friend.*
>
> *You won the lottery, Jack! You get a disorganized jumble of love letters, travel narratives, and poetry, which your sister and I exchanged during our too-brief courtship. I had hoped to present her with the ring in the red box; it is yours now to do with as you please. Keep in mind it's an engagement ring. Don't delay, for destiny may have plans of its own. Don't screw it up, my friend.*
>
> *As for me, I'm burning all my bridges, ready to give karma another try.*
>
> *Live hard, love harder.*
>
> *Risby*

The silence in Jack's office grew oppressive. I wanted to break it and relieve the awkward discomfort of being in the presence of the words written by a man whom I now presumed to be dead. One didn't go climbing in late fall in Alaska and disappear only to show up come spring, alive and all in one piece. My thoughts drifted to the meal he cooked for me—Celia's recipe, he had said—and to his book by Julius Caesar I never returned before he disappeared.

Maybe Risby couldn't live with his guilt for Toussey's blindness. Maybe Risby couldn't live without Celia. Maybe Risby—

"Was there a body?" Jack's voice ripped through the room.

"No," Lucy replied, her eyes still downcast. "No body. Just things."

"Did he seem like he wanted to kill himself?"

She shrugged. "He seemed happy when he gave me the package for you. Like he expected you to receive it. He said to say hi to your guy." She shrugged, confused, not knowing whom that might mean. The reference warmed my heart, and I could feel my eyes itch along with my nose.

Damn spring allergies.

"There was no body… but the land will claim its own. No body, animal or human, will last long in the bush."

"Grizzlies?" I asked, suddenly revolted.

"Among other things." She nodded.

I sat stunned while speculations about Risby's fate abounded. Rick Blanchard offered to take the short woman out to lunch, while Louis mentioned a concert she might enjoy, going on tomorrow in a large Victorian greenhouse—everyone wanted to take Lucy out somewhere and have her try something she'd never see back home.

She gave a faint smile. "Don't take me where there are people. This city is too… too busy for me."

"Would you like to use my apartment?" I asked. "I often stay with Jack. It's empty—you will have privacy."

She thought hard. "If it's not an inconvenience…."

"You're staying at Wyatt's, and Rick's taking you out to lunch," Jack declared as though it was a done deal.

For the first time, Lucy raised her deep brown eyes to mine and smiled.

"Dammit," I said after everybody left, blowing my nose in Jack's now-empty office. "I hate these spring allergies, you know."

He lifted his blue eyes up from a letter Celia wrote while she climbed some obscure, smaller peak in Mexico. "C'mere." He patted his lap and leaned back after setting the package onto the table.

I scowled; I wasn't a dog to come when called, and said so.

"Wyatt?" His voice was plaintive and needy all of a sudden, and I was drawn to him, letting him pull me into his embrace. "Sit up, will ya?" he said, stretching so he could reach past me to grasp the red velvet box. He leaned back and opened it. "It might fit you, you know." His eyebrow was cocked at me, gauging my reaction.

"No way. Too expensive and way too girly. I'd just lose it or trash it."

"Let's see anyway." He removed the white gold and platinum band out of its satin seat and stroked my left hand. "Your fingers are almost as slender as hers."

"But I climb. It leaves them gnarly." My protest was of no use.

Jack exerted himself to force the engagement ring almost all the way down on the correct finger. "Looks good," he decided.

I eyed the ring with as much impartiality as I could muster. It didn't look bad—it didn't feel right though. It was too soon and the opportunity arose in too awkward a manner. "It's beautiful. Too bad, Jack."

"I want you to wear it."

I turned toward him and straddled his thighs, draping my arms around his neck. "I will wear it today. Then tonight we'll put it back in its box and you'll put it in your safe. You could buy a decent condo for that ring, Jack."

His eyes got that wistful, faraway look. "I don't want to pressure you, Wyatt. I know you like keeping your apartment and not always staying with me. You need your space, and I'm okay with that. It doesn't make us any less of a couple, although... although I wouldn't be opposed to a more permanent arrangement."

I nuzzled his neck, my mind reeling with possibilities. The damn ring felt annoying on my finger. I couldn't imagine using my computer keyboard with it on. I knew I'd lose it sooner or later, probably while climbing or hiking somewhere outside. If it had only been attached to me.... "Jack."

"Yeah?"

"I'd like some token of our relationship, too, but it has to be two-way."

His hand stroked my back up and down absently, making me feel warm enough to close my eyes. "What do you have in mind?"

"How about a piercing?"

JACK took the rest of the day off, I collected my laptop, and we shucked our suit jackets so we could better feel the warm breeze. Jack whistled as he took his tie off, smiling.

An hour later, we both had a cubic zirconia earring in our left earlobe, its surgical steel post still making the area feel swollen and sensitive.

"When this heals up, I'm buying you the most awesome diamond earring there is."

"Let's go dutch, buy a whole pair."

He elbowed me in the ribs. "Shaddap. I get to do stuff for you if I want to."

I snorted. "I wish Risby was here. What would he say if he saw you trying to fuss over me?"

"You mean, *when* he finds out I've been constantly fussing over you?"

I stopped on the cool concrete sidewalk, the shadow of the half-leafed tree keeping the eager spring sun off my shoulders.

"There was no body, Wyatt."

"But it's Alaska."

"But it's Risby. Trust me, Wyatt. I knew him well enough to know that right about now, he could be just about anywhere."

SPRING gave way to summer and the summer heat receded, allowing the fall to move in and paint maple leaves with its brush of frost. Jack and I wore our diamond-and-platinum earrings unless we were out climbing—then they kept Celia's ring company in Jack's safe.

We were done with what was probably the last outdoor climb of the season. Chill wind chased us into an eclectic bookstore with a small café. We stood in line, eager to try one of their spicy autumn blends, when my eyes fell onto a familiar outline of a mountain. The drawing of Mt. Denali decorated the dust jacket of a slim volume of poetry. The author's name was Theresa Elias, and her sonnets described many an interesting piece of rock in Alaska. The book's pages emanated the solitude of eternal winter nights and the pain of great love lost. I could just hear the howling, ice-cold winds and feel the frozen rock under my fingertips, lit by naught but the eerie Northern lights.

Demon of Santa Theresa.
Mount St. Elias.
Could it be?

Jack and I bought the volume and settled on a beat-up coffeehouse sofa. I sipped my coffee, nestled in the crook of his arm while he read the verse in a hushed whisper, right by my ear.

The cadence... the word choice... the mood.

After having Jack read all of Risby's poetry to me, it felt awfully familiar. I could no longer contain myself and turned to face him. "Jack. Jack, do you think...?"

He let his mouth turn into a slow, knowing smile. He had a secret and felt obliged to keep it away from the world. "Hush. Here's a good one about Sedna, the Goddess of the Underworld...."

I closed my eyes and sighed, content to be lulled by the smooth cadence of Jack's voice.

STEEL CITY STORIES

A STEEL CITY STORY

WILD HORSES

KATE PAVELLE

http://www.dreamspinnerpress.com

Just about everything KATE PAVELLE writes is colored by her life experiences, whether the book in your hand is romance, mystery, or adventure. Kate grew up under a totalitarian regime behind the Iron Curtain. In her life, she has been a hungry refugee and a hopeful immigrant, a crime victim and a force of lawful vengeance, a humble employee and a business owner, an unemployed free-lancer and a corporate executive, a scientist and an artist, a storyteller volunteering for her local storytelling guild, a martial artist, and a triathlete. Kate's frequent travels imbue her stories with local color from places both exotic and mundane.

Kate Pavelle is encouraged in her writing by her husband, children, and pets, and tries not to kill her extensive garden in her free time. Out of the five and a half languages she speaks, English is her favorite comfort zone.

Contact Kate at www.katepavelle.com for more reading pleasure, or follow her on Twitter at KatePavelle.

Also from DREAMSPINNER PRESS

DIRTY SECRET

RHYS FORD

A COLE McGINNIS MYSTERY

http://www.dreamspinnerpress.com

Also from DREAMSPINNER PRESS

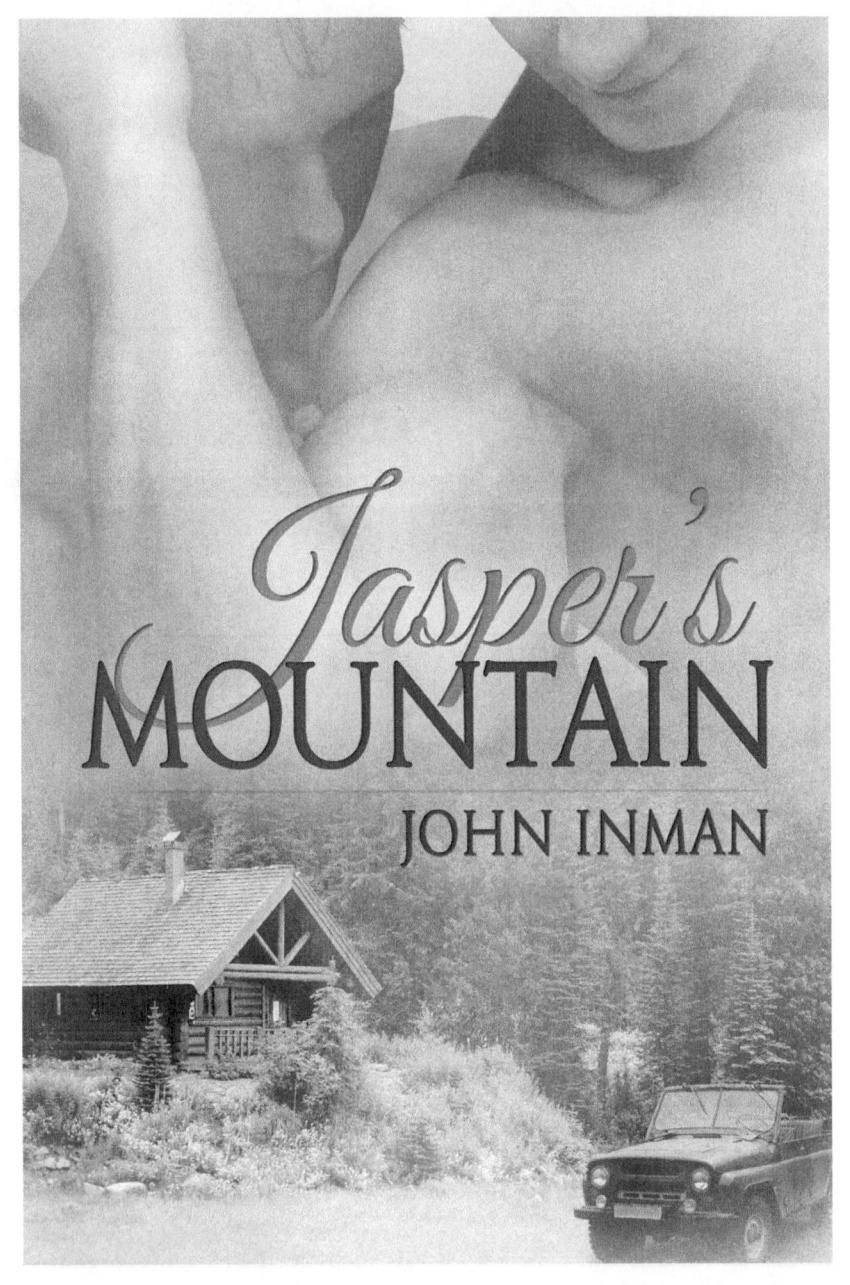

Jasper's MOUNTAIN

JOHN INMAN

http://www.dreamspinnerpress.com

Also from DREAMSPINNER PRESS

A SENSES AND SENSATIONS MYSTERY: 2

Love in Plain Sight
Susan Laine

http://www.dreamspinnerpress.com

Also from DREAMSPINNER PRESS

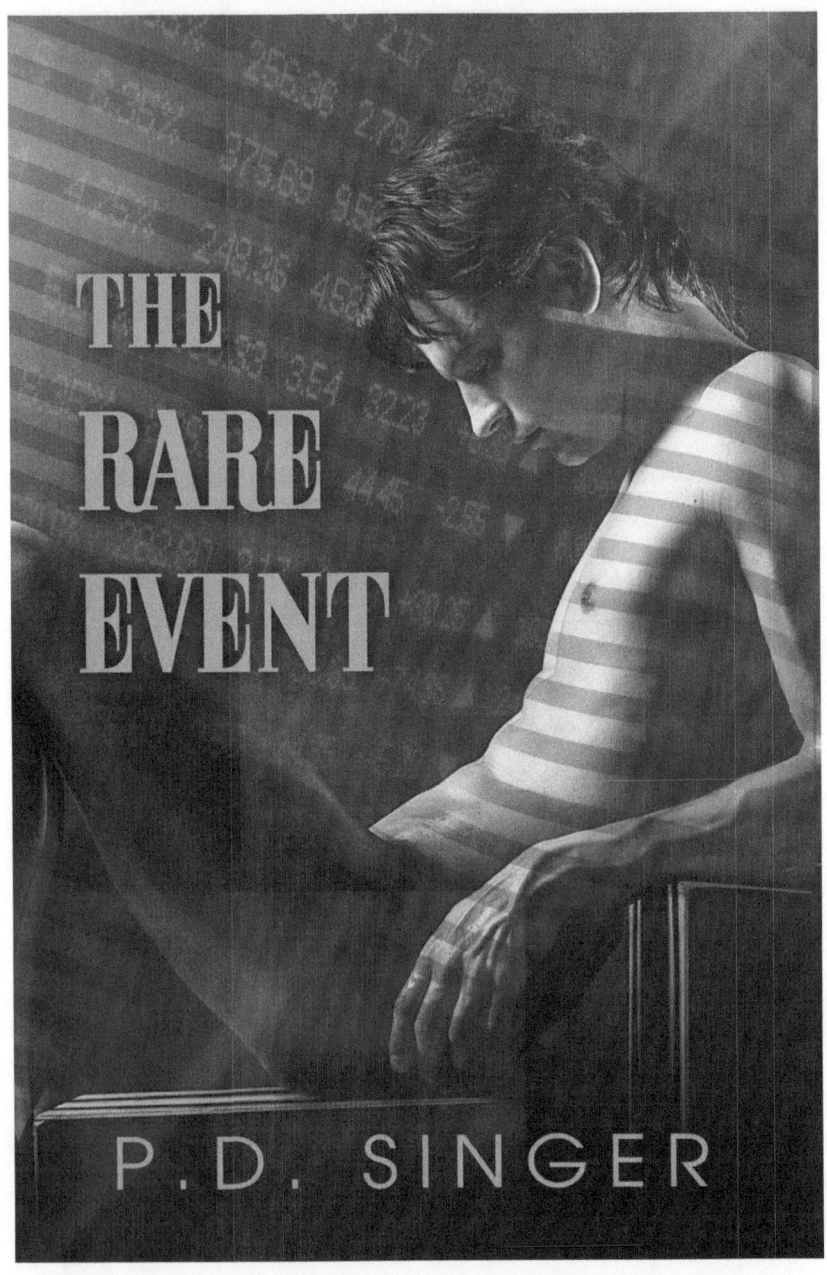

THE RARE EVENT

P.D. SINGER

http://www.dreamspinnerpress.com

Also from DREAMSPINNER PRESS

http://www.dreamspinnerpress.com

Also from DREAMSPINNER PRESS

TIGERS AND DEVILS

SEAN KENNEDY

http://www.dreamspinnerpress.com

Also from DREAMSPINNER PRESS

MAGIC FINGERS

AN AVONDALE STORY

ETIENNE

http://www.dreamspinnerpress.com

Also from DREAMSPINNER PRESS

one small thing

PIPER VAUGHN • M.J. O'SHEA

http://www.dreamspinnerpress.com

Also from DREAMSPINNER PRESS

SINS OF ANOTHER

JESSICA SKYE DAVIES

http://www.dreamspinnerpress.com

For more of the best M/M romance, visit
Dreamspinner Press
www.dreamspinnerpress.com

ation can be obtained at www.ICGtesting.com
SA
70913
0002B/86/P

9 781627 980630